Praise for the
Home Repair Is Homicide
mysteries of
Sarah Graves

"Just the right prescription for a post-repair rest."
—*Orlando Sentinel*

"Everything's Jake—until she starts snooping."
—*New York Daily News*

"With an intricate plot, amusing characters and a wry
sense of humor, Sarah Graves spins a fun,
charming mystery that is sure to make you smile and
keep you guessing right up until the end."
—*Booknews* from The Poisoned Pen

"Charming." —*New Orleans Times-Picayune*

"A winning addition . . . A sleuth as tough as the nails
she drives into the walls of her 1823 Federal home
enhances a clever plot. . . . Many will relish the vividly
described Down East setting, but for anyone who's
ever enjoyed making a home repair it's the
accurate details of the restoration of Jake's old house
that will appeal the most."
—*Publishers Weekly*

"Graves gives us a lively look at small-town life in
charming down-east Maine. Her characters, as always,
are captivating examples of Americana and their
relationships with each other are inspired."
—*The Old Book Barn Gazette*

ALSO BY SARAH GRAVES

The Dead Cat Bounce
Wicked Fix
Repair to Her Grave
Wreck the Halls
Unhinged

Available in hardcover
from Bantam Books:
Mallets Aforethought

TRIPLE WITCH

Sarah Graves

BANTAM BOOKS

New York Toronto
London Sydney Auckland

TRIPLE WITCH
A Bantam Crime Line Book

PUBLISHING HISTORY
Bantam mass market edition / June 1999
Bantam reissue / March 2004

Published by
Bantam Dell
A Division of Random House, Inc.
New York, New York

This is a work of fiction. Names, characters, places, and
incidents either are the product of the author's imagination or
are used fictitiously. Any resemblance to actual persons, living or
dead, events, or locales is entirely coincidental.

ISBN 0-553-57858-8

Manufactured in the United States of America
Published simultaneously in Canada

OPM   16   15   14   13   12   11   10   9   8

ACKNOWLEDGMENTS

Thanks to all who have helped by word, deed, and example, including: Paul Pulk, Judy McGarvey, Steve Koenig, Sandi Shelton, Kay Kudlinski, Brenda Booker of Fountain Books in Eastport, Maine, David and Kathy Chicoine and *Bullet 'n' Press*, Dan Rabes, Don Sutherland, Amanda Powers, Kate Miciak, Christine Brooks, Al Zuckerman, and as always and especially, John Squibb.

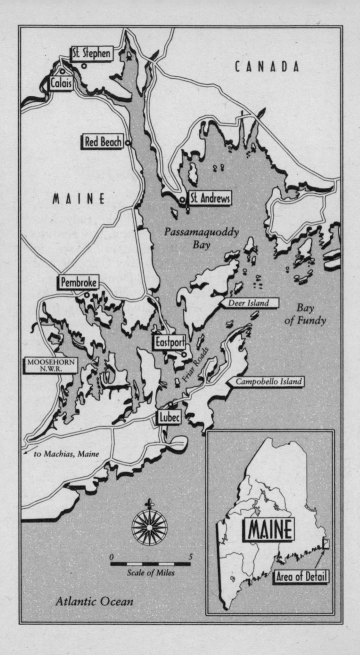

Kenny Mumford's wide, sightless eyes gazed up out of his shroud of wet, green rockweed, on the beach at Prince's Cove. The rockweed covered much of the rest of his face, but we knew right away that it was Kenny. His left hand, flung out loosely behind him as if he were doing the backstroke, had the peculiar, purplish round scar in its palm that anyone in Eastport would recognize.

Kenny always told people he'd gotten the scar when a biker chick, high on methamphetamines, hammered his hand to the shiny metal rim of a barstool after a night of drinking. Others said the drinking part was right but that the nail came from a nail gun, one time when Kenny had had a job.

Now Kenny's eyes were bleached to a pale, milky blue, the result of being soaked in cold salt water. A day earlier, Kenny's boat had been towed in minus Kenny by the Coast Guard, so it was no real surprise finding him there on the beach.

The hole in his forehead, though; that was a surprise.

"Not," Ellie White said thoughtfully, "from a nail gun."

"Right," I agreed, looking at Kenny again. "No nail."

Out on the water, two harbor seals' heads glided smoothly through the waves toward the fish pens of the local aquaculture operation, where a barge was unloading bags of salmon food. Gulls swirled in drifts over the fish pens, waiting for a chance to swoop down and steal floating morsels, screaming impatience.

Ellie crouched, pulling more rockweed from Kenny's face.

"Poor Kenny," she said. "I went to school with him. Up until eighth grade."

Lying in its nest of rockweed, his head looked disembodied. "Is that when Kenny got sent away to reform school?"

It was right around noon, and seventy degrees, which for downeast Maine in late June is practically a tropical heat wave. Ellie was wearing a green-and-white sleeveless gingham sundress with an apple embroidered on the bodice, thin white sandals, and some kind of sparkly purple gauzy stuff to tie back her red hair.

"No. It was when he stopped going to school altogether. He turned sixteen that year, so they had to let him quit. Kenny," she explained, "failed a few grades."

Rising, Ellie took off her sandals and strode into the icy water, gathering her skirt up, while I tried to reconcile Ken's stillness with the rowdy fellow he had been. He was a terror around town, always into some dumb trouble, often drunk and disorderly. Saturday nights you could pretty well figure he'd be blotto, head back, howling at the moon, while the rest of the week he spent trying to parlay his talent for mischief into something besides another stretch of jail time.

Mostly he failed, and it surprised me to realize how much I would miss him. In Eastport, Kenny was as much a fixture as the boats in the harbor, or the cannon on the library lawn.

I called my little black Labrador retriever, Monday, and snapped her onto her lead, not wanting her to nose around the body. By then Ellie was on her way back up the beach, too, and I could see that she had been crying.

I handed her a tissue, and she gave it the sort of long, honking blow that I had come to expect from her; fair-skinned and slender, with green eyes and freckles like a scattering of gold dust, Ellie looks as delicately lovely as an Arthur Rackham fairy princess, and is as tough as an old boot.

We made our way up the embankment through the indigo spikes of wild lupine, back to where I had left the car. There were a few small dwellings widely spaced along the Cove Road, each with a satellite dish and the plundered remains of last winter's woodpile out in the side yard, but I thought it would be best just to drive down to Water Street, to police headquarters, and speak to Eastport's Chief of Police Bob Arnold directly.

To tell him, I mean, that there had been a murder.

 My name is Jacobia Tiptree, and back in Manhattan I was an expert on the care and feeding of vast sums of other people's money, neat slices of which I lopped off in commissions. As a result, by age thirty I possessed more assets than your average small publicly-traded corporation, along with fewer illusions than your average city homicide detective, up to his ankles in blood and accustomed to hearing, pretty much on a daily basis, numerous lies.

Not that I had much contact with homicide detectives. As a class, my clients leaned more toward swift, bloodless acts of financial disembowelment. Meanwhile, I turned out to be good at transforming large fortunes into even larger ones, and talented also at the tasks of (1) getting married and (2) having a baby. Sadly, I was not so adept at (3) realizing that my neurosurgeon husband was a cold-blooded, methane-breathing, sludge-dwelling slime toad whose ability to tell the truth ranked right up there with my own ability to jump off a building and fly.

Finding a medical secretary in my bed did tend to clarify my thinking on the matter, however. And as if that were not enough, once the divorce battle was over my by-then young teenaged son, Sam, began failing in school, smoking marijuana—

—at least, I hoped it was only marijuana—

—and running with a crowd of sullen, secretive little streetwise hooligans.

Fortunately, this was also about the time I found Eastport. The move—from a pristine townhouse in Manhattan to a rambling, dilapidated 1823 Federal clapboard in a tiny fishing village in remotest downeast Maine—

—the house came complete with antique plumbing, ceramic-post electrical wiring so scary it could star in its own horror movie, and weatherproofing that consisted entirely of forty-eight heavy wooden storm windows, each of which had to be fastened up every autumn and hauled back down again in spring—

—was impetuous, impractical, and absurd for a woman of my experience and situation.

And I do believe that it saved my son's life.

"Is that so?" said police chief Bob Arnold when Ellie and I told him of our discovery.

Arnold leaned against the squad car parked in front of the wood-frame storefront housing the Eastport police station. "Sure it was Kenny?"

From the way he said it, lazy and slow, a person who didn't know Arnold might think he might just decide not to do anything about the situation.

But that would have been a mistake. Arnold is a plump, pink-cheeked man with a calm, deliberate way of moving, but he gets from here to there as fast as he needs to.

A few months earlier, for instance, Arnold had arrested a Calais woman whose husband had just died facedown in the main dish at a baked-bean supper. She'd been on her way home to fetch the biscuits she'd forgotten—or that, anyway, was her story—when Arnold spotted her speeding by after hearing the ambulance call on his radio, and put two and two together.

The woman, as it turned out, never got charged with murder, the well-known fact that her husband beat her regularly—

—this, Arnold said, was how he came up with four—

—not being sufficient evidence, and the toxicologists not finding any poison they could identify. So they had to release her almost as fast as Arnold caught her. But nobody ate her dishes at public suppers anymore, which in these parts is still harsh punishment.

"It was Kenny," Ellie told Arnold now. "And," she added to his inevitable next question, "we're sure he's dead."

Arnold frowned, squinting at the water sparkling in the bay. Out on the waves, a couple of speedboats zipped flashily, while up and down Water Street clusters of tourists strolled, eating ice cream, peering into shop windows, and buying bumpah stickahs.

"Well. That's a hell of a thing," Arnold said. "All right. Guess I'd better get cracking."

He glanced across Water Street at the pilings of the boat basin, great towering forty-foot logs set deep into the seabed, supporting the dock. It was dead low tide.

"Better fetch him 'fore the tide is flowing, or Kenny might float away. And someone's got to find old Timothy Mumford, too, and deliver the bad news."

"Oh," said Ellie, freshly stricken. "I forgot about that."

In the entrance to the boat basin, a forty-foot yacht was making its careful way to the dock. The gleaming white pleasure craft's engines rumbled and fell silent, while fellows on deck hauled lines around cleats to secure her against the bumpers.

"Hope they know how high she'll be riding," Arnold said, his eyes narrowing at the yacht crew's spotless white uniforms.

It is a fairly common event here, in summer, when pleasure boaters from away tie up without thought for the tides: the water rises but the boat is held down by the line, with (glub, glub) predictable results.

"I guess," said Ellie, "that I am going to have to go out there. To Crow Island. Maybe if he gets the news from someone he knows, it won't go down quite so hard for him."

"Maybe," Arnold agreed. He thought a minute. "Don't guess it's Tim who decided to pop Kenny, do you?"

She gave him an oh-for-Pete's-sake look; he nodded in reply.

"Yeah. Not much point treating him like a suspect, is there? So you go," he said. "Tell Timothy I'll be out, too, let him know any of the details he might be worrying about. And," he added, "see if he knows who might have had a mad on for Kenny."

"Should I tell him the body will be going to Bangor?" she asked. "Because the church will want to do a service, and if there isn't a body there won't be any graveside ceremony. But we'll still want to take up a collection."

For later, she meant, for getting Kenny into the earth: for a grave at Hillside, and a casket and some flowers, and a decent dark blue suit to bury him in, because maybe he was just a rowdy, uncouth, small-town layabout, but he was our small-town layabout.

"Yeah," said Arnold, "Bangor for the autopsy. Be simpler, they just cremated him, there. All the booze Ken's poured into himself, he'd go like a torch, and Timothy could have the ashes."

Ellie fixed Arnold with a gaze that communicated perfectly what she thought of this idea. "I'll tell Timothy that Kenny will be coming back here."

"Now, Ellie," Arnold began in an attempt to placate her.

"In the ambulance. At town expense," she went on inexorably. "Hank Henahan drives that ambulance to Bangor all the time, to pick up supplies. So this time, he can just pick up Kenny."

Arnold sighed, knowing what Eastport's emergency medical technician would say about driving three hours with a dead man. Hank Henahan was well known for peeking through his fingers at the nervous-making parts in animated Walt Disney movies; he would be glancing in the ambulance's rear-view every half mile, waiting for Kenny to lurch up at him.

"All right," Arnold relented. "I guess I can ride along when the time comes, so the boogieman doesn't get Henahan."

Ellie put her hand on his arm. "Tim will be grateful."

Arnold's round pink cheeks grew pinker than usual. "No, he won't," he answered gruffly. "He'll just moan and complain like always, and threaten to walk off the dock. If I had a nickel for every time he has told me that he is planning to end it all," Arnold went on, "I would be lying on a beach in Tahiti right now, and some other poor bastard would be police chief."

Ellie twinkled at him. "Oh, you would not. If anybody tried to make you live anywhere but Eastport, you would wither away."

"Yeah, well," he allowed. "Anyway, you take care on that boat of yours with the tide running."

"We will," Ellie assured him, turning to me.

"Me?" I said, shaking my head in a way that I hoped was the final word on the topic.

It wasn't.

 Back at my house, I busied myself with a task that obviously needed doing that minute: on the hardwood kitchen floor was a spot of old carpet adhesive that had only been stuck there twenty years or so. Getting it off required boiling water, a paint scraper, and infinite patience, all of which I was prepared to apply forever if it kept me from having to go out on Ellie's boat.

She, by contrast, enjoys narrow channels, swift currents, and all the other hazards with which the cold waters off the Maine coast are furnished. Possibly this is because her forebears were pirates, people whose idea of fun was to wait for a winter midnight so cold that chunks of sea smoke froze solid and calved off like icebergs into the frigid water. Then on a creaking, disreputable boat they skulked out into Passamaquoddy Bay, flying the skull and crossbones and singing dark, ominous sea-chanties, awaiting some hapless vessel—lost in the fog, her crew praying aloud for salvation—to blunder into their clutches.

Too late, the master of the victim ship would glimpse the pirates' dark eyes, torch-lit and glittering with cruelty; too late, the doomed crew would understand the chanty drifting dirgelike over the water at them, and the deck would fall silent for the moment it took to sink into them: that they were dead men.

I dripped more hot water onto the carpet adhesive. In a year or so, I could remove it completely. But Ellie was not about to let me escape into the pleasures of old-house fix-up.

"Let's," she said in a voice that was bright as a knife-edge, "take a picnic." She was not a happy camper, I could tell from the brisk, furious way she bustled around the kitchen, making sardine sandwiches.

Eating food while bobbing up and down on the waves is for me a pointless exercise. I find it simpler and more pleasant just to hurl the sandwiches overboard while they are still wrapped in wax paper. Still, I thought humoring Ellie might be wise; murdered friends bring out the cutthroat ancestor in her.

So we compromised: lemonade and those horrid little oily creatures in flat tins for Ellie, pilot crackers for me. Then Monday started romping and agitating to go, too, so we took her Day-glo orange doggy life vest which she regards as sissified, but she tolerates it.

There was of course no real likelihood of my falling from Ellie's boat and drowning. Still, I gave the kitchen a fond, last look, which was when I noticed a pool of rusty water spreading slyly from beneath the cast-iron radiator.

"Wow," Ellie commented. "Better call George."

She meant her husband, George Valentine. In Eastport, he was the man you called for bats in the attic, frozen pipes, strange bones in the garden, or a plague of red ants.

And for imminent floods. Have I mentioned that the house is haunted? From the front parlor came the sharp whap-whapping of a window shade, snapping up by itself.

I turned the round wooden handle atop the old radiator, cutting off its water supply. "Probably," I said, "George is at the beach, helping to get Ken's body. So if I stayed here, I'd just be waiting around for him. I might as well come along."

Out in the dining room, an old silver spoon that I have put onto the mantelpiece a hundred times dropped to the tiled hearth with a familiar, communicative little *clink!*

Ellie looked assessingly at me. Her campaign to turn me from landlubber to sea dog was ongoing, but it had not escaped her that, under most circumstances, I would rather be anywhere but out on the water in her tiny wooden boat.

This time, though, I was beginning to have a funny feeling, amplified by that spoon and that window shade, something like the intuition that makes you decide to buy a lottery ticket, and you end up winning fifty dollars.

But my sense now that something was brewing didn't feel a bit lucky. I'd have paid fifty dollars to get rid of it, in fact.

And as it turned out, eliminating it cost more than that.

A lot more, starting on Crow Island.

 At the dock, Ellie stepped easily from the pier to the foredeck of her boat, loading our supplies and a gas can, taking off lines and making sure the oars were properly shipped. Finally, checking that the flares and life cushions were stowed under the seats, she started the Evinrude engine.

The decks of the bigger boats loomed like tall buildings as we motored between them: me in the middle, Ellie at the rudder, and Monday perched up in the prow, her pink tongue lolling and her eyes bright with adventure. The red bandanna tied around her neck looked dashing, and her joyfulness made me glad I had brought her.

It was a glorious day, the cool breeze tangy with fish and pine tar and the water very clean so you could see right down to the bottom where sea urchins clung in clusters. Yellow sunshine poured from the azure sky and bounced from the waves, so that the air seemed to vibrate with an excess of light and energy.

Turning back to Ellie, I found she was smiling at me with a look both knowing and mischievous. Getting me out on the water was like pulling teeth, but being out on it was dandy—until she hit the throttle and we shot from the mouth of the boat basin like something being rocketed out of a cannon. I gripped the gunwales, Monday gulped a faceful of spray, and Ellie laughed wickedly, like one of her rascal ancestors.

Crow Island lay between the lighthouse point at Deer Island and Head Harbor on Campobello. From where I sat it was just a dot on the horizon, a rock and a clump of fir trees.

"Want to shoot the narrows?" Ellie waved a freckled arm at Head Harbor, about half a mile off on our right. (Or starboard, as these boating types insist on calling it. If you want to remember which is which, the trick is this: the words *left* and *port* mean the same thing and have the same number of letters.)

The lighthouse at Head Harbor was white and octagonal in the Canadian maritime tradition, with tall gabled windows and a red cross facing the Bay of Fundy. At low tide you could scramble to it by making your way across a great many slippery rocks, down a ladder, and across the tide flats.

"No!" I called back to Ellie. "Just head straight out!"

At high tide, it is possible to zoom between the island and the promontory upon which the lighthouse stands—possible, that is, if you go very fast so your keel stays high on the water, and your aim is very true; otherwise the last thing you hear will be a loud noise, a sort of mingling of *kablooie* and *sayonara*.

"Ellie," I said quietly. I was not shrieking, I was very carefully not shrieking as the lighthouse loomed larger.

Ordinarily, Ellie would not scare me this way, but she was angry about Kenny. The boat sat up smartly atop the waves, skipping over them with the heedless momentum of a hurled stone.

Then suddenly she cranked the throttle down, the boat nearly swamping in the sudden backwash. I waited until the forward roll settled, listening to the rumble of the Evinrude churning in low.

"I'm sorry," Ellie said quietly.

"That's all right. Think of it as medical screening. I mean, if I didn't have a heart attack just now, I probably never will."

Monday looked from Ellie's face to mine, figuring out the emotional subtext, which to a dog is really the only thing that matters. People, too; dogs are just better at admitting it.

"You dated Kenny Mumford a few times, didn't you?" I asked. "When you were in high school?"

Ellie steered us back out into deep water, increasing the throttle just enough to buck the swirling currents and keep us from wallowing in the waves.

"More than a few times. My sophomore year. He had a car, and all he wanted to do was drive."

I waited.

"He was always a perfect gentleman," she added, a bit too defensively, I thought. On the other hand, in my time I have drunk enough Southern Comfort in the back seats of enough convertibles to know when I really ought not to pursue a subject, so I didn't.

"And then you started seeing George."

George Valentine, who if Ellie were in trouble on the

other side of a mile of burning coals, he would hotfoot it over in a heartbeat.

"And then George," she agreed. "I'd broken off with Kenny a few months earlier, so there was no trouble about that."

"But still." Monday stood unsteadily in the boat's bow, her nose twitching in anticipation of land.

"Right. Kenny was important to me."

The boat scraped bottom. Ellie cut engine and hauled up the Evinrude, hopping out as the boat's motion sent it onto the small stones. Monday leapt out, too, paddling around a few times in an excess of doggy happiness before scrambling onto the stony beach, shaking off a halo of sparkling droplets.

I put a foot in the water, cringed, and dropped overboard. The icy wavelets came up only to about my ankles, but froze me to my hipbones, with the deep, aching, wedgelike agony of water that is cold to the point of being truly dangerous; survival time without a drysuit in Passamaquoddy Bay, even in summer and with your head above water, runs about fifteen minutes.

Ellie and I dragged the boat up above the high-water line while Monday had a puppy blowout, which even in her canine middle age still consists of: (1) dashing away full tilt, (2) skidding to a frantic, backpedaling halt like a cartoon character, (3) chasing her tail in a half-dozen mad circles, and (4) repeating the above until a switch flips in her brain and she saunters calmly back to you, the look on her face asking clearly what the hell you think is so funny.

"Hey," said Timothy Mumford. We hadn't heard him coming.

"Hello, Timothy," said Ellie. "This is my friend, Jacobia."

He stood on a grassy rise above the beach, gazing down at us in surprise and alarm. Flanking him

were a pair of evil-looking hounds, one a shepherd mix
with pale yellow eyes and a snaggletoothed grin that
did not look at all welcoming, the other a tan, hulking brute with a missing ear, some god-forbid cross
between a mastiff and, apparently, a Rhodesian Ridge-
back.

"Monday," I said quietly, and she trotted over; she
is a knuckleheaded little Labrador retriever, but no
fool.

The mastiff picked his way deliberately down the
embankment, placing his enormous feet with the deli-
cacy of a deer.

"Nice doggy," I said inadequately.

The mastiff sat, offering his paw and looking grateful when I took it. *Umph,* he remarked from somewhere deep in his big chest.

At this the shepherd gave a little yip of relief and
danced into a play bow in front of Monday; moments
later all three dogs were chasing in and out of the water, having a high old time.

Timothy hadn't said anything. He was a small, wiry
man with thin, silky white hair, skin tanned the color of
moose hide, and anxious blue eyes, wearing a flannel
shirt and overalls.

"Timothy," said Ellie, "I'm afraid we've got bad
news."

His face did not change expression, as if after many
sorrows another one would not come as a surprise.

"Ayuh," he said, leaning on a stick. That was when I
noticed his clubbed foot. "Coast Guard fellers came
yesterday, said Ken's boat come up a drifter."

Timothy turned and hurried as best he could, away
from us up the path through the blueberry shrub, then
halted as if in pain.

Overhead, a pair of brown ospreys circled, scanning
the island for some helpless prey animal to target, to
seize on and pluck out its liver, while out on the water

the ferry to Deer Island plied the channel prettily, trailing a banner of foam.

"All right," the old man said, bracing himself desperately on his stick. "I'm ready."

So then Ellie told him.

 "It's not right." Timothy's voice was a reedy tenor note of complaint. "Poor Ken being done that way, it's not right at all."

His house on Crow Island was a tumbledown scrapwood frame structure, braced and patched over almost every ramshackle inch. Outside, it looked like a movie scene set in a ghost town; inside, the little old shack smelled of bacon grease and dogs.

Lots of dogs: Timothy was a hopeless collector of strays. By the time we reached the house, some twenty of them had joined us; inside, half a dozen more looked up alertly at the creak of the rusting hinges on the screen door.

"He didn't deserve it," Timothy complained again. In the light filtering in through the grimy window, his wrinkled face resembled a mask of tragedy carved from a nutshell. "Maybe he wasn't no straight arrow, like some o' those high mucky-mucks as live in town, but he'ud begun t' change."

Ellie glanced around, mentally cataloguing the old man's needs: blankets, a half-dozen replacement windowpanes, another roll of tarpaper for the roof and perhaps a good cleaning of the stove flue, for while it was summer now, in Maine another winter is always lurking frigidly around the corner.

"Of course he didn't deserve it," she said, her voice full of honest sympathy, making him believe her in a way that I never could have. "Kenny just had bad luck."

"That's right," Timothy agreed stoutly. "But he had things workin' for him, things as was goin' to make him a bit o' money. Ken had a deal goin'. He," the old man protested vainly, as if it might somehow bring Ken back again, "had just hit a good patch."

The dogs watched the old man adoringly, and despite the disorder they seemed clean and well fed. Among them, Monday looked happy and at ease, and not a bit better cared for.

"But I guess that's all water under the bridge, now. What about the arrangements?" Timothy demanded. "I got a bit o' burial insurance for m'self, but t'wont pay nothin' for Ken."

He glanced angrily at me. "And who're you, some snoop from the welfare? Don't you worry, I don't pay for them dogses' grub with none a' your'n."

I opened my mouth to make some inadequate reply, but Ellie got in before me. "No, Tim, I told you. Jacobia is my friend."

"I'm very sorry for your loss, Mr. Mumford," I said, and he accepted this, nodding curtly before turning to Ellie again.

"A man ain't meant to bury a son," he said, his voice rising in grieving affront. "It ain't fair, just when Ken had somethin' going, that bastard come'n shot him."

"There, there," Ellie said, patting his arm in a gesture which, had I tried it, its falsity would have been embarrassing. But coming from Ellie, whose sincerity is as shiningly genuine as a brand-new silver dollar, it looked comforting.

Timothy pulled a kerchief from his overalls and mopped his reddened nose, while the dogs looked anxious at his distress. "I got no reason to live no more," he uttered. "It's all just got to be too much. I should just get my guts together and end it all."

Here we go, I thought, remembering Arnold's prediction: that Timothy would threaten to walk off the dock. It was still pretty heartbreaking, though; he had, after all, just lost his son.

"Only I don't know as who'ud take care o' the dogs," Timothy mourned heavily. "Them as has money enough is awful hard-hearted, nowadays, not like in times before."

He shot a glance at me, to see if I might deny this, and possibly put my checkbook where my mouth was too.

But instead I put my foot there. "What scheming bastard," I asked him, "did you mean? The one who you think shot Kenny."

At which Tim's own mouth clamped shut, his shoulders hunched forward turtlelike, his liver-spotted hands clenched stubbornly in a gnarled hump in front of him on the kitchen table.

"Jacobia," Ellie said in that sweet tone she takes when she wants me to do something important, like shut up and get out of the way, "I think Monday needs some fresh air."

Timothy snorted, and muttered something unintelligible in a tone that could have stripped paint.

"Why don't you take a walk out to the shed," she suggested, "and check on Timothy's dog supplies? That way," she went on smoothly, "the ladies from church can put together a package for the animals, too, when they make cakes and casseroles for Tim."

"Cakes," Tim muttered less sourly, his wish for extinction apparently tempered by the promise of powdered-sugar frosting.

I took Monday and went out, glad for the dazzle of sunshine and the scouring rush of salt air. Poor old Timothy was purely pitiful in his grief, and pitifulness brings out the worst in me.

By contrast, the shed was a cheerful surprise: ramshackle on the outside, all sweet-smelling order within. Sacks of dog chow stood neatly stacked on wooden

pallets beside fresh straw heaped to make dog beds.
There was a pile of emptied food-bags, too, carefully
folded and weighted with a stone from the beach so
they wouldn't get scattered around. The windows were
tight, the old pine floor had been swept recently, and in
a tin box I found a stock of basic animal remedies.

The dog food, Ellie had said, was donated by a local
animal-welfare group. But not vet care; he'd done without something for himself to buy this stuff. I wondered,
if push came to shove for me as it had for him, whether
I would be so humane.

Some time later Ellie came and found me there
sprawled on a hay bale, half-drunk on the sweet smells
of straw and dog kibble. Dogs gathered around me,
pushed against my sides, with Monday jealously holding pride of place under my right arm and a collie nuz-
zled under my left.

"I may never," I told Ellie, "walk again."

She laughed, and began shooing dogs away from me.
"Better not let Tim see. He'll adopt a dozen of them
onto you."

I clambered up, brushing straw bits off myself.
Hanging from the shed's loft window was a counter-
weighted rope for opening and closing the window's
heavy frame, the top length pulleyed over a roof beam
and the bottom one hanging straight down, each length
knotted to a big, bullet-shaped lead sinker.

"Why does he save dog food bags?" I asked, waving
at the pile of them.

"He stuffs them with straw, piles them around the
foundation of his house in winter, for insulation," Ellie
replied.

"Huh. That's smart. How is he now?" Something
about the window arrangement bothered me, but I
couldn't quite put my finger on what it was.

"Tim? Oh, he'll survive. He's talking about killing
himself, but he's always done that. He thinks it makes

people feel sorrier for him. Although," she added softly, "I don't know how I could."

Outside, the tide was turning and the smell of roses floated on a breeze. Timothy was putting things into Ellie's boat.

"His wife died," Ellie said, watching him, "when Ken was little, and then two of his other kids died. One in a car accident, one of meningitis. After that his back went out, so he lost his job and his house. Finally he moved out here, started picking up dogs."

"And now Kenny."

She nodded, picking her way between the blueberry shrubs. In a few weeks you could comb your fingers through the leaves and get a handful of wild berries, their flavor so intense that if you ate them with your eyes closed, you would *see* blue.

"And now Kenny," Ellie agreed, stepping onto the beach where the rising tide left a ribbon of wet stones.

"What's he doing?" I peered at Timothy, who, I realized, was loading his own things into the boat.

"Oh," Ellie said, "sorry, I forgot to tell you. Tim's coming back with us."

"With us? Why?" I had a clear mental picture of the old man hurling himself overboard, and of me having to tow his body back to Eastport with Ellie's grappling hook.

"Because," she answered, "Tim says he knows who shot Kenny. And he says he knows why."

 The Bisley .45-caliber six-shot revolver is an Italian-made replica of an old Wild West killing implement, the sort of weapon you might expect cowboys to be shooting at bad guys outside the saloon.

Back at my house, I brought the Bisley up from the lock box in the cellar and opened the cylinder at the kitchen table. Ellie had taken Tim down to talk to Arnold—Tim wouldn't discuss what he knew, assuming he really knew anything, in front of me—which left me some free time. So I got out the cartridge reloading press, a block of Ball canning wax, and the ketchup, and began creating Fake Death.

While I was melting the wax in a double boiler my son Sam came in, fresh from trying out the sailboat he and his friend Tommy Daigle had just finished building out at Harpwell's boatyard. At sixteen, Sam looked tan, fit, and older than any child of mine had a right to be, and I blinked for an instant, wondering where the awkward kid I'd produced had gone.

"Hey, nice ones," he said, eyeing the cartridges. "They look real. Daigle says he wants to try 'em."

"Right," I replied, thinking of Sam's friend, a smart, sweet-tempered kid who as a weapons handler has all the dexterity of a vaudeville pratfall comedian. "In his dreams, tell him."

"Aw." Sam grinned, rummaging through the cabinets, the bread box, and the refrigerator. Finally he slapped two hamburgers into a skillet and grabbed the ketchup bottle.

"Hey," I told him, "don't use up all of my fake blood."

"Don't worry." He flipped the hamburger patties. "So, could you hit anything with 'em?"

He watched with interest as I slotted a new cartridge into a little plastic hammer, a tool especially designed for the purpose of taking cartridges apart. I smacked the hammer smartly on the table, then dumped the powder from inside the cartridge onto a sheet of newspaper.

"Don't know," I said. "I never got a chance to fire them."

That, originally, was what Ellie and I had been doing, down on the beach at Prince's Cove: checking the targeting trajectory of a cartridge full of wax and ketchup, as opposed to one loaded the normal way, with nitrocellulose powder. The Eastport annual Fourth of July celebration was just ten days off, and in honor of a special guest the town was planning some unusual events.

"So who is this Felicia Abracadabra person, anyway?" Sam wanted to know through a mouthful of hamburger sandwich. With it, he was having a few pickled onions, some smoked Gouda cheese, and a half-bag of Oreo cookies, all washed down with a quart of milk. "And how come you're going to shoot her with fake bullets?"

"Felicity Abbot-Jones," I corrected him calmly, reminding myself that a teenaged boy, in order merely to maintain the basic functions of life, is required to consume enough calories to power a space shuttle liftoff, apparently on an hourly basis.

"And we're not going to shoot her with the fake bullets. We are using them to re-enact a historical battle, down on the dock. She's from Portland, and she is the founder and benefactor of the Maine Endowment to Stabilize and Save Early Structures."

Sam worked out the acronym and guffawed, nearly losing a whole mouthful of milk and cookies.

"You can laugh now," I told him, loading the final cartridge into the hammer, "but when Felicity visits here, it's serious. She's always sent a representative, before. But this year she's coming herself, and if she thinks Eastport looks historically accurate enough, she'll send a year's worth of grant money."

I popped the last cartridge open. "To promote tourism, and all kinds of other stuff that puts cash in town people's pockets."

Sam considered this. "You think she might fund a model boat show? I mean," he went on, "old boats. Galleons and frigates and schooners and men-o'-war, made out of real wood, with real sails and rigging, and real brass fittings, that really float?"

He swallowed his Oreos. "And on the inside, little maps on the chart tables. Little," he enthused, "dragons on the edges of the maps, see, to show where the known world ends, and astrolabes. Working ones, so they can navigate, but scaled to size."

He sat up straight, already raring to get started, and I looked wonderingly at him again: so tall and dark-haired, with my long eyelashes and his father's stubborn jaw, wearing a navy T-shirt, denim cutoffs, and deck shoes. Sometime when I wasn't watching, he went from choirboy soprano and reasonably attractive to baritone and startlingly handsome.

"So," he persisted, with the movie-star grin that was going to be some poor girl's downfall, someday, "what do you think?"

What I thought was that somehow, he had been switched at birth. No one in my family, or even in my ex-husband's, has so much drive. Also, none of us are that good-looking.

"I think it's a fine idea. Why don't you work up a proposal, and maybe some sketches."

His face fell.

"I will," I said, "proofread. And make corrections, if any."

Sam has always been able to design, build, or fix anything. When he was six, he repaired a weimaraner by fiddling around with its back leg, and changing its diet. What he can't do is read or write very much, at least not without some elaborate strategies.

The specialists call his disorder refractory dyslexia, and think it fascinating; Sam calls it a pain in the tail and doesn't. He'd spent the past six months getting therapy for it in New York, living with his father in Manhattan, but had seen little improvement.

But he had learned, apparently, not to care so much.

"Okay. I'll do the genius stuff, give the scut work to you."

"In trade for two nights of dinner dishes. Washed, dried, *and* put away."

Sam groaned, laughing. "My mother, the drill sergeant. But you've got it," he agreed, getting up and carrying his plate to the sink. "So did you test any of your bullets?"

He nodded toward the table, where I had assembled the Lyman hand press. It comes with metal dies custom-made for specific types and calibers of ammunition, so that after you've enlarged the primer pocket and filled it with your load of choice—in this case, layers of ketchup interspersed with layers of melted wax—you pull down the lever on the machine and *ka-chunk!*:

Presto, a handy, dandy little nugget of Fake Death that will explode in what looks like a bloody gunshot wound.

Although, I must add, Fake Death is not to be fired at a person or animal at close range, and also not unless the target wears a bullet-proof vest and safety goggles. Even a dummy bullet can do damage.

"No. We found a body, instead." I said it quietly, but of course there is really no minimizing a thing like that. "On the beach."

Sam turned slowly from the open refrigerator, another quart of milk in his big left hand. I swear if that boy's bones grow any more, he will have to take on a whole new set of specialists.

"Mom." His eyes were mock-horrified. "Can't you find another hobby?" Other than getting involved in murder, he meant.

"We weren't out looking for it. It was just there. With," I added, "a bullet wound in its forehead."

"Dad'll blow a gasket when he gets here and hears about it. Which," he glanced at the clock, "will be in about two hours."

At the mention of my ex-husband, I looked at the

pile of black powder growing on the sheet of newspaper. I could so easily confuse a real cartridge for a dummy, load the Bisley, and . . .

"Where I am concerned," I told Sam, "your dad has already blown all the gaskets he has, some of them several times over."

I pulled the lever on the Lyman press for a final *kachunk!* and one last projectile of Fake Death—we really didn't know how many we were going to need, so I'd decided to make plenty—meanwhile thinking about dinner. Salmon, I thought, with sprigs of dill and little potatoes in butter, and new peas. Afterwards, we would have strawberry shortcake: buttermilk biscuits, tiny wild strawberries no bigger than the tip of your little finger, and real whipped cream.

"So I think that as far as dead bodies go, we will just keep our mouths shut. Your dad doesn't need to know everything I do." I loaded the Bisley with six of the dummies and closed the cylinder.

Whereupon my ex-husband cleared his throat, stepped into the kitchen from the back hallway where he had been standing for who knew how long, and smiled in the reliably infuriating way he had, like a cat whose breath smells of canary.

"Body?" he asked. "Did someone mention a body?"

Owing to his profession, of course he was not fooled by the fake blood on the newspaper. Being a brilliant, death-defying daredevil of the neurosurgical suite, he's quick on the uptake.

"Hello, Jake," he said to me, picking up one of the remaining dummy bullets and examining it with clinical interest, as if it were a tumor.

"You're early," I said.

Of course he was early; he was always either early or late.

"Keeping busy, I see," he remarked.

The son of a bitch.

"Hey," Wade Sorenson said, coming into the kitchen an hour after my ex-husband had arrived.

Laconic and even-tempered, Wade has pale grey, unflinching eyes and a face tanned and weathered by years of being out on the water. His hands, calloused from hauling the lines of countless boats and dinged by the scars of accidents over the years—a wayward propeller blade, a blazing carburetor, the unfriendly jaws of an injured harbor seal he was rescuing—are deft and clever, but I have also seen him reach barehanded into a dock brawl to break it up, with immediate results.

"Hey, yourself." He put his arms around me and I leaned my head on his shoulder. My ex-husband—whose name, appropriately enough, is Victor—had taken his bags upstairs to settle into the guest room, and to speak with Sam. "He's here."

"Yeah, I saw the car. Being his usual charming self?" To punctuate this, Wade made piggy snorting noises into my neck.

I nodded. Those were the proper sound effects, all right. "He's let me know that I'll have to cook specially for him. Free-range chickens, whole grains, and organic bean juice."

Without any warning, Victor had decided that ordinary foods upset his system. He felt his nourishment needed to be mild and pristine, and that I, naturally, should arrange this for him.

"Also his bed linens will need to be ironed every day, but without—and he was very definite on this—any starch. He says his skin . . ."

I was shaking; in under five minutes, Victor can bring me to the edge of a rage so furious, you could boil lobsters in it, but now a gasp of hilarity bubbled up and escaped me.

". . . his *skin,*" I managed, "has gotten *sensitive.*"

You would need to know more about my ex-husband, whose skin would repel buckshot, to understand how funny this was to me.

Wade held me away from him, his eyes crinkled with amusement but examining me, too. "Sam okay?"

I nodded, getting my breath back. "Wonderful. Victor seems to treat him with some kind of respect. I think in another life Sam must have been a snake handler."

Wade peered into the refrigerator and came out with a bottle of Sea Dog butternut ale.

"Yeah," he agreed, sitting at the table, "probably. Don't you get snakebit, though." He was still eyeing me carefully.

"I'm fine," I replied, looking noble while touching the back of my hand to my forehead in a tragic gesture.

"What about you?" I went on more seriously. "Are you really sure you're okay about this? Victor staying here?"

He put his beer down. "Well, it's hard to be jealous of a fellow when you know the woman in your life would like to knock that fellow's block off. But I still can't say I like the way he affects you. The way you always end up kowtowing to him, I mean."

The trouble with Wade is, he is so right all the time. "I know," he went on, warding off my protest, "it's easier not to argue with him, and there's Sam to think of. But there's a limit to what I'll watch you put up with, is all."

"Yeah." I felt myself nodding unhappily. The score so far between Victor and me was him a million, me darned near nothing, and it's hard to step back into the ring with a record like that. But I might have to.

Wade drank some beer. "Anyway, it can't be helped. With the holiday, the motels are full, and besides, if Victor gets comfortable, maybe he won't make a fuss when Sam tells him he's not going back to New York."

Which was the plan; Victor just wasn't in on it yet. He thought Sam was returning to the special school in the fall. But Sam meant to stay here in Eastport, finish high school, then go on to the local boat-building school and an apprenticeship at Dan Harpwell's boat-yard. Dan had Sam figured to run the place for him eventually, a situation that Sam regarded as heaven-sent.

Me, too; it was just the sort of work Sam loved and could do really well. All we needed now was to inform Victor, which was why Sam had begged me to have Victor here. So I'd invited him, and to my surprise he'd accepted at once; I wasn't sure why. Probably he had some nasty surprise up his sleeve, as usual.

"Let me know," Wade said, "if he gives you any real trouble."

"And then what? You'll punch him in the nose?" I stirred a handful of fresh dillweed from Ellie's kitchen garden into the buttermilk sauce I was making to go with the salmon; to hell, I'd decided, with bean juice, at least for tonight.

"No." Wade's eyes twinkled. "I'll take him out on the water with me. Maybe stop off at the Waco Diner for a couple of drinks, after. Introduce him," Wade added, "to some of the guys."

At six foot four and two hundred and twenty pounds, with a chest as solid as the weight bag that prizefighters work out on, Wade is regarded as something of a shrimp by the guys at the Waco.

"You wouldn't," I breathed, enchanted by the idea.

Wade guides big cargo vessels into the harbor for a living, motoring to the vessel on a tugboat, then climbing up a gangway, which is a metal ladder hanging over the rolling sea.

"Wanna bet?" He ran a calloused hand over his wiry blond hair, grinning. Wade knows the rocks and the ledges, the channels and currents of Passamaquoddy Bay better than anyone, which is one of the many reasons why he is Eastport's harbor pilot.

It is also why, if ever he took a notion to, Wade Sorenson could scare the bejesus out of my ex-husband, even without any of the guns that Wade is an expert at shooting and repairing.

"And," he went on, adding to the fantasy, "the fellows at the Waco will explain to Victor that you are their favorite tax preparer, and they would hate to see you distressed, 'cause then maybe you couldn't help them give the 'guvmint' the middle finger, anymore."

It is true that I have become a boon to sole proprietorship in Eastport. Before I came, people thought tax deductions were to be plucked up delicately, like thorned roses, but I must say they have taken well to my own more adventurous attitude, which Wade says resembles the Texas Chainsaw Massacre.

I went over and draped my arms around his shoulders. In the summer he smells like salt water and clean clothes. "Thanks. For sticking up for me, I mean, and for reminding me to stick up for myself. It'll be fine, you know."

He laid his head against mine. "Yeah, you always seem to make sure of that. Hardly leaves a knucklehead like me much to do."

"I'll find something interesting for you, later," I promised him, and he chuckled. Wade keeps his own little house by the water on Liberty Street, overlooking the bay, but when he strides down off the dock with his duffel bag over his shoulder, it is me he is coming home to. The situation suits us.

I was about to tell him about Ken Mumford, but just then Victor came in, his eyes narrowing at the sight of my happiness.

"Well," he remarked waspishly, "isn't this just the picture of domestic bliss." He marched importantly to the refrigerator and opened it.

"Ale?" he inquired, sounding horrified. "Ale is *loaded* with deleterious yeast organisms. And what's this—buttermilk? Blue cheese, and . . . *wine?* Good heavens."

He held up a bottle of Riesling, light and harmless as spring water. "This stuff," he breathed fervently, "is *bad*."

I felt Wade sigh.

"Hargood," I said urgently into the phone. "Don't sell the gold stocks. Hang on, and someday they'll be worth something."

Right, and someday I would go ice skating in hell. On the other hand, even in hell there was the chance of a cold snap, and if my old friend Hargood Biddeford sold his precious-metals stock now, he would miss out on it.

Besides, at the moment those stocks were about as valuable as wallpaper. "Hargood. Don't do it. We'll think of something else."

Six hundred miles and an entire, it seemed, universe away, Hargood Biddeford sat in the study of his New York apartment on Fifth Avenue and sighed heavily. "But Jacobia, they're so low."

"So low that if they get any lower, people won't pay to take them off your hands anymore. *Which* is why it makes sense to hang onto them, doesn't it? You've got nothing to lose."

From out in the dining room came the clink of silver-ware on plates. George and Ellie were there, and Wade, and Sam, and of course there was also Victor, who would ordinarily have spoiled my appetite. But after my boat ride I was starving, so that just the thought of those salmon fillets made me feel faint.

I waved my hand out of the phone alcove, and Sam

came and put my glass of Riesling into it, and gave me a pitying look.

"Harry," I said, "you've got that telephone." AT&T, I meant. "Why not dump a little of that?"

"But," he responded predictably, "it's so high."

Hargood's grasp of investment theory is tenuous. Getting him to take actual profits, for example, as opposed to bailing out of things at the worst possible moment, is a formidable project.

But Hargood also has eight children, whom I adore and whose voices I could now hear piping sweetly in the background. And what with them all having to eat and wear shoes and so on, I could not quite bring myself to abandon Hargood.

I did a series of quick calculations in my head. "Sell," I instructed him, "half your telephone stock."

He gasped. "But Jacobia, that's—"

"Enough," I overrode him, "to run your household and pay all the kids' tuitions for the rest of the year."

Not coincidentally, it was also what he'd lost on the gold stocks, which he had bought without my advice. If as I expected they were still tanked at the end of the quarter, we would sell them and offset his telephone profits.

"Meanwhile, take your income and start buying . . ." I named the stock. "And Harry, don't have any more children. I can only finagle your money a finite number of ways."

There was an ominous silence; Harry's wife is so fertile, I believe she actually goes by the name of Bunny.

"Righto, then," he said quickly, hanging up before I could question him further on the topic of yet another bouncing little Form 1040 deduction.

Back at the table, I took my plate off the warming tray and ate a bite of salmon, pausing while my taste buds swooned. "So," I asked Ellie, "what happened with Tim Mumford?"

Timothy had changed his mind about staying in

Eastport, Ellie had reported after taking him to see Bob Arnold, so she had run him and his belongings back out to Crow Island.

"Well," she replied, "he does think he knows who killed Ken."

Victor looked up with interest. Bullets on the kitchen table and murder at dinner, I could hear him thinking.

"Because when Kenny was in jail this last time—"

She turned to Victor. "Kenny is an old friend of mine," she explained, "or he was until today when we found him on the beach. He'd been shot to death."

Wade merely tipped his head; Sam had filled him in on all this while I was steaming the new potatoes. But Victor looked as if he might have a heart attack, the way he did the day I told him I was leaving him and that, by the way, the apartment and his office and the charge cards were all in his name, not just in his possession, so he could start making the payments on them.

"And," Ellie went on, "the last time Kenny was in jail for D and D—"

"That's drunk and disorderly," I explained *sotto voce* to Victor, whose hand seemed to be trembling. Ellie took pity on him and put some wine in his glass, and he drank it without noticing.

"—he met this other guy, a real bad guy," Ellie said.

"I don't get it," said Sam. "I thought Ken was a bad guy."

My ex-husband nodded approvingly at Sam, forgetting what a bad guy he was, himself.

While the others listened to Ellie, Wade glanced meaningfully at me. The look in his eyes expressed an invitation requiring no clothes whatsoever, and I must say I have rarely felt so fabulous while discussing bloody murder.

"Kenny," agreed Ellie, "was kind of a loser. But this guy, his name is Ike Forepaugh, beats people up and robs them, and he sticks up gas stations with a gun. According to Tim, when Ken was in jail, he met

Forepaugh and borrowed money from him, and also
told him that he—Ken, I mean—had some kind of a
surefire moneymaking operation planned, for when he
got back to Eastport."

The deal Tim had mentioned, I recalled; the way Ken
Mumford had found to make money.

"How'd Tim know?" George asked, helping himself
to seconds. "How would Tim know who Ken met in
jail, or what Ken said there?"

"Ken loved talking about big plans," Ellie replied.
"And mostly it *was* just talk. But this time, Tim says,
was different. He says he thinks Ken was running drug
packages over the border from Canada, in his boat."

At this, Wade and I looked at each other again,
George sat back sharply in his chair, and even Sam appeared impressed.

"Whoa," he said, while his father's lips pressed together in a tight, puritanical line.

"Tim didn't like it, but he says he thinks that's how
Ken was making money. Tim's theory is that Ike tried
to horn in," Ellie went on, "then killed Ken when Ken
didn't let him. Ken wouldn't have known how to handle a guy like that."

"Ken," George objected, "wasn't spending any
money." Which Ken would have if he could have,
George meant.

"Maybe he wasn't spending it in an obvious way.
There are methods of doing things," I said, looking
straight at Sam, "that don't raise an uproar."

Sam got the message; I didn't object to his telling his
dad about his plans. We'd have to, sooner or later; that
was the point of the visit. But I wanted him to be diplo-
matic.

Meanwhile my ex-husband had drawn himself up
into a sour little pickle of self-righteousness. "This," he
pronounced, "is not a very uplifting conversation."

George peered up from his meal. "Hey, Victor," he

said, gesturing at Victor's wineglass, "pour yourself a real drink, why don't you? Might cheer you up."

He took a gulp of his own wine. "I don't think," he added in tones of genuine kindness, "that anybody's going to call you back to the city, make you do any complicated brain surgery, tonight."

Victor looked at his glass, and realized what had been in it. There was a brief silence, the kind that I imagine occurs between the click of the pin being pulled from the grenade, and the moment when it explodes.

"So go on ahead," George said. "Relax. Loosen up."

Whereupon, and to everyone's astonishment, Victor did.

 No one except George would have dared say that to Victor. But George is so good-hearted and plainly without guile, he can get away with almost anything; nor is he afraid of bullies, which is also handy when dealing with Victor.

George's directness, though, can be a problem when it comes to things like that leaky radiator, as I was reminded later in the evening when Sam had gone out, Wade was in his workshop fixing a shotgun, and George was on his knees on the kitchen floor.

"This radiator," he observed, "has bought the farm."

Once upon a time, those words would have paralyzed my heart. But now I only suffered a brief arrhythmia, after which I returned to the problem that arose whenever I hired George for anything: keeping him from turning my old house into the sort of domestic showplace that the Stepford wives would feel right at home in.

"Don't," I said, "even mention baseboard heaters to

me. The day I put baseboard heaters into this house, I will put in fake paneling, acoustical ceiling tiles, and wall-to-wall shag carpet, and I will install fake gas logs in the fireplaces, too."

"All right," he groused. "I get the picture. You split enough firewood, though, you'll get to like those gas logs."

Pict-chah. "I don't see why people from away want to cling to all these old, inconvenient household trappings."

Besides the radiators, he meant tin ceilings, pressed with acorn-and-oak wreath patterns; stovepipe thimbles decorated with illustrations snipped from turn-of-the-century magazines; plaster walls and double-hung windows paned with wavery old glass. To him there was little wrong with my house that couldn't be fixed with Sheetrock and new Thermopane replacement windows, which he wanted to supply at once.

"George," said Victor, sitting with his elbows propped on the kitchen table. "You're a good man, George."

"Ayuh," George said kindly, and went to get his toolbox.

"Do you think he'll be all right?" Ellie asked, meaning Victor, who had opened another bottle of Riesling and was drinking it, studiously and determinedly, out of a jelly glass.

"He'll be okay," Wade said from the doorway; periodically he likes to come down from his workshop and wash the gun oil off his hands. "I'll stay and keep him company, while you two do your errand."

Ellie and I were going out to Ken Mumford's trailer, to pick up a few things for Timothy; Bob Arnold and the state police had already been through it, finding nothing of interest.

"Company," Victor agreed owlishly. "That's what I need."

"You might want to stop at the drugstore," Wade added, "get some aspirin. In the morning, he's going to be one sick pup."

"I," Victor pronounced in slurry sorrow, "am a sick pup now."

 "What was *that* all about?" Ellie asked as she drove her old Land Rover with gear-grinding vigor, gunning it down the dirt road that led to the neighborhood known as Quoddy Village. Here, small frame houses dating from the forties perched on tiny lots laid out in the style of a subdivision.

"I'm sure I don't know," I said, steeling myself against the bone-jarring bounce of the vehicle's suspension.

"Victor's usual drink," I added, "is a double martini. Or it was, before he turned into a health-food freak. And I doubt that the murder of someone he hadn't even met would have upset him. Maybe he just didn't know how hard that wine would hit him."

"He drank," Ellie pointed out, "a whole bottle. He's got to have realized that would have some impact."

The road narrowed and began slanting downhill. "Victor's been pretty mellow for a while, at least since Sam was in New York with him," I said. "He's had things the way he wanted them. But if his intuition tells him that's about to change—"

"Victor has the intuition of a cinder block."

Which was comforting in its intent but not quite true. Victor had plenty of intuition. The trouble was, the things he intuited were always things that you did not want him knowing about.

"I've got," Ellie said, "a bad feeling about him." She

found the landmark she'd been looking for. "Hey, this is it."

Ken Mumford's trailer was located at the back of an acre of uncleared land at the end of Toll Bridge Road, nearly to where the bridge once stood. Now the bridge—and before it, the flat barge-like ferry—were memories, the bright water moving swiftly where carts and carriages once rumbled for a penny.

"Here goes nothing," she said as we started bush-whacking in.

"What do you mean?" I plucked raspberry bramble from my sleeve.

"My understanding from Tim is that Kenny had a dog. A big," Ellie said, "dog. It's why he wanted us to come out here."

"Oh," I said doubtfully. From what I had gathered on Crow Island, Tim's idea of a big dog was the size of a brontosaurus.

"That's what Tim is mainly worried about," Ellie went on. "Who's going to take care of the animal."

Just then the animal in question hurtled from the forest at us: not big as a brontosaurus. No bigger, really, than a Buick.

A Buick with sharp white teeth, two blazing coals for eyes, and a bark like the one you might hear on a nature program whose film has had to be retrieved from amongst the scattered bones of the cameraman, to whose memory the production is dedicated.

I had a second to notice the width of its shoulders, the blocky head atop the thick neck. It was a German shepherd and as it hurled itself I did the only thing I could think of: I ducked.

The dog sailed over me with a *snap* of his massive jaws, hit the brush in a skid, and whirled for another rush at me; then from somewhere up ahead came a whistle and a girl's anxious call.

"Cosmo, heel!"

The only heel this monster wanted was mine, and

with my leg attached. I couldn't see Ellie, but I hadn't heard screaming; it was the only good thing I could think of about the situation.

The girl's voice, again; this time the dog paid attention. With its regal head lofty, bones as big as sledge-hammers, and a coat as heavily underfluffed as fox fur, the dog was—now that it wasn't trying to kill me—magnificent.

"Jacobia, I'm so sorry," Ellie managed shakily, rising from where she'd been crouched. "I didn't know it was a *wild* dog."

"It's not." I watched it depart. "It's a *Schutzhund* dog."

"I don't care what it is. Bob Arnold can just come out here and take it to the shelter, before it hurts someone."

"Wait." I caught up with Ellie. "Whoever called it, the dog obeys her. Sort of," I added.

Ellie looked doubtful. "What if she tells it to attack us?"

"Well, then probably we're dead. But she won't, or why would she have called it off in the first place?"

The girl hadn't called *heel*, I realized. She'd given the dog a command in German, the language in which the dogs were trained.

"Ellie, those dogs are amazing. The training costs a mint, but when they're done, you've got the best body-guard *and* the best companion dog in the world."

Ellie eyed me. "I thought you were scared of strange dogs." But she was pushing with me through the bramble again.

"Not of strange dogs. Just mean dogs. And I like to get it clear which kind I'm dealing with. But this dog . . ."

The path broke through to a clearing. At the back of it stood an old Airstream trailer, the round-shouldered, silver-skinned kind. Somebody had built a deck for it, with steps leading up to the door. Through a stand of trees at the back of the lot, blue water sparkled like sequins on a fancy cocktail dress.

"Dogs like that," I said, "won't hurt you unless they're told to. They won't even eat their own food until you tell them to." It's to keep them from being poisoned; trained for tracking, obedience, and protection, the animals make excellent guards for big estates.

"So why'd he charge us?" Ellie wanted to know.

"Handler error," I guessed. "That's mostly why a guard dog's an insurance liability. And the girl didn't sound very confident."

Lying on the deck, the dog raised its head but didn't move. "We can go," I told Ellie, "right to the foot of the steps." After that, I wouldn't give a pin for our chances. Someone, probably the girl, had told the dog where the line was now.

"You," Ellie said, "seem to know an awful lot about this."

"I worked for a while with a fellow who had them," I said, scanning the trailer again.

There was something wrong with the windows: they were clean, hung with curtains of eyelet lace.

"And," I went on, frowning at this incongruity, "this fellow asked me to keep one for a while. When I was in New York."

Actually, the fellow hadn't asked me to keep the dog. He'd ordered me to do so, emphasizing that the arrangement was for my own safety. My client, it seemed, had made some interesting enemies, and so by association had I.

Clamped to Ken's trailer near the deck was a pulley like the one old Tim used to operate his shed windows, only smaller. Looped through it was a length of clothesline with towels hanging from it. A pang of unease struck me: what had bothered me about Tim's pulley? But the thought faded in light of a new insight about Ken.

"He had a girlfriend. That's Ken's girlfriend, in there."

Ellie looked dismayed. "Oh, I hope someone's called her. I don't want to have to tell her that he's—"

The trailer's door opened suddenly and the girl appeared.

"Get out of here. I'll sic Cosmo on you, if you don't."

She was a small, slender person in her late teens, with a cap of short, white-blonde hair, wearing cutoffs and a halter top. A large, silver-glinting medallion hung from a chain around her frail neck.

"Do you know," I called, "what will happen if you do? The dog will tear us apart, and it will end up being shot."

I took a step. The dog got calmly to its feet. "Look, we only want a few of Ken's personal things for his dad."

The girl glared, but spoke to the dog, who lay down again.

"We're not here to bother you. Although," I added, unable to help myself, she looked so woebegone, "if you want to come back with us, maybe talk about it . . ."

"No. I know who sent you. My father. I'm not going back."

Ellie stepped quickly in front of me. "Hallie, we only want things that mean something to Timothy, to remember Ken by."

"Oh, sure." The girl's mouth twisted. "What about me? What am I supposed to remember him by?"

I spotted a line of scabs on her arm as she fingered the medallion. Then she slammed into the trailer again, emerging a few seconds later with a bulging canvas satchel.

"I hate you! You're all alike. You all just want . . . want . . ."

Fists clenched, she shrieked out a howl of grief. The dog looked up, alarmed, but did not move.

"Cosmo!" She uttered a command, then scrambled off the deck, darted across the clearing, and vanished into the scrubby woods.

After an uncertain moment—I thought again that she didn't know how to handle the animal, that the command she'd given was somehow wrong, or inappropriate—the dog gave up and followed, sailing in among the trees behind her in long, athletic bounds.

Ellie sighed. "Well, so much for social work. Come on, let's get whatever Tim might want and get out of here."

"Who's that girl?" I asked as we went in. Then I stopped, unable for a moment to credit my perceptions.

"Hallie Quinn," Ellie replied. "I should have figured she'd be out here, it's perfect for giving her father a heart attack."

She frowned. "Do you see what I see?"

The trailer was immaculate. "Strange but true. Looks like someone has turned into Holly Homemaker."

"Hallie," my friend corrected distractedly, leafing through some papers on a countertop. "Hey, look at this."

It was a stack of bills: fuel, electricity, and so on. Each was marked "paid" and initialled with a circled HQ, in a childish hand that I figured was Hallie's.

The curtains were certainly her work, also; peeking between them I spotted a big Trans Am with an open hood, an empty engine compartment, and a bad frame twist. Patches of Bondo smeared the body, and the headlights were empty sockets.

"There's the Ken we all know and love," I said. "Tim's full of beans. Kenny didn't have any deal going, or he'd have fixed up the car. He just found a girl willing to clean up after him."

Ellie shook her head. "Takes more than Windex to pay bills."

"Huh. You're right," I conceded. "He must have had money coming in. See any ledger or checkbook? I could get an idea of his cash flow."

She gave a little snort. "I don't think so."

I opened drawers and peered into them: old tide tables, fishing lures, balls of twine. No financial records.

"I guess you're right about that, too. Ken probably didn't even file income taxes."

"He filed," she corrected me quietly, "a 1040-EZ. I've been doing them for him, for years."

I turned in surprise and found her eyes brimming with tears. "*Damn* it. Timothy was right—he shouldn't have died that way."

"Hey, Ellie. I mean, if it's any comfort to you—"

"I know. A bullet in the head—it's the way you'd put down a good old horse. Quick and painless, and I can't do anything about it now. But I wish," she finished earnestly, "that I'd been kinder to him at the end. I was so busy with my life, and being married to George, and all . . ."

Through the window a flash of something metallic caught my eye; the medallion, I realized. Then I saw Hallie standing at the edge of the clearing, gazing wistfully back at the trailer.

"Look," I murmured, and Ellie stepped up beside me.

"Oh," she exhaled. "Let's go, so she can come back."

"She's not coming back." The girl slipped into the brush and was gone. "I thought so too at first, but that bag she took? It's got her things in it. There's nothing of hers left, here."

Ellie frowned. "I said we wouldn't take anything except . . ."

"It's not what we're taking. It's that we're here at all, and even worse, that the police have been. She might have put up with one visit, even from cops. But not two. Did you notice the marks on her arm? Those are needle tracks."

Ellie stared at me, but after a moment she accepted it, aware that I knew what I was talking about.

Back in the city, Sam always insisted he wasn't using any hard drugs. But his friends were, and I got to know the signs. I had hoped I would not see them again, and around him I never did.

"But—" Ellie peered at the cleanliness of the place.

"Junkies can function," I said. "For a while."

I stifled the urge to stride out after the girl. It wouldn't do any good. "Let's just do what we need to, and go home."

So we did: I found a Boy Scout manual and Ellie snagged Ken's fishing rod. In the living area, next to a sofa with a sheet and a blanket neatly folded at one end—the pillowslip on the pillow bore the blue initials HQ, embroidered in a delicate chain-stitch—I picked up a framed snapshot of Tim and Kenny. In the sleeping alcove was a Swiss Army knife. There was a book on the bedside table: Stephen King's *Christine*.

"I wouldn't have figured Ken for a reader."

Ellie looked over, her glance softening. "Ken liked reading. Took him a while to get the hang of it, but he did, finally."

Moments later we were out of there. Leaving the clearing I looked back, still hoping I would see Hallie and persuade her to come with us. But all I saw was the dog; as soon as we'd come out, he'd returned to the deck.

More evidence, I thought, that the girl didn't really know how to control him. Now he lay watching us with eyes that were calmly professional. I felt bad leaving him there, but I assumed he wouldn't have come with us, anyway.

Driving home, we passed the barracks-like building that had housed the Quoddy Dam workers, back in the

1940s when the Navy's never-completed project to produce electricity from the tides had been in its heyday. A two-storied frame structure with dozens of windows, a red-shingled peaked roof, and a porched entrance, the building now stood empty, its shutters hanging askew.

Ellie gazed at it as we went by. "Too big," she remarked.

"What?" I replied, distracted. I'd been thinking of Hallie: how pretty she was. Some of Sam's friends, both male and female, had been pretty, too. Once upon a time.

"Those shutters," Ellie said, "on the barracks. But they're too big for your house. Didn't Felicity Abbot-Jones say last year that she thought all Eastport houses ought to have shutters? And I thought you meant to do something about it."

"Yes," I said, feeling a thud in the pit of my stomach as I remembered: murder or no murder, Felicity was coming—and soon.

Months earlier I had hired a crew to take down my old shutters, most of them irreparably damaged. But now without them my house resembled a woman who has, for some ungodly reason that probably seemed sensible at the time, shaved her eyebrows off.

The difference being that a woman's eyebrows will grow back.

"Good heavens," I whispered inadequately as we pulled into the drive. "I don't even have an extension ladder."

We tiptoed into the house, where the silence was absolute, as if someone had filled the place with anesthetic gas.

"But," I said, peering around—the radiator was gone, and the spot underneath it had been swept, scrubbed, and coated with wax; good old George—"that's not the real problem."

The dining room was empty, and so was the parlor.

No sound came from Sam's room, and Monday was asleep in her dog bed.

"The problem is, I have nothing to haul up there. No," I finished, "shutters. Ellie, where is everyone?"

Ellie picked up a note from the roll-top desk that Sam had found, abandoned in a barn in Lubec. When he brought it home, it looked like a load of firewood, but now it gleamed with all the sanding, staining, and finish-rubbing that he had put into it; it was, he had informed me proudly, bird's-eye maple.

" 'Gone to movies. Victor asleep. Look in refrigerator,' " the note said, and it was signed by Wade.

So I looked, and found a split of champagne, along with two rose crystal glasses that I had admired in a shop in Calais. The card tucked under the bottle read, 'Do not open until midnight.'

"Too bad he didn't put some shutters in there," Ellie said.

"Probably he would have, if they'd fit and he'd had some. Do you suppose we should check on Victor?"

"Uh-uh. If he's dying, I don't want to resuscitate him."

I shot a look at her.

"Oh, all right," she relented. "I guess it wouldn't be so good if Victor stopped breathing. Although," she added, "it *would* mean that he would also stop talking . . ."

"Ssh." I slipped along the upstairs hall ahead of her. A small lamp burned on the guest room's bureau, so we could see his chest slowly rising and falling.

"Okay, he's alive," Ellie said. "Now let's leave him here. Having him at my mercy like this is too tempting."

"Wait," I said. "Just . . . look at him."

Asleep, Victor resembled one of those Botticelli angels that used to get painted on the ceilings of cathedrals. He could be funny, too, when he wanted to be. When he wanted to, Victor could charm the birds out of the trees.

"Right, he looks harmless enough, now," Ellie said. "So does a wasp's nest if you don't know what's in it. Why you put up with him the way you do, I can't understand."

As if in reply, Victor snorted and sat up suddenly, his face twisting peevishly into an expression of anger tinctured with paranoia. Then the alcohol hit him, and you could practically see every blood vessel in his skull reacting to the blow.

"Oh," he moaned, clutching his temples, and saw me standing there feeling sorry for him in spite of myself.

"Well," he snapped, "what are you waiting for? Go get me two aspirin, and some bottled spring water. And hurry it up."

Later that evening, upstairs with Wade, in the dark:

"Move your elbow a little, will you?" I said. "Right, that's better."

We'd nixed the champagne—Victor's presence in the house would probably just make the bubbles go flat, anyway—and then Monday had decided to get up on the bed with us, so now the three of us lay companionably under the quilt.

"I'm going out in a couple of hours," Wade said.

To work, he meant; to go out on the water. The tug often went out to meet a freighter while it was still dark.

A breeze moved the curtains, moonlight shifting in the lace. A foghorn honked at the lighthouse a couple of miles away. Wade put his arms around Monday and me, gathering us in. "Don't worry."

A week earlier, a freighter had capsized off Newfoundland: five saved, sixteen lost. There had been film of the awash vessel on Canadian TV, the craft moving helplessly, being swallowed.

"I won't worry." I made myself smile when I said it.

If anyone is safe out on the water, it is Wade; that's well known. He will come home if anyone does. There is not a woman in town who would say any differently. Then again, there's not a woman in town who will speak of capsizing, who will say the word aloud, not even if you pulled her fingernails out with pliers.

Which reminded me: "Listen, if Ken's boat was adrift, how did his killer get to shore?" Not by swimming; the water was too cold.

Wade's shoulder shifted. "Another boat?"

"Maybe." But it meant Ken had let someone aboard. From listening to Wade, I knew boarding another guy's boat was nearly impossible without that guy's cooperation.

On the other hand, maybe Ken didn't know Forepaugh meant any harm. Ike could have stolen a boat, then put it back afterwards.

"You located," Wade asked drowsily, "those shutters?"

I found his hand and held it. "Over in Dennysville, some guy remodeling a house. I talked to George when he came to take Ellie home, and he says there are shutters in the Dumpster, out back."

I felt Wade nodding in the dark. "Yeah, I know the place. Guy's got every tradesman in town on the job, turn that farmhouse into a palace. You might know him, up from New York. Somebody in the Waco says the guy was a stockbroker, ran into some trouble."

A little pang of something nudged me, but I ignored it. Lots of stockbrokers have run into trouble; it didn't mean anything.

"Funny name, the guys said he had. Something like a tree."

The pang sharpened. It couldn't be. Could it?

". . . birch, alder . . ."

Sure it could. With Victor around, anything could happen. The man spread disaster like a head cold.

". . . willow. That's it—Willoughby. Do you know him?"

Down the hall, Sam slept the untroubled sleep of adolescence, out like a light the minute his head hit the pillow, while in the guest room Victor tossed and moaned, misery seeping from his pores.

"Baxter Willoughby," I said resignedly.

Suddenly, Wade's last waking defenses fell; his breathing deepened, becoming even and slow, and I felt him slide away into unconsciousness. Monday slept, too, paws twitching as she chased, with dreaming whimpers, a dream rabbit.

Which left me alone, thinking about Ken, Hallie, and Tim. By now Ken's body was in Bangor, awaiting forensic autopsy. Timothy was back on Crow Island, grieving for his son. And where Hallie Quinn might have gotten to by now, I didn't even want to imagine.

And then there was Baxter Willoughby, on account of whom my planned expedition to Dennysville didn't seem quite so promising.

I'd never met him, but I knew him well in the way that a skilled accountant knows you by examining your bank records, charge accounts, brokers' statements, and tax filings. I knew of every insurance claim he'd ever made, every parking ticket he'd gotten, the names of his children and the address of the vet where his wife took their miniature schnauzers to be spayed.

He'd been a crooked trader—his name, in fact, had become synonymous with the breed—and when the SEC had gotten wind of him, they'd called me: fast, accurate, discreet.

I'd spent a year creating a flow chart so detailed, it looked like a map of the New York subway system. I'd had phone records, appointment calendars, even the contents of his wastebaskets, all collected by an army of SEC snoops; for twelve months, if Willoughby dropped a tissue, somebody picked it up.

The point of it all was to prove the SEC's suspicions: that over a period of approximately fifteen years, Baxter Willoughby had bilked a whole range of victims out of millions of dollars.

My job was to prove it, and when I was finished, Willoughby went to jail.

13 Early the next morning, I found the paint scraper I'd been using on the kitchen floor and took it out to the backyard, along with a cup of coffee. Hummingbirds flitted among the dahlias in the garden while I spread newspapers along the stone foundation of the house, then began scraping clapboards.

It was too late to get Bill Twitchell to come over, with his mile-high ladders and space-age grinders, to scrape and paint the whole house before Felicity got here. But I could get the loose paint off in spots that were low enough for me to reach, and cover the bare wood with white-tinted shellac. That would protect the wood, and make things look spiffier for Felicity.

I kept scraping until my arm began aching and the rest of the world began stirring: cars starting, dogs barking, the big white garbage truck with the moose painted on the side of it, rumbling down the street.

Trash day: I'd forgotten it. I scrambled to haul the garbage cans out to the curbside, just as Al Rollins swung off the back of the truck to empty them toward the receptacle's gaping maw.

" 'Morning, Al. Thanks very much."

He muttered a reply, his normally cheerful face clouded.

"Something wrong?" Al's good nature is a given, around town.

"Aw, them illegal dumpers got me hopping. Too cheap to get trash picked up like normal people. They go out, dump it in the woods someplace, make a big mess. Then town hall hires me to go get it. And I don't mind telling you it's a lot more trouble, at the end of some godforsaken dirt track out in the wilderness."

"I'm sorry about that, Al. Want coffee? I've got some fresh." Al's pleasant manner has cheered me up on plenty of occasions; I figured the least I could do was return the favor.

"Nah, thanks." He waved at the rest of the street, with the trash cans lined up neatly at the end of each front sidewalk.

"Worst part is, they got me goin' through the stuff. You know," he added at my look of puzzlement, "to find out who it is, doin' the dumping. Boy, what a lousy chore."

"Ick. Well, I hope it lets up soon. And look at it this way, when you find out who's doing it, Arnold will make them stop."

He brightened minutely. "Yeah, that's right, isn't it? Well, see you next week." He swung aboard the truck and signaled to his driver.

"Yeah, see you," I called as it rumbled away. Al's comments about trash-sorting reminded me of Baxter Willoughby, whose trash had been gone through so exhaustively by the SEC investigators, and whose Dumpster was one of the tasks on my agenda for today.

But I wasn't ready to confront any of them yet, so as the garbage truck turned the corner I went inside, got Monday's leash, and took her for a walk along the waterfront.

The air was cool, smelling of chamomile and salt threaded with a hint of woodsmoke; gulls, swooping

and soaring over the water, cried raucous warnings to
cormorants diving for minnows under the dock. Monday sniffed appreciatively as we passed the Waco Diner,
pouring forth a powerful aroma of coffee and pancakes.

Meanwhile, I pretended our walk had to do with me
being a good dog owner. But I was really only putting
off the inevitable.

The SEC guys had sworn up and down that no one
would ever know I'd helped them get Baxter Willoughby. More to the point, they'd sworn up and down
that he wouldn't.

Pretty soon, though, I'd find out how good their
promises were: good enough to get me onto Willoughby's place—and off again—with four dozen pairs
of wooden shutters the cost of which, if I had to buy
them new, would pay off the national debt?

Or only good enough to get me chased off, with Willoughby reading me a profane riot act as I fled?

On Water Street, Henry Wadsworth had unfurled the
green-striped awning over the hardware store window.
Margaret Smythe was watering the red geraniums in the
planters outside Bay Books. And on the boat dock an
army of yellow forklifts beetled around the Quonset
warehouse, getting ready for the cargo freighter which
was due in soon.

Over it all hung the fresh smell of seawater and an
air of incalculable good fortune, the golden state of
grace that was an island summer in Maine. So why did I
feel so lousy?

Not, I realized, because of Willoughby and the shutters. It was on account of Victor.

Wade and Ellie were right: after the way he'd treated
me over the years, my ex-husband deserved a kick in
the pants. Instead I was behaving passively, telling myself it was easier than fighting with him—after all, he
wouldn't be here forever—and that maybe it would
help Sam keep a good relationship with his father.

But the truth was harder and deeper: I loathed knowing I'd been so stupid as to marry him, and disliked other people knowing it even more. Treating him as he deserved, especially in front of witnesses, felt like admitting the kind of mistake whose memory—even years later—can stop you in your tracks, quivering with shamed embarrassment.

Also, I liked being the good guy, the one who could not be accused of keeping an argument going, much less starting it. This, I had to admit to myself, was also part of the reason I'd never dished any real dirt about Victor to Sam. Victor's "heart attack," for instance, when I told him I was leaving . . .

But no, I wasn't going to start thinking about that. What I needed was to behave like a vertebrate, or Wade and Ellie—and probably Sam, too—would lose a lot of respect for me.

As I would for myself . . .

"Hey!" The greeting roused me gratefully from my musings; it was Bob Arnold, coming out of police headquarters.

The dog and I crossed the street to meet him, and he rocked back and forth on his shiny black shoes as I told him that Ellie and I had gotten the things Tim wanted, and would be taking them out to him on Crow Island later in the day.

"Ayuh," he replied, his freshly shaven cheeks looking babyish in the morning sunshine. "That's fine. I got a call from the boys down to Augusta, too, you might want to tell Ellie. They confirmed who that friend of Ken's must have been, that old Tim figures was the one who shot him."

He stuck a toothpick in his mouth and chewed stolidly on it, wanting a cigarette and as always determined not to have one.

"I mean that Forepaugh fellow," he went on. "We'll pick him up, I don't doubt, and I'm going to have another look at Ken's boat, see if there's any evidence Ken was doing anything he shouldn't have been."

I nodded. Something, he meant, that Forepaugh might have wanted to horn in on, like a boatload of smuggled drugs.

"Doubt there will be, though," Arnold added. "You kill a fellow, stands to reason you clean up anything points to your motive, doesn't it?"

"I guess. Who gets the boat?" I wondered aloud. Other than the trailer, which was pretty decrepit and sitting on rented land, it was the only thing of value that Ken had possessed.

Arnold shrugged. "Tim. Or maybe Ken's cousin, Ned. Whichever one of 'em wants it."

He considered this further. "Probably," he decided finally, "it'll be Ned. Crow Island's got a deep enough cove on the north side, bring 'er in, but I doubt old Tim wants the trouble of it, with his foot all bunged up the way it is. And the boat needs a good bit of repair, too. When the state cops hauled it out, they found a big ding in her hull, below the water line."

"Huh," I said. "Any idea how the killer got to shore?"

Arnold shook his head. "Couple possibilities, one being an accomplice."

Monday snorted along the sidewalk, snuffling up bits of old chewing gum and any other items that were even remotely edible.

"Ken had a nice inflatable rubber dinghy stuffed away in the hold," Arnold mused further. "Whoever killed him didn't take it. Maybe didn't find it. Or didn't need it. Whichever."

"There was a girl out at Ken's trailer," I said, thinking about the idea of an accomplice.

"Yeah, I know. Hallie Quinn. State boys want to talk to her, too, but she lit out before they could nab her, yesterday. They'll get her, though. Unless," he added, "I get her, first."

I looked questioningly at him while Monday ate an apple core.

"Her parents have been on me like flypaper," he explained, "to bring her home. Not that they're model citizens, never mind the good front they put up."

"She looks as if she might be having some trouble."

"Uh-huh. Like the desert's got sand. You don't have to dance around it. Her folks've told me they think she's on something."

"That's the reason they want her back?"

He nodded unhappily. "One of 'em. It's the reason I can agree with, anyway. Mostly, it seems like they think she's gotten above herself. Gotten snotty, is how they put it. Or her old man did."

He looked at me, his pale blue eyes undeceived. "You know, if you'd grown up here, you might not think it was heaven on earth the way you do. Damn near fallen off the edge of the world, we're so far away from everything. No excitement, not many jobs, and the ones that there are, they are awfully damned hard work."

He shook his head, turning to gaze out across the flat, blue water to Campobello. "Fine place if you've got a little money, or a way to get some." It wasn't a dig at me, just the simple truth.

"But what girl you think is going to like it," he went on, "hip deep in the cold mud, makin' a living filling a clam bucket, and in winter she wrecks her hands tying Christmas wreaths?"

"I know. It isn't easy." That was one reason Felicity Abbot-Jones's visit was no joke; Eastport wasn't Camden or Bar Harbor. We needed the money she controlled.

Arnold sighed. "Anyway, Hallie's a smart kid. Ask me, she's smarter'n her parents. And like any kid will, she wants things, you know, some of 'em things that the parents never even thought of wanting."

He shook his head worriedly. "But now she's got

herself in a pickle, got herself into that heroin, I think, and what I hear, she can't get herself off. Not," he added, "that I believe she's made much of a try at it. She hasn't gotten to the hurting part, yet, I guess."

Remembering the pale, twisted face peering at me from out of the scrub woods, out behind Ken Mumford's trailer, I thought that possibly Arnold was wrong about the hurting part.

"I don't know where they get it," he declared, "but I mean to learn. And when I do—" He slammed a solid fist into his palm.

Monday pounced on a nugget of toffee and began chewing it, her jaws working with comic industry.

"A little pot," Arnold added, "is one thing. But heroin will be the death of us. This town—"

He gestured at the granite curbstones, antique storefronts, and turn-of-the-century glass windows that comprised the village of Eastport's brave little downtown commercial area—

"We aren't ready for that kind of thing. Crime, overdoses—and once it's here it doesn't ever go away. I'm worried," Arnold said seriously, "and I don't know how to stop it."

Nights in Eastport, you could walk stark naked down Water Street with the Hope Diamond in your hand and no one would molest you. Gossip about you, yes; and Arnold would arrest you, and your name would be in the paper. But nobody would hurt you.

So far.

Meanwhile, Arnold had gotten his wind up. "I tell you, Jacobia, you can take the nastiest guy in town— and till now, I'd of told you it was Ken Mumford—a guy, he thinks a six-pack is breakfast, he's addicted to those dirty 900 numbers, and he's light-fingered around a cash register, too, if you are foolish enough to let him get near one—"

He took a breath. "A real joker. But he won't rob or murder you, and if you are in trouble, he will help you.

That's the way it's been, here. Until," he finished unhappily, "lately."

"Now, Arnold," I said, "don't get all bleak and miserable about it. We're not gone to hell in a handbasket yet. The town's been around for two hundred years, it's hit bad patches, before. We will," I tried to encourage him, "get through this."

What I should have been telling him was to call out the Marines. But on a summer day in Eastport when the water and sky make you feel that things just cannot get better, it is hard to believe they are about to get worse.

A lot worse.

"Yeah, well," Arnold said, "Hallie just turned eighteen, so I don't have to take her home. I don't want to. Her old man hits the bottle pretty good. Hits her, too, is the word in town."

He squared his shoulders. "But I am," he emphasized, "going to bring her in and bust her for possession if I can, and scare her so she tells me where that garbage is coming from."

In the boat basin, the big white pleasure cruiser—her name, painted in swirly gold script on her bow, was *Triple Witch*—still floated, resembling a dream of luxury.

"So if you see her again," Arnold told me, "you let me know. Don't go adopting her like some stray cat, Jacobia, I mean it. I need her to help me or we're going to have a problem around here."

I promised Arnold I would tell him if I saw Hallie again, and we parted in front of Leighton's Variety Store, which was doing a brisk business in hot coffee, doughnuts, and packs of cigarettes for the truck drivers and stevedores gathering by the warehouse.

After that, Monday and I continued out Water Street to the part of town called Dog Island, the white clapboard houses giving way to frame row houses, cottages, and the windswept fields overlooking Passamaquoddy Bay. Across the bay, Campobello sparkled under a turquoise sky, with the swirls of the whirlpool, Old Sow, churning the aquamarine waters in the channel.

Returning through Hillside Cemetery, I let the dog romp among centuries-old tombstones inscribed with the names of early sea captains, a litany of their wives' names, and the solemn stone faces of angels. We paused at the cast-iron planter that once was a horse trough, and at a mound of stones and earth, the remains of Fort Sullivan's powder-house in the War of 1812.

But finally I couldn't delay any longer. At home, the *Bangor Daily News* stuck out of the letterbox, and when I got inside the welcome fragrance of the coffee I'd brewed earlier greeted me.

"Man Found Dead on Downeast Beach," announced the paper's headline. I poured some more coffee and scanned the piece while I drank it, but it reported nothing that I didn't already know.

Except one thing: the reporter had apparently tried calling me. I was mentioned by name as one of the two Eastport women who had found Ken's body, and was described as not wanting to comment—"according to a family spokesperson."

Just then Victor wandered into the kitchen, looking frowzy in a blue-striped bathrobe and slippers.

"Coffee," he muttered, squinting through reddened eyes, and made a beeline for it.

I held the pot away from him, waving the newspaper. "Did you do this? Refuse comment on my behalf, without even telling me?"

Not that I particularly wanted to be interviewed. Keeping my own and my clients' names quiet had been second nature to me for too long, in New York. But the idea of Victor making the decision for me made me want to pop him one.

Victor made a face that I am not even going to describe. "This family," he intoned, "does not need that sort of attention."

He grabbed for the coffeepot, missed, and reached

for the table to steady himself, then sank into a chair. "Head hurts," he said froggily into his splayed hands.

I just stood there holding the scalding-hot coffeepot, gazing at my ex-husband. Then I put the pot down and got out of the house, for two reasons:

First, I really did need to find out about those shutters of Baxter Willoughby's.

And second, if I stayed in Victor's presence for even a moment longer, there was going to be another murder.

 Wade had left his pickup parked in my driveway with the keys still dangling from the ignition, so I took that, figuring that if I did get the replacement shutters, I could haul them home.

What I didn't figure on was the transmission, lurching and grinding unpleasantly, but once I was out of town and cruising on the causeway with the water sparkling on both sides, the trouble went away by itself; the truck apparently liked fourth gear, and motored along happily in it.

Approaching the Passamaquoddy reservation at Pleasant Point, I slowed for the thirty-five-mile-per-hour zone, nodding at Joseph Lookabaugh stationed in his green squad car across from the tribe's local community center. A few minutes later I was headed south on Route 1, with the gearbox grinding in protest again, though Wade hadn't said anything about trouble with it. I put the clutch in and babied it, and eventually Tab A consented grudgingly to enter Slot B, and the engine regained power once more.

Keeping an eye on the oil pressure, the engine temperature, and the rearview mirror, in case any truck parts began falling off and clattering down the highway behind me, I made my way between spruce trees and acres of purple lupine, the tall spikes moving in the breeze like waves.

Crossing the bridge over the river at Dennysville, I glanced down at the water tumbling and foaming over the rocks, feeling the bridge deck thrumming beneath the truck's tires and experiencing a sensation of vast good luck. This was mine: I was not a tourist or houseguest. I lived here.

As if to prove this, Bill Martin's panel truck went by in the opposite direction, the legend DOWN EAST ELECTRICAL CONTRACTING painted on the door. He flashed his headlights as he caught sight of Wade's Toyota, and waved at me as he passed.

I smiled, humming along with the country tune playing on the truck radio. Maybe I was from away, not a downeast native, but people knew me. They even gossiped about me, a situation I did not regard as ideal until Ellie mentioned the alternative: not caring about me. But now that I understood, I was happy for them to know the amount of my bank balance, the color of my bedroom curtains, the date on which Wade first left his truck in my driveway overnight, and even the size, color, and preferred fabric of my underwear.

Which, believe me, everybody in Eastport does know, and I know the equivalent about them. Briefly, it occurred to me that in a town whose gossip network made the Internet look like two tin cans tied together with string, somebody knew something else, too: where Hallie Quinn was getting that heroin.

But then I had to start watching the route George Valentine had described to me, for getting to Baxter Willoughby's house. I'd been out here before, but in November, and summer in downeast Maine is the equivalent of seeing in color after years of black-and-white; everything looks completely different.

Just past the gas station on the far side of the Dennysville bridge, I took a left onto a narrow, curving macadam road leading between ancient maple trees. Next came an old brick schoolhouse with a wooden bell tower, a granite doorstep, and two front doors: one for boys, one for girls. Finally, I spotted the turnoff.

And blinked, startled at the change since I had seen it last. Where a dirt lane had rutted between cedar hedges, now a straight blacktop path ribboned up, the cedars lopped off and hauled off. I had a moment to mourn them before the next shock came.

The house on the hill had stood vacant for thirty years: gathering cobwebs, sheltering pigeons, and rotting away. Wade and I had come out here to look at the place, but it had turned out to be a sad wreck of its former self, too far gone for us to even think of rescuing it.

Now, though, above the vista created by the slaughter of all those cedars, the old house *gleamed:* new siding, new windows, and a new foundation. The chimneys were rebuilt, the front porch demolished and re-created, with white lattice under the deck. The gutters shone and the glass dazzled with expensive newness; from the wide front steps, a flagstone path led around to—

—yes: a glass-topped indoor swimming pool.

Which in Maine was the luxury equivalent of the Taj Mahal; just heating the thing would cost a fortune, and never mind trying to keep snow from collapsing the roof.

After all that, the fact that Willoughby's place was also home to a small army of llamas came as something of an anticlimax.

15 Llamas are South American cousins of camels, smaller and without humps. Here in Maine, they are kept for their wool and as pack animals; sure-footed and with pleasanter dispositions than their larger African relatives, they carry tourists' camping gear on guided expeditions, lending a cheerful, totally spurious air of "roughing it" to the tourists' outdoor experience.

These llamas didn't seem happy, though: their black-and-white or desert-tan coats looked a little ratty, and when I approached the rail fence that enclosed them (that, I gathered, was where all those cedar trees had gone), one of them spit at me.

Fortunately, he missed; llamas, apparently, didn't have the distance on their spitballs that I'd heard camels could achieve. And the animals' enclosure was furnished with a large trough of fresh-looking water, along with a tub generously filled with small brown pellets, like Monday's dog food, that I figured was their chow.

Also, the acre enclosure held only a dozen of the creatures, and in one corner stood a barn that looked aggressively new and sturdy. So I thought they weren't doing too badly, even if whoever kept them wasn't pampering them with lots of affection. After all, not every animal can live like Monday, who likes to lie in bed at night and eat buttered toast while someone reads mystery novels to her; she particularly enjoys the cat characters.

"Hello." In the rural silence I jumped at the voice. Turning, I confronted a tall, silver-haired fellow of fifty, resplendent in blue chambray shirt with pearl buttons, hundred-dollar jeans, and moosehide loafers. He stood smiling at me in the cautious, arm's-length way that people do when they were not expecting you, don't want you, and really would prefer that you beat it.

I had seen Willoughby's lean, ratlike face in a hundred surveillance photographs. Now his blue eyes took my measure as coldly as if he were adding up a column of quarterly profits and not much liking the result.

The question was, did he know me? The llamas looked on with interest. Oh, what the hell, I thought, here goes nothing.

"Jacobia Tiptree," I introduced myself, sticking my hand out. "George Valentine said you had a bunch of old shutters you didn't want, that maybe they were still out back in the Dumpster."

Then I waited, but I didn't see my name flip any switches. Up at the house, a man in a rumpled suit came onto the porch, peering curiously at us.

"Oh, right," Willoughby said at last, seeming to relax a bit. "Those old things. Sure, you want to haul them away, you can have 'em. So, how do you like the place?" He waved an expansive arm.

Now that my eyes had adjusted to the glare of the vinyl siding, I could take in a few more details. The roof was made from the kind of shingles that are intended to look like cedar shakes, but don't. The new shutters were genuine plastic. And the brick chimneys, I realized, were concrete block, false-fronted with brickface. Even the mailbox, intended to resemble wood when viewed from a suitable distance—say, a mile or so—was vintage Rubbermaid.

Still, he wasn't cursing at me, which I took as a good sign. I glanced again at the llamas, to make sure they weren't sporting little wind-up keys. "Um, it looks as if you've poured in a lot of resources," I replied, trying to be tactful.

"Hey, that's for sure," Willoughby preened. "God-damned money pit. Knocking out the old plaster, putting up new Sheetrock cost a fortune, and getting rid of the woodstoves—forget about it."

He gazed proudly at his creation. "And the facilities—who the hell wants a clawfoot bathtub in this day and age? I mean this may be God's country, but you need some modern comforts."

I tried not to wince visibly, then realized that it wouldn't matter. Willoughby was the kind of fellow who, once he thought he had you pegged, forgot about you for all practical purposes. Your function thereafter was merely to nod and make agreeing noises.

Which I did, while Willoughby poured on the charm of the born salesman and gave me a drastically sanitized version of his life history: business in Manhattan, big success, spiritual awakening. Now he meant to enjoy the stress-free life of a country gentleman.

He liked to talk; all good salesmen did, and in his heyday he'd been one of the best. But nowhere in his recital did there appear the little matter of his conviction for securities fraud, or the fact that his spiritual awakening had occurred—as so many do, nowadays— while he was locked up in the slammer.

The guy on the porch coughed loudly, as if reminding us that he was waiting. Willoughby grinned, showing gold dental work. "Houseguests," he confided genially. "The plague of the country life."

In a couple of weeks he was going to discover the real plague of country life, which was blackflies. But I just grinned back at him, relieved that he hadn't tumbled to who I was.

"Well," I said, "let me get out of your way. I'll drive up around in back, load them in, and take off."

The fellow on the porch went back inside, slamming the door.

"Great," Baxter said, distracted. "Have a nice day." Then he hurried away back to the house, his step a little too anxious for the true country gentleman, his chin thrust out determinedly.

To my experienced eye, he looked worried about money. But his money troubles, if any, weren't my problem anymore. All I had to do was get those shutters.

This, however, turned out to be more work than I expected. I got the truck backed up around the house all right. And I found the shutters in the Dumpster, where George had said they would be; as promised, there were forty-eight of them. But George hadn't mentioned what else was in the Dumpster, on top of them:

Wallboard trimmings. Joint-compound buckets. Scrap lumber. Strips of sheet metal, chunks of concrete, splinters of hardwood flooring, and rusty nails, probably dripping with tetanus germs. And had I brought leather gloves, for hauling the shutters out?

I had not. Still, they were there, precious as buried gold. Meanwhile the sky overhead was a clear, perfect blue, with just enough breeze to be comfortable, while across the lawn a flock of robins hopped like an army of feathered groundskeepers, chirping and gorging themselves on the earthworms that were surfacing as a result of the inground lawn-watering system.

Hard work, a gorgeous environment, and a worthy cause: I kept at it for a couple of hours, and just as I hauled the last shutter out I spotted Willoughby and his guest getting into the silver Jag that Willoughby had apparently thought would make a good Maine vehicle. Perched atop the Dumpster's metal side, I watched the Jag purr away down the drive.

Then they were gone, which of course did not force me to snoop. But bird-dogging a guy is a hard habit to break, so I just looked around a little bit.

The first thing I determined was that Willoughby's venetian blinds weren't shut as tightly as he thought they were. From the inside, the rooms probably looked peek-proof.

But from the outside, they weren't, if you stood close to the glass and shaded your eyes with your hands. And what I saw through the blinds confirmed my earlier feeling: Willoughby hadn't changed his spots after his fraud conviction, only camouflaged the smile on the face of the tiger.

Most of the new first-floor windows looked into a standard variety of living spaces, decorated and furnished to resemble an extremely luxurious Long Island tract home. The kitchen featured Jen-Aire appliances, Corian counters, kitchen island with dishwasher, brushed-steel double sinks, and a restaurant-sized Aga cookstove.

None of which I had any objection to; it was only that you couldn't tell what the old house had been like. For all the charm he had left intact—the butler's pantry was now filled with a bank of electronics: stereo, television, CD player and VCR—Willoughby might as well have bulldozed the place and started over.

The black insectile faces of the stereo components seemed to leer at me, and a radium-green flicker caught my eye as I backed from the window. As I did so, I stepped on a heap of brick scraps left over from patio construction, nearly falling into a rosebush.

Regaining my balance, I brushed my footprints out of the rose mulch, the flicker of green brilliance competing momentarily with the demands of the thorns. And then it hit me: what that radium-colored light was.

It was a real-time data connection, the computer display of what was happening on the financial markets, minute by minute and trade by trade. It was the ticker tape.

Fascinating: Real-time connections are expensive, and useful only for traders who need to know *now* exactly what their holdings are doing. Using them, traders play the market like a computer game, buying and selling stock, risking fortunes and besting competitors with the fervor of teenagers blowing up alien battleships.

Baxter Willoughby, after his securities fraud conviction, had been permanently barred from the business.

So what would he need a real-time connection for?

I moved to another window, squinted through the teensy crack between slats of the venetian blinds.

And there, not ten feet away, were six phone lines, another computer terminal, a fax machine, a clock for every time zone in the world, plus coils of cable and hard-wired phone connections that kept the real-time connection glowing.

They were the accoutrements of a high-end money junkie.

But nobody was guarding the store, which meant that whatever he was doing, he wasn't doing it full-time. Which interested me, too:

The major players can barely eat or sleep, so attached are they to the numbers constantly pouring in. A quiver in Hong Kong or a burp in Berlin must be noted instantly, or a year's worth of strategy might go down the drain without hope of recovery.

All this, to me, meant that Baxter Willoughby wasn't back in the big leagues. But he was in something, and as I drove away with forty-eight battered sets of shutters in the pickup bed, I couldn't repress a further twinge of inquisitiveness. For a whole year, I ate, drank, and slept Baxter Willoughby and his criminal doings, watching his every move the way those robins on his lawn spotted worms, targeting and impaling them.

On the road home, I dug the cell phone out of my bag and speed-dialed Hargood Biddeford's Manhattan law firm, and left a voice mail message for him to call me when he was free.

Hargood, way down in Manhattan, was hopeless at finance. But like so many of my neighbors here in Eastport, he was a wizard of gossip. If something was going on in the money world, Hargood wouldn't have a clue as to how—if at all—he should react. But Hargood would know about it, or be able to find out.

And Hargood, bless his heart, loved to tell.

"Writing," Sam explained patiently to his father, who peered over the boy's shoulder, "isn't drawing. Writing has words."

"But if you can do *that*," Victor objected for what, by the look on Sam's face, must have been the umpteenth time, "why—"

While I was out, Victor had managed to pull clothes on and drive to the health food store in Calais, and to pile the results of his trip all over the kitchen counters: bags of buckwheat flour, wheat germ, and pine nuts, bottles of blackstrap molasses and ginseng syrup, sacks of mushrooms and organic vegetables, containers of tofu and cartons of free-range eggs, each so expensive that it ought to have had a dozen rubies glued to it.

Standing by the sink, I filled a glass with cold water and drank it. I'd hauled the shutters from the truck and stacked them outside the storeroom door. Paint chips and wood dust were glued to my body with sweat, my hair felt thick and stiffened with dirt, and my mouth tasted like someone had been stripping old varnish with it, using my tongue as a scrubber.

"What time," Victor inquired, "is lunch?"

"Looks like you've got lots of choices," I told him sweetly, waving at his purchases, and turned from his look of affronted surprise.

Owing to his father's dive into a jelly glass, Sam hadn't yet had the chance to reveal his boat school aspirations. Now, peeking at Sam's work, I saw he was drawing an eighteenth-century square-rigger, complete with sails from flying jib through topgallant all the way down to spanker, which is the triangular one hanging out behind.

Or aft, as the seagoing types insist on saying. I was about to point out to Victor how beautifully Sam was drawing it, and how, just possibly, his talents in this area might be put to use.

But just then the phone rang: Hargood, returning my call. And before I could tell him what I wanted to know, he began describing urgently some fabulous investment tips he had just found posted on, of all godawful places, the Internet.

Hargood read some of the tips aloud. As I'd expected, they included some colossal howlers, such as the idea that following your natural human instincts is a good way to make money in the stock market.

Now hear this: Making money in the market takes research, planning, discipline, and a ridiculous amount of patience, none of which were natural human instincts the last time I looked.

"So this guy," I said, "who is posting these tips: you've got to figure he's making money, himself. But he does not spend his time marlin fishing in Florida, or buying sports teams."

I moved in for the kill. "No, what he does is sit in front of a computer, typing up free advice and sending it out to people he does not know."

Hargood coughed uncomfortably.

"Because," I continued, "he's such a sport. Or possibly it is because he's not really an investing expert. Maybe it's just because he has nothing else to do."

Hargood sighed. "You know," he admitted, "you've got a point. So," he shifted gears speedily, "what was it you wanted to know?"

You've got to love a guy who will drop an untenable position like that. Hargood might not see it all for himself, but he does if you show him. And in court, he is another person entirely, an *idiot savant* of legal beagles.

"What Baxter Willoughby's been up to, lately," I replied. "He seems to have moved up here to Maine, and I'm curious, is all."

"Oh."

When Hargood gets all one-syllabic that way, each word of his is like a pebble dropped into a pool: you can practically feel the ripples moving as his brain processes possible implications. Like I said: he's a *savant,* just not about money.

"Why don't I drop around to my club," he said casually at last. "I haven't been for a while, might be good to look up old chums, and I must admit our friend Baxter has rather dropped off my radar screen, lately, one way and another."

I understood: After Willoughby got sent to prison for fraud, nobody from his old social haunts would touch him with tongs. And Hargood was social with a vengeance.

"Don't go to a lot of trouble," I told him. Nowadays, just mentioning Willoughby could get you dropped from some important guest lists. "I really am only curious."

"Right," Hargood drawled in reply, and I could almost see his nose twitching, sniffing out the reasons behind my request and the facts he might dig up to satisfy it, rich little nuggets of gossip that, to Hargood, were as delicious as truffles.

And nearly as much fun to root out, if like Hargood you were jealous of people who pulled things off, wanting to know every detail of how they did the deals that he, however talented he was at his own occupation, would never have the knack for.

But he could watch, and learn all the teams and their angles, the players and strategies, like the truly committed armchair fan he was. After a bit more chat he hung up sounding cheerful, and I went out onto the front porch to examine the new railings I had recently bought and installed onto the porch steps.

Against all odds, the wood screws I'd used to install the rail mounts seemed to be holding firm in the elderly, two-inch-thick porch planks. I'd have replaced the planks, which were developing some areas of rot, but for what it costs to replace custom-milled two-inch planks nowadays, I could have torn the porch down and rebuilt it out of the Elgin Marbles. And fixing up an old house simply by pouring money into it takes the fun out.

I seized the porch rail, noting with satisfaction that the rail mounts didn't move, and congratulating myself on painting them before installing them instead of afterwards.

You can spray-paint them while they are in place, of course. But if you do, the paint rises up in a cloud and adheres to all nearby windows, providing you with another, much less satisfying project: getting the paint off.

Pleased, I went back to the kitchen to see what I could cook using Victor's purchases that would not poison or gag us—

—by this time, I was getting hungry, too, and if I waited for him I would never get any lunch—

—and eventually I came up with an omelette that wasn't half bad.

Outside, blue forget-me-nots peeped from the shady edges of the yard. The garden sported masses of lemon lilies, the tall, flaglike spikes of delphinium, and purple coneflowers, all punctuated by the crisp, white faces of the Shasta daisies Ellie and I had planted the previous autumn.

"Why," Victor queried peevishly, finishing his omelette, "do you cling to this backwater? There isn't a decent bookstore for miles, or a live theater."

Victor's attendance at live theater, to my knowledge, is limited to the kind that involves the snapping of Spandex and the twirling of gold tassels.

"Bay Books will order you anything you'd like," I told him, picking up my lunch plate to rinse it but leaving his alone.

"Hmmph," Victor responded predictably, while the poppies waved in a breeze that smelled like expensive perfume. "I'm telling you, Jacobia, modern life is passing you by."

Biting my lip, I looked out the window and counted to ten very slowly, praying for strength. Just because I wasn't going to be a plaster saint anymore didn't mean I had to abandon the image for that of a shrieking maniac: Also, I did not want to waste ammunition on a subject like this; it was Sam's arrangements that Victor might try to put a monkey wrench into, not my own.

Whereupon my prayer was answered by the sight of Zenna Henderson, planting her booted feet in a lawn belonging to the venerable Miss Violet Gage.

Until she was eighty, Miss Gage had lived with her mother, because (as she said) her mother was such a fine cook. Now at age ninety, she lived alone, doing her own cooking as well as almost all of her own gardening, only relegating the heavy chores to youngsters like Zenna.

Who was no spring chicken, either, and also no slouch; white-haired and indomitable, Zenna ran Eastport's landscaping service single-handed, driving an old Ford pickup and disdaining such foolishness as riding lawnmowers. For her labors today, Zenna wore a crisp white blouse, blue serge trousers, and pearl earrings, because (as she said) hard work was no excuse for carelessness in personal appearance.

Between Zenna and Miss Violet, I reflected, there was enough strength in Eastport to move Mount Katahdin a foot or so, and some left over for me. Refreshing myself by means of their instructive example, I watched Zenna pull the starter cord on her gasoline-powered edge trimmer, whose roar cut through the afternoon like a chain saw ripping into soft pinewood.

But the trimmer was not loud enough to drown out what Victor said next.

"Maybe it's okay for you," he announced generously. "But it's a good thing Sam's not thinking about coming back here."

I turned suddenly, my good humor vanished and a voice in my brain shouting loudly: *suspicions confirmed.*

Sam hadn't said anything to Victor yet, and I hadn't either.

But somehow, Victor could smell it.

Tim Mumford's body turned slowly at the end of the knotted sash cord, in his dog shed out on Crow Island. A stepladder lay overturned beneath him.

Ellie and I had gone back out to the island as planned to deliver Kenny's belongings. Now Tim's dogs milled nervously around us in the shed, whining. They'd been gathered on the beach at our arrival, like castaways awaiting an uncertain rescue.

"I," Ellie had said upon seeing them, "don't like this."

I hadn't liked it, either, and I liked even less seeing the way Tim's hands were tied behind him, with a slip knot. It made the whole sad thing too imaginable:

Poor old Timothy, heartsick and despairing, climbs up on the stool, puts the noose around his neck and his hands through the loop of the slipknot, steps on the cord to tighten it, and kicks away the footstool.

It was why the cord had bothered me so much, I realized now: because in the back of my mind I'd been seeing how he could use it. I just hadn't wanted to believe it.

"I guess Tim finally went off the end of the dock, just the way he said he would," I told Ellie as we made our way back to his ramshackle dwelling. The dogs trotted hopefully behind us as if, now that we were here, everything would be all right.

Ellie said nothing.

In Tim's shanty, the token items we'd brought from Ken's trailer looked shabby and pathetic. Without Tim, the place itself looked worse, too; its gritty disorder had fallen into simple filth now that he was not present to energize it.

From the cold cookstove I figured he must have been dead awhile, probably since early morning. A small kerosene lantern over the old sink still burned with a guttering bluish flame, dying as the fuel dwindled.

Ellie just stood there gazing at it, her hands at her sides. Her silence was making me uncomfortable.

"Okay," I said, "look. I'll feed these dogs, and make sure they have fresh water. You just wait here, and then we'll go back and tell Arnold that old Tim finally made good on his threat."

Ellie turned, pale and glittery-eyed. "You didn't see it, did you?"

I just blinked at her. "What? Of course I saw it. Tim hanged himself."

"The knot," she persisted. "You didn't . . . but no, of course you wouldn't. Why should you?"

"Ellie, what does the knot have to do with . . ."

Then I got it, sort of. "Oh, no. You're not telling me . . ."

That, you see, is the important thing about a slip-knot: it slips. And Ellie, being like Tim a Maine seago-ing type—

—everyone on Moose Island, or anyone who's grown up here, anyway, knows more knots than a Boy Scout—

—had spotted something interesting about this one.

"For what you are thinking he did," she said, "that knot is backwards. You're assuming he tied his own hands as a kind of insurance, in case he lost his nerve at the last minute."

"So? I don't see what that signifies. I mean, obvi-ously he was upset, or he wouldn't have killed himself. So maybe he just tied the thing backwards, and—"

Her look stopped me. "Jacobia. What he didn't do— that's not the point, and never mind either that Tim hasn't tied a slipknot backwards since he was about two years old."

She made a face. "The point is what he couldn't do, which is tighten that knot himself. The way that knot's tied, stepping on the long end of the cord would only have pulled it looser, not tightened it. It wasn't," she emphasized, *"possible.* Somebody else tied his hands behind him that way. It was a landlubber's knot."

I sat down hard in one of Tim's dilapidated kitchen chairs.

"Somebody," Ellie said, "killed him. And sooner or later I'll know who it was. And when I find out . . ."

She sank into the other of Tim's chairs, lost in thought. Then, startlingly: "Do you have bullets for the Bisley, Jake? Real ones, I mean, not the ketchup dummies?"

I looked at her. "Yes. I've got them."

Ellie nodded, but she didn't say anything more, and I was afraid to ask her.

"Come on," I said to the dogs, and went on out to feed them, leaving Ellie with her hands clasped quietly on Tim's table. Her face when I glanced back was as cold and scary as the deepest bay water, with icy, pitiless currents running beneath it.

Ellie is my friend, and I would do almost anything for her.

But not what she was thinking right that minute.

Out by the shed I found empty kibble trays and a water trough with a scant inch of water at the bottom of it. Tim hadn't gotten to his chores before somebody got to him. Grateful for the work to take my mind off what I'd seen in the shed, I pumped water and hauled it to the trough. The dogs lapped eagerly at it, starting to get their wind back now that someone was caring for them. Once I had the water up to its normal level, I started on the food.

Along the outside of the shed were a number of covered bins, each filled with a different kind of dog kibble, but I had no idea which dogs got which kibble, or even if it mattered. Nor did I see how Tim got the kibble to the trays, which were nailed to a heavy, immovable feeding platform that he had built from wooden pallets.

Stacked away from the bins, though, covered by a tarp, were about twenty fifty-pound sacks, each labeled

Purina. They'd been donated, I supposed, by the animal
shelter and rafted out here, but not yet stored in the
shed. Seeing them, I decided to pass on the bins entirely,
and just haul a whole sack of the new kibble down to
the trays.

Which was how I discovered that the contents were
not what the labels promised. Hefting one, I staggered
momentarily at its unexpected lightness, then tore the
bag open.

Looking pristine and as if they had never been
opened before, the sacks contained money. Cash money
in rubber-banded bundles, each sack comprising—I rif-
fled one bundle, doing the astonishing sums rapidly in
my head—approximately a hundred thousand dollars.

The end of each sack had been glued, so it looked
brand-new. You would have to lift a sack, as I had, to
get a clue otherwise. There were—I scanned the heap
again—exactly twenty of them, which meant old Tim
had been sitting on a fortune.

Whether he'd known it was there or not, I had no
idea. I only knew his killer hadn't found it.

Or I thought I did.

For pure entertainment, even a pair of
murders couldn't compete with two million
dollars in Purina Dog Chow sacks, and by
evening it was the talk of the town.

Down at the Happy Landings Cafe on Water Street,
the rumors flew as thick and fast as the burgers and
onion rings coming out of the kitchen: there were human bones in the bags with the money; other bodies
were known to be buried on Crow Island; and in one
particularly unlikely version of the story, old Tim had
been a satanic-cult leader whose followers gave over all

their worldly possessions—thus the two million—to follow him in the paths of ungodliness.

"Cult leader," George Valentine snorted, seating himself beside Ellie at our usual table, across from Wade and me. "Load of bushwa. Only cult in Eastport's the one worships Wednesday night beano,"—bingo, he meant; it was a Maine thing—"over to the Community Center."

Then for a while we busied ourselves with the menu, even though we knew it by heart. George and Ellie chose haddock dinners with cole slaw, George asking for gravy on the side for his french fries, while Wade and I dared to order the Saturday Night Special, which Wade always jokes is as explosive as the weapon it's named for: pork barbecue simmered to falling-apart tenderness, guaranteed to produce muzzle-flash later but delicious now.

Fortunately, Sam had taken his father out to dinner at the Baywatch, where Victor could eat something a little less likely to bite back, and where he could be spared the Happy Landings' idea of musical entertainment. George had dropped a quarter into the jukebox, and Flatt and Scruggs were highballing through "Foggy Mountain Breakdown" to the disdain of a tableful of high school students bemoaning "that old redneck stuff."

"They caught the fella," said George when we had eaten our dinners and were starting on coffee and lemon squares. These, as done by the Happy Landings, consist of a half-inch crust of finely ground walnuts, two inches of lemon custard the color of morning sunshine, and whipped cream sprinkled with more ground walnuts and a twinkling of lemon zest.

The high school kids had gone out in a gangling herd, laughing and shoving. Several of them were Sam's friends, and I thought again how glad I was to have him home.

"The one who was s'posed to have done for Kenny,"

George amplified. "And for Tim, they're thinking, now."

George will do this: just go silently along for an hour or more, then come out casually with a bomb of information that makes the rest of us stare open-mouthed at him.

"Heard it," George went on stolidly, "at the fire station, that we didn't need to be on the lookout for him anymore."

Aside from his impromptu duties as primary fixer of whatever catastrophe afflicts us—a break in the water lines, a tree on the school roof, or the equitable division of a deer that has been hit by two cars simultaneously on the causeway—George is also the town's volunteer fire chief.

"And," he went on, "I hear the guy, this Ike Forepaugh, had a wad of cash in his pocket, says Ken paid a debt he owed him."

At the other tables, talk of the money and the murders was beginning to flag, replaced by gossip about the other big doings around town: preparations for Felicity Abbott-Jones's visit.

People were sticking cut evergreen trees into holes in their yards, to hide their satellite dishes. They were dumping beach gravel on driveways to conceal neat, mud-resistant macadam. And they were soaking old dilapidated wooden storm windows in Git-Rot, trying to make them solid enough to hang for a few days.

Most of those windows were so rotten that afterwards (and in spite of the Git-Rot, a miracle substance so effective that it will make, for a while, anyway, solid wood out of sawdust and termite droppings) people could spray them off with garden hoses.

But longevity was not the requirement. The requirement was that Felicity not see the draft-proof, watertight, aluminum double-hungs with which most of those old houses were actually furnished—historical authenticity being, in the middle of a Maine winter, pretty chilly.

Ellie listened silently to the talk at our table, and at the others. She had been quiet and subdued ever since we found Tim, and she had not mentioned the Bisley again.

"This is the guy," Wade asked, frowning, "that Ken was pals with? Back when they were in jail together?"

"Ayuh," George agreed. "Told Arnold he didn't know anything about Crow Island. But Arnold says the guy is from down around Searsport way. He probably knows how to handle a boat all right."

"He does," Ned Montague put in from the next table. His face, normally mild as a pan of milk, wore a look of grim anger.

"Ike Forepaugh," Ned pronounced the name scornfully, "was the one who stole that dragger out of Machiasport, couple years ago."

"Hey, Ned," George said expressionlessly.

"Sorry for your loss," said Wade, not turning to include Ned in the conversation, even though Ned was Tim Mumford's nephew, and Ken's cousin, which officially made him a bereaved relative.

Undiscouraged by the snub, Ned turned his chair. At his table with him were his wife, a tired-looking woman with faded blonde hair and a sweatshirt that read I LOVE YA HONEY, BUT THE CAT SAYS YOU GOTTA GO, and his little girls: one the plump, gap-toothed picture of health, the other a wan, grey-faced miniature of her mother, picking sadly at a chocolate sundae.

"Eat that up, now, honey. Daddy bought it for you," the woman urged, as the child stared hopelessly at it.

Ned set his coffee cup on our table, uninvited. "Listen," he said to Ellie. "I know it must have been an awful thing, finding old Tim like that. And finding Ken, too."

Ellie regarded him: a small, pale man with pink-rimmed eyes and hands as soft and ineffective-looking as little paws. His wispy hair was combed to cover the thinning place on top.

"You'll be hearing from the ladies at the church guild," she said. "About the arrangements."

He nodded. "I know I haven't been on the ball about that."

Throughout the afternoon, Ellie had been at my house, on the telephone, doing what Maine women have done for generations without fuss or fanfare: making things happen. There was the hall to be set up, funeral hymns to be chosen, and the church altar to be decorated: lupine, everyone agreed, and vases of *rosa rugosa*.

"That's all right, Ned," Ellie assured him. "I know you've got your hands full."

At the other table, Ned's wife began spooning tiny amounts of melting ice cream into the thin little girl's mouth, while the plump child sighed with exaggerated impatience.

"It's all taken care of," Ellie said with as much kindness as she could muster.

She liked Ned all right as far as it went, but she knew he was a milquetoast. Ned didn't like getting his hands dirty; he turned down good jobs that involved going out on the water, or even onto the dock. The only useful thing he owned was a big old truck with a cargo box that he took out on day jobs, small hauls that ended quickly and paid poorly. So the Montagues were always short of money, and Ellie drew a line between the sort of fellow who couldn't support a family, and the kind who wouldn't.

Ned ducked his head awkwardly. "The thing is, though—"

"Why don't you just come out with it, Ned?" George asked, applying himself to his lemon square.

Ned blinked, startled at the novelty of being addressed by George, then blurted, "I wonder, do you think they'll be able to get Forepaugh? I mean, was there any evidence? That you saw?"

He sucked in a breath. "Because," he added, "it doesn't seem like enough to get anywhere with. Some jailhouse story doesn't prove much."

Wade looked at Ned as if Ned were a small, pesky insect.

"So I was wondering," Ned went on to Ellie, "if you saw anything. Proof. To make sure that guy gets what's coming to him. On," he finished, "the bodies. Or near where the bodies were."

George did not look pleased to have Ellie reminded of the bodies. All the cool, calm industry she had exhibited, getting things arranged: that was her way of handling it. But old Tim was still in her mind's eye, at the end of a rope.

"I don't think there was," she said, turning to me.

"No," I agreed slowly. "You mean, something that belonged to Ike Forepaugh. Something to show that he'd been there."

Ned nodded. "Right. So the murdering bastard— oops, excuse my French—gets what's coming to him."

"I think," George said consideringly, "the cops'll find any evidence there might be. Way I heard it, they're going over Crow Island pretty carefully, and watching to see if anybody shows up, too, looking for all that money."

Wade took out his wallet and examined the two checks on the table. "Guess I'll take care of these," he said, and went up to the cash register. Passing the table where Ned's wife and little girls sat, he picked their check up too, smiling at the children.

Ned didn't notice. "Right. Well, I guess that's all right." His eyes brimmed suddenly with tears. "They were just a couple of bums, Tim and Kenny. Not the sort you really want to be related to. But I was. Those two were my blood relatives—in fact, I was the only living kin that they had."

His lower lip thrust out injuredly. "I'd even been visiting Kenny some, lately."

George looked blandly at Ned. If he had looked at me that way, I'd have simply dissolved in mortification; his blandness, like that of many downeast Mainers, can be very communicative.

But Ned didn't seem to notice. "I'd been going out to his trailer every week or so," he went on. "Make sure old Ken was okay. He was no-account, but he was a good old boy. And I just want to make sure whoever killed them doesn't get away with it."

Ned hesitated. "About those dogs of Tim's. I hear you two," he included me in his glance, "are watching out for them."

I waited for him to say that he would take over this task, but of course he didn't.

"I can't be taking on that mongrel pack, right now." He angled his head back at his own table. "My little girl—"

The word in town was that the child had kidney disease, something that required specialists, but no one knew for sure. Shunned by the Eastport men on account of Ned's uselessness and isolated by the pity of Eastport women, the Montagues kept to themselves; thus their child's health was one of the few topics so far unprocessed by the town gossip mill.

"So I wondered," Ned said, wringing his pawlike hands.

"Ned, don't worry about it," Ellie said. "I'll make sure the dogs are taken care of until we get another arrangement."

"Poor bastard," Wade`said when Ned was gone.

"Ayuh," George Valentine said, sounding unimpressed. "Guess he forgot to leave the tip," he added, dropping a couple of bills beside the mess around the little girl's ice-cream dish.

Ellie looked at me, and made a shrugging face: What

can you do? Ned was . . . well, Ned was a dishrag, that was all.

At the other tables, talk had turned to the latest obstacle in Eastport's race to historical correctness: the big white luxury yacht, parked down at the dock.

"Well, if we can't find out who owns it, how're we gonna get 'em to move it?" Matt Fairbrother, an Eastport town councilman, wanted to know.

Apparently the vessel had gotten tied up in the spot that the historical committee wanted for the pirate-fight tableau, the dramatic presentation in which my ketchup-and-wax bullets were intended to play an important part. But not, it seemed, if they couldn't relocate the *Triple Witch*.

"Don't worry," Fairbrother's companion said. He wore bib overalls, a T-shirt, and high boots turned down low. "I hear them yachts is fragile. Go bottoms-up, you look at 'em cross-eyed."

Dark laughter greeted this statement, and I thought that the *Triple Witch*'s owner had better be found soon or a sinking party could be in the offing. Downeast seafarers can get pretty sniffy about mooring spaces, especially ones occupied by expensive toys.

"Listen, George," I said, taking him aside as we went out. "How are you doing about all this? The murders, and Ellie feeling the way she does."

George set his cap on his head and squinted. "Well," he admitted, "I've been wondering about it myself."

He took a deep, considering breath. " 'Cause what she's all het up about, basically, is an old boyfriend."

"Yeah. And that's why, I guess, I was wondering."

When I was new in town, George came to my house to remove a bee's nest from my attic vent. When the job was done, he was dripping with decades-old honey, the yard was littered with ancient honeycomb, and he'd been stung twenty-four times.

But he wouldn't take a penny. He just said I could

do him a favor sometime, maybe, and not to fuss about it.

"Did you know," he said now, "that she taught him to read?"

"No. I didn't." Those books, I realized, and the look in her eyes when she saw them at Ken's trailer. She'd been proud of him.

"Well, she did," George said. "And I guess she told you she broke up with Ken, couple months before she started seeing me."

"She did say that." Suddenly I knew what he was about to say.

"I'd asked her, though. A number of times. Turned me down. She had something to take care of, she said, before she could."

Wade and Ellie were coming down the wooden deck steps toward us. George watched her, his eyes lighting up at the sight of her.

"She broke up with him," I said, "so she could start seeing you. But she waited a decent interval so it wouldn't be . . ."

George nodded. "A slap in the face to him. She's like that. And I appreciate your concern, Miz Tiptree—"

No matter what, I could never get him to call me Jacobia—

"—but as for Ellie and me, anything she does, or anything she ever wants to do—"

She came up and took his arm confidingly.

"Well," he finished, smiling down at her, "don't worry about me in that regard."

"What are you two talking so seriously about?" she asked, looking from my face to his.

"Old times," he replied comfortably. "And about those dogs of Tim's. I'll do for them until the shelter can find 'em homes."

Because, he meant, he didn't want Ellie out there anytime soon, refreshing her memory of Tim's death scene.

I looped my arm through Wade's as we strolled downtown, while Ellie and George headed up to Calais to see a movie, George hoping it would take Ellie's mind off things and her agreeing to it for his sake.

"Why'd you pay Ned's check?" I asked.

Wade chuckled. "I didn't. I paid his wife's check. You know it'd come out of her household money."

He shook his head. "Carla Montague. Pretty girl, once. Bet she wishes she'd married Kenny instead. She'd be shut of him." Instead of doomed, he meant, to more years with Ned.

I glanced at him. "You're not usually so cynical."

"I don't usually sit at a table with Ned Montague, either."

"You guys sure don't like him."

He shrugged. "It's that constant poor-faced act he puts on. Like he doesn't have anything but feels entitled to everything."

At the dock, Ken Mumford's little vessel the *Drifter* sat at a mooring where the state cops had left it when they'd finished with it, a paint-peeling wooden boat with an operator's shack amidships. "Like that," Wade said, waving at it. "Belongs to Ned, now."

"You don't suppose Ned killed Ken for the boat, do you?"

Wade laughed. "That tub? No, you'd have to be dumber than he is to kill for the *Drifter*. And he won't be any dab hand, fixing her up, either. Boat like that, it needs taking care of."

He shook his head. "Heck, I used to go out after deer with old Ned, bunch of other fellows. He would never bring along the right stuff, end up borrowing from everybody, then act all hurt about it when the other guys got mad at him. Had a decent old deer gun he got from somewhere, he keeps saying he'll bring it over for a cleaning. But I doubt he ever will."

Then he reached out, grinning wickedly, and ruffled

my hair. "Want to go out on the dock and smooch? Give the folks a thrill?"

And me, too, probably. "Why not? I'm already a scarlet woman in this town, on account of you."

"Hey, we aim to please." He slung his arm around me as we made our way toward the waterfront. "So where d'you suppose that two million bucks came from?"

"No idea." My first thought had been Baxter Willoughby. The size of the stash was in his financial ballpark.

But the way it was happening wasn't how Willoughby worked. If he wanted to move money he could do it with all those computer hookups in his house, hopscotching huge sums across continents with a few keystrokes. Actually putting his hands on the cash, for Willoughby, was as likely as Ned Montague plunging his hands into a tub of fish guts; it had never been his style.

Across the water, the island of Campobello shone in the low sun. "Victor say anything to you about last night?" Wade asked.

"About getting so loaded? Nope. Did he to you?"

Wade peered into the water near the dock. "Sort of. Look, the mackerel are running."

All at once, and for a hundred yards in all directions, fish *boiled* to the surface of the bay, hurling themselves from the water in gleaming arcs and landing with sharp slaps. Almost as instantly, men with fishing gear arrived, casting mackerel jigs.

We left the pier to the fishermen—the smooching, I resolved, would come later—and went on past Leighton's Variety Store, where the tangy smell of chili dogs and onion rings drifted up from Rosie's Hot Dog Stand, nearby on the dock.

Wade stopped, frowning; I followed his gaze.

Unaware of us, two young guys from the bunch of high school students we'd seen at the Happy Landings

strode purposefully down the street, looking as inno-
cent as kids who are up to something always do. At the
last minute they cut furtively around the corner and,
they thought, out of sight.

Intent on their business, they didn't notice us as one
boy dug a small packet from his jeans and passed it to
the other one. Then they hurried away in opposite directions.

"Huh," Wade said. "Wonder what that was all
about."

"I hope it's not what I think," I said. "But I'll bet it
is." Briefly, I related what Bob Arnold had said about
hard drugs having found their way to Eastport, and
about Hallie Quinn.

"Hell," Wade said grimly. "That stuff gets started up
around here, we'll be in a pickle."

"We have already had two murders," I pointed out.

"Yeah. And maybe they are connected. To," he
added, "whoever is bringing the damn stuff in here in
the first place. Or was."

"Maybe," I agreed, knowing he meant Ken.

Now that we'd found all that money, it made even
more sense that Ken's "big deal" might have been drug
smuggling. Eastport, so handy to Canada and an easy
run to international waters, was once a bootlegger's
haven so notorious, it had its own rail spur. And Ellie's
pirate forebears hadn't gone out for nothing; they'd
gone after ships whose cargo holds were loaded with
contraband.

So maybe Ken had decided to bring new blood to an
age-old, lucrative Eastport industry. And someone else,
noticing this, had run up the Jolly Roger.

"But it can't be that simple," I told Wade as we
walked back toward my house. "Two million of anything takes organization and management skills. And
Ken didn't have them."

We paused at the corner of Key Street. To the south,
the Lubec bridge was an ink sketch against the fading

sky, while to the north, Deer Island Light flashed an age-old warning: beware.

"So," I said, "what did Victor tell you?"

Wade grimaced. "You're not going to like it."

"That's all right. I'm used to that from him. Lay it on me."

Wade took a deep breath. "Victor says he's tired of being a brain surgeon. It's not special enough. So he's leaving New York."

At this, my heart went into the sort of free-fall normally reserved for parachutists, after the ripcord has produced no activity whatsoever and the reserve chute has failed, also.

"So what's the punch line? What's he going to do to alleviate his discomfort, eliminate his boredom, and make himself feel—" I nearly choked on the word— "special?"

"He decided this afternoon, after his hangover wore off. He's moving," Wade said. "To Eastport."

19 Carrying all the shutters down to the cellar, I could almost stop believing it. And soon, the pain of all that hauling sent me into such a blur of physical misery, I hardly cared.

Still, underneath all the aching and blisters lurked Victor, sharing a ZIP code with me. In fact, there was a house for sale down the street from mine, and he would probably choose it just to be irritating.

Also, it did not cheer me to find that where I'd thought I had forty-eight sets of shutters, I really had only forty-seven.

Irritated, I went out to the yard and scanned for them, stopping for a moment to gaze at the last light of day; this, in an Eastport summer, is the rich, ripe pink of a raspberry soda floated with blueberry sherbert.

Then I checked the root cellar, the primitive corner of the basement where the coal bin used to be, and even the crawlspace under the storeroom, finally spying them sticking out of the trash barrel. Or what was left of them: hinges and splintered louvers. In there with them, stuffed at the bottom, was a belt from my belt sander.

"Hey, Mom?" Sam peered down the cellar stairs at me.

"What?" I yanked the light-switch cord hanging over the workbench where my tools lived. The sander lay out on the bench, not neatly put away as I had left it.

"Who's been messing around down here?" I snarled.

"Uh, Dad was." Sam came all the way down the steps. "I tried to talk him out of it. But he wanted to help."

"He didn't clamp it, did he? That shutter—he just smacked the belt sander down on it."

"Actually, it was kind of funny. The shutter just—"

Sam waved his arms to indicate a shutter in the process of exploding. "I tried to explain to him, but no deal. He changed his mind when he got a load of the belt sander, though. I mean, after he turned it on."

I could imagine. That sander would take the hide off a rhinoceros. But I swallowed my fury; it wasn't Sam's fault. "So, what's he doing now?"

I got two pipe clamps down from the rack and unscrewed them, positioning one of the intact shutters on the workbench.

"Taking a walk. I wanted to get him out on the dock, maybe show him the difference between a yawl and a ketch."

I smiled in spite of myself, remembering how Sam finally taught me this important distinction: when you *yawn* on a *yawl,* you can lean back against the mast, because it is behind you, but on a *ketch* there is no mast to *catch* you, as it is up front.

"But he wanted," Sam added cautiously, "to go look at houses. He's already got his eye on that one down the street."

"Fine," I replied, screwing a pipe clamp tight. With one of these turned down securely at each side, the shutter wouldn't vibrate, so it wouldn't self-destruct when the sander touched it.

I hoped. "Wade told me your dad's plan. So you don't have to worry about that. Have you broken your news to him, yet?"

He shook his head unhappily. For Sam to finish school here would be bad enough in his father's eyes. But the implications of Sam attending the boat school would be—in Victor's opinion—disastrous. He wanted Sam to go to an Ivy League college; not only that, but Victor intended to get Sam admitted a year early.

Which I'd thought couldn't happen, so I'd postponed worrying about it. Ordinarily, students have to wait for their junior year grades to come in before they can apply to college. But Victor had pull at many prestigious institutions and had gotten special treatment for Sam. As a result, during the past school year Sam had—with Victor's help—filled the forms out, and gone to the interviews at six high-powered, very competitive universities.

"No," Sam said. "I haven't told him, yet. I chickened out."

On account of the handicap imposed by his dyslexia, Sam wasn't expecting anything to come out of his college applications. He'd just gone through the process to humor his father, he'd said.

But now the day of reckoning was arriving.

"I can understand that," I said. "Chickening out, I mean. I do it myself when he's around, don't I? Although in your case I'd call it choosing the moment carefully."

Sam's glance was wary. "Yeah, well. He's a forceful guy. He, like, wants what he wants, you know?"

Clearly, Sam wasn't comfortable with this topic. My remark about my own behavior seemed to make him especially uneasy.

"Well, you might as well wait, now," I said, "until he gets a place here. He'll take the news better, once that happens. And maybe your boat school plans will go down easier with him, too."

I put a belt in the sander and pulled on my dust respirator and high-impact goggles. These make me look like an insect from an alien planet, but they are essential equipment; I have no desire to start learning Braille or have a lung transplant.

"Yeah, that's what I thought," Sam agreed. "But it wasn't my idea," he hastened to add. "I mean, I didn't suggest him moving here just so he'd go along with my coming back, and everything."

He sounded so anxious, the poor kid: his father on one side, me on the other. I put down the sander.

"Listen. What you do is your business, what your dad does is his, and if it turns out I have to move to a mountaintop in Peru to get away from him, well . . ."

Sam laughed; I'd threatened the Peru trip often enough for him to know that I was joking. And the normal, lighthearted expression coming onto his face was all the reward I needed for the enormous amount of self-restraint I was practicing.

Just don't be surprised, I wanted to say, *if when you tell your father, he starts clutching his chest . . .*

But I'd decided to be tougher on Victor, not on Sam. Which was why when I had the chance, I didn't say it. I didn't tell Sam, right then and there, the truth about his father.

I just let it go.

"Hey, how about that cruiser at the dock?" he remarked, fiddling aimlessly with some pieces of wood on the workbench. He was, I realized happily, hanging around just to be with me.

"Man, would I ever like to get a closer look at that boat. You think they might let me aboard?"

"Maybe. All they can do is say no. That won't kill you."

"Yeah," he responded. "You," he added, heading up the cellar steps, "look like a bug in that respirator."

Right, I thought as I heard the refrigerator door opening up there, underlining Sam's return to his usual good humor.

Then I settled down to those shutters, and for a wonder, things started going right for a change. I figured I could belt-sand the sides and bottoms, scrape the louvers by hand, glue-and-screw any really shaky sections. After that I could paint them and put the hinges back on. It was a quick-and-dirty fix, but I was out to hang shutters, not preserve them for posterity.

And as I worked I found my mood lightening. There was not after all much structural repair needed; the wood had been good quality, and the old-time craftsmen really knew their joinery. A couple of buzzes of the drill, some white glue and a flat-headed screwdriver took care of the fractured pieces; even the one shutter half that Victor had demolished required no truly major surgery.

The other half still needed replacing, but I decided what the hell: If worse came to worst, I could paint a green rectangle beside one window, and hope Felicity Abbot-Jones was nearsighted.

Once the reconstruction was done I started on the belt-sanding, and I didn't look up from my work until a creak from the cellar steps told me that Sam had come back for me, to offer me a soda or possibly to say he was going out with Tommy Daigle.

But it wasn't Sam. It was Hallie Quinn.

I pulled the bug mask and goggles off. "Oh," she breathed, relaxing a little. "It is you. I thought—"

"Come on," I invited. "I'm not going to bite you."

Tentatively, she took another step down the stairs, the silver medallion she wore flashing in the wash of white light from the fluorescent workshop overheads. In her ears were a pair of little costume-jewelry stud earrings, each shaped like an H.

"I knocked on the screen door. But I guess—" she gestured at the sander—"you couldn't hear me."

The chain on her medallion was like the one I wore: heavyweight, so it wouldn't break. The clasp on mine was the devil to open, but that added to the security; you didn't go taking it off carelessly and leaving it lying around.

Considering that I wore the key to a lockbox containing two guns and a whole lot of ammunition on mine, security was an issue for me. I gathered Hallie felt similarly about her medallion, even though it was nowhere near as likely to go off and kill people. But my appreciation for her jewelry faded as I heard what she said next.

"Listen, you better not go out to Crow Island anymore. You don't know what you're getting into. You and that other lady—"

"Ellie White," I supplied.

"Yeah, whatever. Anyway, people know about you two. That you found the bodies, and that you're—"

"Snoops." Hey, it may not be flattering, but it's accurate.

And, I thought, it was why Hallie Quinn had come to me. She wanted help.

"This isn't funny," she frowned. "You don't know the kind of people you are—"

"Getting involved with. Right. So, Hallie, how much are you using? Your drug habit, I mean."

The question stopped her cold. "None of your business. And anyway, I can—"

"—stop anytime I want to. But never mind that. What do you say we cut to the chase?"

I dusted paint dust off my hands, feeling annoyed. Dealing with Victor, finding a body, and losing a shutter had all played havoc with my stock of patience.

For which I was later sorry. "Hallie, I've eaten lunch with a lot worse people than you are warning me against. So why don't you tell me who those folks are, that you are so worried about, and I'll just go out and wipe the floor with them, tonight."

I didn't say anything about the police wanting to talk to her. She was spooked enough. "Okay? Have we got a deal, here?"

You know, I think for an instant she almost believed me, or wanted to. But then her teenaged distrust of anyone who actually knew anything, or could do anything for her, kicked in.

"I just came to warn you," she said stubbornly, clinging to the control she imagined she had. "Before I leave town."

She reminded me so much of myself at her age, I wanted to throw a net over her, because I was not always confident, sane, and in command of a talent for making the most of other people's money. I know what New York's Port Authority bus terminal is like at night, alive with hustlers as smooth as predatory reptiles. At Hallie's age I was fresh off a Greyhound myself, straight out of deepest coal country, bound and determined to put a world of difference between myself and where I'd come from.

I'd done it, too, but I hadn't been addicted, then or later: lucky. It was the difference between me and Hallie.

"Where are you going?" I asked casually, busying myself at the workbench. "I'm sorry about Ken, by the way. Looked like you two had a decent thing working, the trailer and all. And the dog. What's his name, Cosmo? What's happened to him?"

I was trying for a sympathetic connection, but it

blew up in my face. Her expression clouded, her lips twisting bitterly.

Come on, Hallie, I thought, give it up; you don't have to go through this. It's too much for you, or anybody.

"Look," I said, "wherever you're going, I'll drive you. Or you can stay the night here. Just don't go out there by yourself again, okay? Because if you do, I'm going to worry about you."

I took a step, reaching out. She flinched in response, and skittered halfway back up the steps. "I'm going to Portland, a rehab place, I've got friends there, I'm going to get straight."

The words tumbled out, too fast to be the truth, sounding just like the things some of Sam's friends had told me, back in Manhattan.

"I can't," she babbled, using phrases she'd heard from some counselor, "straighten out here, where I'm exposed to all the old situations, the same old people and temptations."

"Sure." She was as good as gone already.

"So," I brushed non-existent sawdust off the bench, "if you are going, you won't need those people and temptations anymore. So you could tell me who it is you're getting the stuff from."

Hallie's eyes narrowed. They were blue, and her pale blonde hair was natural.

"Was it Ken? Because," I went on smoothly, "I'd like to keep other kids in town from going through what you're about to. The work of rehab and all. Wouldn't you want to help?"

If she gave me a name and it wasn't Ken's, all Arnold would have to do was find the slimebag and slap him—selling to *kids*—into custody, so I could not rip his lungs out with my bare hands before he made it even as far as the county courthouse.

"Yeah," Hallie spat scornfully at last, "it was Ken. Happy now? And since he's dead, maybe you all can decide he was Jack the Ripper, too. I," she announced, "am getting out of here."

She turned, then nearly fell back down the steps at the sight of Sam, standing silently behind her. Sucking in a breath, she shoved past him up to the landing.

"You'd better remember what I said," she grated out. "Don't be stupid, okay? Keep your noses *out*, you and your friend."

Then she was gone; the screen door's slam like a gunshot and her sandals thumping across the porch, out into the darkness.

"Wow," Sam said. "What was that all about?"

I released a sigh. "That was me, being the biggest fool in the world. Damn it, I should have handled her better."

Sam came down and began helping me put the tools away. I'd forgotten what a pleasure it was, having him around.

"Yeah, well," he said. "With Hallie, it's not exactly easy."

"You know her?" I asked, surprised; it hadn't occurred to me that he might. But of course they were nearly the same age.

He nodded. "Seen her. She travels with a different crowd."

"What do you know about her?"

The screen door sounded again, and Victor's confident step crossed above our heads.

"I know her old man whacks her around," Sam said. "Acts like he's concerned about her, a lot of big talk. But he's an animal with his fists. Or so," Sam finished cautiously, "I've heard."

"And you would know all this how?"

"Daigle." Thus the caution: teenaged boys dish the dirt as exuberantly as girls. They just don't want anybody thinking so.

"Daigle's grandma lives next to the Quinns. And," Sam went on, "I know the cops are looking for her, but they're not asking the right people. Not that any of the kids in town would tell."

Of course not: more teenaged code of honor. "What about Ken Mumford? Heard any scuttlebutt about him?"

Sam hung the belt sander on its hook. "Yeah. Daigle says he treated Hallie decent. Not, like, taking advantage of her."

He eyed me sideways to see if I understood, and I indicated that I did in order to save him having to draw me a diagram. It's another trait of teen boys: where their mothers are concerned, they cling passionately to the doctrine of virgin birth.

"He, like, supposedly loved her. But," Sam went on, "Hallie was just using him, like, for a place to stay and so on. What she really wanted was to go to Portland. More nightlife."

Sam shook his head wryly, indicating how well he thought Hallie would survive Portland nightlife. "But that Ken, what a sucker. She even has another boyfriend around here. But Ken didn't know anything about it."

My antennae went up. "She seemed pretty broken up over Ken's death, though. And who is this other guy?"

He snorted softly. "Girls like Hallie are sentimental in a weird way. Like if their cat dies, they never paid it attention, now they're crushed. Everything is all about them, you know?"

He was right, I realized: histrionics were no evidence of affection, or for that matter of anything else.

"Know any more about the mystery boyfriend?"

"Some older guy. But nobody's gotten a good look. A glimpse on the seawall once in a while after dark. It's where they meet."

He tested the blade on an X-ACTO knife, began replacing it. "There's this kid, Peter Mulligan, really ticked off about it. A high school kid, smart as heck but kind of shrimpy. You know, a nerd. He's like, almost stalking her."

If my antennae got any higher they would pierce the ceiling.

"He walks around with really deep books in his pocket," Sam continued. "But what he really does is watch TV. Like, just sits there and watches for hours, when he's not out spying on Hallie."

"But you don't know who this other guy is, the older one. His name, where he lives, or exactly how much older he might be."

Old enough, maybe, to buy dope in a bigger town, Portland or Bangor, then bring it back here for Hallie and her friends to have a taste. After which, I theorized, they would want more.

"Mom." Sam smiled patiently. "You could use these clamps as thumbscrews, maybe strip one of these electric wires and zing me with it. Try to get more out of me. But honest—"

He tipped his head wryly. "Honest, that's all I know."

"Thanks, kiddo. I wish I could've helped Hallie, though."

He stopped. "You offered?"

"Yeah. Told her I'd drive her to Portland, to the rehab."

Sam smiled sympathetically. Heroin was in vogue again, the kids thinking it was safer than crack or amphetamines.

"Then," Sam said, "I guess the next move is hers."

"Right. As usual." I snapped the lights out, following him upstairs. "How'd you get to be such a smart kid, anyway?"

From the front room came the blare of the TV.

Victor's new lifestyle included, apparently, broadcasts of beach volleyball lasting into the wee hours. At the sound of his father's presence a worried expression returned to Sam's face.

"There's a fifty-fifty chance I inherited it," he said.

20

"He what?" Ellie gripped the telephone in both hands. "How?"

Four brief hours after shooing Victor to bed, I awoke to the smell of coffee and pancakes. From the window, I watched the last wisps of night fog trickling away, little gleams of early-morning sunlight reflecting from the streets steaming with moisture.

Downstairs I found Sam eating a big breakfast. Ellie was in the telephone alcove, in my apron, with a load of laundry already running and juice squeezed into a pitcher on the table.

"When did he do this?" Ellie demanded into the phone.

I poured a glass of fresh orange juice and dumped it down my throat, praying for an energy boost. Meanwhile Ellie looked dewy and fresh-faced as always, her hair pulled back in a garish green-plaid scrunchy that set off her turquoise T-shirt and purple sweatpants. On her feet were a pair of bright yellow sneakers, and her earrings were the tiny square-cut emeralds that George had given her for her birthday.

If anyone else wore this outfit it would be ridiculous, but color combinations that blend as harmoniously as a car crash look smashingly well chosen on Ellie, possibly because she shines right through whatever she is wearing, anyway.

Although at the moment what shone through was

bright red fury generously mingled with frustration. *"Where?"* she demanded.

"What's going on?" I asked Sam, pouring myself some coffee.

"Dunno. She was here when I got up, and then the phone rang. And boy, is she mad."

"She made the pancakes?"

He nodded through a mouthful, swallowed. "Uh-huh. George had to go out early, boiler exploded over at the grade school. So she decided to come over and be useful, she said. Man, these pancakes are great. Here, try some."

He poked a pancake-loaded fork at me. "Open the hangar," he crooned persuasively, "here comes the airplane."

A person, I believe, should be allowed to drink a quiet cup of coffee. But I opened my mouth obediently, just the way he used to when I used the airplane routine on him.

The pancakes entered. Whereupon my own eyes snapped open and my taste buds performed the *macarena*. "Hey," I said.

Sam grinned. "Pretty good, huh?"

"I don't understand," Ellie said into the telephone, "how a man in handcuffs, in an official *police squad car*—"

She waved a hand as if brushing away a swarm of unwelcome news. "I have to hang up, now, before I lose my temper."

She listened. "Yes, I will tell her. No, I won't tell anyone else. Thanks for calling."

She smacked the phone down. "Ellie," I said timidly, "these pancakes are delicious."

"Thanks," she replied. "They're made of Victor's buckwheat flour. But try," she went on, "swallowing this. Ken Mumford's old jailhouse buddy Ike Forepaugh has *escaped*."

"You're kidding." I chased the pancake with coffee, hoping the sugar-caffeine jolt would kick in soon.

"On the way," she continued, "to the lockup in Machias. He faked a seizure, got them to undo the handcuffs late last night."

Sam got up. "Gotta go. Daigle's waiting. Thanks, Ellie."

I opened my mouth to ask him where they would be going, what they would be doing, and when he would be back, but by the time I got these thoughts straightened in my head, he was already gone.

"So that's why . . ." I began. Then I realized the other import of what Ellie had reported: Hallie, out on her own with Ike Forepaugh on the loose.

"I am so *disgusted*." Ellie moved a load of Sam's T-shirts from the washer to the drier, and started a load of towels. Besides her culinary acumen, she has mastered the art of making housework fit into the moments between moments, so that in her house every surface is always shining and the air smells of soapsuds and furniture polish, but she is never actually cleaning.

Then she heard what I'd said. "Why, what?" she asked.

It's those in-between moments that I'd like to get a handle on. Somehow I think they make all the difference.

"Why," I said, "Arnold didn't have time to listen to me last night. I called him, after Hallie Quinn left against my advice."

I hadn't enjoyed keeping my promise to Arnold much. It felt like ratting on someone. But now I was glad I had done it.

Ellie looked over at me from the perfectly clean kitchen sink. The mixing bowl was back in the cabinet, and through the kitchen window I spied fresh eggshells out on the compost heap.

"Maybe," she suggested—the griddle had been scoured, and the cabinet fronts were spotless—"you'd better tell me about this."

So I did, including what Hallie had said and the things Sam had told me, and the part about Victor moving to Eastport.

"Which might have a silver lining. If he's moving here," I said, reciting the mantra I'd been repeating for the last twelve hours in hopes it would start sounding believable, "then maybe he won't give Sam so much grief about coming back, too."

"What about his wanting Sam to go to college, though?" Ellie asked. "Don't you think he'll still be difficult about that?"

"I'm not so sure. He's aware that the only way Sam can study is if someone reads the material aloud to him, or puts it on tape."

I drank some more coffee. "He knows Sam wouldn't be able to survive at any of those schools. So maybe he's just been using the idea to bully me. Maybe he'll back off from it."

Ellie made a disgusted sound. "You," she said flatly, "are in denial. Victor's not going to give up his plan so easy. He's been working too hard on it. And when has he ever seen reality until he was forced to?"

She paced the kitchen, folding dishtowels as she went, pausing only to wipe the refrigerator, tie up the trash, freshen Monday's water bowl, and rearrange my spice rack.

"*And* there's something wrong with Victor," she announced. "He's sick, or he's had some disaster. I started to try to tell you the other day, on our way out to Ken's: Victor is different, somehow. And I think it's something serious."

She paused, thinking. "And it's more than him wanting control. He wants Sam to go to college for his own prestige. And he's too stubborn to admit it won't work out, until it doesn't. If it doesn't," she added doubtfully, glancing at me.

"But Sam's not going to get admitted, anyway, is he? That's why I want him focused on a realistic goal, so he's not too crushed by the rejection. Or by getting admitted and failing. That would really hammer his opinion of himself."

I took a breath. "But the admissions people at the schools must realize Sam's too dyslexic to make it in their environment."

"Maybe," Ellie said. She sat down across from me, looking troubled.

"But Jacobia, that's not the point. If Sam comes out with *anything* other than what Victor wants for him, Victor will blame you. And to get Victor off your case, Sam will do whatever Victor says. Don't you see? To protect *you*. To save you from a showdown with Victor."

"That's . . . that's ridiculous," I managed.

Only it wasn't. Victor would do anything to get his way, including the sort of emotional blackmail she was describing. As for protecting me, when I'd moved to Eastport Sam had accompanied me—as I'd learned later—only because I'd said I wouldn't come here unless he did, too.

At the time, it had been Sam's drug habit that concerned me; that, and his ever-present cadre of depraved little pals. But to Sam the trouble centered on me and Victor, and the angry campaign Victor mounted after the divorce, to punish me for rejecting him.

In short, I'd proposed the Eastport move to save Sam, but he had accepted it to save me; his mother had been crying all the time, and he'd wanted it stopped.

Now he was forming a new relationship with his father. But if he saw the bad old days starting again . . .

Well, once again, Sam would probably think it was up to him to do something about it.

"Having his dad here probably seemed like an okay idea while Sam was planning it. Victor, I guess, was on good behavior around him, while they were in New York. But now that it's happening . . ."

Ellie nodded. "Victor's not going to take Sam's ideas lying down. And I think Sam's just going to surrender."

He would, too; he was sixteen, and gallant to a fault. To keep the peace, he would go along with Victor's program until it demoralized him completely.

Or until I showed him that he didn't have to.

Which meant it wasn't going to be enough to triumph in small skirmishes: letting Victor do some of his own cooking, for instance, or snapping off the TV and sending him grumbling up to bed instead of allowing him to keep the whole household awake.

Instead, for Sam's sake—and preferably in his presence—I would have to have World War III with Victor.

And I would have to win.

From the front of the house came a shivery tinkle of glass, as if someone were passing under the pendants of the hall chandelier.

I peeked through my fingers. "Don't tell me Victor is up." I hadn't assembled my tanks and rocket launchers, yet.

"No. I think it's only the ghost," Ellie smiled.

But I didn't smile back. For a long time it had been a joke between us: the idea that my house was haunted. Lately, though, the notion had grown less charming, because the problem I'd begun having was this:

A chill on the stairway or the sense of a presence is one thing. I can tolerate a haunting like that. But once you have physically perceptible manifestations—spoons and window shades developing their own odd behaviors, mirrors that seem to ripple at you when you look into them, and in one unpleasant instance an icy fingertip applied, suddenly and startlingly, to the back of my neck—you are over the edge.

"Maybe," I said miserably, "the ghost will chase Victor away and keep me from having to have a big fight with him."

Whereupon the teaspoon on the mantel dropped to the floor with a clear, brilliant little silvery *ping!*

 Down on the dock, a trio of skin divers ventured into the ice-cold water behind the Waco Diner, to hunt for relics of the days when square-riggers crowded the wharves, and the lamp fuel of choice was whale oil.

"Can of varnish," Ellie recited to herself as we passed the divers, strolling toward Wadsworth's Hardware; she was doing an errand for George. "Varnish, joint compound, silicone tape."

Wadsworth's was my destination, too; I was running out of sanding belts, and if I was going to hang those shutters at all it would be a good idea to put up shutter dogs: the black iron latchlike gadgets that hold shutters open. Otherwise on the next windy day with the shutters all flapping, my old house would appear to be readying itself for takeoff.

As we went in, Bob Arnold sped by in the squad car, looking grim, and I supposed it was because of the escape. Having a guy whom you are going to charge with double murder slip out of your cruiser is embarrassing.

I was feeling grim, too, on account of what Victor was up to, and passing the For Sale sign down the street from my own place didn't help.

The house looked perfect for him: an old Greek Revival, big enough to make him think he was living in a mansion, but in decent repair. There was even a parlor with its own entrance off the pillared front porch, if, indeed, he really wanted an office, or in his case possibly a torture chamber.

So I didn't give much thought to the look on Arnold's face. Besides, the hardware store always distracts me completely with its buckets of galvanized roofing nails, drawers of wood screws and plaster buttons, racks of brushes, tin snips, and linoleum cutters. Way in the back hang the buoys and anchor chains, with links as big around as your wrist, or your head; there are drill bits the size of hypodermic needles, and generators big enough to run a hospital.

In short, it is do-it-yourself heaven. I got my sander belts and shutter dogs, then wandered around waiting for Ellie to make her purchases. Outside, another squad car zoomed by. But I hardly noticed, too busy gazing at a shop gadget I had long coveted: a Dremel Moto Tool, which is a device sort of like a dentist's drill—and with as many attachments—for shaping, sanding, polishing, etching, or otherwise altering the surface of almost anything. You can even cut bone with it, the package advised, which I thought might come in handy if I ever decided to dismember Victor.

Through the store window I saw the tourists begin moving as if in a tide, sluggishly at first. But I was busy, getting the Dremel box down from the shelf. It was richly, satisfyingly heavy, just as I had always imagined it would be, as I carried it to the counter.

But Ellie did not smile and agree with me at once, as she usually did when I decided to make an extravagant purchase. Instead, spotting George through the window and seeing his expression, she ran to meet him and bury her face in his shoulder.

Henry Wadsworth stood watching the scene in some puzzlement, tugging at his suspenders. "Some sort of excitement, over to the dock. You don't suppose that big white boat is sinking, do you?"

From the look on Ellie's face, it would have to be the

dock sinking, not the boat. "Henry, put this on my
account, and ask Charlie to deliver my things, will you,
please? I'll pay him then."

"Ayuh," Henry said with a snap of the suspenders.
"Will do."

I rushed outside. People streamed past me on the
sidewalk toward the waterfront side of the street.

"George, what's wrong?"

George took a deep breath and let it out in a rush,
his arm still around Ellie. "Body," he muttered unhappily. "Some fellows from away rented a boat from
Hugh Crowe. Going fishing, opened their bait bin,
dump the ice in. And there was a body. I saw it."

Which didn't quite account for his discomfort. Over
the years, there are a lot of bodies in small towns, and
in Eastport George had seen most of them.

But this one had knocked him for a loop. "For a
second, I thought it was Ellie," he explained. "The hair.
It looked red."

There is always some water in the bottom of a bait
bin, and George didn't have to elaborate on what had
stained it. I could figure that out for myself.

At the dock, the town's two squad cars idled with
their headlights on and their cherry-beacons whirling, a
state car pulled alongside them. Henahan's ambulance
was moving slowly out past the quonset warehouses,
the forklifts pulling over to make way. A couple of
tourists had gotten out there, too, eager for a glimpse.

Arnold urged them back as the ambulance opened
and a white-sheeted stretcher angled down the gangway
to the finger pier.

A bad thought hit me. "George. Who was it?"

"Young girl from town, you've probably seen her
around."

A man rushed up. "Listen, George. You got to tell
me. You tell me that it is a mistake."

George looked sorrowfully at the man. "Harley. You
need to talk to Arnold, now. You know I would do

about anything for you that I could, Harley. But I can't, not this time. So go on, now, and Arnold will talk to you. Please, Harley."

A scared sort of stillness settled on the man's furrowed face, in its weatherbeaten grooves. He stared at George, the look in his eyes still disbelieving.

"I want," he repeated, "for you to tell me."

Suddenly he turned with an oath and started running, pumping his skinny, bare arms like a sprinter toward the dock.

"That," George said sadly at my questioning look, "is Harley Quinn. It was his daughter, in the bait bin. I guess that Arnold must have called him, didn't want him to hear some other way."

"Hallie," Harley Quinn howled terribly as he ran. "Damnit, Hallie, you get the hell home, now. You get home or you'll get the whuppin' of your young life!"

But, as Arnold confirmed later, Hallie already had.

 "If I had stopped her, she'd be alive right now."

"Jake." Wade put his hand on mine. "You did what you could."

"That's right," Ellie put in. "She wasn't going to listen."

"Yeah." I swallowed some wine. The two of them had taken me to the Baywatch to try, as Ellie diplomatically put it, talking some sense into me. It was almost noon, and we sat at the bar, with sunshine glittering in the glasses stacked against the mirror, glinting in the brass bar rail.

Sunshine that Hallie Quinn wasn't going to see, anymore. My stomach knotted painfully around that knowledge.

"What I want to know is what she was doing down there," Ellie said, sipping a lemon soda. "That's not the smartest place to pick up a ride out of town."

"Yeah, well, she wasn't the smartest kid, was she? Or not in any of the ways that could have saved her life."

I felt a burst of fury at poor, foolish Hallie, so certain that she could take care of herself. She couldn't have been dead, Arnold had told us, more than a few hours. He'd spared us most of the details, but he did say she'd been beaten and strangled. The blood she'd lost hadn't been from a cutting wound, he said; only from her nose being broken.

Only.

"Did she ask you for money?" Ellie wanted to know.

"No." And I wouldn't have given her any; it would have been tantamount to shooting the dope into her arm myself. But if I had offered her money, would she be in Portland, now, instead of in the ambulance with a sheet over her face? And what if I'd called Arnold the moment she left, instead of thinking it over first?

"Jacobia." Wade's tone was serious. "Quit hitting yourself."

"Right." It's like they tell you in the stock market: don't chase your losses. I sat up straighter.

"That's better." Wade slid off the barstool. "Now, I'm going to go finish up that Remington. I guess you two are going to sit here and talk about girl stuff. Needlepoint, slipcovers. How to put on makeup. Stuff like that. Right?"

"Right," we echoed together, eyeing him innocently.

Wade shook his head, undeceived. Since I'd known him, he'd never tried to stop me from doing anything I really wanted to do, and some of those things—in hindsight, anyway—had been pretty foolhardy. But there was a flash of warning in his eye as he left us, and I knew what he'd left unspoken: keep your cell phone handy, keep your eyes open, and don't mess up.

Because he knew I wouldn't let go of it, now. There were just too many things wrong with it. Such as:

(1) Two million dollars on a beach just begging to be taken.

(2) Three bodies—one a young girl's—in a single week.

And (3), the notion that Willoughby's presence in town was awfully coincidental. Maybe cash wasn't his *forte*, but big money and bad deeds were, especially when the two were linked together.

Besides, it kept me from dwelling on the upcoming carnage in my own life: I'd decided I was going to tell Victor about Sam's plans, myself. That way, the fight would begin before Sam could do anything to prevent it. And I was going to win, even if I had to end up replacing Hallie's body with Victor's in that bait bin.

Ellie took another sip of her lemon soda. "So," she said, "how do you think she was planning to get out of town? If," she added, "you really think she was going."

"Oh, I think so. She told me she came to warn us, but she looked pretty scared, herself. And she must have known the cops were looking for her. I don't see how she expected to get a ride so late, though. Do you suppose she already had money?"

Ellie shook her head, anger sharpening her features. "Don't know. All I know is, Ike Forepaugh gets out of custody and Hallie gets murdered. Sounds like a one-two punch to me. If she knew he killed Ken and Tim, then he probably killed her to shut her up."

"Huh. But that means he came back here. Would you, if you were facing a murder charge?"

"I might," she replied, "to get rid of a witness."

"Which would account for Hallie being so scared. What if Hallie and Tim both knew about something Ike and Kenny had going? Something big enough to be worth Ike's murdering all three of them for, so Ike could have it all for himself."

"All," she agreed, "of two million dollars."

"Absolutely. Because you know, it's true there's not enough market around here for two million bucks' worth of heroin. But what if the real market for it wasn't around here? What if this was just the point of entry?"

"Arnold told George that Ken had charts on his boat, for the water out past Halifax. International territory. And on the way back, why would the Coast Guard bother? It's just Ken. Everybody knows him."

I took her meaning: Theoretically, you can't import anything without Customs and Immigration knowing about it. But in practice there's a lot of water out there, more than anybody can patrol. And as Ellie had implied, Ken Mumford was so well known around town and out on the water, he was practically invisible.

"Once you get the stuff on land," I mused, "you could take it anywhere: Boston, even New York. Especially if you used, say, a fish truck. Or something else very ordinary looking, that normally would be making trips."

"Yep." She slid off her barstool. "Listen, I've got to go. I asked them to hold a spot for me, in the *Tides*—"

The *Quoddy Tides,* she meant: the most northeasterly paper regularly published in the United States. I could see a corner of its trim, white-painted Victorian building from here, so cute and sweet you'd have thought a pair of bluebirds lived in it.

"—for Ken's and Tim's death notices." She dropped a ten on the bar. "Keep thinking about it."

Turning, she made her way through the dwindling lunch crowd in the Baywatch, leaving me sitting at the bar with an empty wineglass and a strong desire to just forget the whole mess: Hallie, Victor, everything.

But I couldn't forget the girl in the Port Authority bus terminal. I owed somebody something, for the luck that girl had.

I got out of there.

Think about it, Ellie had said, so I did as I drove back to Dennysville, hoping to replace that half-shutter that Victor had ruined. Ken hadn't been spending much money, but if we were right about what had been going on—some kind of an enormous drug buy that was apparently about to happen when he got killed, with the money on Crow Island all ready to be ferried out to a big boat—he'd had access to an enormous lot of it.

Which just didn't compute. Even a lout like Kenny knew that if you spent a lot, people would figure you were getting it from somewhere, and in Kenny's case they weren't going to figure he'd been made CEO of General Motors. In a town like ours, if he'd even bought someone a drink, someone else would sit up and take notice. They'd figure Kenny had graduated to bigger crimes.

And soon—the Eastport rumor machine being what it was—word would get back to Arnold. Ken would be watched and pretty quickly thereafter, he would be arrested:

End of deal. That would be obvious even to Kenny.

But it wasn't Ken's ability to know all this that I doubted. It was the likelihood—given his booze-soaked character—of his acting on the knowledge, by not spending any of the money.

This led me kicking and screaming to the idea that Ken hadn't known about all that money at all, which pretty much ruled out his having told Ike Forepaugh about it, didn't it?

Passing the Crossroads Restaurant, a low red-and-white frame place that looks like a lowdown hamburger joint and serves prime rib that is to die for, I passed Ned Montague driving a rust-raddled Chrysler, headed back toward Eastport.

He didn't see me, or anyway he didn't wave. In the rear-view, I saw his muffler trailing sparks, bouncing and dragging along on the pavement. This was not exactly a rare sight around here; hard use, salt air, and long winters are tough on cars in downeast Maine, and a ten percent local unemployment rate—for Ned, it was more like seventy-five percent—doesn't help.

But seeing Ned's car reminded me of the one up on blocks, out behind Ken Mumford's trailer, and that reminded me of Hallie Quinn again, stuffed into a bait bin awash in bloody ice water and fish stink. So by the time I pulled into Willoughby's drive, I was ready for a change of scenery, even if the place did look way too glossy and overdone, like a farm whose chief agricultural product is the floral pattern on a bolt of Laura Ashley chintz.

The silver Jag was pulled up outside the garage. Beyond the cedar fence the llamas muttered disgruntledly, glancing at me as if calculating whether or not they could spit that far. As I jumped from the truck, Baxter Willoughby slammed out of the house and barreled at me, looking ready to chew nails.

"What are you doing here?" he demanded. The bulldog-faced fellow I'd seen last time came out, too, and stood on the porch watching us.

I explained about the broken shutter, laying on the gratitude and apologizing heartily for troubling him again. "But I'd hoped I could have one more look in that Dumpster. It would help me out a lot."

"Oh. All right, I guess," he relented. The bulldog man was crossing the lawn toward us.

Willoughby made the introductions bare politeness required by pronouncing a name so quickly that I couldn't catch it, adding the phrase, "consulting client."

Which term, as we both knew, covers a multitude of sins. The bulldog man offered a limp hand. "Good t' meetcha," he muttered.

One of the llamas came over to the cedar fence and spat.

"Ha ha," the creepy bulldog man said creepily.

Willoughby flushed. Even though the glob of spit hadn't reached him, he seemed to feel it indicated a lack of respect. "Someday, I'll use them for target practice," he said darkly.

I wondered why he kept them at all. In my experience, his type usually went in for more decorative pets: exotic felines, or terrifyingly expensive tropical fish.

Looking bored, the llamas turned and walked away.

"You won't shoot those animals," the bulldog man said. His accent was British tinged with a background he had not managed to eliminate: Yorkshire, possibly. "You've paid out too damned much money for them."

He smiled, exposing teeth in a bad state of repair. "You can't," he confided to me, "kid a kidder." But his smile wasn't pleasant and I didn't think Willoughby was kidding.

"Go on, then," Willoughby said ungraciously. "You can have the shutter. Root around in the Dumpster all you want." He stalked away toward the house with the bulldog man following behind, and the two of them went in and slammed the door.

All of which piqued my curiosity, just on general principles. In the Willoughby department I was beginning to feel like an old bird dog; maybe it wasn't my job to retrieve anymore, but I couldn't get the scent out of my nose. Still, trying to find out more now would get me run off his place, minus one absolutely essential shutter, so I went on around back to the Dumpster like a good girl, and climbed onto it.

The day was glorious, just as before: the sun was shining, birds were singing, and there was a little breeze, so it wasn't too hot. I'd brought gloves along this time, and the stuff I'd dragged aside on my last visit was still pushed out of the way, so all I had to do was cling onto a slender metal rung, balance on a heap of drywall scraps, and . . .

Darn: half a shutter, just out of reach. I scooted along the edge of the Dumpster, bypassing paint cans and concrete sacks and noticing that, just by coincidence, I could see into Willoughby's den of electronic iniquity from here. This time the blinds were open, although at this distance the text on his computer screen wasn't legible, just a trio of solid ribbons moving vertically.

Like columns of figures. The two men's heads, peering at the screen, were silhouettes: Willoughby's long and narrow, the other low and flattened like the head of a toad.

Suddenly Willoughby's head came up, turning alertly.

I busied myself retrieving the shutter; when I looked over again, the blinds at Willoughby's den window had been closed.

And that was that. I tossed the shutter into my car and went down the lane, noticing something I'd missed, earlier: the small, glassy eyes of motion detectors where the lane met the road. No wonder Willoughby had bopped outside so fast.

Banks of computers, overseas visitors, big-ticket security items—it was all just so wonderfully, fascinatingly odd that I nearly went back up the lane again, to knock on his door and just ask Willoughby what the hell he was up to.

But instead, as I got on Route 1 heading north to Eastport, my cell phone beeped and I found out.

"Jacobia," said Hargood Biddeford. "Some facts on our friend for you."

"Great. Don't mention the name, okay? I'm on the cell phone."

"Right. Not exactly the most private method of . . ."

Rounding an uphill curve, I slowed for a loaded log truck, its engine roar drowning out Hargood's voice as the truck driver downshifted for the long grade. Had I been born in Maine, this would have been my signal to pass, but I hadn't so it wasn't. Dust from the big rig's tires billowed into the car; I leaned over and rolled up the passenger side window.

"It seems," Hargood continued, "there've been developments in his case, to wit: association with known criminals. Which as you know is against his terms of probation and could get him sent back to prison. If," Hargood added, "you can call that country club he did his time in a prison."

"So, you think somebody put the fix in? Told his probation officer to let him slip through the cracks, as long as he also slipped out of town? In other words, let's let him screw up in someone else's jurisdiction?"

I turned onto Route 190 toward Eastport; the lumber truck continued north.

"Nah," Hargood dragged the syllable out sarcastically. "What gives you that idea, that he got a break?"

Hargood's clients were respectable, middle-class people who'd made, most of them, stupid mistakes: skimming the registers in restaurant chains they owned, or omitting to pay withholding taxes. Usually there was some tragic story involved: a drinking problem or a gambling habit. Only rarely did his clients really scheme to defraud.

But Hargood's clients, unlike Willoughby, went back to jail for clipping their toenails crooked, and Hargood resented it.

"Also," he added, "around here word is he's short of money."

"Really." That didn't fit with those expensive renovations on his house.

On Route 190 I slowed through Pleasant Point, then pushed the speedometer back to fifty for the run across Carlow Island. Here the white pine grew nearly up to the road on both sides of the pavement, with sandy cuts leading back in to the building lots marked by the real-estate agents' For Sale signs.

"Thanks, Hargood. That's very interesting." A bee

bumbled in through my window, buzzed angrily, and flew out again.

"You're welcome," Hargood said happily. "Listen, about that plan you and I were discussing earlier—"

Selling his telephone stock and socking away his paychecks, he meant. The bee buzzed back in and I waved, shooing it away.

"Do it," I said, and the passenger-side window exploded.

 "Now, Jacobia," Arnold said, "let's not go all wild-eyed. We don't know anyone shot at you deliberately. We don't know it was a shot at all."

"Arnold, we have had three murders in three days."

"Well," Arnold conceded slowly. "There is that."

"You think that bullet was out there flying around for fun, and decided to break my car window?"

Arnold frowned vexedly. Neither murders nor escaped prisoners were good for summer tourism, nor were random gunshots.

"We don't," he repeated stubbornly, "know it was a bullet."

I just about flew out of my chair at him, whereupon he spread his hands placatingly. "All right, say it was a bullet. Say our pal Ike is still around, too, not down in Portland or points south the way any sensible escaped prisoner would be."

He held up his fingers. "One, we don't think he's armed. Ken got shot, but with his own little gull-popper—"

A .22, Arnold meant; it was illegal to shoot gulls, but people still did it.

"—we found that on his boat. The other two *didn't*

get shot, which if Forepaugh has a gun, why didn't they? More likely somebody local went out, fired off a few shots for fun. Got," he concluded disapprovingly, "a little careless. Which," he went on, "I am going to find out about, and when I do, there will be a hot time in the old town, tonight."

I wanted everyone to think I was bright-eyed and bushy-tailed, that having a shot whiz through my car window hadn't even fazed me. The truth was, I'd managed to drive back to town all right—fast, to avoid being an easy target—but as soon as I arrived I'd called Ellie and my voice had begun shaking, and she got here in about fifteen seconds.

"Thanks for coming, Arnold. You're probably right. Someone got careless, that's all. Made me nervous."

"Hmmph." Arnold looked disgusted, clapping his hat onto his head. "I find the fella, whoever it was, I'll make him nervous. I'll make him just as anxious as hell."

But at the door he paused, looking hard at me. "You be careful, though. Because I could be wrong about Forepaugh being long gone. About everything I'm thinking, in fact. So you just watch it."

Then he was gone. "So," Ellie said when the squad car had pulled away from the house, "what do you think?"

"Well . . ." I said, biting into one of the fresh doughnuts she had brought to help me get my strength back. Say what you want about Valium and Prozac and all; for nervous shock, there is nothing like a fresh, homemade doughnut.

"I think," I went on, feeling my recovery begin, "what we have here is three hits and a near miss. Hallie visits me, she's found dead, someone takes a shot at me. It's not," I concluded, "trigonometry."

"Arnold thinks you weren't shot at—or not deliberately, anyway—because he doesn't think Ike would have. Or could have, because he doesn't think Ike has a gun," Ellie said.

"Correct. Which makes some sense, actually, because if any weapons had been reported stolen around here recently, Arnold would know about it. And how else would Ike get a weapon?"

I finished the doughnut. "This brings us to: it could be Ike didn't do any of it. Or he did all of it except shooting at me. Or I suppose it could be he really has gotten hold of a gun."

"So which way do you want to go from here?" Ellie asked.

I finished my tea. There was only one course of action that covered all the bases.

"Down," I told her, "to the cellar."

Back in the city, I knew a fellow whose job was to take the Mob's money and put it in banks. Using the proceeds of extortion, prostitution, gambling, drugs, counterfeiting, hijacking, strong-arm, and protection rackets, he bought CDs and Treasury bills: the safe but low-interest kinds of investments normally purchased by people who can barely bring themselves to pull the money out from under the mattress at all.

With his own cash, however, he was more imaginative: He bought weapons, filling his modest Brooklyn Heights apartment so thoroughly with them that he barely had room for furniture, so he used to come to my place and sit on mine.

One day I asked him why, since he never touched any of the mob's cash—

—well, actually he did, but that was much later, and it is another story—

—and since he was so cautious in investing it that he would never lose any—

—well, not unless banks failed and governments fell, which they didn't, and he didn't expect them to—

—he needed enough firepower to wipe out a tank division.

Jemmy Wechsler grinned. And he said: "Jacobia, pure of heart works better when you're armed to the teeth."

Which was why I now removed the silver chain from my neck, struggling as always to work the clasp, so that the small brass key on the chain fell into my hand. Seeing the chain reminded me again of Hallie, and sent another thump of guilt reverberating through my heart.

Then from the lockbox Wade had installed in my cellar, I removed the Bisley. With it I had put in hundreds of hours of target practice; Wade, in addition to being a fine marksman, is a wicked good teacher. By now, I was pretty good with the Bisley.

But the trouble with it is, there is no part of the human body designed to withstand its stopping power. Even a wing shot can result in death, from shock or hemorrhaging.

So, after considerable thought, I'd recently bought a .25-caliber semiautomatic pistol. Along with the Bisley, I removed this unattractive but serviceable item from the lockbox, along with its ammunition clips. Then I examined the smaller gun.

The grey metal surface of the weapon felt cheap and shoddy, which it wasn't. There is just something about an automatic that makes it seem unsporting.

"Yeeks," Ellie said when she saw it. "I didn't know you had that."

"Neither does anyone else but Wade," I said, snapping a clip in and thumbing the safety on. He'd gone over it, checked it for manufacturing flaws, and taught me to shoot it. "And now you."

She nodded, understanding what I didn't say: Hallie

hadn't only been warning me, just before her death. She'd also been warning Ellie. And if anyone tried to hurt Ellie, he was going to find out how unsporting an automatic weapon could be. I put the Bisley in my bag and dropped the .25 in my sweater pocket.

"Arnold might be barking up the wrong tree," Ellie said. "Or rather, there might be more trees to bark up than he realizes."

I'd reported to her my impressions of Baxter Willoughby, before Arnold arrived.

"Still, we can't just tell Arnold that," she added.

"No. His thoughts are set on Ike Forepaugh. Besides, I don't want Arnold spooking Willoughby if it turns out he's in this some way."

"But maybe we could get Arnold's thoughts turning in the proper direction."

"I don't see how."

"Well," Ellie said consideringly, "I don't know how it was back in the big city. But in Eastport if you want a man to come by some information casually, some way that he can turn it over in his mind for a while without going off half-cocked about it . . ."

I caught her drift. "You talk to his wife," I said.

Clarissa Dow was a dark-haired, diminutive woman who'd come to Eastport as an investigator for the State District Attorney's office, and stayed to marry Arnold; she'd also established a small law practice here. Her brisk manner and no-nonsense street smarts had put people off, at first, but now, six months later, they had come to appreciate her hard-as-nails way of handling a legal problem, especially when it was their legal problem.

Climbing the stairs to her office overlooking Water Street, I smelled flowers, and when I reached the top, I saw why: a dozen red roses stood in a glass vase in the waiting area, evidence that Arnold was glad to have her back after her week at a legal convention in Portland.

I sat in one of the wooden straight chairs in the ante-room, hoping I wouldn't have to wait too long; after a moment I heard chairs scraping back, and voices mingling in tones of farewell.

Except for one voice. "I don't *want* to! You can't *make* me! I *won't*—"

The office door opened and a little girl appeared, about six years old and prettily dressed in a plaid smock, white stockings, and patent leather shoes. Flash-ing dark eyes and black ringlets framing a heart-shaped face completed the initial impression of a child straight out of an old-fashioned storybook.

But I knew little Sadie Peltier only too well, and the only story she belonged in was a horror story. Flinging the door back, she stomped into the anteroom and spun around.

"Old witch! I hate you! I'm not sorry, and I won't say I am even if you *kill* me!" Then she raced down-stairs. Moments later, I heard her in the street.

"Do you know what they did to me up there? Well, *do* you?" she was demanding at the top of her horrid little lungs. "They bashed me and crashed me and *smashed* me."

Looking shell-shocked, Sadie's parents staggered from the office and helped each other down the stair-case without a word to me, while Clarissa waved me in.

"Good heavens," she commented as Sadie's voice faded down the street. "People told me about her, but I really had no idea."

"She's a handful," I said. Sadie's parents were per-fectly nice people, and how they had managed to pro-duce the equivalent of a Tasmanian devil was a mystery to everyone. "I gather she has to apologize for some-thing, or somebody's going to sue?"

Clarissa nodded. Since moving from Portland, she had let her hair grow and stopped wearing makeup, except for lipstick. The effect was softer, less the career woman who would eat broken glass for a promotion and more the professional person, actually interested in doing the job right.

Her fingernails, though, were still perfect ovals, always clear-polished. She tapped them thoughtfully on her desk.

"Something like that," she allowed. "Tell me again a little about Sadie? I need some background if I'm going to get her folks out of a mess, and I never quite comprehended . . ."

I nodded. "Comprehending Sadie is like trying to understand a hurricane. Either you're in it and no words are necessary, or you're not and you don't quite get it. Sadie is a *terror*."

A small V appeared above the bridge of Clarissa's nose. "I wonder if she's bad enough, or even strong enough, to fill the entire trunk of a car with . . . well, cat droppings? Because that's what she's supposed to have done, and she even admits it. But I'm not sure I believe . . ."

I had to laugh, although probably to the victim it had not been funny. "Depends on how mad she is at you. If you don't give her candy when she wants some, or you stop her from kicking all the slats out of your picket fence, she might just fill your whole house up with cat droppings. So what did someone do to her, first? That is, what provoked her attack?"

Clarissa looked rueful. "Took away her spray paint. Which she was allegedly using to redecorate a white French poodle. The poodle didn't mind, but the owner did. Seems it's a show dog—the people were visiting in Eastport, just for the weekend—and the dog's out of the running, now, for some important prizes."

"Oh, my. And if she apologizes for the dog *and* the trunk they won't make a federal case out of it?"

"Uh-huh. But if she doesn't—she doesn't appear very

likely to—then they will. And they can do it. The husband's a lawyer, himself."

Clarissa brightened unconvincingly. "Well, I'll think of something. It's not your problem. How are you, anyway? I heard you had some excitement, this afternoon."

Actually, it might be my problem. When Sadie was upset, windows began breaking and small fires began starting, all over town. Still, I was here on another matter.

"Somebody shot my window out," I said. "Arnold thinks it was just careless gun handling."

"But you don't." She sat back a little, her attention fully focused on me, now: another reason people had come to like her.

"No. Or anyway I'm not sure. The thing is, everybody figures that just because Ike Forepaugh was hooked up with Ken, back when the two of them were in jail, that Ike must have killed him."

"And you don't think that, either." Even though she'd been in Portland, Clarissa was fully up to speed on Ken Mumford's murder. People joked that the only thing Arnold could do fast was pick up a telephone call from Clarissa; that, or make one to her.

"I don't know," I said. "I don't see how Ike could've got to shore after killing Ken. The water's too cold to swim in, and if he had some accomplice with another boat, who?"

Clarissa nodded thoughtfully. "But the jailhouse connection is such a good one, and Ike is such a dirtbag, and there's really no evidence for anybody else. *And* he seems to have disappeared, a sure sign of a guilty conscience."

"Maybe. What's his story, anyway?"

She counted off on her fingers. "Drunk and disorderly, resisting arrest, DUI, aggravated assault, armed robbery . . . shall I go on? Those," she added, "are just the highlights."

"Moving right up the criminal career ladder. After all that, murder could be a logical next step."

Clarissa looked thoughtful, trying to decide whether or not to tell me something. "Look, keep this under your hat. We don't need to start a panic. But there's also some evidence he's been around in town, or at least that he's still in the area."

"Such as?"

"A cap that some fellows in town say belonged to him. And a beat-up old bowie knife. They were with a bedroll and some other things in a cave, in the cliffs at Broad Cove."

"Interesting. So maybe he was camped out there."

She nodded. "It does make sense, if you don't want to get caught, to lay low. Not go out hitchhiking or something, out on the highway."

"I guess it does. Does Arnold know this, yet?"

Clarissa shook her head. "Just happened. One of the state guys came up looking for Arnold to tell him, while Sadie and her parents were here. I told the state officer," she grinned wryly, "that Eastport cops carry radios, just like the ones in the big city. After I weaseled the information out of him, of course."

"Of course." Sometime in a previous life, I thought, Clarissa had been a bloodhound. But I was forgetting my mission.

"I don't suppose the name Baxter Willoughby has come up in the investigation? Just . . . hypothetically."

Her eyes narrowed. "Not that I know of. Should it have?"

"No. I mean, probably it wouldn't."

Getting caught once, back in New York, would have made him more cautious. The only way to nail Willoughby for anything now would be to catch him actually doing it; he was not the kind of guy, anymore, who would just let himself happen to come up in an investigation.

"Clarissa, do me a favor, will you? Don't tell Arnold what I'm about to say. Or at least not the way I'm going to say it."

Her eyes grew cautious. "Jacobia, you know I can't promise anything like that."

"Not even if it works out best for Arnold? Because listen, the thing is this: I think there's something funny about Baxter Willoughby. Maybe even something connected to the investigation. But if I mention Willoughby to Arnold, either Arnold won't listen to me because he's so set on Ike, *or* he might go roaring out to Dennysville, demanding to know what's up."

Clarissa smiled, recognizing the truth of this.

"And believe me," I went on, "the prudent thing would be if Arnold could just keep his ears open. With this guy, it would be best not to let him know there's any interest in him at all."

I went on to tell Clarissa about my own history with Baxter Willoughby. I also mentioned that, as a candidate for secret ownership of two million dollars, I considered him top-drawer.

"He's the only guy around here right now with a connection to big money. On the other hand," I finished, "I have no idea why he'd stash two million bucks in cash on Crow Island. And there's other things wrong with him in the likely-suspect department. But if, for instance, he wanted people murdered *and* he had Forepaugh working for him . . ."

"No physical violence in Willoughby's history," Clarissa assumed correctly. The switch from DA's investigator to private law practice had done nothing to blunt her naturally sharp mental processes. "But Ike could take care of that stuff for him?"

"Exactly. If they were connected, that might be the way it would be. The thing is, though, this is all so . . ."

"Circumstantial."

"Very. I could be seeing things where there aren't

any. But if Willoughby is involved in all of it somehow, and somebody scares him without being able to arrest him, then he will scram."

Clarissa smiled, tenting her fingers over the desk. "I see. How about if I bring it up at the dinner table, then, that there is such a guy as Willoughby? And maybe that in the past, he's had big money, and a less-than-savory reputation. So the name will be fresh in Arnold's mind, if it pops up somewhere else? I might get the phrase "flight risk"in there, too, just very tactfully."

"Perfect. I appreciate it, Clarissa." An uncomfortable thought struck me. "You do know that I'm not casting aspersions on Arnold's intelligence."

"Of course I do." Her pale blue eyes, the color of ice on a pond, were luminously intelligent. "Fortune favors the prepared mind, that's all. And sometimes certain minds have to be prepared not to charge in like a bull in a china shop."

She rose from behind her desk. "Thanks for the heads-up."

"No problem. Anything else going on in the investigation you can let me in on? I'd like to tell Ellie, if there is. She's pretty upset about Ken and Tim."

Clarissa shook her head regretfully. "No big breaks, if that's what you mean. APB for Forepaugh, ballistics check on the weapon, toxicology tests on the bodies, all the usual."

Then she changed the subject. "But Jacobia, there's still no reason for Ike Forepaugh to be taking a shot at you even if he does have a gun. And even if he's working for Willoughby—well, *he* doesn't know you've got suspicions about him, does he?"

"No. I haven't given him any reason for that. I don't think he even recognized me when I saw him. He didn't act like he did."

"Good." She walked me to the door. "By the way, Ellie might want to hear Ken's body is coming back tomorrow. Tim's, too."

At my look of surprise she grinned. "The autopsies should've taken longer. But I used to date the medical examiner, back in Portland, and I told him he owed me one for not marrying him when he asked me, and I guess he agreed."

I had a feeling the favor Clarissa had pulled in was a bit more substantial than that. In Portland, she'd been a mover and shaker. But she knew it would mean a great deal to Ellie, having the funerals over and done with.

"Thanks, Clarissa," I said again as I was leaving, thinking I'd gotten my message sent cleanly and efficiently, and without any loose ends dangling. "Oh, and—listen. If the people with the painted French poodle and the car trunk full of you-know-what were to find that both those situations had been fully repaired, do you think they would . . . ?"

"Let Sadie's folks off the hook? Yes. But I really don't see how that could happen."

"I might have an idea. I'll give you a call if it works out. But Clarissa, don't let Sadie know about it."

And that, I thought, was that. But when I reached the bottom step, she stopped me. "Jacobia? There is one small thing more."

"Yes?" I replied, thinking *uh-oh*.

"About the ambulance ride with the bodies?" she went on. "Hank Henahan is awfully nervous about it. Arnold told him he'd go with him. But tomorrow's our six-month wedding anniversary."

She smiled: appealingly. Inexorably.

Inescapably. "And you'd like Arnold to be here for it."

"That would be pleasant, yes. So could you . . . ?"

I felt a sigh of resignation rising from my toes. "Okay, Clarissa. I'll go on the morgue run while you stay home with Arnold and drink champagne out of a slipper."

What the heck, I figured it was the least I could do. If she hadn't expedited those autopsies, Ken and Tim could have wound up not getting released until winter, by which time the earth would have frozen too solidly to bury them, and they would sit around until spring.

So the next morning I set off for Bangor with Hank Henahan in the ambulance, and the trip didn't start out badly: cool, fresh breeze, coffee in a thermos, Route 1 curving south along the coastline toward Ellsworth, through green trees and past blue inlets bright and colorful as Kodachrome.

As I say, it didn't start out badly. But by the time we were through, I was wishing for some of that champagne: one bottle to drink, and another to break over Hank Henahan's head.

"Durned red tape," Henahan muttered as we made our way through what passes for evening rush-hour traffic in Bangor. The Penobscot glittered in late-afternoon sunlight as we crossed the bridge, Hank slowing for the double line of cars heading out of the city. "You'd think we was adopting those poor fellers."

The road ahead was two-lane, with plenty of cross streets, businesses, and other impediments to getting this errand over with. Hank refrained from putting on the siren or beacons, though, partly because he was a good, safe, ethical paramedic who knew his business, and partly because his hands were shaking too hard.

Driving from Eastport had been okay, and pulling into the ambulance bay of St. Joseph's Hospital, where the bodies had been sent from Augusta, had gone like clockwork. I guessed Hank had been pretending he was delivering a live one, not picking up two dead ones. Even the long waiting around we'd had to do, with lunch in the hospital coffee shop and plenty of time to peruse the magazines in the lobby, hadn't fazed him much.

Now, though, his pale, sweaty face and haunted expression were beginning to make me feel like someone in a Stephen King novel. In the book I would be the character who pooh-poohs supernatural horrors, and who subsequently is devoured by one of them.

In my lap lay the large manila envelope of paperwork we'd gotten at the hospital. The secretary in the pathology department there had made a point of telling me not to lose it, as among other things it contained copies of the autopsy reports for me to give to Bob Arnold. The envelope was stamped CONFIDENTIAL in large red letters.

Which I ignored, removing the sheaf of papers as Hank gaped in dismay. "They don't," I told him, "come to your house and shoot you for this," and he harrumphed disapprovingly but didn't offer further objection.

Scanning the autopsy reports, I found Kenny's to be what I expected. There were a lot of exotic latinate phrases, but they all boiled down to *gunshot wound to the head*. Tim's, however, was a surprise.

He hadn't died by hanging. He'd been dead when somebody put him up there, of a heart attack that happened while someone was in the process first of strangling him and of finishing the job by smothering him. Probably with a pillow, the report said; the fabric weave was imprinted in his skin. Thumb bruises showed on his neck, partially obscured by the rope marks but not entirely.

Which cleared up a small mystery I'd been pondering: how had somebody gotten Tim onto his makeshift gallows? Surely he'd have seen what was intended, I'd believed, and would have fought like a dozen demons, yet there hadn't been any marks of a struggle on him, or any sign of a blow to the head to knock him out.

Now I understood: he'd already been dead, and the ligatures were all applied later, in part perhaps to cover up the thumb indentations. So at least we didn't have a torturer on our hands.

Only a multiple murderer.

Meanwhile, we continued heading to the back of beyond with a couple of corpses in tow, as evening gathered around us.

"What was that?" Hank glanced fearfully in the rear-view.

"The plastic." I stared ahead. Just a few miles more and we would be out of the Bangor area, with only tourists and small-town local traffic to contend with.

"They're rolled," I added, "in plastic. Taped and zipped in bags. They couldn't get out if they tried."

I meant this as reassurance; instead, the idea of Ken or Tim trying to get out of their wrappings made Hank's eyes widen unhappily.

"Oh, Lord," he mourned, "I feel like I'm going to faint."

Which, even in what in Bangor passes for heavy traffic, wouldn't have been a good idea. "Hank. Get a grip on yourself. I hate to break it to you like this, but dead is dead. D-E-A-D. If you want a scary idea, think about us ending up in a ditch."

Hank was a sandy-haired bruiser with a square, solid jaw and shoulders that bulged like beef roasts, but right then he looked like a little kid. "I can't help it. When I was a boy, my grandma told stories. I think she gave me a complex."

If she had, I thought—unjustly, as it turned out—it was the only complex thing about Hank.

"And it ain't true, neither, what you said about deadness. I got a personal experience."

He glanced hopelessly into the rearview again. "Oh, Lord, that damn bag is moving."

The ambulance swerved toward the shoulder, surprising a pair of pedestrians who seemed to think we were trying to drum up business. One of them shot a middle finger at us as we missed him by inches.

"Pull in," I ordered Hank firmly. "Right there, in the driveway of that store. Put the brake on, turn the key off, and take some deep breaths."

Hank obeyed shudderingly. "I can do it," he gasped faintly. "Just let me get my nerves back together."

Another small crackle of morgue-issue plastic emanated from the back of the ambulance: Ken or Tim, settling from the sharp turn we'd made.

Hank moaned. "You city people," he managed between juddering inhalations, "think you know everything. Why, I could tell you a story about your very own house—"

Only a hundred and thirty or so miles to go, and it was already past six o'clock. "Hank, get out of the driver's seat. I'll take the wheel."

"But I'm the only one who is supposed to drive the—"

"Do you want to break the rules, or do you want to be going through the Moosehorn Refuge in the middle of the night with these two?"

The Moosehorn is barren and desolate-feeling even in bright day, the narrow road winding between granite cliffs and under old trees that seem to be stealthily reaching down for you.

"There will," I added, "be a full moon."

"Ohh," Hank groaned defeatedly, and moments later we were back on the road again.

"Now, what was it you were telling me about my house?"

I doubted I could unscare him entirely, but if I could get him talking about dead folks other than those we were transporting, he might be a little distracted. And as I'd hoped, he warmed to his favorite subject immediately.

"Ain't nothing to tell," he began, but this is the standard Eastport way of beginning a story, so I was not discouraged.

He cracked the window, pulled a pack from his pocket, and lit a cigarette. "Mind?" he asked, glancing at me.

I'd have let him sniff chloroform if it would calm

him down. "Nope. You said your grandmother used to tell you stories."

But he didn't answer, just sat there shaking and smoking. We were out of the suburbs, now, shooting for the hill towns between Bangor and Ellsworth. After that it was a long poke of curving blacktop, the danger of a moose wandering out onto the road ever present; if you hit one of them, it could be all over for you.

"Want coffee?" I asked as the lights of fast-food places in Ellsworth twinkled garishly in the thickening dusk.

Hank shook his head as we took the turn away from Blue Hill and Castine, up toward the real downeast.

"My grandma," he offered finally, beginning to answer my question an hour after I'd asked it, "she told me one about the Holbrook House. You know, that big old captain's mansion on the way to Lubec, it got turned into a bed-and-breakfast."

He chuckled grimly. "Guess the tourists get their money's worth *there*, all right."

"Why, what do they get?" The road wound through crossroads towns: church, post office, country store.

"Old Captain Holbrook," Hank related, "back in the 1800s, he went to the South Seas, and when he got there, he got all hooked up in some heathen religion. Not the regular religion the people there had, but some real old, evil kind. Came back with all sorts o' trinkets, gold and jewels. Each of 'em by itself would've made the old captain rich. An' they did, too. But," Hank paused significantly, "they had a price."

I sneaked a sideways peek at him. "And the price was?"

"The price," Hank intoned heavily, "was his soul. The beings as had bought it from him, well, they come and took it. He used to go out on the water in a dinghy, to communicate with 'em, so folks said. An' finally, one night, the dinghy went out but when it came back he wasn't on it."

He took a breath. "Out of the sea they'd come up in darkness, those strange awful creatures, all that way from them heathen islands they must've swum. Folks who was there, and ones heard of it afterwards, they said those heathenish beings plucked his soul from his living body, as he had promised it to 'em. And the screams he gave out, they all said, while the beings did it. The screams was purely horrible."

We were in the real country, now, through Milbridge and climbing into the blueberry barrens south of Machias. Hank spoke up again, his tone matter-of-fact.

"You don't want to spend the night there, is all I'm saying. He don't show himself to everyone, that captain, but if he does, he comes in your dreams. And the dreams," Hank emphasized, "ain't ones as you will ever forget."

Behind us on the stretchers, the two wrapped bodies rode silently, their bulk in the utility light of the boxy compartment now shadowy and portentous-looking. Machias went by in moments: first the college, then the bridge over Bad Little Falls, the short business street and Helen's Restaurant. Once we got over the smaller bridge in East Machias we were in the boondocks again.

The full moon was rising, coming up out of Penobscot Bay like a coin dripping silver. A flock of black cormorants vee'd across the indigo sky, heading for evening shelter. A too-fast curve—I touched the brake pedal—made the plastic shrouds of the dead men whisper and crackle.

"Oh, mother," Hank muttered, getting nervous again. "Out at night, haulin' a couple of corpses, under a full moon."

"If you light another cigarette," I began irritably, "it's not those corpses you'll have to worry about. They don't have to breathe in all your—"

"Look out!" Hank gripped the dashboard.

You don't see their eyes in your headlights or their bodies in your way. All you see are the moose's legs, looking too long and spindly to hold up that massive body.

I hit the brakes, spun the wheel, and yelped as the tires hit the shoulder, bounced, and swerved us up toward a big pine. A moment later the front end of the ambulance bounced off the tree's trunk, nosed around wildly, and smashed into another with a vicious thud, stopping us suddenly.

After that, the only sound was a loud hissing, there in the pitch-darkness. I knew we hadn't hit the moose—the impact, I've been told, is unmistakable—but if he was still out there somewhere we couldn't see him, or anything else.

"Why aren't there lights?" Hank cried in a sudden panic.

I just sat, feeling like a computer that has crashed and needs a minute to boot up again.

"I . . . don't . . . know." I was pretty sure I wasn't bleeding, and nothing hurt very badly. I'd banged my knee on the dashboard and the steering column had broken off on impact as it was designed to do, smacking me in the chest but fortunately not impaling me.

The seat belt had saved my bacon. Too bad it hadn't saved the radiator; as my eyes adjusted to the darkness I could see that the hissing sound was engine coolant, boiling up out of—I suspected unhappily—the cracked engine block.

"Oh my gosh, where's the light?" Hank fumbled in the supply box, found the flashlight and snapped it on with fingers made clumsy by terror. Being Hank, however, he didn't use it to make sure that I, his living companion, was all right. He shone it into the rear of the ambulance, to check that neither of his deceased passengers was creeping toward him.

"Oh!" The shriek Hank let out was terrible. "Oh, oh, oh—"

I grabbed the flashlight and aimed it where he was looking. "Damn it, Hank, I've had about enough of your silly—"

Our passengers were gone.

26

"Hank, they're out here. They've got to be out here."

A mosquito the size of a B-52 took an enormous bite out of me, causing me to be grateful for the multitude of little brown bats swooping and flapping all around me, feeding on the mosquitoes.

Or almost grateful; after the story I'd heard, a bat under a full moon was not the most reassuring image I could think of.

"That," Hank replied quaveringly, "is what I'm afraid of. I *know* they're out here, somewhere."

We kept trudging, shining our flashlights—Hank had found a second one and given it to me—into the shallow ditch along darkened Route 1, in the Moosehorn Refuge. Behind us the back doors of the ambulance still gaped wide, blown that way by the impact and now impossible to close.

When the doors burst open, the stretchers—each with a body on it—had flown out. The stretchers had wheels, so if they had hit the pavement, they could have rolled.

"You sure you're okay?" I scratched a fresh mosquito bite.

"Yeah. Little bounced around, that's all. Sure wish a car would come along, though."

"Hank, you better pray we find those bodies before one does. Do you know what kind of story this is going to make in Eastport? Lost the dead guys—they'll hear 'em laughing at us in Canada."

"Come on," the paramedic replied defensively, "it's not our fault the damned—*gurk*."

That was the sound he made, leading me to believe that at least the dead guys weren't lost, anymore. And I was right: when I reached Hank he was holding one hand over his mouth and aiming a flashlight with the other, gazing down goggle-eyed.

Ken Mumford wasn't on his stretcher any longer. He wasn't in his body bag, either; a broken pine bough had ripped hell out of that. And he wasn't in his plastic morgue wrappings; they'd come apart on impact.

Also, owing to the postmortem surgery that had been done on him, to track the path the bullet took in his head and so on, he was not looking very attractive. The big line of heavy black sutures where his hairline had been sewn back to the top of his face, plus similar stitches put in to hold his eyelids and mouth shut, reminded me irresistibly of a B-movie zombie in the moment just before the creature clambers to its feet and begins shambling toward you.

I grabbed Hank's shoulder. "Come on. You don't need to see this." I sat him down in the ditch by the ambulance.

"Hank? Listen to me, Hank. He's dead. Really. There's not a thing he can do to hurt you. You don't have to be scared of him."

"I'm not scared."

I shone the flashlight past him, so I could see his face. But in the glow it was not fearful, as I'd expected. Instead it was gentle and full of sorrow.

"I've been an ambulance guy for twenty years," he said, seemingly apropos of nothing.

But I understood: Evil beings, or haunted houses, or bodies in bags lying silent behind you—all those things were the stuff of Hank's nightmares: the awful unknown.

What he'd seen just now, though, was different, and in Hank's job he saw it all the time: the face of someone he'd known all his life, after catastrophe.

A tear rolled down his nose. "I wish those things didn't happen to people," Hank said.

Just then a pair of headlights shone out of the dark at us, and not long after that we had bagged up Ken again, found Tim, and were riding toward Eastport in an old grey Econoline van with the legend, "S & M Remodelers, We'll Whip Your House Into Shape!" lettered in white script on the side.

Only after we were moving did I learn that the van had an engine problem, limiting its top speed to twenty-five carburetor-clogged miles per hour. Which was when—

—owing to the fact that the van only had one seat and the driver was presently sitting in it, so Hank and I had to sit in the back with a dozen gallons of paint, two extension ladders, a toolbox, and four disassembled sawhorses, plus the bodies—

—I really did start wanting that champagne.

 "He never did tell me anything about my house," I complained to Ellie the next morning. "Or about his supposed experience with the undead."

The Waco Diner consists of a counter and a row of booths with a long, narrow aisle between, leading back to the kitchen. On the wall behind the counter hangs a magic-markered menu, a mirror with plates and glasses stacked before it, and a color TV.

"People in Eastport are like that," Ellie said as we made our way to a booth and sat. "They might talk a blue streak, but they won't soon tell you anything really personal about themselves."

Which was actually a welcome change from the city, where I'd listened to people at cocktail parties relating the gory details of their psychoanalysis, five minutes after I'd met them.

"Or," she added significantly, "about your house."

I looked up sharply. My own house had been owned by a sea captain once, too.

"Ellie, do *you* know things that you haven't—?" But just then the waitress arrived.

"What'll ya have, girls?" asked Dolly Henderson, navigating the narrow aisle with three loaded plates and a tray of brimming coffee cups balanced on her arms.

At a good six feet tall, Dolly has black, curly hair that she hacks off with scissors whenever she happens to think of it, a big, hulking body whose soft parts sway alarmingly this way and that way, and a wandering white eye that stares past you even while she is looking straight at you.

But Dolly sees more with one good eye than most people do with two. That was why, the morning after my ill-fated trip with Henahan—I was a little sore but otherwise suffering no ill effects—Ellie and I had come to visit Dolly.

"Just coffee, please," I said as Ellie and I slid into one of the red leatherette booths.

"And maybe a little conversation, if you've got time," Ellie added. Now that Ken's and Tim's bodies were back, she was more set than ever on finding out what happened to them. And Ellie was not the type to sit back and let someone else do things; while they remained to be done, she would be in there pitching.

"Hey, I always got time for talk," Dolly cackled, setting our coffees in front of us. "Who d'you want the scoop on?"

"Well, we're wondering what you might have heard about Ken, lately," Ellie said quietly.

Dolly's bushy eyebrows waggled up, down, and sideways, her stray eye pinwheeling as she glanced at me.

"He came in, weaseled a few Cokes out of me here and there. Sometimes had a load on, sometimes a hangover. Sometimes not."

I let Ellie do the talking. As she'd said, people from Eastport don't take kindly to talking personally about themselves or their own, in front of people from away.

Which I would be, even if I lived here until my dying day. I had not grown up in one of the old houses, with a family whose family business all the other families knew. I hadn't been under a lens of inspection and evaluation from the moment I was born, so that everyone would know what to expect of me just the way they did of one another.

"Kenny," Dolly said, her voice turning gentle, "was a poor, sad soul. And you know why? Because Kenny never gave up. It was always something. The next time, he would hit it big. You know?"

Ellie nodded. "Tim said that, too. That Ken had another big deal in the works. And you know, all that money they found out on the island, you have to wonder if that was connected to it."

Dolly shook her head. "Kenny didn't have two cents, I know it for a fact. You think he'd a let that boat of his go to ruin, he'd a had any money? He kept it floating, all right, but even that he did mostly on old, used parts he begged off'n fellows who felt sorry for him. I stood right here an' watched him do it."

Back behind the counter now, Dolly put the coffee-pot on the warmer coil and dumped the old grounds. "Kenny started payin' his bills when that Quinn girl took up with him. I know 'cause he'd run a tab up on me, and one on Jim Krill runs the diesel pump, over to the dock. Also he got the power turned back on, out to his trailer. But she was behind it all, and he never had any to spare."

She gave a sniff of disapproval. "Thick as thieves they was. I don't know what she saw in him. It wasn't his bright future."

Two men in overalls and boots came into the Waco, settled at the counter, and peered up at the menu, finally ordering pie and sodas. Dolly served them with her usual brisk, cheery efficiency, trading jokes and wisecracks before returning to our booth.

"I do know," she went on, "Kenny decked one of the Peltier boys, teasin' Ken about jailbait. Gave that boy a good shiner. He didn't like nasty talk about that girl. Funny, you wouldn't think Ken was anybody's knight in shining armor."

Ellie's glance softened, and I remembered what she had said about Ken being a gentleman. "I guess everybody's got their good side," she said. "Even Ken."

Dolly's clear eye fixed on Ellie. "Maybe so. But everybody's got their dumb side too, and that went double for him. You ask me, that girl was usin' him. Cute little thing, and smart as the dickens. Maybe too smart, seein' how she's ended. But what'd she want with a fool like him?"

She blew a breath out. "I been lookin' at people's faces a long time, and what I know is, Ken Mumford was hopeless in love with her, and she let him be in love with her, 'cause he had something she wanted. And that is the long and the short of it."

"Dolly," I said, remembering Hank's story again suddenly, "did he ever talk about a dinghy? Buying one, I mean. An inflatable."

It just didn't seem like something he would have, and Ellie had agreed with me when I'd asked her about it.

Dolly blew a breath out through pursed lips. "Hell, no. Them things cost real money. And that reminds me." She stuck her plump hand into her apron pocket and came out with a five-dollar bill, thrusting it at Ellie.

"I hear you're taking up a collection for the arrangements. You put this in," she finished brusquely, turning away.

"Thanks, Dolly." Ellie put the money in her bag, and made a notation on the yellow pad she was carrying around with her.

"Hey, Ellie," said one of the fellows at the counter as we passed on our way out. "This here's for the Mumfords, too." He opened his wallet and shelled out liberally, as did his partner.

"Christ, can you believe I'm gonna miss the dumb son of a bitch? And what d'you suppose is gonna happen to that old boat? An' that rust-bucket car he was always bitching about tryin' to get the money to fix up?"

"Ned got the boat," the other man said, "for all the good it's gonna do him. It's too bad about that car, though. Kenny set high store by that vehicle, even after he lost his license on that last drunk charge. Guess by now it's hardly worth haulin' it to the dump, way it's sat."

Outside, we squinted in the afternoon brilliance, sunshine slanting down from the sky and caroming off the water.

"I guess Hallie figured Ken was somebody safe to stay with," I said as we walked up Water Street. In the back of my mind those shutters still hovered ominously, like a flock of albatrosses.

"Maybe," Ellie replied. Out on the bay, a couple of fishing boats bobbed jauntily, their fresh paint jobs bright watercolor splotches against the blue water and their engines a low grumble at this distance.

"Funny, though," she added. "She must have had other places she could've used as crash pads. If that's what she was doing."

"Probably. But what else could it have been? Sam says they weren't sleeping together, according to the teenage grapevine."

"And the couch in the trailer did look slept on, didn't it?" Ellie agreed. "You just didn't think of anybody wanting anything from Ken, though. Because he didn't have anything."

Up Water Street, the shops and restaurants and the Motel East gave way to small cottages set cheek-by-jowl along the inlet overlooking Sea Street. At low tide the rotting wooden skeleton of the old boat ways, where new-built wooden ships once slid into the water for the very first time, poked through the inlet's calm surface like the stubs of broken teeth.

"It puts," Ellie admitted, "a different slant on it, the idea of Hallie using Ken."

By then we had reached the Quinns' house, a white frame structure whose aggressively neat exterior showed the effects of constant maintenance: crisp new siding shingles, shiny gutters, freshly pointed chimney, and bright white squares of concrete forming the front walk. Flower beds bloomed with marigolds, and even the water in the birdbath looked freshened that morning.

It should have been attractive, but instead it was faintly off-putting, too neat. Every window shade was lined up perfectly with every other one, and a little white sign tacked to the front door ordered visitors to WIPE FEET.

The woman who came to the door resembled Hallie, if you didn't count the pink nose, tear-swollen eyes, and a thirty-year age difference. They didn't look as if they'd been easy years and the upcoming ones weren't going to be, either, her face said. Peering through the screen, she looked wildly from me to Ellie and back, as if still hoping we might have come to tell her that it was all a mistake.

As usual, Ellie got around the introductions with ease and grace; before I knew it, we were in a terrifyingly clean living room, being served a terrifyingly polite cup of tea. But this time it was my turn to do the talking.

"Mrs. Quinn, Hallie came to visit me just before she died."

Mrs. Quinn gasped, her hand going limply to her throat. "You saw her? Harley," she called out harshly, "come here! This woman says she saw our Hallie!"

He came into the living room, his face full of grief, anger, and abruptly freshened aggressiveness. "Who are you?" he demanded. "What was she doing with you?"

I tried to make allowances for his bereavement, but all I could think of as his beery breath gusted into my face was that I understood why Hallie had wanted so badly to get away from him.

"She came to tell me I might be in some kind of trouble, if I tried to find out more about the Mumfords' deaths. She came to try to help me."

His lips pulled into a snarl. "She'd be sticking her nose where it didn't belong. That's like her. But you didn't think to hang onto her, did you? I oughta call the cops and turn you in."

"Harley," his wife pleaded, "let her say what she's come to tell us."

I was already calculating the time before Ellie and I could get out of here. "I came to tell you how much I regret not doing more for Hallie when I saw her," I began. "I tried to get her to stay with me, or to let me take her to the drug rehabilitation place in Portland."

At the mention of drugs, Quinn's face reddened in new fury. "You shoulda called me, I'm her father! I know how to handle—"

He stopped suddenly, perhaps realizing that the only ones who would be handling his daughter now would be preparing her body for burial. But the effect didn't last.

"And I wanted to ask you," I went on, ignoring his outburst, "about . . . well . . . I feel bad about not offering her money. I feel now that if I had, she might have been able to leave town. That's what she was talking about doing. So—"

"She had money," Mrs. Quinn interrupted dully.

He shot her a look that promised her a beating, as clearly as anything I've ever seen in my life. *Just you wait,* that look said bullyingly, and I swear he enjoyed her flinching at it.

But she went on talking. "I don't know where she got it, or from who. I tried to get her to tell me, but she wouldn't. When she was with that Mumford fellow, I went out there."

The veins bulged in Quinn's stringy neck. "You went there. You knew where she was and you didn't. Tell. Me."

"Hallie was a bright girl," she went on, with what strength I could not imagine. "But she and her father had tempers."

She looked up, pathetically. "I thought some time away would be good for both of them. They could get over their pride, let things settle down a little."

You could feel it in the room, the slapping and screaming, him roaring out ultimatums and Hallie shrieking her defiance. You could feel it on your skin, like acid.

"So you let her go whoring to that bum," he went on, his tone ugly. "And you *kept it a secret from me?*"

His fingers opened and closed convulsively, as if he wanted to wrap them around someone's throat. I recalled suddenly that Arnold said Hallie had been strangled, that the beating had been only the beginning.

"Harley, what would you have done if I told you?" Mrs. Quinn asked. "The last time, you broke her eardrum."

Quinn reared back in exaggerated affront, shocked not so much at the accusation as at her saying it in front of us, and at the reproach in her tone. I got the feeling that reproach was not something he encountered on a daily basis.

Meanwhile it was obvious that she didn't care anymore: what he did to her, what might happen after Ellie and I were gone. The worst had already happened.

"Should I," she asked her husband, "have let you kill her?"

He got up. "You and I will talk," he pronounced ominously, "at another time."

He left the room. The refrigerator door slammed. Then came the unmistakable snap of the pop-top on yet another beer can, and the thump of footsteps on the cellar stairs.

Mrs. Quinn looked up at us. "I'm sorry. He's upset. I should not have said that to him."

She might as well have been wearing a big Kick Me sign. "Well," I said, getting up, "please accept my sympathies. I thought I ought to let you know I had seen her."

And to try—unsuccessfully, as it turned out—to find out where Hallie's supply of money was coming from.

I picked up my bag, tried to come up with some comment to ease our way out. Somehow I didn't think "gangway!" was exactly appropriate. But I didn't see how I could just leave Hallie's mother like this, either. She was cruising for a bruising the minute we were gone.

So I pulled one of my cards out. "If you need anything," I began. "Any help." I glanced significantly in the direction her husband had gone.

But she waved me away, avoiding my gaze and refusing the card. "I'll be all right."

Sure, I thought helplessly. A few more steps and we would be in fresh air, free from the sad, oppressive atmosphere of the house. I could practically smell the sea breeze, everything in me yearning for sunshine and escape.

But at the door, Ellie stopped short.

"Can we," she inquired gently, "see Hallie's room?"

"This," I told Ellie, "is ridiculous."

We climbed the narrow stairs, which were covered in torn brown shag carpet. The paneling was wood-grained Contac paper, scarred to expose the particleboard beneath. Quinn's efforts to keep his house in repair extended only to the portions of it that others might see; the comfort of his family, clearly, was not a concern.

"We're not going to find anything useful in her high school yearbook," I said, "or her makeup table. She would not have left anything here for anyone to find."

As we went down the narrow hallway my momentary glimpse of the Quinns' bathing area did not raise my spirits. Soap and a scrub brush can only go so far; after that you need paint and new fixtures, ceramic tiles to replace the cracked ones, and a shower curtain held up by something other than twists of coathanger wire.

"Patience," Ellie advised, as we approached the door Mrs. Quinn had described to us. We'd left her downstairs obsessively washing the teacups.

"Probably if he finds a dish in the sink, he smacks her," I muttered.

This, you see, is the trouble with carrying a loaded weapon: meeting a guy like Harley Quinn, whose head just absolutely begs to be blown off. Grimly, I followed Ellie into Hallie's room.

And stopped, feeling a small sigh escape me.

The curtains pulled back from the glitteringly clean windows were the same delicate white eyelet we'd seen at Ken's trailer. But while Ken's place had been clean, this was another ballgame entirely, so spotless Victor could have done surgery in it. And that wasn't the half of what Hallie had managed to accomplish.

The walls were covered in floral wallpaper, the trim and the closet door enameled crisp white. Spread across the bed was a white handmade sampler quilt, the patterns bright primary colors, the border dark blue. The rug was thick blue wool, the bedskirt crochet-edged.

On the night table stood a white china lamp, a vase of wilted flowers, and a book: *On the Road,* by Jack Kerouac.

Hallie had done all this herself, I felt sure after seeing the bath and her parents' spare, motel-like bedroom, and knowing it stabbed me with another sharp pang of regret over her death. But her creation also made me wonder again about money, because this stuff didn't come cheap.

Meanwhile, Ellie made straight for the night table and pulled a drawer out, setting it on the quilt.

"What are you doing?" I whispered, glancing at the doorway.

"I had a nightstand just like this when I was Hallie's age. There's a shelf." She reached into the opening where the drawer had been, felt around, and pulled out a manila envelope.

Inside was a sheaf of lined paper, pages torn from a spiral notebook. The pages were covered with writing.

" 'Why can't you accept that we belong together?' " Ellie began reading aloud. " 'I will never stop loving you. You think you can keep secrets, but I am always watching. You can't escape so why not embrace your fate?' "

And more of the scary same, including descriptions of how the writer had peeped in her window by climbing a tree, each letter signed in a boyish scrawl: "Peter M."

"Mulligan," I said, remembering Sam's description of the kid who was "stalking" Hallie. "Peter Mulligan."

"Sounds pretty intense. And creepy. 'Embrace your fate.' Who does he think he is, Edgar Allan Poe?"

"Sam says he's a nerd. I'd say he's reading beyond his grade level, all right. But I can't say much for his penmanship."

The writing, literate in spelling and sentence structure, was otherwise the equivalent of a drawing made by a disturbed child: a bizarre mix of upper- and lower-case letters leaning forward and back, pressed down so hard that in places the pen had gone right through the paper. It was as if Mulligan had not just written the words, but carved them.

Footsteps sounded on the hall stairs. Swiftly, Ellie shoved the letters into her bag and the drawer back into the nightstand, as Mrs. Quinn entered.

"Isn't it beautiful in here? She could do that. Want something a certain way, make it that way. It wouldn't occur to her to think she couldn't."

Mrs. Quinn bit her lip. "I don't blame her, you know. For wanting to go somewhere, be somebody."

She picked up the book from Hallie's nightstand, glancing at it with puzzled sorrow before putting it down. On a low shelf stood Hallie's other volumes: Ayn Rand, the *I Ching*, and *Why I Am Not a Christian* by Bertrand Russell. I bet old Harley had blown a gasket when he got a load of that one.

If he ever had. Gazing around again, I felt that it was probably rare for him to come in here, that the feminine decor, perfectly worked out to the last detail, had been a sort of talisman against him.

And on second look, I saw the other striking thing about the room that Hallie had imprinted so heavily with her personality: monograms.

Like the earrings she'd been wearing when I last saw her, nearly every object here bore initials—usually Hallie's alone, but sometimes entwined with others, almost always accompanied by a date. Stitched, carved, painted, engraved; she had personalized the quilt squares, lamp bases, pillows, even the stuffed cat reclining at the head of her bed. Mrs. Quinn saw me looking at it.

"Hallie and the boy she was seeing won that, at the State Fair two years ago." She picked it up and showed me the stitched letters and numbers memorializing the event.

"I don't know where she got her obsession with initials," the dead girl's mother went on. "But from the time she was a tiny thing, she put them on practically anything she touched. Yours, too, if you were with her when she got it, or found it."

She put the stuffed cat back in its place. "Hallie wasn't sleeping with that Mumford fellow," she added. "She had another boyfriend, I don't know who. Mumford, she had some reason why she hung around with him. Maybe because he let her boss him around. But the other one—"

She stopped, frowning over how to say it.

"You think," I hazarded a wild guess, "that this other man, whoever he is, he's probably more like her father than Hallie realized."

Mrs. Quinn glanced up gratefully at me, our eyes meeting in the dresser mirror. "Yes. Someone determined, but . . ."

She shook her head. "Hallie loved Portland, went there all the time. Hitchhiked, though I warned her a hundred times against it. She had friends there, and they were bad enough. But this fellow, whoever he is . . . she must have thought he was strong enough to get her out of here, into the life she wanted. But I think she didn't know, yet, what she was really seeing."

Mrs. Quinn's reflection in the mirror laughed defeatedly. "Oh, aren't we all just such fools?" she asked.

But she'd long ago stopped expecting an answer.

Outside, I resisted the impulse to rush home, take a shower, and wash my clothes. The atmosphere that hung like a toxic cloud in the Quinn house seemed to have seeped into my bones.

Ellie, however, was having none of this. "I want a word with this Mulligan fellow," she announced. "He sounds like some kind of real weirdo."

Passing the Mexican restaurant with its bright strings of Christmas lights looped around the houseplants that grew like jungle vines in the windows, I inhaled the sweet aroma of corn tortillas frying in lard, fresh fajitas smothered in shredded beef, and the pot of black beans and rice that the cook kept simmering on the stove. Next door, Frank's Pizza tempted me with similarly delicious odors, reminding me that I had not had lunch.

Fortunately, the picnic table outside Rosie's Hot Dog Stand is a great place for keeping an eye on the kids who hang out on the seawall across from Leighton's Variety.

Also, Rosie serves hot dogs smothered in cheese, onions, and chili, tucked in a roll toasted to light, crispy perfection, then slathered in real butter. The whole thing arrives on a cardboard holder to keep the spicy-hot chili from falling off before you have managed to devour it; with it come a Pepsi and onion rings.

Ellie said she wasn't hungry. "Also, I don't have a death wish," she commented at the sight of the chili, rich with meat and beans and redolent of hot pepper, onions, and tomato.

The cheese was thick and cheddary. "Victor would have a heart attack if he saw this," I said, glancing around in case I could spot him and make him look at it.

"Victor," said Ellie, "is having a midlife crisis. You know, wondering about the meaning of his existence."

"I could tell him what his existence means." I crunched into an onion ring. "But I don't use that kind of language."

Ellie scanned the seawall across from Leighton's.

Half a dozen high school kids stood there, drinking sodas and smoking the cigarettes that Arnold would fine
them for if he saw them. But he wouldn't because they
all had teenager radar, a sixth sense that let them detect
his approach from a mile away.

"Which one is Mulligan?" Ellie squinted. "I don't
see anybody who looks strange enough to have written
those letters."

They all looked strange to me, because I am too old
to comprehend the dress code of baggy jam shorts,
loose-laced high-tops, and T-shirts so ragged they resemble fishnets.

"Wait a minute." I spotted a pair of khaki trousers, a
knit polo shirt, and a pair of loafers. "That's him."

I gulped some Pepsi, and tossed the hot-dog wrappings in the trash. "You want weird? That—"

I angled my head at the kid's neatly trimmed hair,
the book stuck into his back pocket. "That's weird."

The other kids eyed us coolly from beneath lowered
eyelids, moving aside to let us pass. But the boy I'd
spotted walked away as we approached, as if remembering an urgent errand.

"Wait," I told Ellie. "Let's not scare him too far off
by chasing him."

Instead we went into the store, where I bought a
Bangor newspaper whose front page trumpeted "Murder in Eastport." Outside, we loitered by the door as if
we had nothing better to do but watch the tourists.
Finally, we strolled casually back.

"So," I said to the cluster of boys smoking their cigarettes, "any of you know Hallie Quinn?"

They looked at each other. I might as well have been
talking to Willoughby's llamas.

"Come on, guys. I'm not trying to get you in trouble.
Hallie Quinn? Anybody?"

"Uh-huh." One boy flicked his cigarette into the
street.

"Too bad about what happened to her. Any of you see anyone giving her trouble? Last night?"

No response, except for the sidelong looks passing between them: Who is this woman and why is she hassling us?

"Because," I went on, "she was a friend of mine."

Shrugs all around, faces as blank as squares of wallboard.

"I'd like to know what was going on with her, is all. Not to get anyone in trouble."

They knew how to talk; just not to me. So they responded by shutting down, all except for one boy, older and sharper-looking than the rest. He had a fox face, dark hair, and long, ropy arms poking out from a regulation T-shirt.

"Ask Mulligan," he said, and the other boys laughed.

I turned to fox-boy. "It doesn't look as if Peter Mulligan wants to talk to me."

A few yards away, the clean-cut kid we had spotted lingered, glancing over at us while trying to act as though he weren't.

"He'll talk to you." The boy pulled a Marlboro from his T-shirt pocket and lit it, squinting against the smoke in a perfect, unconscious James Dean imitation. "He'll dance you around first. That's how he is. But he will, 'cause he's such a candy-ass little suck-up."

The boys laughed again, unpleasantly, moving away in a pack as a beat-up Chevy pulled alongside of them, rumbling and roaring its engine. They piled in and were gone.

Mulligan scowled, but by waiting we'd let it seem as if he were making the choice, so he didn't run when we approached.

"Idiots," he said, watching the car pull away. The look in his eyes said he wished he were in it. But he might as well have wished he were on the moon; guys like Peter Mulligan, scornful and superior, never got to ride in cars like that.

"Yeah, well," I told him consolingly, "someday when you've got a great job and you're driving your Mercedes, they'll still be trying to keep that piece of junk on the road."

He brightened, straightening. "That's right. I'm going to college. In two years. I've already started visiting campuses."

"Very good. Listen, Peter, I'm sorry about Hallie. My son, Sam, says you and she were pretty close. You must be upset."

"Sam." He frowned, as if trying to slot the name into his memory banks. "Oh, right. In the tech program. Yeah, I remember. He works on boats."

He said this as if it were as significant as collecting Pez dispensers. "Some of the guys in the technical program are smart, though," he assured me patronizingly. "In their own way."

"Yeah, he's smart in his way," I replied, and of course I didn't swat him with my rolled-up newspaper. "But about Hallie."

Mulligan's face clouded abruptly. "If she'd listened to me," he said, his fists clenching, "if only she would have *listened.*"

"About the drugs, you mean? And her other boyfriend, not Ken Mumford but the other guy, the older man?"

He looked up, startled. "How do you know about that?"

Across the street, another bunch of boys had collected, looking on with interest. Peter wasn't doing himself any favors with his peer group, talking to us. I angled my head minutely at them. "Why don't you meet us down on the breakwater in a minute?"

Not that I thought Mulligan was missing out on his chance to be captain of the football team, but we didn't have to help him in his bid to be chosen Most Likely to Get Stuffed into a Locker.

"Those losers," he pronounced with too-elaborate disgust. But he agreed to talk with us in a place where we would not be under such direct observation, and a few minutes later he did.

 "Hallie loved me. She was confused, but she did. She knew I was the one who would be there for her, that I was the only one who really cared."

Because you told her so about a million times, I thought but did not say. *Because you followed her, and spied on her.*

Ellie walked on down the breakwater ahead of us, carrying the letters Peter had written in her shoulder bag.

"And this just proves it," he went on. "That she should have listened, and done what I told her. If she had, she'd be alive."

He leaned on the rail overlooking the water, staring down to where the waves slopped against the weed-coated rocks.

"Did she say where she was getting the drugs?"

"No. She wouldn't talk to me. I wasn't wasting my time on that stuff she got into. I," he asserted loftily, "am too intelligent for that."

But not quite smart enough to realize that a girl might not like being stalked.

"Anyway," he went on, glancing around as if fearful of being overheard, "it's all my fault. I heard her the other night on the seawall. With some guy. They were arguing."

I stared at him. No one else had mentioned seeing

Hallie after I did. "Peter, have you told Bob Arnold? Or your parents?"

He shrugged, ashamed. "I can't. If I do, everyone will know I didn't go down there, and stop it. But he must be the one who killed her, and if I had gone—"

His shoulders shook, under the polo shirt. I put my hand on his arm, but he flinched roughly away.

"But she should have listened," he insisted. "The way she acted to me, she made me afraid to go down and butt in. I bet it was that other guy she'd been seeing. I'd tried, but I could never catch them together. And now she's dead."

I thought about the beating Arnold said Hallie had endured. "Peter, if you had, whoever did it might have killed you, too."

He scrubbed at his eyes. "Do I have to talk to Bob Arnold?"

He was sixteen or so, but his imploring look was like a ten-year-old's, pleading not to have to go to school. In his heart he was just a pathetically lonely, mixed-up kid.

"Don't you want to help catch who killed her?"

"Yeah. Yeah, I do." His look hardened. "And killed those other two guys, I bet, the Mumfords. Don't you think?"

The expression of superior scorn returned to his face, mingled with something twisted, off-kilter. "Although," he confided, "if somebody was going around here killing people, he missed the one I'd like to knock off."

Sensing that the interview was ending, Ellie strolled back toward us, stopping along the way to speak to people she knew. Ellie knew almost everybody in town.

"Really?" I inquired of Peter. "And who is that?" I was thinking about the letters he'd written, the obsessiveness they betrayed. That, combined with the look in his eye, made me feel uneasy about the welfare of Peter's enemy, whoever it was.

"Somebody's selling dope," he snarled, "not just pot but heroin, and *that's* who should have gotten killed. It's only a couple kids hooked on it, now. Maybe half a dozen. But it'll be more, and they're too *stupid* to see."

Just for an instant, his face was a mask of adolescent fury: a child's rage, the strength of an adult, and no self-control.

"And I *hate* it," he went on. "It took Hallie away from me. I don't know who's doing it, but if I find out, I'll—"

I wondered if he had any idea who it was he really hated: some faceless drug dealer? The boys who scorned him, picked on him and made fun of him? Or perhaps himself?

"Peter, you said the killer missed the one who really ought to have been killed. Does that mean it wasn't Ken Mumford selling the heroin? I mean, do you know for a fact it wasn't?"

"No," he admitted. "I don't know it for a fact. But I never thought it was him. He was just too . . . I don't know. Harmless, or something. Why, do you think it was?"

I sighed; oh, for a shred of actual, solid information. "I don't know either, Peter. Listen, can you talk to your folks about this? Or a guidance counselor, somebody at school?"

He made a rude noise. "None of them," he said, "are on my mental level. My IQ is in the genius range. So I have," he confided unnecessarily, "a hard time communicating my concerns."

Maybe, I wanted to say, you could write them some letters. But that would have been too cruel.

"Thank you," he said, nodding to Ellie as she joined us, "for giving me a chance to ventilate my emotions. I'm feeling a lot of stress. I'll go and confer with Chief Arnold."

"You do that, Peter," I said, and he strode off: head high, practically whistling now that he'd ventilated his feelings. Personally, I was glad it was me carrying a weapon and not Peter, or I'd be worried about him ventilating something else.

Or someone. Then I got a look at Ellie's face.

"In the park at Shackford Head this afternoon," she burst out, "two tourists were mugged and robbed. One of the people on the pier just told me, some guy *menaced* these tourists and ran away with their wallets."

I looked around: blue sky, sparkling water, salt-fresh air. That kind of thing didn't happen here, and certainly not at the state park at Shackford Head, a wild, remote area where the most menacing event in recent history was the sighting of a black bear urging a cub up the hill toward a raspberry thicket.

"Has Arnold heard?"

"Yes, he's up at the Happy Landings with the tourists, now, trying to get them calmed down enough to get information out of them. I understand he's fit to be tied."

He was, too. By the time we got home, Arnold's squad car was parked outside my house, where he had gone looking for George.

"This is it," Arnold said explosively. "I have had it."

George was there, too, tinkering with the valve stem on the new radiator. "I don't suppose," George asked me, "that you have any chewed-up chewing gum?"

Once upon a time, a cast-iron radiator cost a few dollars and required no attention whatsoever, other than being painted gold or silver if you wanted it cooler, and white if you wanted it hotter. Nowadays, a radiator costs hundreds of dollars, and needs more maintenance than a zoo animal. At the moment, this one was behaving like a zoo animal, too: hissing and spitting.

"Because," George went on, "I think I'd better repack that valve stem, and I used up my packing over at the grade school."

"I'll go," Sam offered, looking up from the table

where he was working on the sketch of the square-rigger, complete with miles of hemp lines and acres of canvas sheets.

"Hey, Arnold," George remarked. "I hear you found some more of that illegal trash, out South End way."

George understood the seriousness of the situation. But he thought going along normally was a good approach to most things, until positively shown otherwise.

"Yeah," Arnold replied disgustedly. "Household trash. Some cheapskate can't put it out for the truck like civilized people. Al Rollins is going through it now."

He took an outraged breath. "But that is the least of my concerns, right this minute. I have had it to the eyes, damnit. There are not going to be any more murders. Or muggings. Or *escapes*," Arnold said thunderously, glaring around at us. "I am here to *guarantee* you of that."

We all nodded obediently, because it was what he wanted: for all of us to agree with him. After that, he would go back out and do his job, but right now he needed—as Peter Mulligan had put it—to ventilate.

"Do you," Sam asked George, "want valve-stem packing? Or chewing gum?" He put his sketches into their folder and removed them from the table, planning ahead for dinner.

George looked at the radiator, thinking about what it said in his plumbing manual versus what he knew from fixing radiators all over town for fifteen years.

"I'm not going to tolerate any more of this nonsense," Bob Arnold declared. "I am going to put a stop to it here and now."

George took his gimme cap off and examined it, still thinking about his decision.

"There is not going to be more upset in Eastport," Arnold predicted forcefully, "or any more crime wave. Not at *all*."

"Chewing gum," George said. "It'll work a lot better, is my professional prediction."

So Sam went out to buy a pack of Wrigley's, all of
which he promised to chew to the proper consistency
on the way home. And although I felt doubtful, wondering if a roll of packing from Wadsworth's might not
be the better choice, in the end George's prediction
turned out to be right.

Unlike—unfortunately—Bob Arnold's.

 The way to a man's heart is supposed to be
through his stomach, and since I had never
found any other route I decided to try it with
Victor; maybe I could soften him up before I
lowered the boom on him. So for dinner we had avo-
cado-nut loaf, a tofu-based herb sauce, baby carrots,
and whole-wheat oven rolls, all of which turned out to
be a satisfying meal that even he ate without any complaint.

"Soapstone sinks," he enthused over dessert, a com-
pote of strawberries and blackberries.

In the house he was thinking of buying, he meant; in
which he would become my neighbor.

"Butler's pantries, and fireplaces—lots of fireplaces,
one in every room!"

For what it would cost to bring those old chimneys
up to code, you could heat the house by burning bricks
of money and still end up considerably ahead. But
Victor for once in his life was in a wonderful mood, and
no one wanted to spoil it.

Or anyway not right this minute.

"So, George," Victor asked, "what do you think it
would take to get a Jacuzzi into that house? With," he

added, "separate tub and shower stall, maybe a steam cabinet, twin lavatories. That's all, nothing fancy."

George smiled, visions of full employment until sometime in the next millennium dancing in his head. "Oh, I don't know," he replied, spooning up strawberries. "Shouldn't be too difficult."

Compared, say, to building the Egyptian pyramids by the original labor-intensive methods, with maybe a few of the hanging towers of Babylon added on. Just getting a Jacuzzi unit up the staircase would be an interesting project, and at the idea of hooking it to the jerry-rigged network of old pipes that must be the house's plumbing, I nearly inhaled a berry.

"The question is," Ellie put in, "and only if you don't mind my asking: what are you going to *do* here?"

Victor looked surprised. "Do? Why, I'm going to do surgery. Because back in the city there's a neurosurgeon every half-block, but here, it's special. It'll probably take a little time to get my credentials transferred, but after that—"

"Victor," Wade put in. "Have you visited the hospital yet?"

Wade had taken to behaving as if he were Victor's uncle, mostly on account of wanting things to go well for Sam and me.

"Well, no," Victor harrumphed, irritated. "But I'm sure it's a fine, perfectly modern—"

"Dad?" Sam put his hand on Victor's shoulder. "Listen. It is a good hospital, for where it is, out here so far away from everything. But, Dad, they transfer compound fractures."

The implication being that it didn't matter how good a surgeon Victor was. To do his job, he needed a very high-tech support system: special instruments, teams of technical staff, cutting-edge therapeutic techniques, not to mention an intensive care unit wired like the control room at NASA. The hospital in Calais is excellent, but it's not set up for that stuff.

Which meant that Victor, so spoiled by the big city that he imagined all ninety-bed regional care facilities possessed the same sophisticated diagnostic imaging systems he used in New York, might not be staying in Eastport after all.

Not that it was going to save him from the conversation I had planned for him. Still, it was a pleasant prospect.

"All," Victor asked Sam intensely, "compound fractures?"

"Well, no," Sam admitted. He'd done volunteer work there. "Not all of them. But the terrible ones, the trauma-center ones where big bone ends are actually all mangled and sticking out, they put you in Hank Henahan's ambulance to Bangor. And the bad head cases go on a helicopter from Quoddy Airfield."

Personally, while I am eating my dinner, I do not want to hear about bone ends sticking out. But it was worth it if it got rid of Victor.

"They stabilize you," Sam continued. "Then they ship you. Somewhere bigger where they have, you know, a lot more technology."

Delighted as we all were to think that we might soon be seeing the back of Victor—his good humor was a freak thing, believe me, like a rain of frogs—it was sad to see his dream busted.

Or I assumed it was, anyway, for one brief, shining moment.

"Well, then," Victor asserted, lifting his head and gazing imperiously at all of us. "I'll have to change my plan."

Tra-la. But then his tone alerted me.

"I'll have to give up being a neurosurgeon. After all," he went on, smiling at me as if he had not just trashed my own dream, which was to say goodbye to him, "you changed your life, Jacobia. Why shouldn't I change mine?"

Because, I thought nastily, *there is no backhoe big enough for all your bad karma.*

"Work," Ellie ventured, "is scarce around here. I mean, for a man of your specialized talents."

Lying, cheating, bullying, tyrannizing . . . the list just went on and on. The only other thing my ex-husband was qualified to be was Attila the Hun.

"Then maybe," Victor said, "I'll retire. Enjoy," he went on, absent visible irony, "the simple life."

With, of course, the assistance of that Jacuzzi.

"I might write some poetry," he said. "You know, I've always wanted to try my hand at poetry. Never had time."

This, naturally, being the only obstacle between himself and a Pulitzer. Victor thinks old Burma-Shave signs are the height of linguistic cleverness.

"But the important thing I'll do," he said, "is get to know Jacobia again. Heal," he added tenderly, "our estrangement."

Wade turned slowly, with a look in his eyes that should have incinerated Victor right on the spot.

Whereupon I thought: There once was a jerk from the city, whose plans for my life were not pretty, and lest you think I was waxing excessively bitter may I just tell you right here and now that my ex-husband Victor no more wanted to heal our estrangement than I wanted multiple stab wounds.

This was a scheme. What he wanted was to torture me, and he had happened upon the perfect method.

"So," Victor said, "I'll just have to reconsider my options. Think it over. Take my time, reinventing myself."

He smiled, hideously. "You won't mind if I stay for a while longer with you and Sam, will you, Jacobia?"

Wade watched me carefully.

"Not at all," I said, and a gleam of triumph lit in Victor's eye, while Wade looked disappointedly away.

I took a deep breath. "Stay as long as you like. I

want to talk to you in private after dinner, though. We need to get a few things straight around here. About Sam, and about your behavior while you're in my house."

A silence descended as everyone—especially Sam, who looked thunderstruck—waited to see how Victor would react.

"Fine," he agreed at last, blithely, as if whatever I might have to say to him couldn't possibly be very important.

But, as a small smile curved the corners of Wade's lips, we all saw Victor's gaze waver a fraction.

Score one for me.

 Later that night, the town had two burglaries and another mugging. By the time Hank Henahan got the ambulance back home again the local people had organized into citizen patrols, willing and able to stomp out everything from misdemeanors to major felonies.

Well, maybe not particularly able, I thought, peering out the guest-room window the following morning.

Victor and I had not after all had our fight scene; pleading a headache, he'd rushed upstairs after dinner.

Which was par for the course, for Victor, and precisely what I'd expected; when he knew you wanted to talk with him, he never wanted to, especially if you sounded determined. He wasn't around now, either; somehow he'd managed to get up and out of the house without my noticing.

Frustrated, I scanned the street to see if I could find him, spotting instead Miss Violet Gage tottering up the hill with a long umbrella in her hand, gimlet-eyed and ready to bonk someone.

The menacing effect was spoiled, however, on account of her having put her corset on over her dress. She was frightening, all right, but not in the way she intended, and at the sight of her I went hastily out to meet her, and brought her inside.

"It's all organized," Miss Gage gasped flusteredly, gazing around my kitchen as if she might spy some most-wanted criminal, and bring him to justice. "Ned Montague has got a list, and he is going to assign us all to patrol our territories."

I gave Miss Gage a cup of tea, and took the umbrella away from her; as long as she was holding it Monday would not come into the kitchen, not even to eat her breakfast.

"Nice doggy," said Miss Gage.

I had spent the previous evening until past midnight in the cellar, working on the old shutters, so I was feeling toxic from the late night and also from the knowledge that my ex-husband was still under my roof instead of under a granite monument.

Pouring a cup of coffee, I sat down across from Miss Gage. She smelled of talcum powder, chamomile, and sassafras tea, and her face was as sweet as a sugar doughnut.

"Are you sure Ned meant you should personally go out chasing criminals? Because," I added tactfully, "I should think that with your knowledge and awareness, your experience, you might be best utilized in the planning area. The strategy, and so on."

Miss Gage looked gratified. "You are quite right . . . oh, what is your name, again?" She shook her head vexedly. "Never mind, it'll come to me. But I must discharge my civic duty. Age is no excuse when one's community is threatened. Our very way of life, my dear, is under attack."

She drew herself up seriously. "No Gage has ever shirked his or her responsibility where defense is concerned, not since those red-coated bastards marched in here and stole our freedom!"

She said it the Maine way—*bahstads*. "This," she breathed dramatically, "is war!"

A button popped ringingly off her corset.

"Yes. Well. Probably it is," I said. "But still, I can't stand to see your talents wasted this way so I wonder," I ventured, "if I might help."

You had to go carefully with Miss Gage; she was a dotty old lady but not a bit stupid, and she knew when she was being inveigled.

"Y-e-es," she drawled skeptically, eyeing me from under the brim of her big straw hat.

"My thought is, I might replace you on the front lines. Take on, as it were, the actual military portion of the activity."

She lowered her eyelids. The effect was wickedly knowing and wildly attractive, reminding me that Violet Gage was the belle of the ball in that excellent year, 1932.

Meanwhile I do very much like intelligent old ladies, and the dottier the better. A little misarrangement in the corset department, I feel, is as nothing in the grand scheme of things.

"Freeing you," I went on, "for the brain-power part of the program. Where Ned," I added delicately, "might just require a bit of . . ."

"Shoring up," she supplied crisply. "The boy is a fool."

"Ah, yes. Well. That's one way of putting it, I suppose. At any rate . . ."

I searched my mind, trying to think of some further way to persuade her that at her age, racketing around chasing juvenile delinquents or worse was as good a way as any to land herself in the hospital for a hip replacement; they did those, in Calais.

"And of course you would be doing me a great favor, too," I went on, feeling that I was babbling, now, and sure that at any moment I would insult her, or worse, hurt her feelings.

"Because you're right, we must all do our duty, and I would not want to be accused of . . ."

"Quiet, girl. Quit blithering. I understand, and I accept."

When I turned, she had taken off the hat and was carefully straightening the black grosgrain hatband. In the light slanting in through the kitchen window her hair was the color of an autumn leaf, red with white frost on it.

She placed the hat on her head and regarded the front of herself. "I don't recall this dress lacing up this way. How," she pronounced, "curious."

Then she looked up at me, shrewdly and humorously, as if, having tolerated the quirks and missteps of others throughout her long life, she would now be as charitable about her own.

"I wonder," she said, "if you might perform another small service. I seem to have left my glasses at home, or I would do it myself."

"Of course, Miss Gage," I said, feeling humbled and proud that she should trust me this way. "Stand up, and we'll make the adjustment."

So she stood, holding out her slim, graceful arms, her head held high with the big hat perched on top of it, while I undid the many tiny buttons of the corset. When I had finished I put it into a paper shopping bag for her, and she received it gravely.

"I believe," I added, "that at some time I must have borrowed your umbrella."

Miss Gage, as we both knew, never lent her umbrella.

"Thank you." She smiled graciously, accepting it. "And now I must go home, and prepare for the mission. Plans and strategies, attacks and counterattacks." She made way for the door.

"Meet at the corner of Shackford Street," she instructed, "eight sharp. Mind you're not late. Bring a flashlight. A heavy," she added with considerable charming menace, "flashlight."

But at the door, she paused suddenly. "Who is that man?" she asked. "Not Wade Sorenson," she added. "Everybody knows him."

They not only knew him; they knew he and I were an item and had been for nearly two years.

"The one I mean is so," Miss Gage hesitated, ". . . dubious-looking."

Ah, that one. "That," I told her, "is my ex-husband."

"Ex-husband?" she repeated. *"Ex?"* She hefted the shopping bag with the corset in it as if weighing the implications.

Then, decisively, she came to her conclusion, one that buoyed me all through the rest of that long day, and into the frightening night.

"Smart girl," Miss Violet Gage said.

 That evening at the corner of Shackford and Middle Streets, a small group of citizens bent on defending Eastport against a crime wave had already gathered. As promised, Miss Gage had supplied a list of territories matched to the volunteers, and Ned Montague passed these around with much harrumphing and bossing.

Ellie and I drew a plum route: out South End to Sodom Wharf, back County Road to Hawkes Avenue, up High Street, and home. If we saw anyone or anything suspicious, Ned ordered pompously, we were not to try to handle it ourselves; we were to go to the nearest house and phone Bob Arnold, who would come in the squad car.

So we set off, heading first through a low, hilly area of apple trees and lupine, the bay glittering in the moonlight on our left and the railway bed on our right. The tracks were long gone but the wooden ties still lay in the earth, and the night was so silent you could almost hear the engine chuffing as the eye-beam of its headlight rounded the curve, strafing through the foliage.

Near Johnson's Marina we paused to look down at the lights of town, on a backdrop of water and twinkling stars. Here and there flashlights of other patrol members glowed briefly as they moved among the quiet houses.

"This isn't going to work," I said, gesturing at them. "They'll do it for a while, but pretty soon people will go back to normal life. And even if they don't, we don't want to patrol the town, do we? We want a town we don't have to patrol. The way," I finished, "it used to be."

"That's what George said, too," Ellie responded quietly.

From a distance, the flashlights resembled candles. We walked in silence a little longer. Then:

"Ken let me drive," she spoke up again suddenly. "A long time ago, he let me drive his car."

She smiled in the moonlight, remembering. "It was a Mustang convertible, and he had fixed it all up. It was red, and it looked just like new. Kenny was a pretty good scrounger," she added, "even back then, and Tim hadn't lost his job, yet. So there was a little money between them."

Across the bay, the lights on Campobello spilled out onto the water like streams of metallic paint.

"So we went for a ride, up to Woodland, out on Route 214. And after a while, he pulled the car over and said we should switch places. It was a night like tonight. Cool and bright and you could look right on up into forever, it seemed like."

At the foot of Pleasant Street, Mavis Gantry's garden spread over the humped-up earth and smooth granite shoulders of rocks overlooking the water, the silvery mounds of the succulent plants iridescent under the moon. Paths of stones and beach glass wound through the garden, shining rivulets among the plants.

"So you switched places," I prompted as we climbed the hill to Poverty Rock. From here, you could see north to New Brunswick and south past the islands, their dark shapes jagged with firs, to the lights of Lubec afloat on water bright as pewter.

"We did," Ellie said. "And I thought he would be nervous. He knew I'd never driven before. I thought he'd sit close, so he could grab the wheel if he needed to."

At High Street we turned left, toward Sodom Wharf and the ruins of the old salt works. The structure's dark, oblong shape was jagged at the roofless top where courses of crumbling bricks had fallen away, pierced with silver rectangles where light from the water reflected up through the empty, ominous-looking windows.

"But he didn't," Ellie said. "He sat back, looking at the sky."

We walked on, until at the curve in the road we stopped, catching our breaths and looking out over the water.

"I drove," she continued, "all the way to Caribou that night. It was dawn by the time we got there, and my father was wild when I finally called him. He made me," she remembered, "put Ken on the phone, to yell at him, too."

From the curve of High Street, the old salt works is the only human construction you can see, three stories high and as big around as half a city block. In its bleak and barren decrepitude, the salt works looks as if the shell of a building from a major city has been transported here to this pristine seascape, for what reason no one could imagine.

"So your father talked to Kenny." Now we were on County Road: farm fields gone to grass, fences of rusting barbed wire strung on leaning cedar posts, an empty cellar hole or a pair of pine trees marking the spot where a working homestead used to be.

"He talked to him, all right," Ellie said. "Lots of 'yes, sir' and 'no, sir' out of Kenny. And then there was a long time when Kenny just listened, while my dad about chewed his ear off."

Crickets chirped in the sweet-smelling darkness. Ellie's dad and her mother, too, were gone, now, buried at Hillside.

"And Kenny," Ellie went on, "when he was done listening to my dad, he said to him, very respectfully: 'Sir, I don't know if you noticed. But it's July, and it won't be July for very long. Pretty soon it will be winter. And it was an awful nice night.'"

We passed Vernal Potter's red cottage, hunkered down amid stacks of scrap lumber all sorted for size and condition. Vernal's old coon hound, Rascal, bayed a greeting as we went by.

"It was, too," Ellie said wistfully. "An awful nice night."

Ahead, the lights of the convenience store at the corner of County Road signaled the approach of civilization. We'd seen nothing suspicious, and I thought again that we probably wouldn't.

"Was your father still mad when you got back?"

"No. He'd told Ken to tell me everything was okay, and that I should eat a good breakfast before we came home. So we did," she finished, laughing. "Sausages and eggs. We were *starved*."

Her laughter faded, and I knew what she was thinking: no more nice summer nights or big breakfasts for Kenny Mumford.

We turned onto Purcell Avenue, a narrow, winding

road leading down into a little hollow of older wooden houses with mostly older cars parked on the street out front. Here and there a few lights still burned in the kitchens, but by now it was past ten and folks were turning in for the night.

The street had the hushed, preliminary feeling of the moments just before a dream, or a nightmare. "So basically you're avenging him," I said. "Is that it? By trying to find out who?"

She nodded emphatically, just as an explosion of barking, growling, and general canine intimidation erupted out of the dark at us, followed by the energetic clank of a chain against a post.

"Oh, Christ," I said, my heart punching like a fist against the wall of my chest; as you may have gathered, posts in Eastport vary widely in their age and condition. "Not another dog."

Ellie aimed her flashlight. "Not," she corrected, "just any dog. I think it's Cosmo."

A woman's voice shouted from an upstairs window; the dog fell silent. Just then Ned strode out of the gloom at us. "Who's that?"

He aimed his own flashlight at our faces, but his battery was dying so the effect was perhaps not as paralyzing as he wished.

"It's just us," Ellie said as he hurried toward us.

"Oh, well, then." He switched off the flashlight.

"Is that Ken's dog?" I asked. "I wondered what happened to him."

"Yeah," he said. "Too much dog for me, though. But I've got a fellow out in the country, has a lot of property. I think he'll take it."

"So how is it going with the other patrollers?" Ellie asked.

"They're fine." The officiousness returned to his voice. "Seems like we accomplished our mission for tonight. Everything is nice and quiet."

I'd wondered why Ned would bother doing anything for the town; it was so much like work. But now I thought I understood: he was loving this. It made him feel important.

"This is what it takes," he went on. "Decent citizens scare the lowlifes right back into the woodwork."

"Ned?" His wife's voice came from the upstairs window again. "Ned, what are you doing out there in the dark?"

"I'm trying," he replied in tones of strained patience, "to keep order in this town."

A porch light went on, showing Ned's lawn. At one side stood a couple of trash cans overflowing with bagged garbage; the rest of the lawn was a broken ankle waiting to happen, littered with plastic toys. Where, I have always wondered, did the toy manufacturers find those virulent shades of orange and blue: in a psychopathology textbook?

Ellie had begun looking at him oddly, and following her gaze, I noticed that his sweater had . . . stuff on it. Lumps of stuff clung here and there like lint, or dried grass clippings.

Also, he kept fingering something in his sweater pocket.

I had the sudden bad notion that maybe I wasn't the only one toting more than a heavy flashlight, and the idea of Ned with a gun gave me some pause.

(Which parenthetically brings me to the gun thing in general, and I suppose I do have to say something about it. So here it is:

1) We have had guns in this country for over two hundred years, and

2) we have had television sets for about fifty years, and

3) before television, kids didn't take guns to school for the purpose of mowing down their teachers and classmates, and

4) now they do.

Your assignment: figure out the variable.)

"Anyway," Ned went on, "I've found work driving my truck. So I'll be hiring another fellow to go out to Crow Island and do the necessary for Tim's bunch of strays, you can tell George."

But when he finally took his hand out of his pocket, the pocket didn't sag: no gun. I breathed a quiet sigh of relief.

Ellie's eyes were still on Ned's sweater. What *was* that stuff, anyway? Then, in an inspired maneuver, she slung a casual arm around him. "You're doing a fine job of keeping the peace, Ned," she said, and when we got home we immediately examined the stuff she had lifted from his sweater.

Picking apart the fibers twined together like flax strands or rotted hemp string, we poked at the green, oddly familiar-looking bits thickly distributed among them, bits flecked with black and a rich, bluish white, like fine stationery.

"Fur?" asked Ellie, using the end of a pencil to separate the strandlike stuff as we sat at the kitchen table.

"Not fur," I answered. "More like hair. And what's that other material?" Then suddenly the lightbulb in my head went on and I saw it:

That green. A *familiar* green. The color of . . .

Money.

 Much later that night, Wade put aside the pair of lovely old Italian dueling pistols he was appraising for an antiques dealer in Camden, and we went downstairs to work on the shutters.

Funny how harmless they had looked, back in the

Dumpster. But as the day of Felicity's arrival loomed, that shutter pile grew taller and more ominous.

"What say I take all the hardware off?" Wade suggested.

"Great. Makes them easier to burn."

He looked at me, his eyes amused. "Scrape," he instructed gently. "We can finish in a few hours."

He put a CD in the player: Bela Fleck playing "Metric Lips," an old banjo tune from the New Grass Revival group, before Bela put together the Flecktones. The plunkety sounds echoed liquidly in the low-ceilinged cellar, spreading on my heart like salve; Ellie's story about driving with Ken had made me feel frightened and sad, regretful over the way good things go by.

And then, hefting one of the fragile old objects, Wade said: "Look at this. These things are dowelled, not put together with screws. Man, somebody built these so long ago. Built 'em by hand. It's great that you managed to save them, Jacobia."

Which was what I needed to hear, and he knew it; he is like that. Renewed, I applied the chisel to the shutter's surface.

The trick, when you are chiseling off old paint, is to aim the blade at an oblique angle relative to the grain of the wood. Chiseling with the grain will inevitably dig up a splinter, and the splinter will run deeper and deeper until it makes a groove you will never be able to sand out, while chiseling across the grain digs a square, toothy gouge, as if some ratlike animal has been munching on the wood.

Wrapping a thick rag around your chisel thumb helps, too, unless you are actually trying to get one thumb to swell up twice the size of the other. But after a while I fell into the rhythm of the work, monotonous and hypnotic, comforting in that there was no strategy to it, only the long, slow doing of it.

Meanwhile my brain kept working the ideas of money and hair, nibbling at them as insistently as the constantly moving blade of the chisel, but with less result. I didn't notice when Wade went upstairs, but I did when he came back with two bottles of beer.

Gratefully, I accepted one of the icy bottles and laid it against my head, before taking a long, scouringly cold swallow. "Thanks. Couple more evenings, we'll be ready to paint."

He looked surprised. "Jacobia. You've been down here six hours, and so have I. We can paint these shutters tomorrow, second-coat 'em, too."

I blinked and glanced around wonderingly, coming out of my trance. "Six *hours?*"

But there they were: all the shutters, their louvers scraped clean. On the floor, old green paint scrapings lay in drifts.

"I've been taking them away as you finished, putting new ones in front of you," Wade said. "It's wicked late, but you were going so well, I hated to stop you."

He had done half of them himself. "My hero," I said.

"That," he chuckled, "is the idea."

He'd been changing the CDs, also: now it was the Dillards, complete with lots of sweet, swoopy fiddle flourishes. Wade grabbed me and waltzed me around the cellar, ducking where the old pipes hung down, until I was breathless and laughing.

"Stop," I begged, clinging helplessly to him, giddy with the music, the late hour, and half a bottle of beer.

Tiptoeing upstairs, we kept humming the waltz tune, our arms around each other and our heads close together like a couple of teenagers. Silence from down the hall, Sam and Victor both asleep. In my room, pearl-colored dawn light flooded in through the curtains, as I closed them.

"Now I've got you," Wade said comfortably.

No question about it.

So it was full daylight before I sat up and realized: long fibrous strands and chewed-up bits of stuff.

The llamas had gotten into some money.

Living alone on a picture-book saltwater farm overlooking Passamaquoddy Bay, at age fifty-five Berenice Waugh was a flower child for the nineties: by day the quintessential organic farmer and keeper of rabbits and llamas, by night the maintainer of a voluminous e-mail correspondence with wool-raising enthusiasts and textile artists all over New England.

So Ellie had informed me when I called her to tell her my idea about the material clinging to Ned Montague's sweater.

"Llama hair," she said as we drove toward Berenice's house. "What's Ned doing with llama hair?"

"He is driving," I replied, "a truck. His truck, with Baxter Willoughby's llamas in it. My question is why? And why with money? Because it's starting to seem obvious now that there must be a connection. Don't you agree? With the money, I mean, from Crow Island."

Turning off Route 1 onto the shore road, we drove between farmhouses whose window boxes were brilliant with red petunias.

"He takes the llamas for rides?" Ellie asked puzzledly.

We rounded the long turn uphill between dark stands of pines, coming out along a fenced acre where white-faced cattle all stood facing the same way, their heavy jaws rotating in slow motion.

"Well, no," I said. "But they don't walk to Willoughby's. He must buy them somewhere, and bring them home in a truck. Wouldn't you think?"

"I suppose. Still, they don't ride up in the cab, I don't imagine, so how would they get their hair all over Ned? And what does the money have to do with it? Who lets llamas eat money? And," she finished, "what does Willoughby want them for, anyway? The llamas, I mean."

To our left, a log cabin with matching outbuildings perched on a hilly rise. Sunflowers lined the driveway, their huge yellow heads aimed east like a row of bright faces, into the morning.

"Maybe Ned loads them into the truck, and that's how he gets close to them. And maybe Willoughby thinks gentleman farmers need livestock. Or maybe," I added, remembering the perfection of his place, "he keeps them for the atmosphere. Like outdoor furniture."

Ellie sniffed. "Pretty expensive furniture. A llama is a fairly exotic animal. I'll bet it has an exotic price tag."

"Willoughby," I assured her as we passed the log cabin's mailbox and turned up the drive, "is an exotic guy."

Up ahead, I spied rabbit hutches, a tractor, and a watering trough. Everything looked spiffy, freshly painted and gleaming in the summer morning. By contrast, three hours of sleep and a breakfast in the company of my ex-husband had shorn me of whatever girlish energy I had temporarily possessed.

"After dinner tonight," I'd told him firmly, and he'd shot me an "oh-yeah?" kind of look, then gone on drinking his orange juice.

"With Sam," I'd continued, stifling an urge to smack him. "We're going to have a conversation about a few things."

"Such as?" he inquired dismissively.

I didn't want to get into the meat-and-potatoes of it right then; Sam had gone out of the house before I got up. I wanted Sam to see me sticking up for myself, to know he didn't have to do it for me.

"Such as the way you've been behaving around here," I told Victor. "Treating me like the maid, and this house like a motel."

Victor had smiled at me, recovered from the uncertainty he'd shown at the dinner table two evenings earlier.

"You know," he'd said softly, with a hint of menace, "I've been taking it easy on you for Sam's sake."

Well, no; that wasn't quite why, and I wouldn't have called it taking it easy on me, either. But keeping up a halfway decent front made it easier for him to pretend I was the crazy one, so he rarely showed his truly mean side in front of anyone else.

"After dinner," I'd repeated. "And Sam will be with us."

Then I left the house before I could succumb to temptation, and give him the only meal he really deserved: a knuckle sandwich.

"Berenice Waugh," Ellie said now, "knows *everything* about llamas. I'm sure she'll say something useful."

I got out of the car and stopped, struck by the small green paradise Berenice Waugh had created. In the dooryard, mint plants grew profusely from an old washtub. Potted herbs tangled together on the porch rail, and the backyard was a botany lesson: ginseng, goldenseal, aloe, yarrow, and echinacea were among the species names printed on the stakes in the growing beds.

Everything was silent. A marmalade cat stood and stretched in the sunshine by the cellar doors. Then I spotted the llamas, their coats as smooth and flawless as ranch-raised mink, peering from a corral. Not a one of them looked ornery, or curled a lip to spit.

The back door of the cabin flung open abruptly and a bundle of merriment whirled out into the yard at us. "Hello, hello!"

Berenice was a short, round figure in blue denim coveralls, a red flannel shirt, and enormous hammered-copper earrings. "Ellie, so good to see you. And this must be Jacobia, welcome!"

Her hair was thick, bowl-cut, and pure white, a fringe of bangs stopping short above a pair of bright blue eyes. More copper braceleted her wrists, which at first glance looked plump but were actually just very

thickly muscled. Her hands, strong and capable-look-
ing, sported clean square-trimmed fingernails.

Inside, Berenice moved mail-order catalogs from one
chair and a black cat unceremoniously from another.
"Sit. I'm waiting—"

—she bustled around the kitchen: wood-burning
cookstove, a bright-red pump handle on a venerable old
sink, and an enormous galvanized kettle simmering on
the woodstove's firebox—

"—for a communication."

The room's decor included peace symbols, yin-yang
diagrams, and a deck of tarot cards. The window cover-
ings were made from strips of bamboo, and a curtain of
multicolored glass beads divided the kitchen from the
rest of the little bungalow. On a shelf above the sink
were jars of strange-looking substances: curled-up
mushrooms, dried leaf fragments, greyish bits of moss.

"Here, dear," Berenice said, setting a steaming cup
in front of me. "Drink this tea. It'll make you feel better."

I glanced questioningly at her, but Berenice only
smiled, as if medicating women who've been rebuilding
shutters, carousing with indestructible boyfriends, and
facing down demon-possessed ex-husbands were for
Berenice all part of a good day's work.

The liquid in the cup was yellow, and it smelled very
bitter. Hesitantly, I looked at Ellie.

"Ginseng," she informed me. "Try it." Her green
eyes flashed mischievously.

Oh, well, I thought, that couldn't hurt me. I'd had
ginseng in soft drinks, for heaven's sake. The flavor was
like that of an aspirin tablet, after the tablet has been
sitting around for fifty years. I took a swallow.

Whereupon every nerve ending in my body woke up.
My eyes snapped open, my sinuses cleared, and long-
buried memories burst from the depths of my brain like
suddenly-activated newsreels.

Berenice eyed me benevolently. "Try some more. It works much better," she added, "when it's fresh like this."

Her smile was enigmatic, and I understood suddenly that her flower-child days had begun in the sixties, and that she had probably picked up plenty in the way of pharmaceutical knowledge.

That garden, I realized; those plants. Whatever I'd thought I knew about ginseng was gone, swept away in a wash of alertness.

"Thank you," I said, noticing that the colors in the glass-bead curtain seemed much brighter and wondering whether Einstein had felt like this when he was coming up with his theory.

Something mechanical rattled to life over in the corner, sounding like a cross between a nail gun and a threshing machine.

"Ah," Berenice breathed, satisfied. "There it is. I e-mailed a friend in Australia this morning to ask her if she would make me a new spinning wheel."

Which reminded me: Yarn. Llamas.

"I wonder," I began, "if you know anything about—"

"Baxter Willoughby," Berenice supplied, tearing her message off the old daisy wheel printer. Noting my puzzlement but not the reason for it, she explained:

"I fixed the computer to print out all my e-mails when they arrive. You see, I like to save all my letters, and if I don't do it right away, I know that I never will."

"Admirable. But how did you know I was going to ask you about Willoughby? Did Ellie tell you?"

"No, dear." Berenice took out a hand-rolled clove cigarette and lit it, suddenly looking nowhere near so benevolent. "Everyone who comes to visit has been asking about him lately, it seems. Dear mysterious Baxter is a puzzle in the llama world."

"Llama world? What's that, another new Disney theme park?" The ginseng was making me feel witty.

"I mean the little community of people," Berenice clarified patiently, "who raise them, keep them for pets or as pack animals, or utilize their wool. There aren't very many of us, and we keep in touch. Well," she amended, "there are lots of us all over the world, but in Maine, just a handful."

"I see," I said. Trust Ellie to know who in all of Washington County could give you the lowdown on anything, even llamas.

And give it, apparently, with some relish. "Willoughby," Berenice said, "tells people he's selling those llamas for pets. But nobody is buying them. I would know, if they were."

She poured us all more tea. "Would you," she queried acutely, "buy an expensive, exotic animal from some newly arrived fly-by-night, someone who offers no pedigree, no assurances, no proof of anything resembling a well-thought-out breeding program? No," she finished indignantly, "veterinary certificates?"

"Well, no," I admitted. "Actually, probably I wouldn't."

Probably, I wouldn't buy one at all. But I didn't think it would be polite to say so, so I didn't.

"Indeed," she pronounced crisply. "Furthermore, if he isn't supplying himself with new animals—which, if no one is buying the old ones, naturally he isn't—what is he doing with them?"

"I'm not quite sure I follow."

Berenice looked severe. "If he's not trucking new animals in every couple of weeks, then he is trucking the same animals out, and then trucking them back. And I'm sure he is doing that—I've been to his place twice, trying to get straight answers out of him. Once I saw them being loaded off."

She sipped her tea. "I was also there to check on the animals' welfare, of course, which to my surprise was not bad. He's doing the minimum necessary, in my opinion, just to keep meddling old women like me from causing him trouble."

"But why? I mean," I added, "why truck them around at all?"

"My question precisely." She shook her head in disapproval. "Loading them onto a truck every week or ten days—maybe it's a wool-production experiment, but if it is I don't see the point of it. Stress only makes their coats ragged, and makes them spit."

"How do you know that's how often he does it?" Ellie asked.

"And," I remembered the strange stuff stuck to Ned's sweater, "what do they spit, exactly?"

Berenice looked wise. "I know because Ned Montague's truck goes into the gas station on Route 190 in Eastport every two weeks like clockwork. But," she added significantly, "Willoughby pays the bills. One of the fellows who works there is a friend of mine, Adam Franklin. He says it's for a trip check: tires, signals, fluid levels. That sort of thing. As if someone wanted to be sure not to break down."

I could think of another reason, but I let her go on.

"That makes sense," she continued, "especially in summer. Llamas are extremely sensitive to heat—you don't want to stall on a hot day. And to answer your other question, llamas spit what they're chewing. Saliva. Or saliva mixed with chow pellets. Like whistling with a mouthful of crackers."

The daisy-wheel printer rattled to startling life again, and she glanced at it before going on.

"They do it when they're feeling annoyed. Or if they're very annoyed, they'll spit their stomach contents, but you won't have any trouble identifying that. It's ghastly—even the animals don't like it. You'll see them curling their lips in distaste."

She frowned consideringly. "Look, I'd like to know

what's going on over there, too. If it's something that's bad for those creatures, I intend to put a stop to it."

"I wonder," Ellie put in thoughtfully, "if they mark down the mileage, every time that truck gets checked."

"Ellie," said Berenice. "What a brilliant girl you are."

 Bay City Mobil is the kind of small-town gas station that when you go there to get your car fixed, they don't fix it if it doesn't need fixing, and if it does, they give you a ride home. Pulling in, Ellie went to see if Adam Franklin was on duty.

When she returned, she said, "Bingo. They note the mileage. And it's always the same, he says. Twelve hundred or so."

"New York City," I said immediately as we pulled out. When you live in a place as far in the hinterlands as Eastport, you always know how far away everything else is.

"So we can give Berenice her answer, anyway," I added. A fresh wave of fatigue washed over me. "We still don't know why the beasts are being shuttled, but at least we know where."

"Jacobia," Ellie said. "I think your ginseng has worn off. It isn't the llamas we're interested in. It's the truck."

Boink. I thumped my fist on my forehead. That's the trouble with ginseng: it has the half-life of a subatomic particle, and when it wears off you feel like pond sludge.

"Oh," I said. "Right. Um, did Adam happen to mention the next time it's scheduled to come in?"

"Tomorrow night. What say you and I go back to Willoughby's after it does, and see what all goes into it?

Because if you ask me, this Willoughby guy is sending more to New York than llamas."

Me, too, now that she'd mentioned it. I yawned hugely. "Like, for instance, illegal drugs?"

"Possibly. It would make some sense. Let's say the contraband comes in here, maybe on Ken's boat, and a little of it leaks into the local market. But the majority of it would have to go somewhere else, where there are more people."

"But if Ken's not bringing it in anymore," I objected, "why is Willoughby still making trips?" And there was something else, something I was too thick and muzzy to fasten onto.

"Don't know," Ellie said. "Maybe that's what we'll find out. So, have we got a plan?"

I was so tired, I'd have agreed to getting blasted from a cannon if I could close my eyes while doing it. "To-morrow night," I agreed. "We'll go down there and snoop our brains out."

Being very careful meanwhile not to get them shot out; the memory of that whizzing bullet remained vivid despite my fatigue. But Willoughby had been miles away when that happened, and anyway he wouldn't be expecting us to be skulking around in his expensive un-derbrush nor would Ike if he was still nearby.

So Ellie dropped me off and I went into the house, intending to lie down for a year or so, but instead I discovered that Victor had made good on his threat to attempt a career switch. While I was out he'd tried plumbing, cooking, and, apparently, demolition.

As a result, the yellow plastic bucket that usually lived under the kitchen sink stood, disorientingly, on the hall floor. Ranged alongside it was every single plumbing tool I owned—George is a fine plumber but I can't very well call him at two A.M., which is when the worst plumbing disasters in my house always occur—and a new roll of Teflon tape.

Really, I should have fixed that sink drainpipe

sooner, or asked George to do it, but the bucket had gotten so familiar, and best of all it worked.

Now, though, that unopened roll of tape was a bad sign. Doing your own plumbing without Teflon tape, which you wrap around the threads before screwing the pipe back into the fitting, is like jumping out of a plane without a parachute: possible, but the result may not be all that you had hoped for.

The suicidal plunge metaphor continued—somehow everything about Victor seemed to summon it, lately—into the kitchen, where the cabinets stood open and the counters were covered with utensils. In the sink, a pile of dirty dishes teetered crazily, and on the stove a pan sputtered, blackening a substance that once upon a time had been a pound of butter.

From the basement came an unfamiliar sound: Victor, singing. There was a brief silence as he heard my steps cross the floor. Then he bopped up the stairs and sauntered into the kitchen.

"Beautiful day." He inhaled deeply and pressed his fists to his chest, radiating good humor. "Sam's gone out again, to help some fellow rig a ketch. Whatever that is."

He frowned briefly, then shrugged the thought off; since he didn't know it, it couldn't matter.

"Meanwhile, I thought I'd take care of a few chores around here," he continued expansively.

The tap was dripping, and from under the kitchen sink came a trickle of greasy water, spreading out over the kitchen floor. I turned the stove off as calmly as possible, and faced him.

"Victor, we're going to have our talk about your guest status a little early."

It screwed up my plan, but if this sort of thing continued there would not be a house for him to be a guest in, or for me to live in, for that matter.

"Sorry about the mess," he went on as if I had not spoken, "but I also decided to give you a hand downstairs. Earn my keep, you know. Make myself useful around the place."

In the middle of my thinking about how he could make himself useful (submitting himself to taxidermy would have been my first choice) it hit me what he must have been doing: those shutters.

"I put the hardware back on for you," he continued.

When he got like this, it was like trying to talk to the Energizer Bunny.

"Now I'll whip up the dishes, so you—oops." Elaborately, he looked at his watch. "Oh, gosh, I'm really sorry, Jacobia. But I've got an appointment with a real estate agent in five minutes, to look at another house. I'm going to have to dash."

Face him down, everyone said while I was married to him. Show some backbone. So I'd tried it and the result was always just like this: a barrage of passive-aggressive crap that made the effort seem not worth making. He grabbed his sweater from the hook in the hall and pulled it on speedily.

"Tell you what, I'll make it up to you. I'm going to cook dinner, tonight. And no more health food. I've given that up. It doesn't suit my new lifestyle."

Thus the blackened pound of butter. "Victor, you don't put the hardware back on until you—"

Paint, I was about to say, but he stopped me.

"By the way, I noticed that the screw holes were shabby. So," he finished brightly, "I drilled new ones for you."

It was a good thing I didn't have the drill in my hand right that minute. He was always this way: just when you'd gotten to the point of cornering and confronting him, he weaseled out of it.

Also, something about what he'd just said sounded funny—not ha-ha funny—but I was much too disorganized by fatigue and fury to identify it.

"Thanks," he said, his hand on the screen door, "for

being such a sport. It's best for Sam, you know." He grinned. "In the long run."

Victor's eyes, which were green flecked with hazel just like Sam's, positively glittered with malice.

"Sam says you've really started coming around, about me. I mean, in your outlook toward me."

Sam had made no such comment. For one thing, Sam knew the only reason Victor wasn't lying drowned at the bottom of a well somewhere was that we had city water.

"Hey, you never know," he finished slyly. "Maybe some day we will even get back together again."

In my worst nightmare and after I fixed the damned plumbing. Oh, how I wanted to kill him.

"Damn it, Victor, you come back here this minute and—"

"Toodle-oo," he sang out cheerfully, making sure all of my neighbors for blocks around could hear. "See you soon."

The screen door slammed. Victor was whistling. He was like a rabid animal: you couldn't get hold of him, and when it came right down to it, you didn't want to.

But I had to. Somehow, I really had to.

Glumly, I gathered my wits together, putting the bucket back under the sink and doing up those greasy dishes, and discovering, as usual, that almost any mood can be cleared by enough soapsuds and hot water.

After all, maybe Victor would fall through a floor in one of those old houses he was looking at. For Victor—

—whose only real skill or state of grace lay in his uncanny ability to open up the heads of other human beings, and repair whatever flaw he found therein—

—it was a distinct possibility.

Cheered, I started on the drainpipe, but here I encountered more difficulty, because, like so many people whose only previous contact with plumbing repairs involved complaining about the bill, Victor thought that if you tightened a connection securely enough, it would not leak. But the key to successful plumbing repair isn't force; it's finesse, especially in an old house like mine, where the application of a hairsbreadth too much torque is often enough to pull the pipes right out of the walls.

Still, once I had taken the trap section out, cleaned it, and put on the appropriate amount of thread tape—two wraps all the way around, pulled tight so the threads bite into the Teflon—the whole thing went together again fairly easily. Which made me wonder why I hadn't taken care of this problem earlier, so I could use the bucket for the leak under the bathroom sink.

Victor hadn't yet taken an interest in that, possibly because the first thing you see when you open the cabinet under the bathroom sink is a collection of cleaning products, and of course he wouldn't have gotten past any of those.

Giving the pipe nut a last gentle turn with the wrench, I got up feeling confident that the challenges vouchsafed to me so far were within my ability to handle.

So when I went down to the cellar to see what Victor had meant by his remark about the screw holes, I was feeling a sense of light, pleasing buoyancy, of having escaped a myriad of troublesome—and for Victor even possibly fatal—household disasters.

And then I actually saw the hardware on those shutters, and the problem was this:

Victor had taken the craftsmanlike approach: he had drilled new screw holes.

On the wrong sides of the shutters.

The hardware was on, all right: all one-hundred-and-ninety-two hinges and ninety-six latch-halves of it, solidly and securely.

And backwards.

Arriving home to find me in high dudgeon, Wade had bundled me and the Bisley into his pickup truck, and driven us out of town. Now we were standing behind Bud Abrams' mobile home, on the neat half-acre at the end of a back road in the town of Pembroke.

"*So*," I said, "I backed all the screws out—thank God for the electric screwdriver—and filled up the screw holes with plastic wood. Tomorrow morning I can finally paint them."

"Why not tonight?" Wade asked sensibly.

Bud had put a firing range into the terrain: steel backdrops with target butts in front of them, spaced out over the hillside behind his place. To each side, maples and spruces gave the range a private feeling and soaked up sound.

"Um," I said. "Actually, I'm going to be busy tonight."

I filled him in on the plan.

Wade listened bemusedly. "You don't think Baxter Willoughby killed the Mumfords and Hallie Quinn, do you?"

"Well, no. It seems too hands-on for him. He strikes me as the kind of guy who would hire other people for the heavy work. There wasn't any violence involved in his previous crimes."

I checked the Bisley's firing chambers, saw the six dummies there, and closed the magazine.

"But if I found out he was shipping contraband to New York, I could tip Bob Arnold to alert the state police, so they could go down there and catch him at it. And to save himself, he'd probably tell them who else was involved."

Wade nodded. "What do you suppose he'd do, if he caught you two at it? Assuming you're right and he's behind it all, that is."

"Probably something drastic," I admitted, "if we're right and if he caught us snooping around."

But it was the only method I could think of to find out more about what was going on out there. I know enough law from talking to Hargood Biddeford to understand that, to get a search warrant, you need probable cause. And probable cause was precisely what Arnold and the state cops would never get—especially since they were still all focused on the legendary Ike Forepaugh—unless Ellie and I snuck in and got some.

Leveling the revolver, I squeezed my hand around the grip. The weapon fired with a loud, concussive report that scared nearby starlings out of the trees; even with my ear protectors on, it was the kind of noise that made my chest thud.

Fifty yards away, a bright splotch of ketchup spread over the head of the silhouette printed on the target sheet.

"Huh." Wade scratched his head. "You adjusting?"

"Nope. Sighting normally. These dummies don't drop as fast as I thought they would."

"Right. I expected the trajectory to be a lot different. But hey, that's what we're out here for."

By this he meant that a cartridge with powder in it is heavier than one that is loaded with ketchup and wax, so momentum ought to carry it farther before its flight line starts dropping. But in practice, fifty yards wasn't enough distance for that sort of effect to show up.

Or so our experiment with these cartridges indicated. It was important, because we would be shooting dummy bullets at people—albeit ones covered in protective gear under their costumes—and we didn't want to hurt them.

Wade took the Bisley, sighted it, and fired five more shots. Five splotches circled the silhouette head with a ketchup halo.

"Okay," he said judiciously. "I'll try some more before the day of the tableau, to make sure. But I think we can shoot them normally, at the distances we'll be working with. Tell everybody, though, no hotdogging."

No unscripted firing or getting in the way of the weapons for any reason, he meant. At greater distances, these slugs could drop suddenly out of their expected trajectory and there would be a lot of people around. We didn't want any trauma.

Just to be sure, we ran through a half-dozen more cartridges, with the same result. Aiming the Bisley with the dummy cartridges in it would be the same as firing real ones.

With, of course, one important exception: the result.

"Let me just try something," I said as Wade began clearing up to leave. Loading the revolver again, I waved him out of the line in front of the target area. "Come back here with me."

I carried the Bisley onto Bud's deck, where Bud's wife Tillie had set out lawn chairs, a table, and citronella candles to ward off blackflies. Ordinarily, they would be here: Tillie offering glasses of lemonade and showing off her new square-dancing dress—at seventy, she had the fastest feet in four counties—and Bud giving Wade a few shooting pointers, because while Wade was a very good marksman, Bud Abrams was supernatural.

Today, though, the two old people had gone to Heaven, a town way up past Woodland, in Aroostook County, because Bud was also a sharp, lively, and enormously popular square-dance caller, and the state championship contests were being held there.

I got my sight picture from the deck, looking down the blue barrel of the Bisley. If the slug didn't drop in the first fifty yards, what would it do in the second fifty? The silhouette-head wavered as I hesitated, then steadied in the middle sight picture.

Then I just raised my aim a fraction, heard the smack of the report, felt the weapon jump hard all the way up my arm.

A bright bloom of ketchup obliterated the target head.

Wade's eyebrows raised appreciatively. "Nice. Hundred yards? So, how much correction?"

"I aimed above the target butt. Double the distance, that sucker drops. We need to tell people, be careful." Somebody trying to knock off a stop sign or paint ketchup on a seagull could put someone's eye out.

He nodded, frowning. "You know what? I think the only ones firing these guys are going to be you and me. Because it's a great idea, but you know, it's just too dangerous."

I reloaded the Bisley with dummies while he finished clearing up the firing table. Then we put the box with the weapons and unfired cartridges into the bed of the truck. As usual, shooting had cleared a couple of days' worth of irritation; Victor and all the repressed fury associated with him seemed, suddenly, ridiculous and irrelevant.

"You're right," I said as we drove back toward Eastport. "We don't need to be putting guns into anyone's hands. No sense taking that kind of risk."

I stopped, hearing what I'd said. Meanwhile Wade drove easily, with his elbow out the window; not a care in the world.

And not commenting.

"You think it's too dangerous, don't you? Willoughby's place, I mean. You think I'm out of my mind."

He glanced sideways at me, grinning. "Yeah. That's why I like you, though. You're not a slave to your inhibitions. Well," he amended, putting his hand on my knee, "one of the many reasons."

I slid over next to him. "We could use a driver."

"Think so? Somebody for backup and lookout?"

"Little insurance policy," I wheedled, "couldn't hurt. I could carry a cell phone. You could have another one. We got into trouble, it wouldn't be too difficult to summon reinforcements."

He squinted, thinking. "Tell me again why you're doing this?"

"Because Arnold thinks Ike Forepaugh killed the Mumfords and Hallie. And maybe he did. But I'll bet he didn't come up with the idea himself."

I paused, gathering my thoughts. "I think maybe Willoughby really has changed his spots. He didn't used to like cash, but his situation has changed. A smuggling operation could replace a lot of the money he lost by going to jail, paying fines and losing his trading credentials."

We took the curve onto Carlow Island. Two state patrol cars stood on the sandy berm, their cherry-beacons whirling, evidence that the search for Forepaugh had not yet been given up locally.

"And," I went on, "if they catch Forepaugh first, he'll say somebody put him up to it. But Willoughby will know, you see, that Forepaugh has been caught."

"So if and when that happens, he'll destroy any evidence he can. Including evidence of a smuggling operation. Which you think Tim and Ken and the girl all knew about, and maybe Willoughby had Forepaugh kill them so Forepaugh could take over the heavy work?"

"Right. Ike Forepaugh being a more experienced— and so from Willoughby's point of view much more long-term useful—bad guy."

Wade made a noise. That's another thing about him: he can find the hole in your argument faster than a blackfly can find the hole in a citronella fog.

"Yeah," I agreed without him having to say it. "That's the shaky part. Ken was a drunk, Tim was an old blabbermouth, and Hallie was an eighteen-year-old girl, so one of them should have spilled the beans sooner. And how would Willoughby know anything about Ike Forepaugh, anyway?"

"That's easy enough. Ken brags to Forepaugh, who bullies Ken into making the introduction. Then Forepaugh muscles in, with or without Willoughby's blessing. Unfortunately," Wade finished, "for the Amateur Hour."

We took Clark Street back into town, passing Charlie Bower's row of quonset greenhouses, made of heavy, clear tarp stretched over arched support poles. A row of cars stretched out Charlie's driveway, as women from town carried flats of pink geraniums, blue pansies, purple asters, and yellow zinnias back to the trunks of their vehicles; with Felicity Abbott-Jones due to arrive in a matter of days, there was a lot of camouflage still to accomplish.

"And maybe," Wade said as we sailed down the hill toward the foot of Clark Street—

—ahead in the bay, huge whitecaps foamed atop the chaotic waves formed by the whirlpool, Old Sow—

—"maybe they just didn't have the chance to let it slip to anyone what they were up to, before someone eliminated them."

Downtown, flags snapped briskly over the heads of the milling tourists getting an early start on the holiday weekend. Children on bikes zoomed in and out of creeping traffic, and if the air did not yet smell of popcorn and cotton candy, the carnival atmosphere suggested that it should.

On Key Street, the cannon in front of Peavey Library was being given a final polish. "Know what Willoughby was raiding in New York before they caught him? Pension funds. People who worked all their lives for a decent retirement."

Remembering it made me mad all over again. "Know where those folks are spending their golden years? Flipping burgers. Trying to earn enough money so that their own happy meals don't have to come out of a cat food can."

Wade pulled the truck over sharply. "Hey, isn't that Sam?"

Over by the band shell, a dozen or so teenagers were shouting and carrying on like . . . well, like teenagers.

But Wade was already halfway across the lawn, and seeing his urgency, I followed. By the time I got there, the kids had formed a ragged circle around the main attraction: two boys beating the tar out of one another.

Rather, one doing all the beating and one getting beaten: the aggressor was Peter Mulligan. Sam's arms were around Mulligan's neck, hauling the boy backwards, but Mulligan's own arms kept windmilling, punching the boy he knelt on. The victim's face was already bloody and swollen, his hands making ineffective flailing motions as Mulligan punished him.

With Sam's elbow still around Mulligan's throat, Wade grabbed his legs and they lifted him while he cursed and tried to struggle away. Through the mess Mulligan had made of him, I recognized the victim: one of the boys from behind Leighton's a few days earlier, the one who had passed the packet of something to the other kid.

"Buh-bastid," he gasped, and spat a wad of blood.

"Get back," I snapped at the kids, and they moved away, their faces expressing fear and shock. A punch or two among boys wasn't a rare occurrence, but this went way beyond squabbling.

"Jesus," one of the boys behind me said. "That Mulligan, he just went nuts on Corey Banks. Banks didn't even say anything to him, Mulligan just started trying to kill him."

Arnold's squad car screamed up and drove across the lawn, bumping to a halt by the band shell. "What the hell," he uttered as he got a look at Banks, and at Mulligan still struggling.

Sam's boat gear and duffel bag lay in a heap where he'd flung it. "Pete," Sam said, trying to get the squirming boy to look at him. "Hey, man, it's over. Come on. Earth to Mulligan."

Mulligan twisted his head around and tried to bite Sam on the face, whereupon Wade raised Mulligan and held him at arm's length, and smacked him with his open hand.

"Settle down," he barked, "or I'm going to knock you out just so you'll quit it."

Mulligan sagged, all the fight suddenly draining away. His eyes focusing, he gazed wonderingly around, as if unsure what had happened or how he'd gotten here. Lifting his hands, which looked as if they had gone through a meat grinder, he winced.

Then he sat down on the library lawn and began to cry.

Shaking their heads in embarrassment, the other kids moved away, while Arnold bent over the Banks boy to assess his injuries.

"Come on, Banks, try to sit up," Arnold said. His tone was kind, but his eyes were narrowed with anger and disgust. "You took a beating, that's all. Let's see if we can get you moving."

With an effort, Banks obeyed. He was a big, strapping kid with wide shoulders and a thick, muscular neck, a football player during the season. I knew his mother, a cheery little person whose husband had run off a couple of years earlier, and whose small-business plan—a local cleaning woman, she'd invented a spot remover she said was sure-fire—I had advised on.

Seeing Banks made me remember my promise to Clarissa, to try to help get Sadie Peltier's folks out of their legal difficulties. I'd been thinking of Mrs. Banks when I made the promise, but now I thought she would probably have her hands full with her son.

I glanced at Mulligan again, surprised that a kid so much smaller than Banks could have done so much damage. Not for the first time, I thought Mulligan had a lot of potential for mayhem.

"All right, you sit here, now," Arnold told Banks. "Get your wind. One of you kids run down to the Happy Landings," he ordered, "get Banks, here, some water."

The kids looked at each other.

"Go," Arnold repeated, the razor-wire in his voice cutting through the spell of inertia they seemed to be under.

"Christ," he muttered, "you'd think they were on the moon. Now, what the hell was this all about?" he demanded of Mulligan.

Peter Mulligan sobbed monotonously. "Banks," he managed to say through the little gasps of his weeping. "It's all his fault. Look," he demanded, "at his arms."

Hearing this, a look of new fear passed across Corey Banks' battered features. He wrapped his arms around himself.

Mulligan sniffled deeply. "Ask him," he went on, his phrases interrupted by small shudders, "who robbed those people in the park. He's broken into some houses, too, where the summer people didn't come this year. I bet he's still got some of their stuff."

Banks gazed stonily away, the pain of his injuries apparently fading by comparison with what he was hearing. "That's bullshit," he mumbled to nobody in particular.

Arnold shot him an admonishing glance, then returned to what Mulligan was saying.

"He's using heroin. I don't know where he's getting the stuff. The same place Hallie was, probably."

"Heroin?"

Mulligan nodded. "Uh-huh. Paying for it by doing crimes."

Corey Banks struggled to his feet and attempted to limp away.

"Sit," Arnold snapped without looking at him, and Banks sat.

"Hey, I'm the one got beat up," he complained.

His arm came up shakily to take the paper cup of water one of the other kids brought grudgingly to him.

"Get in that squad car," Arnold told Mulligan. "In

the back seat. And once you are in there, don't move an inch."

"You lock him up," Mulligan said, climbing unsteadily to his feet and glaring at Banks, "you won't have any more muggings and burglaries and all. You'll see."

"Oh, I see. Uh-huh. And how about assaults? People getting clobbered, they're walking across the library lawn. We going to have many more of those?"

Mulligan's gaze dropped. "I'm sorry," he muttered. "I lost my temper, that's all." He went and sat in the squad car.

Arnold sighed deeply. "Lost his temper. Jesus." He turned to the other boy. "Okay, Banks. Hold out your arms, let's see 'em."

Banks looked up, his expression all injured innocence. "Hey," he protested, "that's against my rights."

Arnold's expression as he gazed down at Banks was one of deep skepticism, mingled with a clear and obvious desire to swat Banks into the next county. "Yeah. And I could go over to your house, ask your mother to let me look at your room."

Banks pushed up his shirtsleeves. Arnold stood looking at the boy's arms in a silence that lengthened until Banks couldn't take it anymore.

"All right?" he demanded. "You got your rocks off, staring?"

"Shut up, Banks," Arnold replied, and turned away.

"Hey!" Banks cried out, suddenly aware that he had lost his privileged victim status.

"I'm gonna press charges, you know," he yelled. "I wanna make a complaint. He broke my tooth, he can't do that. And he can't say that stuff about me, he's got no proof. I got a skin condition, is all. Hey, I know my rights!"

Arnold spun on him. "Yeah, you've got rights. You've got a right to be watched by me every minute of the day and night from here on out. And you've got a right to press charges. So you want to make a complaint against Mulligan, there, you come down to the station later on, and bring your mom with you. We'll talk it over. We'll talk it *all,*" he emphasized, "over."

Banks's bruised chin jutted out truculently, but he appeared to recognize the foolishness of any further discussion. The squad car backed away across the lawn to the street, with Mulligan in the back seat.

"Do you want me to call someone for you?" I asked Corey Banks when it had gone. "I could call your mom. Or you could come up to our house with us and call her from there."

He was at the moment a terrifically unattractive young man. But he was also another mother's son, and despite the fact that he wasn't as injured as I had feared, I couldn't just leave him.

"No," he responded sulkily. "Get away from me."

I had a flashback of Hallie Quinn, telling me the same. But I couldn't force him. So I got into Wade's truck, and when I looked back Corey Banks had begun limping painfully across the library lawn with his arms clutched over his chest, alone.

38 "He would do it for me, if our positions were reversed."

We had finished writing up the arrangements for Ken's and Tim's burial service, scheduled for July third when many people who had known them would be in town. Now Ellie and I were sitting in my front parlor, working on the lists for the Fourth of July events.

Rather, Ellie was working and I was worrying.

"He wouldn't just let me go, like I was nobody." She tipped her head at the activities schedule. "I think we'll keep people busy with all this. The tourists will get a run for their money."

Which was putting it mildly. The Fourth of July festivities began at dawn with a flag-raising service down on the dock, and ended nobody knew when. There was a salmon supper on the Baptist Church lawn, strawberry shortcake on the library steps, tours of a Navy warship, and a performance by the Marine Band Choir. There were children's activities, too: a karaoke contest, a pet parade, a talent show, and of course the fireworks.

Also, there was Felicity Abbott-Jones's visit, in whose honor George Valentine had just finished replacing the metal quonset he usually used for tools, in favor of a temporary—very temporary—ancient-looking wooden shack.

If she stayed out of the shack, George had remarked, Felicity would think it was an authentic eighteenth-century construction, and if she went in it would probably fall down on her head, and no one would have to worry about her, anymore.

"Ken would find out," Ellie persisted, "who killed me."

"That's because Ken didn't have anything better to do." I was getting cold feet about the Willoughby expedition.

Ellie looked sorrowfully at me.

"Oh, all right," I relented. "Ken wasn't as bad as Benny Joe Stottlemeir, I'll give him that much."

Benny Joe Stottlemeir was a legend in Eastport. As a boy, he put bees and dry straw into Mason jars, then lit the straw on fire. He tossed dogs into wells, hung toddlers by their heels, and taped stray cats to the undersides of parked cars, to wait for the fun when the engines got started.

Later on, people sent their daughters on round-the-world tours, just so they would not marry Benny, who was pathologically handsome and who in spite of his claim of having killed two men—some said five—could be personable when he chose to be.

But Benny's luck ran out when a man who could not afford to treat his daughter to the wonders of the world—or perhaps just felt stiff-necked about the notion of paying for such a tour, just on account of Benny—began suspecting Benny of introducing his daughter to wonders of another sort entirely.

The result: Benny, dead of a gunshot wound. It was only a hip shot but he was gone when he hit the ground, which demonstrates what I said before about the Bisley; it's not the wound that'll kill you, but the shock.

"Benny Stottlemeir," Ellie said quietly, "was mean. Kenny was only foolish. Do you think fifty quarts of whipping cream will be enough for the strawberry shortcake?"

I thought a minute, envisioning the steady stream of locals and tourists trooping up the library steps, all wanting dessert to top off their afternoon meal of grilled salmon. The shortcake was made with home-made biscuits, not the sponge cake stuff you can buy at the supermarket, and the strawberries would be fresh, hulled and sugared, sliced into blueware bowls.

"Seventy-five," I said.

"Anyway," she went on, writing on her shopping list, "when I look down in that grave, and the first shovelful of dirt falls on Ken, I intend to be able to tell him who put him there. And that," she finished, "is my final word on the subject."

When people say something is their final word on the subject, more words are usually forthcoming, but Ellie is a Mainer born and bred, so there were none.

Wade had gone with George to find out if the old horse trough from Hillside Cemetery could be moved to its original spot in front of the bank building for Felicity's visit. They meant to tie up some ponies there, tame ones suitable for a children's-ride concession, thus creating yet another holiday activity while also furthering the cause of historical correctness.

Upstairs, Sam was huddled in his room with Tommy Daigle, where they were mending an old turnbuckle salvaged for use in tightening the shroud on their sailboat. While they worked, Sam was trying to convince Tommy that a muffler was a necessary item of automotive equipment for his old jalopy; Tommy wanted to spend the money on a raccoon tail.

And Victor, once again, was already in bed. He had come home from his real-estate trip looking thoughtful, quiet in the storm-on-the-horizon way that in the old days forewarned a tantrum and now cast an air of ominous silence over his end of the dinner table. In honor of the warm weather, we'd had cold couscous with shrimp, chilled leek soup, a fruit salad, and breadsticks, after which he had gone upstairs without a word to anyone.

"What do you suppose is really wrong with him?" Ellie asked. "Because I still think there is something. Beyond the usual, that is. And more than trying to make a career switch."

Ellie is the one who understands most how troublesome Victor can be. She was around when he sent me a dozen apples and a note, inviting me to guess which one was poisoned. She was there when he phoned every ten minutes for six hours, hanging up each time I answered, and when I took the phone off the hook he called Arnold to say there was an emergency at my house and that Arnold should send a SWAT team. And she was present when Victor, upset that I had allowed Sam on a fishing trip—

—Victor regards fishing as an activity more simian than human, on a level with tail swinging and flea picking—

—arrived brandishing an emergency order of custody removal, and demanding that I hand Sam over. Fortunately he was drunk at the time, so Ellie could step up and snatch the order of removal away from him, and burn it in the sink.

"What's wrong with him is, I confronted him on his behavior and told him I intended to have it out with him. And I told him I wanted Sam to be there."

Ellie looked at me as if I'd reported taming a Bengal tiger.

"But he doesn't want to," I went on. "For one thing, it would show his true colors to Sam. Victor's finessing Sam, so a blowup's too blatant for his purposes. Probably we've seen the last of him for tonight."

Ellie frowned, poring over her list. "It's early. He could wait until Sam goes out with Tommy, and then come back down. Of course," she added, "we *could* manage not to be here . . ."

"Oh, sure. Trap me in a squeeze play. Either I get to go to Willoughby's, or I can get stuck in whichever level of hell Victor turns out to be landscaping for me."

She shrugged. "We can avoid Willoughby if we're quiet and careful. As for Victor, though, I'm starting to think he is like the poor, whom we shall always have with us."

Now there was a ghastly thought. Before I could reply she got up and went to the hallway, returning with a canvas satchel. I saw a flashlight sticking out, a spare cell phone, other items stuffed down into it.

"Come on," she said. "I've put together our kit. Equipment for trespassers. And I told Wade to meet us out front at eight."

Grumbling, I pulled on the navy sweatshirt she thrust at me, and pulled the watch cap she offered over my hair. She wore a dark cotton pullover, dark pants, and a scarf, all of which made her appear dashing and slightly madcap; together I thought we resembled Lucy Ricardo and Ethel Mertz.

But she was going, and I couldn't very well let her do it alone. "Is this how Kenny got you to go with him to Caribou?"

I hitched the satchel over my shoulder. "Just kind of muscled you and bullied you, and swept you along, until you felt you had no choice?"

Ellie stopped, gazing out the dining room window toward the water. On the horizon hung a nearly full moon, its glow the bright orange of a forest fire. That moon was going to light Willoughby's place like an arena.

"Ken Mumford," Ellie said, "never bullied or muscled."

 Flying down the highway on a clear summer night in the back of a pickup truck, you forget about air bags and seat belts. The sky is enormous, and the stars wheel around like the glass shards in a kaleidoscope until you feel you will fall right up into them.

Wade had one of the cell phones; I had the other. I pressed the COM button on mine.

"Yeah." He angled his head slightly toward me. "What?"

"Wade, if he catches us I'm going to leave this open, so you can hear what's happening."

"Sure, but he's not going to catch you. I've been thinking."

"And?" I tried to keep the skepticism out of my voice.

"Worst case, you'll create some commotion."

We'd make a commotion, all right: the kind that gets you tossed in an unmarked grave. This wasn't Wall Street, where when somebody catches you doing something, they call the Securities and Exchange Commission. This was downeast Maine, where security was provided by yard dogs, barbed-wire fences, and buck-shot.

At least Baxter Willoughby didn't have any yard dogs.

That I knew of.

"So I figure," Wade said, "I'll make a ruckus right up front. Drive up the driveway, tell him my dog jumped out of the truck bed, took off across his property. That way, he hears any unusual noises, he'll think it's the dog."

"Smart. But if you're there they might not do whatever they are planning for tonight."

Ellie had called Ned's house, asking for Ned, and his wife had said Ned was gone and wouldn't be back until tomorrow: bingo.

"Good thought," Wade said. "Tell you what, I'll racket around a while, then tell him I'm giving up, the dog'll have to find its own way home."

"Uh-huh. Then, if anything unusual happens, he'll still think it's your lost animal. Instead of us two lost animals."

Wade grinned. "Want to know why I'm doing this, don't you?"

Ellie looked sideways at him, but said nothing. In the soft glow of the dash lights, her face was implacable.

"Yeah, I do."

"Ever ridden in a truck bed at night before?"

"No, but what does that have to do with—"

He pulled the truck to the side of the road, saying something to Ellie that I couldn't hear, then swung into the truck bed with me. Ellie threw the truck in gear—it ground a little, going in; I should have said something to Wade about the transmission, I realized belatedly—and we were moving again.

"Lie down on the floor," Wade instructed.

I did. He lay down beside me, and I rested my head on his chest. "Look up," he said.

The night sky filled all of my vision, enormous and

flooded with moonlight. A meteor streaked across it like the flickering slash of a scalpel. There was no wind, just the rush of the air moving on the truck's sides, the engine noise muted and distant.

"Now," Wade said, "the way I see it, you made your decision. Ellie wants to do something, wants it bad, you decided to help her. I respect your choice. And I could decide whether to make it a little safer or not. Simple as that."

Which for Wade it was, unlike in the city where there is always another layer of machination, another motive beneath the ulterior motive. With Wade, what you see is what you get.

"You had to come back here to tell me that?"

He pulled me against him. "No. I wanted to be here with you."

"Sneaky devil." Another shooting star streaked through the sky. "I wish I could get things to be that simple with Victor."

"Yeah, well. I've been meaning to say something about that, too. I know what I said about not kowtowing, but I don't want you to feel you have to go head to head with him just because I—"

"It's not that. It's Sam. I don't want *him* thinking he's got to do things that aren't right for him."

The truck slowed, pulling to a halt under an aspen tree whose leaves shimmered like coins. Wade jumped out and reached up a hand; I hit the ground with both feet, bouncing around a couple of times, overwound with my own energy.

"I'm glad you came," I told him, keeping my voice low. "All of a sudden I'm really nervous."

"Nothing wrong with being nervous," Wade replied. "Trick is, knowing what to be nervous about."

He looked around, picked out the glimmer of light at the top of the hill: Willoughby's house.

"Speaking of which, we're here."

40 We waited in the shadows at the foot of the long drive while Wade took the truck up. In a moment, a light went on at the garage end of the house, and the sounds of men's voices floated on the night air, one of them Ned Montague's.

Which was when I realized what I'd forgotten. But it was too late to worry about that. Ten minutes passed while Wade called and whistled, chasing the nonexistent animal. Then silence.

"Okay. The stage is set." Wade backed down the driveway again and his face appeared through the driver's-side window.

"What'd Ned say? He knows you don't have a dog."

"Yeah," Wade whispered back. "And if he had any brains he'd know that if I did, I wouldn't let it ride in the back of a pickup any more than you would. So I finessed him, said I was trying out a dog I was thinking of buying, it got lost around dusk. Do you know," he added, "how to make Ned's eyes gleam?"

"No," I frowned back, puzzled. "How?"

"Shine a light in his ear," Wade replied, and drove away to wait. I saw the brake lights glow, and the tail-lights wink out.

And then we were on our own. We picked the worst, brambliest spot full of barberry and raspberry canes that we could find to enter the property, a place where not even a security-systems installer would risk his hide, in case Willoughby had more detector gadgets.

Picking the thorns out of our own hides, we scanned toward the big house. "There," Ellie pointed, "is the barn. The llamas must be inside."

"Drat." The main door of the barn was in the animals' paddock and brightly floodlit. "How are we going to get in there?"

The idea was to sneak inside and wait for Ned to load the llamas. That way, we could check around the barn and get a view of the truck's cargo area, too, when he opened the back of it. But I'd rather have crossed a minefield than that floodlit paddock.

On the other hand, last time I looked, they weren't lighting up the exercise yards of maximum-security prisons with that much candlepower. The major-league illumination argued strongly for the notion that Willoughby was—or had been—keeping something important in that area.

Ellie marched away from me, striding up the hillside.

"Hey," I whispered after her, "where are you going? We need to figure out what we're doing, not just blunder in."

"I'm not blundering. See that barn?"

"Yes, of course I do," I answered, exasperated. "It's got all those lights on it, for heaven's sake. That's the problem."

"It's the same barn George just disassembled. The quonset. So he could put the shed up. George built that quonset from a kit."

"Fabulous, but that doesn't—oh." I hurried after her.

"Lights around front by the big overhead doors," she went on. "But that style of building has a hinged door in the back, so you don't have to open the big doors if you don't want to, just to go in. And *that* door doesn't have any lights near it that I can see. It just backs out onto the underbrush. Which probably means," she finished sadly, "a lot more brambles."

"Ouch." I tripped on a root hump left over from Willoughby's clearing of the cedars, and nearly went flying. "Bad enough he ruins the scenic beauty, he's got to create a pedestrian hazard?"

"Ssh. Get down." Ellie crouched suddenly as figures appeared on the porch of the big house: Willoughby and the British fellow, peering down the hill in front of them. In the stillness, their voices carried.

"See anything?" The British guy.

"Not yet. These goddamned locals and their dogs. Hard to say who's stupider, the people or the animals."

"Right." *Roight.* "Humans won't piss on your leg, though."

"Dog won't either, if I see it."

"Fancy a bit o' bull's-eye practice, eh?" The British fellow laughed unpleasantly.

Smack! The concussive report of a gunshot rang out, some small-caliber weapon by the sound of it, followed by a vivid, ker-whanging ricochet. I'd never heard that sound before except in the movies; Willoughby's pot-shot had hit a granite outcropping.

"Criminy," I breathed. "He's taking target practice on us!"

"No, he's not. Stay down."

"Thought I spotted him," Willoughby said. "But maybe not."

"What're you going to tell the poor fellow, then, when 'e comes back looking for 'is animal?"

A sound of Willoughby's contemptuous breath through pursed lips. "By morning he'll have forgotten it. These types have no . . ." He searched for the phrase. "No continuity of thought."

These types. For a heartbeat, I thought about shooting back, then remembered again that I hadn't brought the pistol or the Bisley with me. It was among the many reasons this jaunt made me nervous.

But as Wade had sagely pointed out, creeping onto somebody's property to snoop around is one thing; doing it while carrying a concealed weapon is another. And while I was reasonably sure we could evade Willoughby, I was equally sure that if I were caught trespassing *and* carrying a concealed weapon I wouldn't evade Bob Arnold.

I hadn't known Willoughby would be shooting.

"Look," Ellie whispered. "They're going inside."

The men on the porch peered into the night one last time, then went into the house. The British man's whinnying laugh hung in the night air, then faded until the darkness was silent again.

"Come on." Ellie scuttled forward.

Ned's truck was parked alongside the house, near the garage, when we reached the back of the quonset. Here a litter of empty feed sacks, scraps of straw, and plastic buckets made an obstacle course of the last few yards between us and the metal structure.

"Try the door," Ellie whispered when we had made it through, and I reached out to, then drew back at the last instant.

"If it were me, I'd alarm this door," I said.

Just then, the truck started up and began backing toward the quonset, on a dirt track that ran alongside the fenced field past the house. From inside the barn came uneasy rustling sounds, as the animals heard the truck and knew it was coming for them.

"Damn. I don't see any wires and even if I did, pulling them would surely be enough to set the alarm off."

"Never mind," said Ellie. "We'll let Ned get us in there."

Pulling the brim of the watch cap over her face, she revealed the eye, nose, and mouth-holes cut into the headgear while I gazed at her in astonishment.

"I saw this on TV, once," she said, thrusting another cap at me. "Put this on, and do what I do."

"I don't think seeing it on TV really qualifies us to—"

"Ssh." She gestured sharply at me. "Here he comes."

Oh, for pete's sake. I pulled the cap down and crept forward. Montague was slowly backing the truck the last hundred feet or so, its tires jouncing in the rutted tracks previous trips had made. He set the parking brake, leaving the vehicle running, and got out to fiddle with a keypad on the front of the building, to one side of the overhead door.

A faint beep signaled the disarming of the intruder alarm, after which Montague raised the door. Peeking around the corner, I saw a ramp inside; it was how the animals got from floor level up into the cargo box of the truck.

"Now," Ellie whispered, "get ready."

Ned got into the truck again, and let off the hand brake.

"Go," Ellie urged, and rushed ahead of me, keeping low to avoid being spotted in Montague's passenger-side mirror, slipping through the narrowing space between the truck's rear bumper and the door opening, and vanishing into the darkness of the building, away from the truck's backup lights.

"Criminy." She was lithe as an eel, but I wasn't nearly so graceful. Planting my foot on the approaching rear bumper I lunged up and vaulted clumsily over it, landing in a heap on what turned out to be the llamas' communal dung pile.

Fortunately, animals who eat top-grade chow pellets produce output nearly equal in refinement to their input. Or so I managed to console myself as Ellie grabbed my shoulder, yanking me out of sight just as Montague's face appeared in the door opening.

At the rear of the building, the animals clustered unhappily. One spat halfheartedly and bleated as I shouldered past him, but it was only saliva, not the truly ghastly, unbelievably odiferous stuff they began aiming at Montague, when he approached them.

"Hey," he protested. "Come on, you guys, you know me."

Another llama spat horridly, curling his lip back afterwards in distaste.

"Aw, come on." Ned sounded disgusted, now, as well he might. Truly, it made your eyes water, just being within sniffing range.

"It's not like I'm gonna torture you. Look, I got your water in there, I got the walls all fixed up with wet rags, keep you nice and cool, and there's plenty of fresh air.

You know I take care of you, 'cause Willoughby would shoot me if I don't. We're just going for another ride."

As he spoke, he kept moving toward the rear of the quonset. Ellie and I crouched behind some bales of straw. Grudgingly, the llamas began moving toward the ramp leading into the cargo box.

"That's right, get along," Montague urged them.

His soothing tone might have made me believe that whatever else he was—lazy, easily discouraged, chronically morose, and not precisely a full-fledged genius— Ned was at least a decent guy around animals. Then I peeked up over a straw bale and got a look at his face: tautly grimacing, like a man who really wanted to punch something, but didn't dare.

Ned finished getting the animals into the truck. Then came the *thunk* of the cargo box doors closing, and the heavy metallic slide of the bolt slamming home. And then . . .

Nothing. Ned's footsteps did not go away as we expected. The overhead doors didn't close. He just stood there.

Listening.

Almost immediately, though, his footsteps sounded once again in the quonset. I could feel him peering into corners, his sullen little mind having picked up on something.

The dung pile I'd landed in. Maybe it didn't look right to him. Or maybe the atmosphere in the quonset wasn't the same; not just animals. He wasn't brilliant, but he sensed it—something different, something wrong.

And then Ned Montague must have just thought *oh, the hell with it*. The truck door slammed. The truck pulled away a little, stopped, and he came back to pull down the overhead. I heard the faint beep-beep of the keypad for the alarm system, as the code keystrokes armed it again.

At last the truck departed, its engine growing fainter

as the vehicle made its way across the pasture, down the long drive, and out onto the paved road. We waited until the sound disappeared.

"Interesting," Ellie whispered.

"Yeah. Really." I snapped on one of the flashlights. "You get a look inside that cargo box?"

She nodded. "Water buckets, wet rags. Nothing else. I'm not sure," she added, "what that means."

I pulled out the cell phone, called Wade.

"Montague's coming. We're okay, here. Do me a favor? Follow him for a while, see if he stops anywhere, puts something else in that cargo box?"

"You got it." He broke the connection.

"Maybe," Ellie mused frowningly, "he had it in the cab."

I shook my head. "Not enough room. A bale of marijuana, for instance, means a bale." I thumped a straw bale for emphasis. "A load of cocaine or heroin wouldn't take up so much space, I guess. He could have packed it in the body of the vehicle, or hidden it on the underside, somehow."

I took a deep breath of the now-fetid air inside the quonset building. With the overhead closed, the olfactory result of the llamas' antagonism was mind-bendingly disgusting.

"But we found all that money on Crow Island," I went on. "And that, to me, means somebody is moving more weight."

I stood up, feeling my muscles crimp. "But we didn't spot it, and I've got a strong notion it's not in here."

Briskly, Ellie produced a large jackknife from her satchel. She cut the twine holding the hay bales together, one bale after another, plunging her hand into the center of each.

"Nothing." She scanned the quonset interior, sending the beam of her flashlight along floor, walls, and rafters. "And nowhere else, it looks like, to hide anything substantial. You think we bothered him, somehow? Something's here, and we're just not seeing it, but he picked up on something that made him feel sort of . . ."

"Hinky," I supplied. "Yeah, I know he was getting a funny hit off this place at the end, there. Nothing wrong with old Nedley's nerve endings—he definitely sensed something. Bottom line," I finished, "I think Ned is too lazy to follow his instincts."

Or we'd have been facing Baxter Willoughby and his buddy, by now. I kicked the remains of the dung pile: nothing beneath. "But he was on his way out of here by then. If he was loading anything, he'd have loaded it already."

The straw was pretty fresh, and so was the animals' water. Berenice Waugh was probably responsible for that; her interest had put Willoughby on notice that he'd better be good or the pet police would be making unscheduled visits, disrupting his newly assumed gentleman-farmer habits and in general annoying him more than somewhat.

I looked around again, aiming the flashlight for the edge of a trapdoor, or a compartment hidden in the quonset structure; nothing. "And I don't think he'll stop anywhere, either. I wanted Wade following, to rule that out. But Willoughby wouldn't risk keeping a stash of something important anywhere but here, where he can keep an eye on it, until it's in final transit."

Ellie sat on one of the hay bales. "And Ned," she agreed, "wouldn't want to be loading it anywhere else, either. Crow Island was one thing—except for us, I'll bet no one but Tim or Ken has been out there in at least a year, other than just to pick Tim up or drop him off, with dog supplies. But with a warehouse over here on the mainland you run the risk of someone seeing you."

I thought about Willoughby, the way he had moved money around like some sort of evil magician, staying one step ahead of the SEC until it took a person like me, somebody who was bonehead stubborn and had a mean streak—who but for the grace of God, in fact, would be as bad as he was—to ferret him out. By the time I had him, I'd admired the guy nearly as much as I'd despised him; Willoughby was one slick son of a bitch.

"But if Willoughby and Ned *aren't* doing anything along those lines," Ellie went on, "why *is* Ned driving those llamas to New York?"

"We don't know, yet." I kept peering at the quonset, examining its solid construction. Small windows pierced its arching sides, which were sheets of heavy-gauge metal bolted together at intervals. "But we're going to."

The windows, fortunately located out of view of the house, allowed ventilation for the llamas, although at the moment it was not nearly as much ventilation as I would have enjoyed. Hurricane Andrew, for instance, would have freshened things sufficiently. Each window opening was covered with heavy steel mesh fastened from the outside, probably with more rivets. The locked rear door was steel, in a tempered-steel doorframe, and the overhead door was bolted.

Just to top things off, Wade was miles away, and the low-battery indicator on my cell phone had chosen this moment to start blinking. I tried it; nothing.

"Well," I said, rubbing my hands together cheerfully to cover my despair. "Interesting situation, here."

"You mean, Ned not loading any contraband?" Ellie asked.

"No," I replied patiently. "I mean being in a steel building with locked, reinforced doors, and the doors have alarms on them."

If Montague keying in the re-arm command hadn't confirmed it, those wires coming in through the wall right along the doorjamb would have. I aimed my flashlight beam at the color-coded strands. In a high-security facility like a bank, a cash-courier's central dispatch or a brokerage house, the wires would have been shielded, but Willoughby's paranoia hadn't extended that far.

Just far enough to cause us a steaming heap of trouble. "That television show you watched happen to demonstrate how the heroes got out?"

"Hmm. I think they went to a commercial at that point."

"Wonderful. Any ideas?"

She thought. "Yes. We need to make the alarms go off."

"Are you out of your mind? If that happens, Willoughby and his buddy will come down here and . . . oh, right. Okay."

She began pulling straw bales apart. "Here, help me spread this out, here. We need to be ready when it happens."

"What if Willoughby notices the straw isn't baled up?"

"He won't," Ellie replied confidently. "If he's the kind of guy I think he is, he doesn't pay a lot of attention to the animal-care details. He's probably got people for that, right?"

We finished pulling the bales apart. "Ready?"

"As I'll ever be. Roll your cap down over your face."

She grabbed a fistful of colored wires. "Here goes nothing." Then she cut them with a swipe of that big jackknife.

Somehow I expected pandemonium: bells, sirens, and flashing strobes. But nothing happened. We dove for the straw piles, buried ourselves hastily, and lay there in silence.

"Do you think it's working?" Ellie shifted uncomfortably in the straw. "Oof, this stuff is itchy."

"It's working. And keep still. That itch is nothing compared to the rash you'll get if he finds us."

She quieted obediently. Moments later, hurried footsteps and men's voices sounded outside. Cursing and fumbling followed.

Then the overhead door rumbled heavily open. I squinched my eyes down hard into narrow slits, in case Willoughby's flashlight beam reflected in them. Big lights glared on.

"That idiot," Willoughby snarled, stomping around angrily. "He must have screwed up the alarm somehow."

"I dunno," the British fellow replied. "They are supposed to be rather foolproof. Or so the manufacturers attest."

"The manufacturers," Willoughby shot back, "have never met a fool like Montague. The flunky I had doing the boat trips turned out not to have a driver's license, and when I found out I made him find someone who did: Montague. On the plus side, however, Montague is just stupid and cowardly enough not to try anything."

"Like making off with a bit of the shipment?"

"Yes. Just like that. Fortunately, our friend Mr. Montague is more cowardly than greedy."

"How," the British voice asked, "are you going to replace the bigger bit you've lost? Bosses aren't going to be happy with that news, you know. Not happy at all."

"I realize that," Willoughby snarled. "Don't worry about it."

His boots thudded nearer, stopping a few inches from my face. "I've got it all figured out. It's why Montague is making another trip, tonight."

Keep talking, I thought at him, but he didn't. I couldn't see if he was still holding the gun he'd fired earlier, either. But probably he was. After all, he was out here checking on an alarm.

Still, it was now or never. I hadn't known what kind of chance we might get, and this was the best we could hope for. So I reached out with both hands, grabbed his ankles, and *pulled*.

"Now!" I hissed at Ellie, jumping up at the same moment as Willoughby hit the floor hard on his shoulder blades.

"Unnh," he groaned painfully as the two of us erupted from the straw heap.

"My word," the British fellow breathed, but I had to hand it to him; instead of backing off in surprise, he stepped forward, trying to block us.

"Say, just a moment," he began officiously, holding up a hand in the manner of a proper British bobby, trying to direct traffic out in front of the Albert Hall.

His eyes, though, were blankly murderous, and suddenly I was much more frightened of him than of Willoughby, gun or no gun.

"In your dreams, bozo," Ellie said, and charged at him, putting her head down and butting him in the midsection so hard, I was willing to bet his long-dead ancestors felt it.

His head snapped back, his arms flew out sideways, his body doubled over, and his legs collapsed as he crumpled to the floor in a moaning, incapacitated heap.

I found it all deeply satisfying, but I didn't get to savor it for long. Just then a gun went off—in the quonset it sounded enormous—and another ricochet whanged off the overhead door.

Which is how I learned that no matter how fast you are running, you can always run faster. Hurtling over tree stumps, vaulting granite outcroppings, I tore downhill through a night so moonlit it looked coated with quicksilver, hearing Ellie ahead of me and waiting for the painful inevitable.

He couldn't be *that* bad a shot, could he?

But no shot came. We reached the bottom of the property and darted across the road into the comparative darkness of an old apple orchard, thick with hanging branches and tangled bittersweet vine. Improbably, there was nothing but silence from behind us.

"Keep moving," I said, unwilling to believe that Willoughby would give up so easily.

"Do you see them?" Winded, Ellie forged ahead of me through long grass and thickets.

I glanced back. There must have been light panels somewhere near the quonset; the outside of the house, the barn area, and the entire length of driveway were now all lit up like an airport.

Nothing moved on the property. "You don't suppose he went in and called Arnold, do you? To report trespassers?"

"Uh-uh. I don't think he knows who we are. He didn't get much of a look at us, and in the masks—"

"Right. And that's what he wants. To know who got in there so he can find out why."

We kept slogging as fast as we could, but not running full tilt anymore; the trees made it too dark for that.

"Make for the road if you can find it," I said quietly. "Wade will be coming back, sooner or later."

"Okay. You know, though," Ellie added, sounding doubtful, "I don't think I know which way—"

Damn; me either. In our hurry, we hadn't paid attention to direction, just taking whichever way looked expedient. Now in the shadows with the branches casting weird, wavery shapes so that the ground beneath our feet seemed to be moving, we'd gotten . . .

"Lost," Ellie pronounced unhappily. Up ahead was an avenue of enormous old spruce trees, lining a dirt farm road that once led out from the orchard. The area under the trees was inky black. To the left and right, walls of brambles rose head-high, supported by what at one time had probably been a rail fence.

"I," Ellie announced, eyeing the darkness under the spruce trees, "do not want to go in there."

I squinted at the brambles again, but it was clearly a no-go. A couple of thorny barberry bushes was one thing, but that mess barred our way as surely as if the old split-rail beneath it was electrified.

"Me, either," I said. "But we can't very well go back. Look at it this way, the farm road probably led to the main road. So if we follow it that's where we'll go, too."

"I guess," she said, sighing. "Not," she added stoutly, "that I'm afraid of the dark."

Of course not. But the cavern yawning ahead of us was what I imagined Jonah saw, while he was being swallowed by the whale.

"And I don't think a flashlight is a wise idea," I went on. "Willoughby and Company are probably still back there somewhere."

"Not," said a voice at my shoulder, "exactly."

The gun barrel's tip pressed expertly against my temple, cutting off my yelp of surprise.

"Turn very slowly, please." The voice was the British man's, dead as ashes and elementally frightening.

Willoughby came out of the darkness and shone his flashlight at me. "Jacobia Tiptree. You came for the shutters, didn't you? I felt that I recognized you then, but I thought it couldn't be."

"You should have paid more attention," the British guy said.

Willoughby ignored this, his brow knitted. "Don't I remember, you were an associate with one of the larger . . . accounting firms? No. Banking? Something, I'm certain of it, in the financial area."

His gaze was amused. "Something," he repeated softly.

Which was when I knew he knew.

 "I don't understand it," Ellie said an hour or so later when we were back to my kitchen. "Why would he chase us, and even hold a gun on us, just to let us go?"

I put my hands around a mug of hot tea dosed with

whiskey. "He didn't let us go. Wade showed up, that's all, and heard me make that noise."

At, I might add, the last possible civilized moment; things had been promising to get ugly. But when you have to stop by the side of the road at night, to fix a truck—

—that balkiness I'd noticed turned out to be a quart of transmission fluid in the process of signaling its absence—

—it's difficult, riding to the rescue in timely fashion. On the other hand, we'd only been a hundred feet from the road, so at least Wade had been able to find us.

"Willoughby knows we aren't going anywhere," I said. "More to the point—"

I swallowed another gulp of the hot toddy. It had taken a belt of the straight stuff to get my teeth to stop chattering, and not only because I'd ridden home in the back of the truck.

"More to the point, he knows who we are. Who I am. And that was what he wanted. For now."

Ellie put her face over her cup and breathed in the vapors. "I thought that awful British man was going to shoot us both, even when Willoughby said not to. His finger was absolutely trembling on the trigger."

But not trembling nervously. More like he could barely restrain himself from experiencing the pleasure of it. In the end, Willoughby had been forced to take the gun, to avoid an accident.

And then there was the way Willoughby's eyes changed, once he recognized me, becoming so cold and reptilian I'd nearly expected a snake's tongue to come flickering from between his thin lips.

Wade poked his head out from the refrigerator, where he had been rummaging. "What do you mean, knows who you are? Why would he care? Why would you be of any special interest to Willoughby?"

"Well. It's never been something I've liked talking about."

For one thing, who would believe me? Nowadays, I hardly believe it, myself, that once upon a time I controlled so many of other people's dollars, whisking them off to be invested in pesos or pounds sterling, yanking them into yen or depositing them in drachmas when a flicker on a computer screen signaled a shift in the exchange rates, halfway around the world.

That being before I became the SEC's favorite dirt-digger-upper.

"I sent Baxter Willoughby to jail," I said. "I ruined him. Because of me, his name is mud in financial communities all over the world, not to mention the fact that he's legally barred from trading even if anyone would knowingly do business with him."

"Yeah? How'd he find out?" Wade took a bite of the sandwich he'd constructed. He couldn't have looked calmer if I'd confessed to bringing a lost pussycat back to its owner.

But then, Wade has been out in twenty-foot seas, rescuing day-trippers who think the phrase "mariner's warning" does not apply to pleasure boats. So he has a sense of proportion.

"I don't know," I answered. "It was supposed to be a secret. Nobody was supposed to know. But Hargood has been asking around about him. Maybe Hargood asked the wrong person, and word made it up here."

"Which means?" Wade washed down his bite of sandwich with a swallow from a bottle of ale.

"Which means he's got it in for me big-time. *And* he knows I'm snooping around in his business again."

"You think he'll come after you?" Wade's tone was serious.

"No. If he'd wanted to kill me, he could have, before you arrived."

"What if we told Arnold what we do know," Ellie mused aloud, "and the police stopped Ned. Did a thorough search of that truck."

"First of all," I objected, "they won't do it without cause, and we still can't give them any. But more to the point, even if he was going to pick up something, he won't do it now. You can be sure Willoughby will be on the telephone to Ned. Probably already has been."

I let a breath out, in exasperation and exhaustion. "No, I'm afraid all we've done is tip him off. He knows his little game is blown. What the *hell* is he shipping to New York, anyway?"

Just then Sam stuck his head in. "Anybody seen Dad?"

"No, I thought he was upstairs, asleep."

He shook his head puzzledly. "He was. I'd looked at him, and he was sleeping like the dead. But then he came down again, after you guys left. I asked him if he wanted to come out with me. But he said he'd rather stay ashore while I went with Harpwell on the *Eric*."

Dan Harpwell's boat, he meant: a 32-foot wooden sailing vessel modeled after the old Norwegian patrol boats that used to haunt the most treacherous coasts in the worst weather, looking for mariners in trouble and helping them out of it.

"Harpwell wants me to start getting a feel for it at night," Sam added. "He says I need to be able to, that sometimes you have to move at night under power."

Built in 1925 and equipped with her original Buffalo 12-horse engine, the *Eric* was Sam's ideal cruiser, and in the rare instances when Harpwell had the opportunity he was teaching Sam to sail it single-handed.

"Maybe," I offered, "your dad's gone back upstairs?"

"Nope. I looked up there again."

"Car's not outside," Wade said. "Maybe he went for a ride. Although it is past midnight," he added doubtfully.

"Probably he's somewhere on the island," Ellie offered. "There's not much sightseeing to do on the mainland, after dark."

"And he couldn't be down at the Baywatch, or in a bar. On a weeknight, they're all closed up by now."

Sam's tone was intensely concerned, which I thought was odd. But at the time, I didn't give it much thought. I just went along with what he obviously wanted: to find Victor.

"Maybe we could take a look for him," Sam said to Wade, "just on the island."

I thought that probably, feeling suddenly at liberty without Sam, Victor had found some pretty tourist girl to listen to his lies. He could be parked out at Harris Point with her right now, just the two of them and a bottle of wine cooler.

"We'll find him," Sam said as they were leaving, sounding as if he were trying to convince himself.

Sounding worried, and strangely guilty, too.

It wasn't until later, when it was too late to do anything about it—other than the one thing I should have been doing all along—that I found out why.

42 "So," Ellie said when they had gone, "let's go downstairs and paint a couple of shutters. I'm too keyed up to sleep, and George is at a bachelor party for one of the guys down at the fire station. He won't be home for hours."

"Okay." I cleared the table, fed the scraps to Monday, and followed Ellie to the cellar where the shutters awaited us.

"I cannot believe," I said as I turned on the work-lights and tuned the radio to the AM all-news station—late at night we can get some pretty distant signals, including CBS—

"I cannot *believe*," I repeated, meaning Victor, "he didn't stop to think that hardware positioning through more clearly. I mean, can you imagine what would happen if he did things backwards inside people's brains?"

Ellie looked up from the workbench where she was securing one of the shutters in the bench-mounted vise, cushioning it first with a piece of chamois so that the vise jaws would not bite into the soft old wood.

"Huh," she said thoughtfully. "I wonder. You don't suppose that's what happened, do you? I mean—"

She paused, thinking it over, "Do you think maybe Victor made a mistake? In surgery? Something," she added, frowning, "harmful, or even fatal?"

I laid my own shutter flat out on the workbench, then took a paintbrush for Ellie and one for myself from the rack at the back of the bench.

"Not," I pronounced, "bloody likely. You know Victor. He's Mister Drive-You-Nuts Perfectionist. He's so focused in the operating room, he once worked through a fire alarm that turned out to be an actual fire. They evacuated most of the hospital, and he never even knew anything about it."

"Hmm." Ellie smoothed paint onto the shutter, working with her usual deftness. "It would explain why he's been even more nuts than usual, though. I've seen him wild before, but I've never seen him . . . ditzy."

She thought a minute. "First health food, then no health food. First a neurosurgeon, then not a neurosurgeon. Goes to bed, gets up again and goes out. As if he's trying things out one after another. As if," she concluded, "he is unsure of everything."

I'd been so focused on the Sam problem, I hadn't thought much about the bigger picture, but now I considered it.

"You're right. The whole wine-is-bad-for-you, I'll-drink-two-bottles-of-it act was very strange, even for Victor. And this idea of his moving here: taking him out of Manhattan would be like taking the clam out of the chowder. It's just—"

I gestured with the paintbrush. "There's nowhere

here where he could work. And he's not going to take
up poetry no matter what he says."

I thought further. "No matter how much he wants to
punish or torture me, *or* blackmail Sam with the idea
that he *will* punish or torture me . . ."

"He wouldn't screw up his whole life to do it. Even
Victor's not that messed up and self-destructive."

Steadily, Ellie applied paint to the shutter. "And not
only that, instead of taking the first opportunity to
throw a hissy fit . . ."

"He keeps avoiding it. As if secretly all he really
wants is for me to be nice to him."

"As if," Ellie said quietly, "he *needs* you to be nice to
him right now, and doesn't know any other way of
making it happen."

I put my brush down. What could possibly make
Victor feel needy? "You know, there's somebody I can
call about this. And at this hour she'll probably be just
getting home from work."

I went upstairs and made the call, looking up the
number in the old address book I had kept back when I
lived in New York. The phone was answered on the
second ring, and my party sounded bright and alert, so
I knew I hadn't woken her.

I asked her my question, told her why I wanted to
know, and listened. Then I thanked her, promised to
keep in touch—which I wouldn't, and she knew that,
but it was okay—and went back down to the cellar.

"You nailed it," I told Ellie, still feeling stunned by
what I'd heard. "I just spoke to the head nurse in
Victor's operating room. I used to know her, back when
I lived in the city. While I was married to Victor."

Last time I'd called her, it was to say that if she had
to have an affair with my husband, that was one
thing—wrongheaded as I might feel she was being—but
leaving her nightie under my pillow was beyond the
pale, and she should stop it immediately.

And she had, and we'd even met for coffee a few

times, after she'd wised up and Victor had left her for an X-ray technician.

"Anyway, she says what happened was not Victor's fault, but the kid's mother—the kid had a huge head injury with internal bleeding, and he died—thinks Victor must have made a mistake. And so, she says, does Victor."

"Wow," Ellie said softly. "So that's what's put the hitch in his git-along."

"Knocked him for a loop," I agreed. "The next morning he took a leave of absence, starting right away, said he didn't know if he was coming back. So that," I finished, "is Victor's tale of woe."

"No wonder he didn't have his mind on these shutters," Ellie said. "Having a young patient die . . ."

I shook my head, picking up the paintbrush again. "Every surgeon loses a patient, sometimes. It's the nature of the job. They've got to accept it in order to be able to go on working."

"But it never happened to him before?"

"Actually, it has. Victor takes the worst cases. It's true he only loses ones nobody else could save, though. And it's never happened like this, with people accusing him of things. And even worse, him accusing himself."

Then in a corner under the workbench I spied a shutter I had missed, one with Victor's hinges still in it.

"Drat." I hauled it out and noticed something about it, still thinking of Victor: so inappropriate. So infuriating, and such an unhappy little duck. There was only one thing he did well, and as if to compensate for his other failings, he did it brilliantly.

His spatial sense was perfect; it was why he always knew where he was, inside people's heads. So the way he'd put the hinges on told me he'd been seriously distracted; obsessing, most likely, over whatever had happened in that surgical suite.

And it told me something else: the thing that I had been missing.

I took the shutter to Ellie. "Check me on something. Look at this, and think about Victor, what he did to it. And while you're doing that, remind yourself of what we were saying a little while ago, about Baxter Willoughby and his truck runs."

Ellie took the shutter and examined it. Then a look of sudden understanding appeared on her face.

"Backwards. We had it backwards."

 The next morning, Victor's bed had not been slept in. Arnold promised to be on the lookout for him but didn't sound especially worried; Victor, as everyone kept saying, was a grown man.

"I don't suppose," Ellie suggested when Wade and Sam had gone out to look for Victor some more, "he left a note anywhere?"

"No." Irritably, I poured coffee for both of us. "That would qualify as ordinary consideration. They drum you out of the club he belongs to, for that."

"Anyway, let's review," Ellie said, biting into a doughnut. "Willoughby's not smuggling anything to New York. What he's doing is using the trips with the llamas to smuggle something back. And that something is money."

The doughnut vanished. My theory is that Ellie burns more calories in the act of eating than are contained in the food, thus maintaining a level of slenderness that some would describe as elegant and others would call evidence of witchcraft.

"Fine," I replied. Anything was better than thinking about all the trouble my ex-husband could have gotten himself into, and the grief that could come of it. "The question is, why?"

"That's where Kenny came in, I'll bet," Ellie went on. "He was taking it out to a bigger boat, and from there," she finished triumphantly, "it went out of the country."

"But for *what?*" I persisted. "Aside from us not thinking Ken had any money, usually when you send somebody millions of dollars you expect something *back*."

The phone rang, and I jumped to answer, hoping that if Victor had been in an accident it had rendered him speechless; I knew from experience that Victor as an invalid was even more powerfully annoying than Victor when he was healthy.

But it wasn't about Victor. It was Hargood Biddeford.

"Jacobia," he said, "I've finally realized: you're right. Buy low, sell high—why, it's positively brilliant! And that's why on Monday, as soon as the banks open, I'm going to buy *bhati*. Lots and lots," he emphasized, "of *bhati*."

Well, he had the theory right. But buying *bhati*, which are the currency of Cambodia, in hopes that their value relative to the dollar will go up anytime soon is like buying straw in hopes of spinning it into gold.

"Hargood," I said, "if you do that, I swear I'll sue to have you committed. There is no upside to a load of . . ."

The obvious dawned on me. "Hargood," I said, "I'll call you back. Meanwhile, what I suggest you do is buy Toyota. The common shares."

Then I hung up, secure in the knowledge that only Japanese citizens are allowed to buy Toyota, but Hargood would keep trying for quite a while, which would keep him busy and (I hoped) out of trouble until I could get back to him.

"Money," I said when I got back to the kitchen. "He isn't trading anything for all that cash. The cash *is* the trade. He's just getting it out of the country. Which means it's dirty. That is, proceeds of criminal activities," I explained.

She tipped her head. "Why would criminals like to get money out of the country?"

"To launder it. Willoughby's broke, from paying fines and legal expenses. He can't make money in the money business anymore because he's barred from trading. But the crooks are probably rewarding him pretty handsomely because he knows how to help them get their own money back into circulation. Bottom line, besides not having to explain how they got the cash in the first place, it is a way of avoiding taxes."

"They pay taxes on crime profits? So much for blackmail, so much for drugs, et cetera?"

"No, they don't. And that's a crime, too. See, it would work like this: you truck the money here, get it out onto a ship. The money goes overseas, into a cooperative bank in a country where the law protects depositors' identities. Someone powerful there is in on the deal, so the bank will take the deposits in cash. Then it comes back, but not as income, just as an account transfer. It looks as if you already own the money, get it? And you don't have to pay taxes just to move money, only when you earn it."

"But Willoughby's been in trouble before," she objected, "and he's so famous in the money world, somebody would probably know if he was doing that. Wouldn't they?"

"Right," I conceded. "But maybe that's where the British guy comes in."

I thought a minute. "Sure. All that electronic investing gear out at Willoughby's place—that's it. See, he's not just getting it out of the country for them. He's the brains. They're investing it after they get it into the foreign account. Willoughby's name is never on it."

Ellie nodded. "So what's he doing *here?* The British guy."

"Could be his bosses want someone around to keep

him honest. Keep him from trying his old tricks, this time with their money."

I laughed, remembering my old buddy Jemmy Wechsler, the mob's banker. "Get your hand caught in the cookie jar with those guys, the next game is to see how slowly they can cut it off. That's probably why Willoughby's hell-bent on replacing the stash from Crow Island."

A car pulled into the yard, but it was only Sam being given a ride home by Tommy Daigle, who in defiance of every possible Motor Vehicle Department rule and regulation—and several of the laws of physics—had not only gotten his old jalopy started, but was driving it around.

Ellie got up and poured herself more coffee, and offered some to me. "But what about Ike Forepaugh? Do we think he *didn't* have anything to do with any of it, now?"

"I don't know, anymore. Because I've been saying all along that Willoughby doesn't like to get his hands dirty, and that's still true. He's not the physical type. He's in cash because he doesn't have a choice; it was the job that was available, probably, so he took it. And even though he has a weapon, he let his British pal take over the gun-waving duties last night until it looked like things might get out of hand. Now, *he's* a possibility—"

In fact, if it weren't for Ike Forepaugh, I'd have said it was a certainty. Once in a while you find a dead fish lying on the beach, its pale eye goggling coldly up at the sky, and the pallid gaze of our buddy from across the Big Pond put me irresistibly in mind of that fish—

A new thought struck me. "But you know," I mused, "the most noticeable thing about Ike Forepaugh, lately, is his absence. I know Arnold is looking for him, but I don't think he's *digging* for him. And that is what may turn out to be necessary."

The idea of someone lying dead somewhere sent me

back to the topic of Victor. "I wish I knew," I burst out, "where that son of a bitch *went.*"

"His car," said Sam, "is on Water Street. He's not in it."

I hadn't heard Sam come in.

"He's not back in Manhattan, either. I called the super in his building. Could you please," Sam added with stony politeness, "not call him names anymore until we find him?"

He tossed an envelope carelessly onto the kitchen table.

"Sam, I apologize. It's just that your father and I—"

"Hey, he drives me nuts, too. But what am I gonna do? He's my dad. It's not like I can trade him in for a new one."

I said nothing.

"Anyway, Daigle and I are going to ride around a little more, see if maybe we can spot him."

He glanced up, a flash of apology in his eyes. "I'm sorry about that crack I made. It just popped out. I didn't mean it the way it sounded."

That I'd traded his father in on a better model, he meant. I nodded at him, letting him see that I understood, that of course I forgave his remark.

Which I was trying to, but what Sam said next wiped out all thought of it.

"This is my fault," he burst out. "I didn't tell you the whole thing. He didn't just go out for no reason last night. After you guys left, I sat him down and told him I wasn't going back to New York with him. That his college plan's a bust, that I'll never make it at any of those universities he wishes I could go to."

His eyes narrowed unhappily. "I told him I'm staying here and if he gave you any trouble about it, he'd have me to deal with."

So Ellie had been right about Victor coercing Sam, using me as emotional hostage. Sam had picked up on it, too. But then, while I was still trying to find the right moment to trigger a nuclear meltdown, Sam had simply confronted his father, honestly and directly.

Whereupon Victor of course went immediately to Plan B: the massive guilt trip. And Sam didn't understand that part of it.

Yet.

"What did he say when you told him?" I asked.

"It was weird. He didn't say anything. He got up and walked out, and that's the last I saw of him. I feel awful about this."

Suspicions confirmed. Until you caught on to him, Victor could make you feel lower than worm droppings. He'd never tried any of this stuff on Sam before, though.

"Maybe I shouldn't have told him. Maybe I even made the decision too fast. Anyway, I shouldn't have been so hard on him."

He looked up in appeal. "I'm going to tell him I've changed my mind, when he gets back. I mean, what could it hurt?"

The pain of giving up his own plans was visible on his face. "Only, if anything's happened to him—"

"Sam. All you did was speak realistically to your father. I mean, about your actual chance of being admitted to an Ivy League school. Which you know is unlikely, and all the rest follows from that. You told him what you're going to do in real life. The one, I mean, that you are actually living."

Something proudly rebellious sparked in Sam's eyes, as if for a moment I were the one bullying him. But then his look returned to one of misery. "It's my fault," he repeated.

I took a deep breath. This was it: truth time. Never mind that Sam wasn't going to get admitted to college anyway. He had the right to make his own decisions without feeling guilty or pressured, and I wasn't going to watch him dancing at the end of Victor's strings, jerking any way that Victor yanked him.

"Sam," I began gently, "do you remember when I gave your dad some bad news, too? When I told him I wanted a divorce?"

Sam nodded. "Yeah. And he almost had a heart attack over it. That's another reason why I feel so—"

"Sam, listen. I never wanted to tell you this before. But your dad faked all that. I found the drugs he was using to bring on the symptoms and the irregularities on the cardiac monitor."

Sam stared at me.

"I took the drugs away from him," I went on. "That's why he got better so fast. He was trying to make me feel guilty so I'd do what he wanted. And now—"

At Sam's expression I decided that when Victor did show up, I would kill him myself. "Now," I finished, "your dad's doing it to you."

Sam's face grew still, but I knew what he was thinking. In six months of living with his father, he'd believed they'd come to some mutual accommodation, some kind of respect. He comprehended as well as any youngster can how things were between Victor and me. But he'd thought that between himself and his father, it would be different.

That was the way Victor always got you, at the beginning: by making you believe you alone were the different, special one.

Maybe in his heart of hearts it was what he believed, too.

At the beginning.

"I'm sorry, Sam," I said. "I'm so sorry about all of this."

"Yeah," he replied. His voice was impassive, his look at me rejecting any comfort, and he went out without saying any more.

When he was gone I sat down heavily at the kitchen table. "I feel like an axe-murderer."

Ellie watched me sympathetically. "You thought it

would be easier, didn't you? Having a big explosion with Victor would have been a lot less painful than this."

"Right. This little moment. So quiet, and it went by so fast. All Victor was doing was softening him up, that whole six months."

"He was going to find out sometime. Sam, I mean."

"That he can't make Victor into some kind of strange, quirky guy who although he may have a lot of odd behaviors, can still be a friend? I mean a real friend, someone Sam can trust not to use him and manipulate him and—"

A dull, familiar pain the size and shape of a thumb-print was starting behind my forehead. I got up from the table.

"Yeah," I finished flatly, "he was. Going to find out. And he'll get over it. Sam's going to be just fine."

I pushed my chair in, carefully not hurling it through the kitchen window. "It's not the end of the world, finding out about Victor."

But I was remembering the day I had.

As an afterthought I picked up the envelope Sam had tossed onto the table, only now noticing the return address and that the envelope had already been opened.

And how thick it was. The sheet covering the sheaf of papers inside was cream vellum with a rich-looking Yale University seal at the top.

Congratulations, the letter began.

Something about swinging a wrecking bar always makes me feel better, so after reading Sam's letter I went up to the third floor, where I put on my dust mask, safety goggles, and work gloves. The wrecking bar, a three-foot length of heavy tempered steel, smashed violently into the old plaster wall.

Chunks of plaster clattered down onto the bare board floor, which until recently had been covered with antique linoleum, not vinyl but the real stuff, made of linseed oil and cork bits spread on burlap and allowed to dry.

This I had saved, intending to use it on closet floors if I ever managed to put in any closets; one of the benefits of living in a very old house is the way it cuts down on wardrobe expenses, there being nowhere to put nonessential clothing items.

At the moment, all I needed was sackcloth and ashes. *How* could I have believed no Ivy League college would want Sam, a boy who at age twelve had invented a gizmo that chased cockroaches not only from our otherwise fancy upper East Side townhouse but out of the whole building, back in New York?

More broken plaster clattered down. In the old days they put horsehair in it to make it stronger; now the hairs fell in tufts onto the floorboards. Ordinarily they made me think of long-ago green pastures, but now they only reminded me of glue factories.

What must Sam think of me, that I had sold him so short? And that I had as good as lied to him about Victor, or so he must believe.

Around me, the third floor of the house shimmered silently in the summer sunshine. These were the servants' rooms, each with a makeshift mantel, a stovepipe thimble and a storage cubby with a tiny door like the door in a fairy tale. A long-ago chimney fire that broke through to the roof resulted in a flood here, once upon a time, and it was the wreckage of this that I had been working to repair.

I wondered if the servant girls were here then, if their few things were ruined. I wondered if, when they heard the alarm, they ran down the flights of stairs barefoot and weeping foolishly, to the kitchen, where the mistress of the house would scold them and order them silent, her own heart hammering dreadfully.

I wondered if Sam would ever speak to me again. His father's illness had terrified him; probably he blamed me for that terror and for letting him believe things about Victor that were untrue. Sam must feel a fool, I realized, and think it was all my fault.

I swung the bar again at the portion of old, unsalvageable, collapsing plaster I was bent on replacing. Then without warning a bright thing flew shiningly out of the hole at me, landing with a metallic *clink* on the bare floor.

It was a spoon, a silver teaspoon. The last time I'd seen one like it, bright silver in an elaborate pattern with a filigreed *M* on the handle, I'd been putting it back on the mantel from which it had again fallen, down in the dining room.

Possibly, I thought, there were two spoons: one there, one here.

But even then, with the bright morning sunshine pouring in through the tall, wavery-glassed windows, I didn't think so.

Not really. I put the spoon in my pocket.

44 "Has Sam come back yet?" I asked Ellie.

While I was upstairs, Ellie had wiped down all the kitchen woodwork with Murphy's Oil Soap, washed the windows, and begun making pesto out of approximately a bushel of fresh basil, which was what had been in the paper bag she'd been carrying when she arrived.

"No," she said. "Victor, either."

Out on the counter were a bottle of olive oil, a head of garlic, a chunk of Parmesan, and a pile of shelled walnuts. She had stripped the leaves from the basil and was stuffing them into the blender with the rest of the ingredients, and the kitchen smelled like heaven.

"You know," she said, pouring olive oil into the blender, "we're operating on a lot of blue-sky theory in the Willoughby department. What we need, which we can't seem to get, is facts."

She let the rich, green mixture puree to a thick paste. "We need," she finished, "Ned Montague."

Spooning pesto into a freezer bag, she sealed it and put more ingredients into the blender, for another batch.

"I say we tell Ned that we know more than we do. Fake like mad, get him confused, tell him he's going to get blamed for all of it, murders included, unless he tells us absolutely everything he knows, or even thinks he knows."

"I doubt he'll tell us anything, anyway. And what's to stop him from telling Willoughby, afterwards, and Willoughby sending his British buddy to silence us? The way, maybe, he did the other three?"

Ellie frowned. "Well, there's that little gun of yours," she offered. Her confidence in me can be frightening.

"But no matter what happens," she went on, "we need facts. Because when we do go to Arnold and the state police, they'll need enough to be able to act fast, won't they?"

She dusted her hands off. "So," she finished, "do you want to call Ned? Or shall I?"

In the end, I let her do it. And while I was right about Ned being summoned back from his trip—he answered the phone, Ellie said, which he couldn't have if he'd gone all the way to New York—I was wrong about him giving us the silent treatment.

One ultimatum from Ellie and one half-hour later, he was in my cellar, spilling his guts.

45 "I have a little girl," Ned Montague said aggrievedly. "She needs an operation. Where was I going to get the money? These guys who work the docks, or on boats, they're bigger than me, stronger. You can't make money as a dockworker, anyway. Not," he finished, "real money. The kind Willoughby's got coming out of his ears."

He looked up, his eyes gleaming weakly under the cellar worklamps. He'd insisted we come down here before he would talk, as if we'd wired the kitchen for secret recording, or something.

Which if I'd thought of it, I would have. But I hadn't.

"So I said I'd drive the truck for him. What's the harm? Everything was okay," he added sullenly, "until you two came along."

He turned toward me. "What the heck were you doing out there last night, anyway? He was already nervous, and now that you've got him all hot under the collar, there won't be more trips for a long time, maybe never. And what do I do for income? Huh? Answer me that."

"So you were getting paid to bring loads of money back in the truck, with the llamas for cover in case you got stopped."

He shrugged miserably, in assent. "I didn't even know it was money, at first. I don't see how you two found out all this."

"That's why the trip checks," I went on, not telling him we were guessing. "To make sure you *wouldn't* get stopped on a silly violation like a bad turn signal or faulty brake light. The llamas were in case that happened anyway, just extra insurance."

"What about the drugs?" Ellie asked. "Have you been making a little spare change off those, too? Maybe," she added, "Ken had some left. Out at his trailer, after he died."

"Wait a minute," I said, "let me make sure I've got this. Ken started out doing a little dope smuggling."

Something about that still didn't sound right to me, but I let it go for the moment. "Then Willoughby hired him. Same deal, but now Ken's doing it in reverse: smuggling money out."

Ned nodded.

"Once Ken was gone, you picked up the last of the heroin and sold it. Heroin that he'd been selling to kids around town, good kids basically, messing up their heads." Nope. It didn't sound right at all.

Ned gazed shamefacedly at the cellar floor. "Yeah, I got rid of the last of it. Found it when I went out there, stuffed in the glove box of that old car, sold it around, but only to the people who'd already been buying it."

Great. Like that made it okay.

"But I didn't," he pleaded, "know how bad it would be, with people doing crimes to get the money for it. I just thought, hey, dumb kids want to get high, what do I care? And there isn't going to be any more. So I thought, what's the point of wasting it? But I don't know anything about any of that other stuff. Tim and Kenny, or the girl."

"Hallie," I said. "Having some trouble remembering, are you, Ned?"

He nodded hard. "Well, I'm nervous. If any of this gets out, I could be in a lot of trouble. Even though all I did, *all* I did, was drive Mr. Willoughby's truck. Hey, after it got loaded in New York, I never even looked inside."

He looked back and forth at Ellie and me. "Never even," he implored, "got *out* of the truck while I was down there. No," he emphasized, "personal involvement."

"So who killed them—Ken, Hallie, and Tim?"

"Ike Forepaugh," he replied reluctantly. "It must have been him. Way I figure, Willoughby hired him to do it."

"Why?" Ellie demanded. "Why would Willoughby want Ken dead?"

Ned sighed heavily. "I think he figured Ike was a better guy in the long run to do those boat runs. He was tougher and smarter. Not, you know, like Ken. And if any bigger things came up, problems, Ike was equipped. He's a real bad dude."

"Willoughby didn't want Ken around after he fired him," Ellie theorized aloud. "Ken might talk about the whole thing, and get Willoughby in trouble. So he wanted to get rid of him."

Ned nodded sorrowfully. "I guess that must have been it."

"What about Tim and Hallie?" I pressed. "Why would Ike kill them? Was it also on Willoughby's orders?"

He shrugged. "I don't know about the girl. But maybe Willoughby told Ike to get Tim, too, in case Ken had been talking to the old man."

Tim had indeed been blabbering about Ken's "big deal." It was possible Willoughby had gotten wind of this.

"Bottom line, you drove a little truck and you sold a little heroin, and that was it," I said.

Ned began nodding again. "That's right. I just—"

A sound from the cellar steps interrupted him. "Isn't that enough?" Peter Mulligan inquired harshly.

He was carrying a hunting rifle.

"Peter," I said gently, much more calmly than I felt. "Peter, where did you get that?"

He glanced at me, annoyed. "Upstairs. I found it."

"Here?" That couldn't be right. Wade secured firearms, his own and any repair items in the house, at least as thoroughly as I did. So I thought Peter was confused, which considering the size of the weapon he was wielding did not reassure me.

But where he'd gotten it was less important than what he meant to do with it, just at the present moment.

"Peter, I want you to put the gun down."

He didn't, and he didn't take his eyes off Ned, either. "You killed her. Ultimately, you're the reason she died. And because of you my life is over, too. I lived," he declaimed tragically, "for Hallie Quinn."

Ned's eyes looked ready to pop out on springs. "What do you want?" he sputtered frightenedly.

"Shut up. I've been listening to you," Mulligan said. "I've heard what I needed to hear, that you sold heroin to Hallie. I begged her to get off it, and after Ken Mumford turned up dead, I thought finally she would. No more supply. But *you*"—he spat the final word venomously—"you kept selling it to her."

He aimed the rifle. "You were behind the drugs all along."

Which made, actually, no sense whatsoever. Until he got the job driving for Willoughby, Montague hadn't had two extra pennies to rub together.

And neither had Ken. But Hallie had.

That glove box, I thought, in that old car. Ken's trailer, so isolated, would have been perfect. Her room's expensive decor, her not selling the silver medallion, yet having enough money to buy drugs and go regularly to Portland . . .

Ken had been doing the smuggling part, all right. But Hallie had been the brains of the operation, I'd have bet anything.

"I told her," Mulligan ranted, waving the gun around, "I told her what would happen. That night on the seawall, I tried telling her one last time. But—"

"Peter," I interrupted, "You didn't tell me you talked to Hallie that night. You said you heard her arguing with someone else."

Nobody had mentioned finding the medallion on Hallie's body, either. "But it wasn't someone else. It was you, wasn't it? She was on the seawall that night, arguing with you."

Suddenly he looked trapped. But fortified by the fire-power he was holding, he tried bulling his way through it. "*He* was the reason. I *told* her how much I loved her, I *tried* to make her see. She didn't want to stop using and it was because of *him*."

But I didn't think so. "What did you do to convince her, Peter? Did you touch her? Maybe slap her, try waking her up to reality the way you did Corey Banks? Did you," I proceeded carefully, "try pounding some sense into her?"

Just for an instant, that dead face came back to the land of the living. Peter looked at me, the way a drowning man looks at a life ring.

"Did your hands end up around her neck somehow? And somehow, by the time you had finished trying to convince Hallie to listen to you—Peter?" I asked it very gently.

"Peter, when you looked into her face for the last time, to see if she believed you . . . Peter, was that when you realized that Hallie was dead? Did you take the medallion, to remember her by?"

His face crumpled. "Hallie," he muttered.

"Peter, do you have it now?"

Montague made a move.

"Get away!" Peter yelled, swinging the rifle at Montague.

"You're lying," I snapped at the boy, trying to bring him back to me. "Hallie wanted off drugs. She just didn't want you."

I was lying, too, partly. She hadn't wanted anything but a way out of the small town she was stuck in, and she thought the money she was making would give it to her, with a little assist from Ken Mumford.

But if Peter would turn towards me, Ellie could jump him. Or if push really came to shove I could shoot him. The little .25 semiauto was right there in my pocket, and loaded; after the previous night, I thought I might never go anywhere without it again.

The Bisley was out, too; even full of dummies, it looked plenty threatening, which I'd thought might come in handy. Trouble was, right now it was upstairs in my bag.

Besides, I didn't want to point any gun at this kid unless I had to.

"I read your letters to her, Peter. Kind of short on things to amuse yourself with, aren't you? Nothing to do but follow her around, spy on her. Like one of those stalkers you read about in the papers. That's what people will say. Just another pathetic, delusional little sap."

"Shut up!" He screamed it, his adolescent face taut with rage as he turned to me. "He made it happen, it wasn't my fault, it was all because of him!"

He started toward Montague again, the rifle swinging wildly. Suddenly Ned moved faster than I'd have thought possible, seizing one of the heavy wooden shutters I'd been working on and bringing it down with a sickening *crack* onto Mulligan's head.

Mulligan dropped as if shot, a trickle of blood leaking from his nose and another from his ear.

"Oh, my God," Montague breathed. "He was going to shoot me!"

"Well, he's not going to shoot you now, is he?" I snapped. "Get upstairs and call an ambulance."

I knelt over Mulligan as Montague hesitated. "Listen, all the things we were talking about. Can we maybe forget about all that?"

"Get up there!" I bellowed at him, and he started to. But just then, a familiar voice sounded from the top of the stairs.

"Good heavens. What in the world are you people doing?"

It was Victor.

"The boy is hurt," I told him. "Can you help him? We can call him an ambulance, but—"

But how long would it be before it got here, and once it got here, where would it take Mulligan? The nearest big-time surgical facility was, as I had emphasized to Victor in another context entirely, three hours away. Looking at Mulligan, it was clear to me that by then he wouldn't be a candidate for any kind of surgery other than the variety performed on autopsy tables.

Montague pushed past Victor, going to make the call.

"Wait. I'll need you to tell them some things, when you talk to them." Victor surveyed Mulligan, then came down the stairs and crouched over him, glancing at the broken shutter.

"This is blunt trauma?"

"Uh-huh. The kid was waving a rifle, not making much sense. So Montague bonked him. He hit him," I added, "pretty hard."

"No harder than I needed to," Montague protested injuredly. "No harder than I needed to, to defend myself."

"Shut up," Victor advised him pleasantly. "Or I'll cut out your *lingua glossa.*"

"That," I informed Ned Montague, "is your tongue. Now get on that telephone, before I—"

"I'll give the orders here," Victor said. But his tone was meditative, and he wasn't actually doing anything.

"Where were you?" I said it quietly.

"Sitting in an old house," he replied. "Thinking."

He kept looking at Peter Mulligan, seeing, I supposed, the other boy: the one who died on his operating table. If I'd had a cattle prod, I'd have zapped Victor with it to get him moving.

Also, I just wanted to hurt him. "I told Sam all about your heart attack," I said.

That got him. "You *what?* I thought we weren't going to—"

"Badmouth each other," I finished. "I changed my mind."

He wasn't used to this sort of thing from me. "Look here, Jacobia, if you think you can make me do anything I don't want to—"

But suddenly that was just what I thought I could do.

Victor had been manipulating me, counting on my view of myself as the good guy, as Sam's protector. But what had I ended up protecting, except my fine opinion of myself?

The truth was that I'd been so worried about my own image, I'd let Sam walk right into an emotional munitions dump.

I opened my mouth. The words came out fast, as if they'd been waiting for the chance.

"I don't care what happened to you in New York. I don't care about the self-indulgent drama you've worked up over it. I don't care if you drop dead right here in this basement. I'll bury you where the coal bin used to be, and get on with my life."

He stared at me, dumb with shock.

"You're going to help this kid here right this minute," I said, "or *I'll* tell Sam what you did that time in Central Park."

Victor winced; even he didn't think making a homeless man sing for a dollar was very praiseworthy.

"How about it?" I demanded. "And then there was the time—"

"All right." He frowned impatiently, trying to minimize what I was doing to him. "I swear I don't know what's wrong with you, lately, Jacobia."

"There's nothing wrong with me. There's something wrong with him." I gestured at Mulligan. "Get to it."

Whereupon Victor gave in and thumbed Peter Mulligan's eyelids open. "Look there," he commanded, trying to regain some semblance of his dignity. "Tell me what you observe."

"One of his pupils," I said, "is larger than the other. Not much larger."

"Not yet," Victor agreed. "But it will be. Soon."

Upstairs, we could hear Ned Montague gabbling into the phone. Ellie had gone up too; now she brought towels and a pan of water.

"I couldn't think of what else you might need," she said.

Peter Mulligan began making harsh, gasping sounds. Absently, Victor lifted the kid's chin up, and Mulligan's breathing eased. In the distance, a siren approached; Henahan, coming to confront his real-life demons.

"Victor," I said urgently. "What's going to happen?"

"If the pressure inside the skull isn't relieved, the brain in there will get crushed to death. He could survive. But he would have the functioning potential of a rutabaga. I said," he went on as if to himself, "that I wasn't going to do this stuff, anymore. And under the circumstances . . ."

He glanced around at the primitive cellar, still stalling. "*Under* the circumstances, I doubt that anyone would fault me for sticking to my resolution," he finished.

And that really was just the absolute final straw: Victor, looking down at this kid who might die and wondering how it would affect *him*.

"You never meant to do neurosurgery here, did you? Your idea of moving here—besides just annoying me—it was so you wouldn't have to. You knew the hospital here wasn't equipped for your kind of work. All your talk about it, that was just blowing smoke."

"You don't—" he began indignantly.

I ignored him. "Because your other patient died," I said, "and you're afraid it was your fault. Or worse, that people think it was. That's why you don't want to do anything, now. It reminds you of your embarrassment. And of your fear."

He fell silent, his face expressing surprise that I knew.

"Victor," I rushed on, "do you think there's something special about you that means you're *never* going to fail at anything? That you're never going to lose anyone who might possibly have been saved?"

He answered slowly. "No, Jacobia. I know about

losing people. I just never knew that I knew it. Until," he added quietly, "I came here and saw how happy you and Sam have turned out to be. And saw what I'd lost. When Sam faced up to me and made his case to me last night, that's when it all fell together for me."

He shook his head ruefully. "Sam's his own man, now. He proved it. I won't make him go to college if he doesn't want to."

Well, you could have knocked me over with a feather. To cover my confusion, I went right on being furious with him.

"Victor, you do what you have to for this kid on the floor, and you do it right now or I'll make you sorry."

I thought hard for a second. "I'll tell Sam about the time you FedExed your mother a fetal pig with a wooden stake in its heart, because she wouldn't stop sending me birthday cards after our divorce."

A little rueful smile played around his lips, reminding me of the old days when I'd first met him, before I was hip-deep in his pathology and only knew him as bright and charming.

"Playing hardball, huh? Same old Jake," he said, kneeling by Mulligan.

As he did so, a shiny object peeped from his pocket, and it occurred to me suddenly that something else unusual might have happened, the night before. Sam had said that he'd looked in on his father, that Victor had been sleeping like the dead.

"What woke you up?" I asked. "Last night, when you got up and went out . . ."

Victor laughed oddly. "Why, I rolled over onto this."

He put his hand in his pocket, and I knew what was coming.

He brought out the silver teaspoon. "Did you put it there? In my bed? As a sort of joke, or something?"

"No." I stared at it. "It must have fallen into the laundry."

That was an unlikely explanation, but not as unlikely as the truth, which I had no intention of offering.

"Just do what you have to for Mulligan," I said,
taking the spoon from him as Montague came to the
top of the stairs.

"Right." Victor turned back to the business at hand.
"Ellie, spread those towels over here. Montague, run
and get my shaving kit. Make sure you bring along the
straight razor."

Everybody leapt to obey as he bent over the injured
boy; his name isn't Victor for nothing.

"You," he snapped as Arnold appeared on the cellar
stairs. "You somebody official?"

Arnold nodded, bemused at Victor's tone.

"Get that helicopter from the airfield over here,"
Victor ordered, "tell 'em we're going to Portland. Tell
the guy from the ambulance he's going, too."

Montague hustled back with the shaving kit. Swiftly,
Victor began removing Mulligan's hair. "I'll need an IV
setup for this kid, and an oxygen tank. Move it. We
haven't got all day."

Moments later, Victor had exposed Mulligan's scalp.
"Get in here," he told Ellie, "with one of those towels."

She complied: looking like a flower does not prevent
her from having the tensile strength of steel cable, in
emergencies.

Swiftly, Victor made a cut with the straight razor,
producing a wash of blood, then probed delicately with
his finger. "Uh-huh. Well, I guess there's no doubt
about it."

He checked Mulligan's pupils again, and saw, apparently, what he expected to see. Then he looked up,
searching for something.

"There it is. Jacobia," he ordered, and when I saw
what he was looking at my stomach took a lurch. But
he was definite about what he wanted.

"Jacobia, hand me that power drill," Victor said.

"Good golly bejesus," said Ned Montague for the fifteenth or twentieth time, sitting at the kitchen table drinking a beer. "Did you ever see anything like that before in your life?"

Arnold had accompanied the ambulance to the airfield and supervised loading the helicopter. But he'd said that he wanted to hear Ned's story as soon as he got back, and that if Ned told it properly—no hiding things, no embroidering—Arnold would see that Ned didn't get into too much trouble over it. Stay put, Arnold had told Ned firmly.

So Ned had obeyed, but Arnold hadn't returned immediately, as I'd expected. Probably one thing had led to another as it often did in Arnold's busy—too busy, lately—day. As a result, Ned had been hanging around for hours; I hoped he wasn't expecting to be invited for dinner.

Speaking of which, it was nearly time for it and Sam wasn't home yet.

"Ellie? Did you ever see anything like that?"

"No," Ellie replied shortly to Ned. "I'm going to find George and fix him some supper," she told me.

"Send Sam home if you see him," I called as she went out.

Ned took a swallow of his beer, looking satisfied. Watching him, I had the feeling that I ought to be asking him something. But the experience of holding Mulligan's breathing passages open while Victor drilled a hole in the top of the kid's head had wiped everything else out of my own.

With the relief of pressure in the skull, Mulligan's pupil size had equalized. This, Victor had said, was a good sign, but it didn't guarantee anything. Victor had also informed me that if Mulligan died after Victor drilled a hole in his head with a power drill, Mulligan's parents could sue Victor for everything he had.

"So I hope you're happy, Jacobia," Victor had said

tightly, which was when I knew that the aberrant little moment of normal human feeling we had shared was exactly that: an aberration.

Outside, the sky was brightening in a last blast of sunset brilliance: high, puffy cumulus clouds the exact same pale yellow as french vanilla, each with a heart of ripest pink.

"You know," I said, "Sam really ought to be home by now."

Wade put his hands on my shoulders. "Hey, it's not like Sam doesn't know his way around town. He'll show up any minute."

"Yeah. But . . ."

I'd made some calls. "Tommy Daigle's mother says Tommy dropped Sam off down at the dock. But Dan Harpwell says he hasn't seen him, that he's not on the *Eric*. And that was hours ago."

Montague watched us interestedly, his eyes beginning to get a little bleary with the beers he had consumed.

"Golly bejesus. Did you ever—"

"See anything like that. No, Ned, actually I haven't."

Worry made me snap at him, but it didn't faze him. He just took another sip of his beer.

"I saw Sam and Tommy earlier," Wade said. "The two of 'em, when we were all still wondering where Victor was. Probably," he added reassuringly, "Sam got interested in that big cruiser, the *Triple Witch*. Maybe talked her crew into letting him aboard like he planned. Now he's forgotten what time it is."

That sounded reasonable; Sam would have killed for a close-up look at the *Triple Witch*. Maybe he'd seen Victor too, and knew he was okay.

But when he heard Wade's theory, Ned looked uncomfortable, downing the rest of his beverage in a single tip-up.

"Ned," I said to him as the look on his face came into focus. "What do you know about this?"

He stared innocently at me. "Nothing. How would I know about it? I mean, know about what?"

"The *Triple Witch*. When Wade mentioned it, you looked like somebody poked you with a pin."

His gaze skittered guiltily to the phone. "Nothing," he repeated, sounding frightened.

And then I understood. "Wade," I said slowly, hearing my own voice as if from a distance. "Did the guys at the dock find out who that cruiser belongs to? When they were trying to move it?"

Wade shook his head.

"Because you can tell them," I went on without waiting for him to reply further, "that I know who the owner is."

I couldn't even feel my feet touching the floor, but somehow I got across the room, leaning over the kitchen table to confront Ned Montague sitting there like some evil little toad.

"You didn't just call the ambulance, did you? When Victor sent you up here, you called someone else, too."

"No!" His face was ashen.

Now I understood why he'd obeyed Arnold's order to stick around with only perfunctory complaining: it suited his purposes. He'd been told to stay by someone else, too, to keep an eye on us.

"Mulligan was about to say something more when you hit him. What was it, Ned? Why did you take the risk of clobbering him?"

"He was going to shoot me!" Ned whined.

"No, he wasn't. Another second, and Ellie would have had the rifle. You hit him to keep him from saying something about you. Something about what happened when Hallie died."

Unnerved by our emotional voices, Monday sat up and barked.

Then I had it. "You," I told him quietly. "What Peter said was partly true. Hallie *was* arguing with someone else, when he came along. You're the "older guy" she was seeing. Hallie was arguing with you, because you stole her drug stash from where she hid it, out of Ken's old junk car."

Cornered, Montague got all blusteringly defensive. "You can't talk that way to me!" He made as if to get out of his chair.

I reached out and pushed him hard. "Sit down and shut up. I hear another word out of you, I'm going to shoot you with this."

I took the little weapon out of my sweater pocket. In the suddenly silent moment that followed, it looked ugly and deadly.

Like the orders Ned Montague had been following.

"You called Willoughby. Right after you called the ambulance, you called him and told him what we knew."

Wade came back from the phone alcove where he had been making a call himself. "Registration for the *Triple Witch* is in New York State," he said. "Principal owner Baxter Willoughby."

His gaze still fixed on Montague, he went on. "The guys at the dock say the *Triple Witch* weighed anchor, half an hour ago."

Turning, he saw the gun in my hand and stopped. "Well," he murmured. "I see there's been a development."

Montague eyed Wade hopefully for about half a second. But Wade didn't ask me to put the weapon down, nor did he do anything else to make Montague believe that he could divide and conquer. So that Montague, after that fragile instant when anything could have happened, slumped in his chair.

"Call Arnold, please," I told Wade. "Find him and tell him we need him here right away. Then call Ellie and tell her we need her, too, and please not to wait until after she cooks dinner for George. Tell her," I added, "George can eat here if he wants to. If he's got any appetite after he finds out what's happened."

Wade did as I asked, then returned and without any warning slapped Ned hard on the side of the head.

Ned yelped and cowered pitifully, cringing as Wade raised his hand again.

"What's the plan, Ned?" Wade asked.

"I don't know! I don't know anything—"

Whap. "You think I'm going to let you get another kid killed? Think I won't smash your teeth down your throat?"

"I'm telling you, I don't—"

Wade closed his fist meaningfully.

"Wait!" Ned cringed, blubbering. It was awful to watch, but not as awful as what I feared might be happening now, out on the water.

"Okay, look." Ned was breathing hard. "I was just supposed to watch you, so he could get a head start."

"Willoughby?" I put the gun into my bag and slung the bag over my shoulder, worried about what I might do with the weapon if I were holding it and Ned told me anything too terrible.

"Y-yes. He doesn't even care about the money anymore. He just wants to get away."

"The money we found on Crow Island?" I asked. "That was his stash? But what was it doing out there?"

Ned gulped a frightened breath. "Willoughby stockpiled cash. I'd bring it from New York, he'd stash it in his barn, and then when there was a big bunch of it, Ken took it out on his boat."

He frowned, appearing to think hard. "But he must've gotten nervous after he had Ken killed. If anyone came asking questions about Ken, I guess Willoughby didn't want the money to be around his place, just in case."

That made some sense, especially if the deaths were part of a general reins-tightening program: shut big mouths, remove incriminating materials, etc. "So he told you to find another hiding place."

Ned shook his head. "No. Ike—he told Ike to do it.

And it was the last I ever saw of Ike, so until you two found the money on the island, I thought *he* had taken it."

"But now the police have it, so Willoughby owes some very nasty guys some very big bucks," I theorized. "Money he's got no way to repay, and no time to figure out a way, either. Which he knows, because you called him and told him. So he's running."

Ned nodded. "I helped flush him out, actually," he ventured.

"Yeah, Ned. You were a big help," I told him sarcastically, and he withered at my tone; under other circumstances I might have found it satisfying.

"What about Sam," Wade demanded again.

"Willoughby knows Arnold will be onto him about the murders, too," Ned replied, "about hiring Ike for them, I mean, and for all I know killing Ike, afterwards."

I stared at him.

"Well, Ike hasn't showed up, has he?" Ned said defensively. "Anyway, Willoughby's snuck away from that British guy who was watching him. He's got your boy—said he heard from the crew on the *Triple Witch* that the kid had been hanging around. He told 'em to invite him on board."

He gulped, sniffling. "So I guess that's where he must be."

Wade seized him by the collar. "With Willoughby on the *Triple Witch,* headed out to sea? What's he going to do with him, Ned?"

"Nothing! He promised . . . he promised he wouldn't hurt him!"

Wade let go of Ned's collar; Ned slumped, fingering his throat. "Willoughby says the British guy's on his way back to New York—that he's already called *his* bosses. But they'll be too late. And Willoughby's promised to set your boy adrift in a life raft, as soon as

Willoughby's safely away. So the kid'll be all right. Mr. Willoughby *promised.*"

Great: a promise from Willoughby. Somehow I didn't think I could put much faith in that.

Because I'd ruined him.

Twice. And he knew it. And now . . .

Now it was payback time.

Wade seized Ned by his shoulders and held him for a moment, visibly deciding whether or not to break his neck. Then with a sharp exhalation of revulsion and dismay, he shoved Ned into his chair again. "You don't *understand,*" Ned wailed.

But I did understand, although of course by now it was way too late: for the Mumfords and Hallie Quinn, for Ike Forepaugh, and possibly for Peter Mulligan, too.

I only hoped that by some unlikely chance or blessing it was not too late for Sam.

 Ellie pulled the Land Rover to a halt and swung out of the cab. I grabbed my satchel containing my cell phone, the Bisley, and the smaller weapon; for this kind of emergency I had not known what I might need, and I'd have brought along an elephant gun if I'd had one.

She was already in the boat by the time I got onto the finger pier. I jumped in, she gave the starter cord a pull, and we were away. Aiming the boat past the dock's end she turned to starboard, gunning the Evinrude; the boat's prow lifted, then settled as we ran northeastward, toward the light on Deer Island.

The water was as bright as aluminum foil, the moon overhead so luminous that it blotted out the stars. But to the southwest at Lubec, an ominous pale curtain turned the bridge lamps to smeary gleams, and on the horizon the clouds marched, darkly threatening, into Passamaquoddy Bay.

I waved at the ominous-looking front. Ellie nodded in reply. "I checked the weather radio," she called. "Line of squalls. We might have to make land, later. But we're okay for right now."

Fabulous. Even if Willoughby kept his unlikely promise and set Sam adrift, a life raft wouldn't last long in heavy seas. And Sam was a good swimmer, but you don't have to drown, around here, to die in the icy water; even in summer, hypothermia can get you long before your energy gives out.

"Wade's down at the Coast Guard station, now," I shouted over the roar of the outboard. The boat slammed through the increasing wave action as we approached Old Sow. The whirlpool, shoving and sucking with the force of a billion gallons of water, can lift a ferry six feet out of the water, then slurp it swirlingly downward the same distance. There is even an Old Sow Survivors' Club.

Which, I gathered, I was about to join; Ellie made no move to avoid the worst of the turbulence, and I swallowed my protest.

"We see his lights, I'm going to get on the phone to him."

Willoughby, I meant; under the threat of another headslap from Wade, Montague had given me the number to raise the *Triple Witch*.

"I've got to try," I shouted, gripping the gunwales as the water beneath us churned, "to negotiate. It won't do any good in the long run but it might stall him."

The Evinrude's prop whined as it flew up out of the water, strained and gurgled laboriously as it bit into the chop again. A green wave rose up and slapped me chillingly in the face, filling my mouth with salt.

"Right," Ellie called. To handle the boat in this water was a muscle-busting task, but her voice betrayed no trace of the strain she was putting forth. "There they are."

The *Triple Witch* looked lit up like a Christmas tree. "They're beyond Head Harbor's light."

"I see." Ellie's reply was grim, underlining what I already knew: zooming around Passamaquoddy Bay in an open boat was one thing in daylight and good weather, something else in darkness with a line of squalls marching in. We could follow for as long as our fuel lasted, but if we did, we'd be too far from shore to make land when the storm hit us.

Ellie gunned the Evinrude through the last turbulence, then cursed as we struck a vicious eddy. The boat swerved, tilting as water hammered over the stern, twisting the wooden craft nastily before sucking it abruptly downward. For a horrid instant the seas loomed *above* me on both sides, preparing to swallow us.

Then we bobbed up as, capriciously, the bay spat us out again. When I looked back at Ellie, she was drenched, her red hair plastered to her neck, her white fist gripping the throttle.

"Golly bejesus," she grated out through a clenched grin.

The fog advanced stealthily, thickening as it came, and the new calm settling on the water felt unnatural. Dead ahead, the tall white shape of the Head Harbor lighthouse loomed like a ghostly pillar, its brilliant beam strafing the rocks and the entrance to the harbor. Between the jagged rocks of the lighthouse promontory and land's end was a wide patch of inky darkness.

"I'm calling," I said, fumbling for the cell phone, "before he spots us and does something hasty."

I didn't let the thought continue as I punched in the codes. Willoughby was going to set Sam adrift, all right, but I doubted he'd bother with a life raft. Sam's only chance was to be alive when he hit the water, and for us to get him out before the cold killed him. Otherwise, he was—

"Fish food." Willoughby's voice came clearly through the cellular, full of its usual arrogance. "That's what this kid of yours is going to be, if you keep being uncooperative."

I swallowed hard. "Come on, Willoughby, you can't expect me not to try to get him back. That's all I'm doing out here, so why don't you just let me come and get him?"

"No." He snapped it out furiously. "I said all I want is to get away clean, and I meant it. I said I'd drop the kid in a raft. And I'll keep my promise," he lied smoothly, "unless you get in my way, Jacobia Tiptree."

He said my name as if spitting out mouthfuls of filthy stuff. "The way," he added chillingly, "you did, before."

"Listen, Willoughby, all that was just business. You had a job, I had one, too. You know how it is, nothing personal."

As soon as I'd said it, I wished I hadn't. To Willoughby, his business *was* personal, and so was his hatred of me. I could hear it in the bitterness of his reply.

"Sure." His chuckle was like a drop of poison. "But that's not how Dysbart sees it. I can't replace that money. His bosses have recalled him while things are in an uproar here. But he'll be back to kill me if he can. It's his job."

"Dysbart?" The name rang a bell, ominously:

Never seen, shadowy and deadly, an enforcer. When I'd had the guard dog, back in Manhattan, it was Reginald Dysbart the dog was guarding against.

Willoughby's voice changed threateningly. "Just stay back. Let me hear that engine of yours throttle down."

I waved at Ellie; she twisted the throttle lower. The little wooden boat slowed sickeningly, keeping me from getting nearer to Sam. Keeping Willoughby where he wanted to be: in control.

"I don't have to get much farther. I've got a plane waiting in Canada, you don't need to know where. So just stay back and I'll read you our coordinates, so you can locate the life raft."

He read me the numbers and letters that would place him on a chart; I scribbled them, squinting as the gathering clouds pulled a shroud over the moon.

"I'll signal you. And then you can come and get him where I've put him into the water."

It wouldn't be that easy even if Willoughby did what he said. Once they got here, the Coast Guard could use the coordinates to create a search sector. But the currents were terrific, the tide was flowing, and the wind kept rising; Sam could drift quite a distance before anyone found him.

If they did. Time was what I needed; time and a clear thought. What did this bastard want?

Revenge, of course: to hit me where it hurt. He wanted to see Sam go into the water, but more, Willoughby wanted *me* to see it.

Then he would be happy, because Baxter Willoughby at heart was the equivalent of a playground bully. It wasn't enough just to do bad things; someone had to know.

That was how I'd caught him the first time; he hadn't covered his tracks quite well enough. Willoughby always had wanted someone to know how clever he'd been, how powerful he was.

So: he was a bully and a braggart, and he was impatient. None of these qualities, combined with his current desperation, made me feel confident of our prospects.

But they were something. "Throttle up," I told Ellie. "Let's get out there right now."

In the last of the moonlight, her eyebrows went up, but she did it. "Hey," Willoughby's protest barked from the cell phone.

"We're coming out," I told him. "I want to see my

son alive before I agree to anything. Once I do, we'll back off. We won't interfere with you. But first I want to see Sam on deck, under a light, so I know it's him and that he's okay."

Grudgingly, Willoughby assented. But I heard the falseness in his voice, the hint of glee he was too thrilled to be able to conceal. It was working out just as he'd hoped; I was chasing him, he thought, until he'd caught me.

In only a few minutes, he could have his precious revenge. He could watch me as I watched my son die. For that, I knew, was what Baxter Willoughby intended: to make sure Sam never came out of the icy water again.

Up ahead, the light at Head Harbor solidified into a slowly revolving silvery sword, cutting through the darkness. I could see rocks at the foot of the promontory, waves crashing against them, sending up gouts of foam.

Ellie steered suddenly at them. "Get up in the prow," she ordered quietly. "Do it," she said.

"But—" I waved the cell phone. "Willoughby's waiting for us. We don't have to—"

"Waiting, yeah." Her voice was harsh with skepticism. "Not a brilliant move on his part, though. Do you want to give him time to figure that out, and change his mind?"

The cliffs rose up on either side of us. It was just past half-tide. The thunder of the water through the constriction between island and promontory rose over the sound of the Evinrude. Beyond, the *Triple Witch* idled, illuminated by her deck lights.

"Have you ever really done this before?" I yelled, trying to keep the panic out of my voice.

Ellie shook her head vigorously.

"No. But Kenny did. Half-tide or higher, he said. Kenny," she finished, gunning the engine harder, "told me all about it."

Straight ahead, the narrows yawned at us, dark, and studded with jagged rocks. The boat lurched forward, as from its bottom came a sickening scrape that sent me scrambling up onto the bow, clinging frozenly as Ellie trimmed the engine, yanking its prop up so it spun in empty air, howling.

There was a crunch, like a bone breaking. A wave caught us, sending the little boat careening. Overhead, the lighthouse loomed massively out of the darkness, its lamp a white, wide-open eye, its tower a tilting club about to smash down.

And then, unbelievably, we were out of it. The boat shot ahead as its prop bit water again, hurling me in a heap off the slippery prow to the floor. As I hauled myself up I saw Ellie's fist thrust into the spray, a grin of defiance on her face, and I heard her laugh of triumph. In that moment, despite the water seeping between the floorboards, I was glad we had done it.

But then reality set in again. "Drat," Ellie said, spotting the seeping water. We were approaching the *Triple Witch*.

"Whatever you're going to do, don't waste time," she said. "We've got about twenty minutes, ten of which we'll need getting ashore, preferably before those squalls hit."

She waved to starboard. The clouds were nearly upon us, wind gusts already slicing foam off the wave tops. A spatter of chilly drizzle slapped me, tasting of salt.

The *Triple Witch* rose alongside us, white as a glacier. "Back off a little," I said.

Ellie reversed the engine, and with a low gurgle the little boat pulled back. Now I could see Baxter Willoughby peering over the cruiser's side at us, surprised and annoyed.

Just that one glimpse of his face told me Ellie had been right. Willoughby had done the math on his little plan, realized that the deluxe brand of revenge he coveted might cost too much. Better, he'd decided, to get away clean and fast.

If we'd waited, taken the time to go around the narrows, Sam would already have been in the water, Willoughby's look said.

But now here we were.

"Hope he's got his affairs in order," Willoughby taunted.

Behind Willoughby, I spotted the terrified face of one of his crew, some poor twenty-something kid still sporting the last of his spring-break Florida tan. The face vanished suddenly; so much for any help.

Then Sam walked out onto the foredeck.

Blindfolded, and with his hands tied behind his back.

The way we were situated in the water relative to the *Triple Witch*, Sam was only about thirty feet away, and getting nearer by the moment. But he might as well have been on the moon.

"Keep walking," Willoughby shouted, and Sam did, one careful footstep after another.

Then I saw the glint of the weapon in Willoughby's hand. As he turned to make sure Sam was doing as he'd ordered, I stuck my own hand into my satchel and came up with the Bisley.

Damn. The boat lurched, sending my bag tumbling away from me. It came to rest at Ellie's feet. In it was the little .25 caliber semiautomatic.

The one with the real bullets in it. We'd raced out so fast, I'd forgotten completely about the dummies I'd loaded into the Bisley, back at the firing range. And now I couldn't get at the satchel again without Willoughby seeing me do it.

"I could try," Ellie muttered.

Shooting at Willoughby, she meant. She wanted to, very badly. But that wouldn't do a lick of good. I didn't need her to shoot *at* him; what I needed was for her to hit him.

And she couldn't. The distance and heaving water

only made it worse: moving sight picture, moving target.

"Thanks anyway," I muttered back. "But in this mess, I'm not even sure that I can hit him."

Sam loomed over me; he was almost at the tip of the *Triple Witch*'s prow. I had no idea how he was keeping his balance.

"You've seen him," Willoughby crowed. "My side of the deal."

Which had always been a sham. He wasn't leaning over the side anymore. He was amidships, where he could be certain of hitting his own target. And where I couldn't hit him.

From far away came the whine of the Coast Guard's *Zodiac*, cutting through the rain at us. A sudden burst of wind blew us sideways and hit Sam hard, making him totter.

He was there, clearly in view, and Willoughby wasn't.

One chance.

"And *now*—" Willoughby's voice was exultant. When the *Triple Witch* heeled over in the next gust, I glimpsed him trying to draw a bead on Sam. Then he was gone again and all I could see was my son, like the silhouette on a paper target.

I raised the Bisley as our little boat bobbed up and down, and so did the *Triple Witch*. The wind was blowing harder, now: another way for the unsteady sight picture to be made more meaningless, the bullet carried sideways.

But I didn't think about that. What I thought about was the dummy bullet, filled with wax and ketchup: the way that, at fifty yards out on the firing range, it had missed the center target by only about three inches.

And I thought about a landlubber's slipknot.

It wasn't something I wanted to count on, but Sam didn't move when I shouted. He couldn't hear me through the rising storm.

Willoughby appeared again, leveling the weapon, vanished. The Bisley jumped in my hand, its report swallowed by the roar of wind and water.

Sam went over the side.

Almost instantly, Willoughby's face showed again, twisted in rage. "You bitch!" he shouted, leaning over the rail, not knowing quite what had happened, only that I had somehow spoiled his fun.

I fired again, fast, and it was easier this time: straight up, not much distance, the movement of the little boat in synch with the bigger vessel.

A bloom of crimson exploded on Willoughby's shirt. He straightened, his hands patting weakly, dabbing at the red stuff.

Ellie hit the throttle, unmindful of the cold water rising to our ankles; the little boat wasn't going to last much longer.

"Sam!" I shouted into the sheets of icy rain.

Waves as sharp as arrowheads raced at us, driven by the wind. Every whitecap came up masquerading as a face, and wasn't.

"Sam!" No sight of him, only the water, slamming us against the cruiser's side and hauling us out again as the Evinrude struggled and the break in the little boat's bottom widened alarmingly.

Ellie grabbed a flare from the box under her seat and fired. Its sudden chemical brilliance sizzled upward, arcing against the violence of the storm clouds and reflecting a sick, sodium-yellow glare off the heaving water.

Minutes went by. I couldn't hear the *Zodiac* anymore, and there was still no help from the crew of the *Triple Witch*. And then:

"Mom . . ."

A ghastly, waterlogged whisper. In the next instant, a hand flopped bonelessly over the side of the boat, and I grabbed it and pulled hard.

"Sam!" The hand was followed by the rest of him, clambering and choking, his body a shivering mass of gooseflesh, his teeth chattering uncontrollably with a rattle like dice being shaken in a cup.

The blindfold had come off. His eyes were rolled partway up into his head. His hands clenched stiffly in front of him, corpselike, as his muscles, too chilled to respond to signals from his nervous system, achieved a single position and stuck there.

"We've got to get him to shore," I said, but I knew it was too late to do it in our boat. The water in it was up to my knees, and I couldn't feel my feet anymore, only a dull aching that transformed to hammering agony the minute I noticed it.

An odd whine filled the darkness around us, a sound I didn't recognize. All I knew was that the break in the boat had gotten suddenly much larger. We were going down.

Bright light blinded me. Ellie threw a life cushion at me. The Evinrude foundered and conked out. Then we were floating, the little boat sliding away underneath us, leaving us in the water.

Sam gasped once, his body spasming powerfully, and I lost the life cushion trying to hang onto him.

Then I lost him, too. I wanted to swim but the cold paralyzed me, punching a fistful of frigid salt water down my windpipe. I was sinking, drowning and disbelieving, fighting to the surface, sucking in a frantic breath of air.

Turning all the while to try to spot him, my eardrums still pierced by the whining sound. Somewhere Ellie was shouting, then not shouting. The life cushion smacked me and I clutched it in arms that had frozen lumps at the end of them, not hands.

In the next instant, hugging the life cushion, I was not drowning anymore. But Sam was gone.

Sam.

Wade stripped the wet clothes off me and muscled me into a bathtub on board the *Triple Witch*. The warm water in the tub felt scalding, but it could not penetrate the misery iced into my bones.

All I could do was weep and wish I had drowned.

"Drink this." Wade thrust a cup at me, then pressed it to my lips when I couldn't hold it.

I spat the spiked hot drink out into the bathwater.

Wade kept talking, saying things I couldn't make sense of. I thought he'd been saying them for a while. But I could only see Sam falling, feel him slipping away from me.

"Jacobia. Listen to me. We got him aboard the *Zodiac* before we found you. It's why *you* couldn't find *him*. Ellie's in the next cabin, she's okay, too. Now will you drink this?"

A shudder went through me. "You're not just saying that? You wouldn't lie to me?" I searched his face.

"As God is my witness, I saw him. I've pulled guys out of the water, Jacobia. He needed attention. But he'll be all right."

I pressed the cup against my mouth, and forced myself to try drinking. A little of it managed to go down.

"The Bisley . . . did I hurt Sam? I didn't see where it hit him. I was afraid I might have put his eye out."

Now that I wasn't dying, or Sam, either, I saw the richness of the *Triple Witch*'s bathing facilities: gleaming fixtures, a huge porcelain tub, ceramic tiles. Heaps of towels embroidered with the monogram *BW* piled on a chair upholstered in gold brocade.

"I got his wet stuff off him," Wade said, "and wrapped him up in some blankets before the *Zodiac* left. I didn't see any marks on him anywhere. I looked him over pretty good."

I swallowed more tea, as Wade ran more hot water into the tub. "Maybe the water soaked the ketchup off," I said.

Wade squinted puzzledly at me. The worst of the chill I'd suffered was seeping out slowly, so that now I was only shivering instead of shuddering.

"I didn't," he repeated, "see that Sam was hit anywhere."

I couldn't stop shivering, though. "What about Willoughby?"

Wade turned away momentarily, then looked straight at me.

"Willoughby's dead. The blow to the chest, from the dummy bullet. I didn't get a very good look at him. But from what the medic aboard the *Zodiac* said, the impact stopped his heart."

At his words a terrible feeling came over me, as if I had taken what I thought was a simple step, and instead walked off the edge of a building.

"I killed him? You mean, I shot him and killed him? But I'd never meant to—"

I wanted to go back, put the tape on rewind, just run it all backwards and try it all over again.

Not shoot anybody. Or not kill anybody. In the heat of the moment I'd been ready to, but the moment had passed. In the end it had been enough to think that I could kid a kidder if my bullets were loaded with wax and ketchup.

But now the joke was on me.

Later, in the adjoining stateroom, I found Ellie pulling on a monogrammed sweatsuit that didn't fit her.

Shakily, she managed a grin. "Sorry about the bumpy ride. I guess the water was deeper out there, back when Kenny did it."

Or maybe old Kenny had been full of beans. But I was not going to say that to her now. "The ride was fine. You got us there. That's what counted."

I sat on the bunk, feeling the cruiser's engines rumble into life, noticing the tiny lurch that meant the craft was moving. Ellie peered into the gilt-trimmed mirror, brushing her red hair.

"You were right about Willoughby. He could have killed us when he caught us, out at his place," she said. "Or let that British guy do it, before Wade got there. But he didn't."

She gave a last critical squint at her face and turned. "Like you said, he wasn't the physical type. Not until you had him backed into a corner, and he had a personal reason to hurt you," she said, "did he really get dangerous."

But somebody had.

"So I guess there's one more conversation I still need to have," she finished mildly.

She sounded so serene and untroubled, you'd have had to know her well to realize what she meant by the innocent-sounding word: *conversation*.

But I did. Know her pretty well, I mean. And boy, was I ever glad she wasn't planning to have that conversation with me.

 The recuperative powers of a sixteen-year-old boy are miraculous; by the time we reached my house a few hours later, Sam had telephoned to say that he was fine, he was hungry, and he was coming home just as soon as the doctors at the hospital in Calais finished marveling over him.

By the way, he added, did we have any lunch meat? Because what he was really hungry for, if I could arrange it, was a good old-fashioned hero sandwich.

"Sam," I said. "I'm so sorry. That I had to shoot at you, I mean. But it was the only way I could get you off the deck of that boat, out of Willoughby's line of fire. I was just terrified that I would put your eye out. But I couldn't help it."

Silence over the telephone. "Uh, Mom? Listen, I don't want to, like, ruin your confidence in your marksmanship or anything."

Behind me, George Valentine came in whistling and grabbed Ellie, and hugged her hard, and waltzed her around the kitchen.

"But," Sam said, "you didn't shoot me off that boat."

"I didn't?"

"Mom," Sam said patiently. "I've been on boats before, you know? I like, kind of know my way around them."

Which, for Sam, was like saying that monkeys know their way around trees.

"I knew," he went on, "where I was. Out on the bow, there. And I couldn't hear you, but I heard him yelling at you, so I knew you were nearby. Boy, was I glad about that."

I swallowed hard. "So?"

"So when I finally did hear you and smelled water beneath me, I jumped. I knew," Sam finished, "that you would save me."

"What about the rope?" I asked quietly, wanting suddenly to change the subject. "The one around your hands?"

"Hey," Sam replied scornfully. "That jerk, I saw him fumbling with the line. He couldn't tie a decent knot to save his life. I was never worried about that."

And then it hit him. "Hey. You mean you *shot* at me?"

"Never mind," I said, thinking about my son jumping blindly into the water with his hands tied behind his back, confident that he could get out of a landlubber's knot.

And that I would save him. "Do you want mayonnaise on your sandwich, or mustard?"

And he said both, so I phoned Leighton's to ask if they could put one together for me, and then asked

George if he could go pick it up, and he agreed to, remarking that he was feeling a little peckish, himself, and should he also pick up a bag of doughnuts and some Coca-Colas while he was there?

"And then—" Ellie's voice came from the kitchen— "*then* we all landed in the water!"

Ned Montague reacted with amusement, as she had intended. After all, driving a truck wasn't an awful crime; especially if, as he insisted, he hadn't known till near the end what was in it. We couldn't prove Ned had sold any heroin, either; it was his word against ours. And even Mulligan hadn't been sure it was Ned on the seawall, the night Hallie died.

It was Willoughby who'd tried to kill Sam, Mulligan who'd as good as confessed to killing Hallie, and the dreaded Ike Forepaugh—according to Ned, anyway— who was responsible for the Mumfords' deaths.

So that Ned, despite our earlier anger at him, was feeling good again. Arnold had jollied Ned along while we were out on the water, too, assuring Ned once more that nothing he'd admitted to—if, that is, he cooperated now—would be used too harshly against him.

"Haw-haw," Ned said. "You girls must've been fit to be tied."

He pulled the pop-top on another beer can and guzzled. "Good thing that Coast Guard boat was on its way. Hate to have to drag a couple pretty things like you outta that cold water, drowned."

The porch door opened: Arnold, returning from talking to the *Triple Witch*'s young crew. When she heard him, Ellie took the beer can from Ned. "No, you wouldn't hate it," she said.

She emptied the can into the sink. "In fact, Ned, I think that's exactly what you would like. After all," she went on, "you have already tried killing Jacobia, once."

Ned blinked, puzzled by her tone, and by the sudden change in the atmosphere. "What? Hey, what're you saying?"

Arnold stepped into the kitchen.

"You shot at her," Ellie said, "with your hunting rifle. The one Peter Mulligan found right here in this house, while you were in the cellar. But whose was it? Not Wade's, or Jacobia's. And it had to come from somewhere."

"Wade," I remembered aloud, "told me you once had an old deer rifle."

The gun was now in Arnold's office, locked up as evidence until he could decide who was going to get charged with what.

Ellie aimed a steady finger at Ned. "*Which* you had brought to use on us, if you couldn't talk your way out of the mess you were in, and if you could, you'd say you brought it for Wade to check it out for you. That's why you left it upstairs, so you didn't have to commit yourself until you knew which way the conversation would go. Isn't that right?"

Ned flushed, realizing suddenly that he had been in Arnold's custody—or ours—since we found out he'd warned Willoughby.

"The same rifle," Ellie went on, "you probably used to kill Ike Forepaugh, because if no one ever found Ike he'd keep getting blamed for everything, wouldn't he? Suspicion wouldn't turn," she finished meaningfully, "to you."

"Gossip was true, for once," Arnold said. "There's a body been dug up on Crow Island and it sure looks like Forepaugh."

Arnold turned slowly. "Met him after he got away from us, did you, Ned? Maybe he even called you for help. You tell him you would drive him somewhere, get him out of town? Want to bet we match a bullet?"

"You ever register that old rifle, Ned?" Wade asked.

"Y-yes," Ned replied, too scared suddenly to lie. "But—"

"When you saw Jacobia heading for Dennysville that morning," Ellie pressed on, "when *you* were on your way back to Eastport, you jumped to the conclusion that her trip must have something to do with Ken's death, because *you* had a guilty conscience. And you got scared, so you decided to take her out of the picture."

"You didn't go all the way back to town. Instead you hid in the brush on Carlow Island and waited for me to come back," I said, recalling now having seen his car that day.

"But," Ellie finished, "you're not a great shot. You missed."

Montague stared. "That's—that's not true!"

"You'd already started insinuating yourself into Ken's life," Ellie said, "when he started paying his bills with the proceeds of the drug trips. Ken was keeping his head down pretty well, but you smelled money and wanted to know where it was coming from."

Ned made a disparaging sound. "Nickels and dimes, from that little blonde's dope deals. She'd met some guy in Portland, he wanted her to distribute. She'd lined Ken up for the boat work. They were the criminals," he protested, "not me."

So I'd been right. It was Hallie behind the drug smuggling.

"Nickels and dimes were more than you were earning," Ellie pointed out. "But then Ken made his mistake. He let you in on his bigger deal, didn't he? Because Ken didn't have a driver's license and Willoughby couldn't tolerate that."

Ned's soft lips pouted sullenly. This was all too accurate for his comfort.

"There you were, having to share this great racket with your loser cousin. Who'd miss him? And you needed the money. So Ken had to go," Ellie said, "because you wanted the whole thing for yourself. Then Tim started talking about Ken's 'big deal,' the only one Tim knew about. He meant drug runs for Hallie, but you were afraid he meant the money runs and you couldn't risk that."

She took a deep breath. "On Willoughby's orders, you took his money stash out to Crow Island and hid it in plain sight, ready for the next leg of the journey, using the dog food sacks Tim had saved up so carefully. That must have been when you killed Tim."

But Tim's dying, I thought, hadn't been on Willoughby's order. Why hide money at a death scene? No, the old man's "suicide" had been all Ned's idea. The guy was as bluntly purposeful—and as blindly stupid—as a tunneling grub.

The old man might know something. Besides, Ned wanted the island. Case closed.

"You even used Ken's boat to get out there," Arnold said, "didn't you?"

Ellie and Arnold had figured it out long before me. It was why Arnold had kept Ned calm all evening; so Ned wouldn't run.

"That trip was a way to get the money away from Willoughby's place, where it was making him nervous, out into a convenient spot," Ellie went on, "*and* it was a dry run with the boat, for you. A short run before you had to attempt the big project."

Ned had begun to sweat, his eyes darting anxiously around the room. But Arnold blocked his only escape route.

"What you didn't realize," Ellie added, "was that anyone would try to take care of Tim's dogs, because it wasn't something you'd have bothered doing. They weren't valuable dogs like Cosmo. You didn't think anyone would find the money or Tim's body so fast."

"But I *told* you, if anyone did all that, it must've been Ike. This—this is libel! Or slander! Isn't it?" Ned turned, his eyes appealing to Bob Arnold.

"Right, Ned," Ellie said scathingly. "I guess Ike Forepaugh probably kidnapped the Lindbergh baby, too. And after that, he shot himself, and buried himself. Quite a guy."

"Crow Island," Arnold added, "makes a better place to start from, if you're smuggling something. Set out from the cove at the north end of it, nobody on shore here sees your heading."

"Tim wouldn't have suspected you," Ellie said, resuming her attack. "With his crippled leg, he must have been an easy victim. And I guess you're the only guy besides Willoughby in fifty miles, can't tie a decent slipknot. And then there was Hallie."

Her eyes shone with anger. "First you sweet-talked her, gave her gifts, probably. Made promises. She was too young to know that a guy like you couldn't really do anything for her. To her, you probably looked like her ticket out. Didn't you?"

Ned squirmed at her tone. "Then you started blackmailing her for those nickels and dimes, I suppose," Ellie went on. "If she didn't pay, you'd tell Arnold. That's why she kept meeting you."

"But after Ken died," I put in, "you took it all. You found her stash in Ken's car and appropriated it, just the way you did his boat."

Montague looked trapped. "You can't prove any of this. You just want somebody to blame for it. And with *you* here—"

He glared at Arnold. "I think I ought to have a lawyer."

Arnold shook his head innocently. "Me? I just stopped by for a cup of coffee. Haven't asked a single question."

"Yeah, well, I'm not saying anything more." Montague's chin thrust out belligerently as he got to his feet again.

Ellie stepped up to him. "Ken Mumford," she told him softly, "was a loser, like you thought."

She stuck her finger in Ned's chest. "But you know

what? He had dreams, and I remember them. He was worth ten of you."

Before he could stop her she'd reached down into his jacket pocket, and I saw her fingers close on something there.

"Hallie argued with someone that night on the seawall," she told Arnold, still staring at Ned. "But when Mulligan approached, that person faded into the shadows. After that, Hallie rejected Mulligan again. But Mulligan never really said he killed her, did he? She sent Mulligan away," Ellie said. "And then . . ."

Her hand came out of Ned's pocket, her fingers wrapped around the silver medallion.

". . . someone else killed her, tipped her body over the seawall, rolled it to the water of the boat basin, and dumped it in the nearest bait bin. The question is, why? There was no reason to move that body."

"Or," she turned to Ned, "was there?"

His face had gone fishbelly white. "I wanted—" he began.

"Shut up, Ned," Wade advised, his expression one of disgust mingled with pity.

I took the medallion from Ellie. "You know, this chain is just like the one I wear," I said. "I noticed it when Hallie came over here. And it's the very devil to open. Especially," I added, "if you can't see it. Say, in the darkness on the seawall. And the nearest light is under the big lamps, by the boat basin."

"I only wanted it back," Ned said sullenly. "It's silver. She'd just end up shooting it in her arm. Only she wouldn't give it to me."

"Still, why risk being seen near her body afterwards just to get a piece of jewelry?" I asked.

His answering look at me was hateful.

"Because," I theorized, "the risk of leaving it was even greater? As it would be, for instance—"

I turned the medallion over. "If your initials and Hallie's were scratched on the back."

And there they were. Good old Hallie: maybe she wasn't the brightest bulb in the chandelier, but she was consistent: initials everywhere. And the way it turned out, she might as well have carved an "M" for *murderer* in Ned's forehead.

"You're related to two of the victims," I said. "You couldn't afford to be linked to a third. Once she was dead, you *had* to get the medallion."

"You don't . . ." he began hopelessly.

I tossed the thing at Arnold, who caught it without taking his gaze from Ned. Like I say, Arnold can be quick when he wants to be.

He hadn't spooked Willoughby, even though I felt certain Clarissa had told Arnold all that I had reported to her. And although while Ned was here with us, Arnold had stayed away doing all the other things he had to do, he'd showed up double-fast when we'd called to say we were leaving Ned alone.

And he was here for the finish. "How'd *you* know?" I asked him, as he applied his handcuffs to a silent, subdued Ned Montague.

Arnold snapped the bracelets shut. "Wouldn't say I *knew*. But it was the gash in Ken's boat for starters. And the dinghy. Ken would never've had such a thing, but there it was, stowed up like it'd always been there. I kept asking how those things linked."

"You can't *prove* . . ." Ned protested weakly, but Arnold just talked over him.

"Simple answer that covered everything was that somebody'd got out to the boat on the dinghy. Killed Ken, then grounded the boat by accident."

He turned Ned around a little more roughly than was strictly necessary. "Somebody had to change his plan, jump off, walk home. Meant to use the dinghy to get away but he couldn't, and he sure didn't want to be seen dragging it. So he stowed it, make it look like it belonged."

"It wasn't my dinghy," Ned objected. "I never had one. Never even saw it."

"Really?" Arnold responded, and dropped his bombshell.

"So how come we found a receipt for it in the household trash you dumped, out at South End? Stuff with your name on it, receipt all torn in pieces, but we put it back together, me and Al Rollins."

Arnold shook his head scornfully. "Your problem, Ned," he finished, "is that you are a cheap bastard, and a greedy bastard. And also, you are a dumb bastard. Should've spent the money Willoughby paid you on something for your kids, 'stead of that dinghy. Or you should've burnt the receipt."

I remembered the overflowing trash cans out at Ned's place. But Al Rollins had just collected. The trash wouldn't have been there if Ned hadn't been disposing of it some other way. Dumping it, for instance, illegally.

"You suspected him all along, didn't you?" I asked Arnold. "That's why you stuck so hard to saying you thought it was Ike. And why you downplayed my getting shot at. So Ned, here, wouldn't suspect he was already on the hot seat, and maybe take off before you could get him dead to rights."

Arnold shrugged. "Something like that. Because look: after the boat's run aground, later the tide comes in, frees the boat up, she's found drifting. So I asked myself, who around here could ground a boat like that? A scrape's one thing but nobody hits hard enough to make such a dent on purpose. Because sure, it floats now, but sooner or later it'll cost money to fix. And when I added up two and two, Ned kept making four. The receipt only put the frosting on it."

Arnold glanced at Ellie, meanwhile giving Ned a small shove. " 'Course, it didn't hurt, you mentioning Willoughby to Clarissa, then I find out who's driving the truck for him. Ned being hooked up with Willoughby *and* being the lousiest boat handler in Washington County *and* being a guy who will pollute the whole world with his trash, just to save two lousy bucks a week . . ."

He sighed. "Come on, buddy. And if you're thinking of doing anything else stupid, keep in mind that I'm carrying my service revolver. I don't want," he added with quiet emphasis, "any more prisoners escaping."

"Hey, Ned," I called as they prepared to depart.

I couldn't help it; I just had to know. "How'd the llamas get into the money?"

Because first it was out on Crow Island, and after that the cops had it, for evidence. It had been a couple of days between the time that money was at Willoughby's, and the llama spat it at Ned. So . . .

Ned turned, replying bitterly. "They didn't. That slime-gob you saw on me the other night? And I knew it, I *knew* you'd seen it, and I *knew* it would get you going. Both of you are just so damn nosy. But I couldn't *do* anything about it—"

His fists clenched in thwarted fury. "It wasn't even Willoughby's cash on my sweater. That was *my* money. I'd dropped a dollar bill I was planning to use for the tolls, on the way to New York. One of 'em grabbed it. Chewed it, and—"

Nothing like a well-aimed spitball to ruin your day. And, in Ned's case, your whole life.

He looked poisonous. "It was the llamas I should've used the damn rifle on, not—"

Then he stopped, realizing what he'd almost said.

"Everybody gets away with everything. Everyone but me," he complained on his way out the door.

I could have argued the point. For one thing, I was going to be in a lot of trouble about Willoughby, once it got sorted out exactly how he'd died. I was betting on involuntary manslaughter, and although under the circumstances I would probably be off the hook about it eventually, getting off would be no picnic.

More sobering, though, was the growing knowledge that I would never be off the hook about it with myself.

And at that moment—and ever since; not a day goes by that I don't think about Baxter Willoughby—the only one I wanted to talk to about it was Kenny Mumford.

Even now I remember him downtown on a Sunday morning, parked on the bench in front of Wadsworth's hardware store, red-eyed and miserably hung over. Thinking, maybe, about some of the things he had done, maybe even wanting to change them.

Wishing; knowing he couldn't.

I think Kenny would understand.

50 The Fourth of July celebration was muted that year, by the murders and by the arrest of Ned Montague. We didn't have the pirate-battle tableau, either, on account of Fake Death having turned out not to be so fake, after all. And finally, on the morning after Ken Mumford's funeral, Felicity Abbot-Jones turned out not to be what any of us had expected.

"Fishing boats," she noted, glancing with approval at the vessels bobbing in the little boat basin.

She was a large, gorgeously flamboyant woman of fifty or so, with flaming hennaed hair, blue eyes peering from behind thick-lensed tortoiseshell glasses, and a brisk manner.

"Real working ones, not just rich men's toys. How," she finished, making a note in her notebook, "authentic."

Driven by Ellie, accompanied by me, and not seeming to notice the discomforts of Ellie's old Land Rover, Felicity directed us to Estes Head, where the construc-

tion of a brand-new, 635-foot dock for container vessels was nearly finished, the men working on it earning
triple-time on account of the holiday.

Pile drivers thudded, cranes swung on flatboats, and
trucks beetled hurriedly around the massive site; the
Estes Head project was thoroughly modern, and Ellie
and I held our breath.

"Progress." Felicity jotted appreciatively in her notebook. "The nineteenth century was an age of progress,
you know. Oh, yes, this is *most* encouraging."

I looked at Ellie, who carefully didn't look at me, so
as not to burst into giggles. We'd been prepared for a
gargoyle who would deprive us of indoor plumbing,
any and all conveniences that ran on electricity, and
central heat, but now it seemed we should have hurried
to install Victor's Jacuzzi.

Next we proceeded to Prince's Cove, where from a
barge near the fish pens men hefted sacks of salmon
food, tossing them onto rafts from which the food
would be scattered to the salmon swimming below. Felicity observed with interest an activity that amounted
to farming the ocean, an enterprise hardly conceived of
in the 1800s.

"Very," she commented, "ingenious."

Just then a jalopy *ooh-ooh-gahed* into the turn-
around just above the cove. In the old car were Tommy
Daigle and my son, who seemed to have recovered ad-
mirably from his near-death experience.

Oo-ooh-gah, the jalopy's horn blatted again. The car
varoomed out the drive with a clatter of loose fenders, a
clank of rotted tailpipe, and a rumble of old, almost
certainly illegal muffler.

"Young people," Felicity breathed, turning to gaze
happily at us. "How delightful for you."

She jotted in her notebook again, while Ellie and I
glanced at one another in amazement.

"I am *so* glad," Felicity said as we drove back

toward town, "that you have not put on an inauthentic false front for me."

Considering that all of the town's home businesses had taken down their commercial signage, that all TV satellite dishes had been covered, moved, or camouflaged, and that the computer with its public Internet connection, located in Peavey Library, had been replaced with an old manual typewriter salvaged from a yard sale, I thought this was not strictly true.

On our way up Water Street, we passed a kiosk on the library lawn; in it, Corey Banks's mother was selling bottles of Clean-All, the spot-removing formula she had invented. Ordinarily, this might not have been the most ingenious marketing strategy. But she had added a twist:

Nearby, Corey was busily cleaning the trunk of a Cadillac, using his mother's cleaning solution. Everyone in town knew what he was cleaning out of it, too: cat droppings. From the sidewalk, little Sadie Peltier looked on in a fury, stomping her foot and shaking her fist at passersby, an unwitting advertisement for the miracle cleaner.

Also on the lawn was a miniature French poodle, pure white and without a trace of any paint on it; with the animal, feeding it tiny dog biscuits, sat Clarissa Dow.

Clarissa waved happily at me as we went by, and so did Mrs. Banks; the cleaning solution was selling like hotcakes. Corey did not look so pleased, but I figured he would cheer up later, when he found out about the college football scouts who were coming to look at him.

Noting the boy's size and quickness and his obvious need for direction, Bob Arnold—an alumnus, to my surprise, of Purdue—had made a couple of phone calls. He'd also sat with Corey while Corey suffered through heroin withdrawal, and arranged the boy's counseling and medical follow-up.

Like Arnold had said: in Eastport when you need help somebody will help you.

"Isn't that enterprising?" Felicity approved as we passed the cleaning-solution kiosk; so far, so good. But there was another hurdle yet to clear: we were about to drive past my house.

Turning onto Key Street, I got a clear, heartsick look at the results of the shutter project. George, Sam, and Wade had worked until nearly dawn getting them up there; it was not until close to four in the morning that I had heard the extension ladder being lowered, signaling the end of their labors.

Unfortunately, they couldn't see very well while they were working, because it was so dark, and as a result they'd hung the shutters upside down, so that when it rained the water would run *in* through the louvers instead of *out*.

As a system for irrigating nineteenth-century clapboards—leading, eventually, to their becoming unpaintable and having to be replaced with (gasp) vinyl siding—it was perfect, and I had no doubt that Felicity would notice the problem immediately.

"Stop," the dictator of historical correctness demanded. "Will you *look*," she breathed, "at *that*."

Miserably, I gazed at the ridiculous shutters. They could be taken down and rehung, of course. The problem, Wade had assured me with some chagrin, could be easily corrected.

Just not in time for Felicity's visit. "I know they're not quite *proper*," I began, then realized: she wasn't looking at the shutters at all.

She was staring at the house down the street: the one with the double parlors, separate entrance, and wide pillared front porch. While we were out, the For Sale sign had come down, replaced by a white wooden placard hanging from two new gleaming brass chains.

In black lettering, severe and dignified, the placard read: Victor Tiptree, M.D., Physician & Surgeon.

Felicity squinted through her glasses, the lenses of which were thick as Coke bottles. "A doctor," she breathed, gratified. "This is an excellent development. A doctor in town."

Given who the doctor was, I didn't feel so sure. I thought that, given a choice, the townsfolk would have picked an old-fashioned general practitioner, complete with a black bag and kindly manner, over a high-tech neurosurgeon with a screw loose.

But Felicity was convinced. "Industry. Progress. Young people. And," she finished, "a doctor, setting up practice here."

Content, she sank into the Land Rover seat, so uncomfortable that it could have doubled as an instrument of torture. But she didn't seem to mind; in fact, she seemed to enjoy it. She was, I was coming to realize, an enjoying type of person.

"I believe I must give Eastport my highest recommendation," Felicity said.

Then she glimpsed the front of my old house: bright white clapboards, crisp, dark green trim, and green shutters, each and every one of them clearly and obviously upside down.

Felicity blinked. Her forehead creased faintly. She adjusted her thick-lensed glasses, then tried peering over them without success.

"Lovely," she murmured obliviously. "Just lovely."

She turned to me. "Now," she pronounced, "where is this young man who wants to talk about a boat show? And where are the lemon squares I've been hearing about, and something called a Saturday Night Special?"

We drove on.

That evening, Wade and I went out for a moonlight ride on his boat, the *Little Dipper*.

"So," he said, draping an arm over my shoulder. "Looks like old Victor's really decided to stick around."

On the calm water, the moon's reflection lay flat as a disk of silvered paper. "Uh-huh. He's discovered the pleasures of being a big fish in a small pond."

Which wasn't, I supposed, very charitable; Victor had saved Peter Mulligan's life.

Wade's arm squeezed around me. "Don't worry. If he's planning to get a neurosurgery department going up at the hospital, he'll be too busy to be a fly in your ointment."

"I suppose," I said, not feeling convinced. "But I'm never going to get things straight with him, am I? He's always going to be . . . unfinished business."

"If you could've got it straight with him, Jacobia, you'd probably still be married to him."

Which was a good point.

"And," Wade went on, "he *is* out of the guest room. I guess that's as much progress as you can expect to make at one time, with Victor."

Which was also true. "Has Sam said anything more to you about Yale?" Wade asked.

"Not yet." Another letter had come, detailing Yale's program for making its studies accessible to dyslexic students.

A whole new world; maybe he'd want to try it.

And maybe he should.

"What," Wade spoke up again after a little while, "ever happened to the dog?"

"Cosmo? He's back in the kennel in Portland where he came from in the first place. Arnold called every police K-9 unit in Maine until he found its original owner."

To our north, the light at Deer Island flashed steadily. "If I'd thought about it more, I'd have realized the dog tied Ken Mumford to Willoughby," I said. "Because Cosmo wasn't just any dog. He was an expensive dog. It took big bucks, to buy him."

Wade nodded thoughtfully. "Willoughby equipped Ken with a dog to help guard the money when it was in Ken's possession. But what about Ike Forepaugh? How'd he ever hook into it? And how did a guy like Willoughby know Ken Mumford at all?"

The dark shape of a minkie whale slid gleamingly out of the water, then vanished again into its own cold, fluid element.

"Ike showed up to get the money Ken owed him. When Ken got killed, suspicion naturally fell on this newly-arrived famous bad guy. Which worked fine for Ned, as long as Ike stayed missing and presumably on the run. So Ned made that happen. As for Willoughby knowing Ken . . ."

I took a deep breath, let it out again; this part was sad. "Willoughby's house. That he's remodeled, so you can't even see what it used to be? Guess who it used to belong to, back when you and Ellie were just little kids and Ken was a few years older?"

Wade put the heel of his hand to his forehead, "Oh no. Don't tell me it was—"

"That's right. Tim Mumford. When he was working, and his wife and kids were all alive. In the old days, before all Tim's troubles arrived, and long before Ellie even knew him, Ken lived in that house. It's nothing anyone bothers mentioning anymore, but people were talking about it, Ellie says, at Ken's funeral. That's how she found out."

"Maybe Kenny went out there to have a look at the old place, before it was gone forever," Wade said contemplatively.

"Thought he'd revisit what was lost when Tim went broke," I agreed, feeling bad about it.

So many things are tied into money, it seems: getting it. Keeping it. Not having enough.

Especially that. "Instead," I said, "he'd have met Baxter Willoughby. And once he did, everything else just . . . happened."

Wade shook his head. "You know, if he hadn't got caught, Ned would have ended up trying to take Ken's boat out to hook up with a big vessel. Guy can't even tie a decent slipknot, he'd have found out how bad he needed money. Bad enough to drown for."

Just then my cell phone *thweeped*.

I dug it out and listened without saying anything, holding it for a moment to Wade's ear so he could hear, too. Then, still without speaking, I pressed the disconnect tab, closed the phone up, and moved the little power switch to *off*.

"How is he?" Wade asked, having recognized the voice.

A call from Hargood Biddeford was getting to be a frequent event. Bunny was not only expecting; she was having twins, and Hargood was beginning to panic over the need for a bigger hutch.

"In a scramble as usual. Got out of gold, thinks the market's too risky on account of the Asian factor—"

That was my punishment for aiming Hargood at Toyota.

"—now he wants to get into commodities. You know, things that people burn, build with, or eat. He wants to know if I know anything about hog bellies."

Wade chuckled quietly. "And do you?"

"I know you can't build with them. Which is more than Hargood knows."

Actually, I knew a fair bit more than that. "But for now I think Hargood and his troubles can wait."

"Yeah. Guess we'd better head ashore." Wade began preparing to get the *Little Dipper* moving again.

"There was another thing I was wrong about," I

said. "Why Ken never took any of that money and spent it."

"Ken only spent what Hallie gave him or Willoughby paid him. Nothing more," Wade said slowly.

"Even the money Ike had in his pocket when they caught him," I agreed, "was legitimate. Ellie's settling Ken's affairs, and it turns out that Ken had started a bank account. Two hundred bucks, all withdrawn the day before he died. He'd been saving to pay the debt he owed Ike."

"Which Ike would otherwise have taken out of Ken's hide."

"Correct. But even with that over his head, he didn't touch any of Willoughby's cash. And it was for the one reason that never even occurred to me."

Wade started the *Little Dipper*'s engine; a pale burble of turbulence spread out on the moonlit water behind us.

"Ned told Arnold Ken didn't even know he was running drugs. He was just doing what Hallie wanted, because he was in love. And he didn't take the money," I finished, "because it didn't belong to him."

Wade came over and stood with me at the rail, the boat just sitting there idling, poised between water and sky.

"He was," I concluded, feeling that I was pronouncing Ken Mumford's epitaph, "a decent guy."

 Back at my house, Ellie was waiting for me in the kitchen and the coffee was on, which I suppose should have alerted me.

"Here," she said, putting a dish of strawberry shortcake in front of me on the red-checked tablecloth.

"I don't need this," I said, eyeing the whipped cream. Unlike Ellie, I do not burn five hundred calories just blinking my eyes.

"I got a call from Felicity a little while ago," she said, ignoring my protest as she dug into her own short-cake.

The coffee was ready, and I poured us some. It was late, and Wade had gone straight up to bed; he'd be out on the water again in only a few hours.

"Felicity? As in Abbott-Jones? But I thought she was—"

"Right. In Lubec, getting rid of the rest of the grant money."

Lubec was the next town down the coastline: small, isolated, and just as interested in grant money as East-port.

"*And* on the way there, somebody told her about us, and about the murders," Ellie added.

If there was one thing we hadn't wanted Felicity knowing about, it was the murders. We didn't think she would find them at all authentic or progressive. We'd kept quiet about them, and so, we had hoped and ex-pected, would everyone else.

But now I guessed not. "So I suppose she's changed her mind and decided Eastport's too deadly to be de-serving?"

Darn. And after all that work, too. In her dog bed, Monday yawned hugely and stretched, eyeing us with muzzy contentment, then turned over and went to sleep again.

"Oh, no," Ellie replied. "She thinks it's fascinating. She *loves* mysteries—on the phone, she actually sounded a little bloodthirsty."

"Oh," I replied, brightening. Yet another reason to like Felicity. "And was that," I inquired, "the only rea-son she called? To congratulate us for being so fascinat-ing?"

"Um, not exactly," Ellie replied, "it seems that she

and her entourage had just visited the meat market in Lubec. You know the place I mean? And the guy who ran it?"

I knew, and I caught the past tense, too. And so in a manner of speaking had he, I guessed suddenly.

The market had been a good idea: organic beef, pork, some lamb, and a lot of poultry, all locally raised with no antibiotics or other chemicals in the feed. In a world that was worried about E. coli and mad cow disease, the fellow who'd owned the place had started looking like a genius ten minutes after the market opened.

"Somebody cut him up with a cleaver," Ellie said. "Carved him, wrapped him, and put him in the walk-in freezer. Felicity thought we might be interested."

Just then Victor strolled in, spied the shortcake, and made a dash for it; he was sleeping in his house but still eating at mine, until George finished modernizing his kitchen.

"You know," he said seriously to me, "the cooking around here is awfully plain."

Studiously, I turned my attention back to Ellie.

"And I am interested," she went on, "because the thing of it is this: the victim's wife has a garden. Flowers, vegetables, and—"

She paused, emphasizing the next part. "Herbs, some quite exotic. Exotic enough to use for murder."

I began to see where she was going. "I get it. You think—"

"Murder?" Victor's eyebrows knitted disapprovingly. "I don't think you should get involved in any more—"

"Victor," I said. "If you don't shut up, there'll be another one right here at this table. Okay?"

Victor swallowed shortcake. "Okay."

Not that his cooperativeness had any hope, long-term. But it was fun while it lasted. Furthermore, he had located a pediatric research program that would treat Ned Montague's daughter's rare kidney disease for free, and pay her travel costs.

And he had sat down with Sam and discussed the fake heart attack—not fully, and not very expertly, but I thought sincerely, and Sam was taking it that way, too. So for the time being Victor had bonus points.

"Let me get this straight," I said to Ellie. "The butcher has been laid with the packages of chicken quarters in the freezer. And the winner of the arrest warrant is . . ."

I paused, touching my fingers to my forehead in parody of a mind-reading act. "The butcher's wife."

Victor blinked, his shortcake-laden spoon stopping halfway to his mouth. "How did you know that?"

"Because," I replied meaningfully, "when a husband gets done in with a cleaver, it's always the wife."

"Oh." He got up hastily. "You know, I think I'll take this shortcake home with me. Give you girls a chance to talk."

With that, he vamoosed.

"Maybe instead of a divorce you should have bought a carving knife," Ellie commented. "Scare him into good behavior."

"If I had, I'd be serving life without parole. So anyway, why is the wife doing it a problem?"

"Well, when they arrested her, she was holding the cleaver in her hand. And wearing a bloody butcher's apron."

"Sounds right to me."

Ellie nodded. "But remember the Calais woman whose husband used to clobber her? Until she poisoned him to death? Or so the authorities were convinced."

I remembered: the guy at the baked-bean supper. "But they couldn't find any traces of poison in the food. Or at the guy's house. Not anywhere. So—"

"So she got away with it." Ellie looked down at her hands. "I am not supposed to know about this. But according to Berenice—"

Ah, yes, the delightful Berenice, lover of llamas and queen of the backyard psychotropics. I made a mental note to get more ginseng, next time I wanted to resemble a Fourth of July rocket.

"—the substance that was used in the poisoning—"

"—came from the garden in Lubec," I finished.

I got up and went to the open window. *"But if you've got a garden full of untraceable poison, why chop a guy up with a cleaver?"*

"My point," Ellie said, "precisely."

Outside, the moon was setting behind the fir trees. A breeze moved, smelling of salt and woodsmoke.

"Maybe," I offered, "we should try to find out."

"Or maybe," said Ellie, "we shouldn't."

From the dining room came a bright, musical little *ping!*

Which in the end was how we decided.

MALLETS
AFORETHOUGHT

A
Home Repair Is Homicide
Mystery

SARAH GRAVES

ABOUT THE AUTHOR

SARAH GRAVES lives with her husband in Eastport, Maine, where her mystery novels featuring Jacobia Tiptree are set. She is currently working on her seventh novel, *Mallets Aforethought.*